The Changeling

Alison MacLeod

The Changeling

St. Martin's Press ⋈ New York

Library of Congress Cataloging-in-Publication Data
MacLeod, Alison
The changeling / Alison MacLeod.
p.   cm.
ISBN 0-312-14564-0
I. Title.
PR6063.A2498C48   1996
823'.914—dc20   96-25854   CIP

First published in Great Britain by Macmillan,
an imprint of Macmillan General Books

First U.S. Edition: December 1996

10 9 8 7 6 5 4 3 2 1

Acknowledgements

There are many works that proved invaluable in my research into early-eighteenth-century living. However, I am especially indebted to the following histories of piracy: *A General History of the Robberies and Murders of the Most Notorious Pirates, and also their Policies, Discipline and Government*, Captain Charles Johnson (1724); *The Tryals of Captain John Rackham, and other Pirates*, printed by Robert Baldwin (1721); *Pirates of the West Indies*, Clinton V. Black (1989); *Between the Devil and the Deep Blue Sea: Merchant Seamen, Pirates and the Anglo-American Maritime World 1700–1750*, Marcus Rediker (1987); *Pirates: Fact & Fiction*, David Cordingly and John Falconer (1992); *Pirates*, David Mitchell (1976); and *The Pirates*, Douglas Botting (1979).

for Hugh

'. . . some may be tempted to think the whole story no better than a novel or romance'.

(Captain Charles Johnson, in *A General History of the Robberies and Murders of the Most Notorious Pirates*, 1724)

Book One

Chapter One

I pulled him from a sea of blood. I grabbed his small, straining shoulders and willed him into my hands.

His head wore the caul like a hood. 'He'll never die by drowning,' I said to her. I was light-headed, giddy almost, as though we had somehow, the two of us, outwitted death that night; as though Sally wasn't already dead.

I kept the caul. Later, I would lay it to dry in the cold December sunshine. I would press it between stones I had heaved from the field. I would fold it into the shape of a wind-shot petal and tuck it below the cradle cloth. Hood of mother's blood.

That night though, his face was blue. Even in the dull light from the smoke-hole, I could see it was blue as I pulled the caul away. He only needs air, I told myself. I laid a trembling hand on his chest. I waited for the rise and fall. Then I saw the cord twisted around his neck.

Memory is a false thing. Even now, it insists on a paring knife – the one I used for potatoes and carrots – there on the table behind me. I need only reach for its rough handle, and I'm turning the child over, easing the blade under the cord, fixing it with my thumb, and cutting. Sometimes, it's not the knife, but my own hands, grasping the small ankles and swiftly unwinding the tangle as if it were nothing more than a knot in a skein of yarn. But, in that moment, nothing was as it should have been. There was only the stink of my fear, and my teeth ripping the cord.

He breathed at last, spluttering blood.

I wiped him clean. I weighed him in my arms: healthy for eight months. I tried to begin again. I tried to forget the weight of Sally's legs, slack on my shoulders. I tried to forget the emerging head: a fist of flesh, the demand of bone. I carried the lamp to the table and replaced its burned-out wick. I covered the rush-strewn floor in soft flannel and laid him down.

I counted toes: ten. Fingers: ten, clenched and angry. As he wailed, I babbled above him, all the while searching for a mark on the face, for down on the spine, for a nub of a tail where only a tailbone should be. I found nothing – nothing except a fold of soft flesh between two thrashing legs.

She was not the boy I had promised Sally. She was a stranger who had cosied herself on the right side of her mother's swollen belly; who had dreamed of Sally's right breast till it grew heavier than the other; who had willed the dangling needle to trace a line and not a circle on the air. She had flouted all signs. She had come true despite me.

I wound Sally's ruined body in a sheet. I laid the newborn in the cradle beside the blood-soaked bed. I rocked her with the edge of my foot, and I let her cry as morning crept up to the cottage, frost-bitten.

Were it not for Sally, my mouth would be as quiet now as an unmarked grave. Were it not for her, I'd know what's what and him from her and her from it and it from the devil, as an old woman should – and I'd not be telling tales.

The Tale of Cross-Eyed Sally

She came all the way from the Ballyhoura Hills where Limerick meets Cork in a heave of black earth and black cloud, where hill turns into sky and sky turns into muck. Small wonder then that the girl didn't know who or what she was about when she turned up one day, looking for work. I found her sitting on my overturned slops pail, sucking on a small round of butter and smiling as though she were eating the sun.

I said, 'Shoo!' like I would say to a stray, but she only wrinkled her brow and sucked a little slower. I said get, go on, and on your way, but she hugged her bruised knees tight. So I said, 'Will you have some bread with your butter then?' and she looked up, mild as May, and said, 'If it's no bother.' That's when our eyes first met, or rather didn't, because hers were crossed, as if they'd been charmed by the tip of her nose.

4

She followed me past the turf stack and the rows of cabbages that had been half trampled by our solitary cow. She was just a slip of a thing, without hose for her legs or even a shift as far as I could see. Sure enough, when we turned the corner and the wind caught her skirt, I glimpsed the white rounds of her buttocks, and saw she was more woman than girl.

Inside, everything was dark. There was only the peat fire, low in the hearth, and the blue hole of sky in the roof. When my eyes grew accustomed to the shadows, I found her at the cradle, rocking my little one, my only girl, with the tip of her foot. I tended to the bread, wrapping my hands in wet rags and lifting the upturned pots from the burning mound of turf and dung. I turned, ready to tumble the new loaves on to the table, but as I did so I saw she was crying. She was staring at my daughter's tiny face, and tears were spilling down her cheeks.

'Leave her be,' I said, unwinding the wet rags. Fear was climbing up out of my belly and clutching at my lungs. 'Take your bread.' I ripped off a steaming hunk and dropped it on the table with burning hands.

As she ate, I asked her who she was, where she came from. She was shy with words, hardly looking up from the table as she spoke. I listened, nodded patiently, waited for something more. Silence lodged itself awkwardly between us. I stood up, was wiping my hands on my apron, straightening the kercher on my head, when she stumbled into speech. 'I want to stay here. With you.'

I tried to smile. 'Sitting on my slops pail is one thing. Settling in on my peace of mind is another.'

'I don't take up much room,' she said.

'We're already seven in this room. There's the little one over there and five boys besides. There isn't any room to take.' She finished her bread and licked the butter thoughtfully from her fingers. 'There's more bread,' I tried.

She looked up, her eyes bright with the light of the fire. Standing over her, I could see my own reflection swimming in their skewed centres. Her voice was so quiet I could hardly hear. 'I've got your future fixed in my eyes. I've seen your old-woman face in my dreams.'

5

I laughed. 'That's nothing that I don't see in the shine of the water butt on sunny days.'

'No,' she said, and her voice was firm. '*Old.* As old as winter.'

I looked her straight in the eye. 'How dare you come into my home mouthing lies.'

She stood up, about to run. Then she saw my little girl, stirring in her cradle. 'I wish I were. I wish I were telling lies.'

I got to my feet, my hands going for her narrow shoulders. I was going to shake my old-woman face right out of her pale blonde head. I was going to send her running all the way back to Limerick. Instead, I fell back on to the bench. 'Just who do you think you are?'

'Nobody.' She was staring at the floor.

'I want you gone.'

'I can't. Don't make me.'

'What do you mean, you can't?'

She was chewing her lip and it had started to bleed. 'Your future's the only one I know. The only one I can see.'

My future in the eyes of a cross-eyed girl. My laugh was empty. I went to the door and stood there on the bright edge of day, just breathing.

When I turned at last, she was at the cradle, crying softly so I wouldn't hear, and, this time, I knew. She wasn't tearful on her own sad account. She was weeping for me – for the dark dream of my future – and the sight of it moved me as though she were weeping Virgin-tears.

'Sit down,' I said. Suddenly, I was afraid, that my future would disappear with her, that I'd be left like a blind woman, groping in the sun.

I bent to the cradle and took my little one in my arms. I just held her, winding her on my shoulder. I said, 'You can stay till you find work in Kinsale. After that, you'll live out.' My words were slow and deliberate, as if I was making a bargain.

Sally nodded, and so it was done, tied like a knot I couldn't figure.

Sometimes still, I daydream it all coming undone: Sally on the pail, sucking butter, and me inside, dallying over the sticky rounds of dough, making a slow Cross-of-Jesus on each loaf with the keen edge of the knife. My mind grows easy as I work, so easy that I never venture out, sniffing the air for heavy weather, and I never find Sally, smiling as though she were swallowing the sun.

In every tale, there's another, one that breaks out between the words we speak and the words we would bury.

She says, 'I'll give you another some day. I'll give you my own when she splits me in two.'

I knock her to the floor.

I am moving to the cradle, picking up my dear one, my little girl who never had a name, whom the priest would not christen while her father slept in the bed of another. I hold her to my breast. I kiss her cold baby lips for dear life. It is morning and she won't wake up. I press my chafed nipple to her mouth. Why will she not suck? Her tiny limbs are so cold. They won't rub warm.

I nibble her ears, her neck. I smother my face in the round of her belly, in the small of her back. I press the sole of her tiny foot to my cheek, to my lips. I take it in my mouth. I would swallow her whole if I could birth her again, but her body's already as stiff as a husk in my arms.

She died even as I slept. She drowned in the tears of a girl who trapped my future in her eyes; a girl I wouldn't let go of for fear I'd be blind. Even now, the memory leaves me winded, like a boot-blow to the gut.

In this tale, I cradle the cold baby-ghost of her in my arms, tucking the coverlet around her feet. I sit on the edge of the bed. I would sit there for ever, only she begins to grow heavy. Heavier. I shift her on to my shoulder, wrap my arms around her back and bottom, but I cannot hold on. Her legs grow warm and squirm against me. An arm curls tight as a creeper around my neck. Fingers pull at the hair that escapes my kercher. A hand pummels my breast. I manage to shift the weight again, this time to my knee. A ruddy face looks up at me. A bubble of drool wobbles on the child's lips.

'I do not want it!' I yell. 'I want my little dead girl. Where is my little dead girl?'

There is no reply from Sally, who lies in a heap on the floor. There's only the lusty cry of the child on my knee. It wriggles and I can hardly hold on.

'Why is it not swaddled?' I demand.

I already know the answer. Mother Midnight used to whisper it when I was just a girl: you cannot swaddle a changeling, she'd say. It cannot be bound. It will not be still.

I have gathered precious water from the rain butt. I have warmed it before the fire. I wet a soft piece of flannel and lay the child on the bed. I loosen the clout. (It is only a child.) I unknot the flannel bulk – and stare. Even as I look, it's slipping between one sex and the other, like a fish slips between the waves.

I turn away, stunned. I reach for the bowl of water. When I look to the bed again, it's gone. Vanished. So is Sally. I'm alone with only the deceits of memory and an old wives' tale telling itself in my head.

It frightens me.

I want my little dead girl.

Chapter Two

Sally stayed. I kept my word and wouldn't have her go, not even when the wind blew through the cottage, rocking the empty cradle in the dark and leaving me for dead.

I never made a sound. There was no name to shape on my lips, and the silence of it was like a gag in my mouth. When Peter, my eldest, tried to move the cradle, my eyes said all. It stayed by my bed.

My five boys slept on the earthen floor in front of the hearth, each in his habitual place, covered with clothing and woollens. Peter, then Finn, his face white in the flicker of the fire, Sean, Michael and Eoin, now my youngest. Sally shared my bed. I remember the softness of her feet on my bare leg – feet that had walked from Limerick to the coast – and those too-soft soles made me uneasy.

But the longer she stayed, the less I wanted her to leave. Winter had passed and the trees were budding green. Spring had come and no one had mentioned her going. Not me, not her. And I let her sleep with one arm curled round my waist. She was my talisman now. Her soft breathing was mine. Her quiet dreams were my safe future. Sometimes, I stroked her hair.

The boys hated her.

Peter, now twelve, had made himself the man of the place since his father had left. He said, 'She's not welcome here. You must tell her to go.'

I was at the stale-urine tub, whitening the linen. 'She is welcome here because I have told her she is.'

'I don't like the way she looks at you. She thinks you belong to her.'

'And I don't like your voice.' I thrust the linen deep into the

9

tub with a long beechwood stick. 'She is a girl without a home. She means no harm. And she helps me with meals and fetching the water and looking after the hens and the cow—'

'She's curdled the milk, twice. She's bad.'

I hit him with the stick. 'Go on, get back to that field, or you'll have more to worry about than curdled milk, my son.' His face darkened, like a bruise.

Even then, I couldn't have imagined – how could I imagine? – Sally pinned on the turf stack, Michael on one arm, Sean on the other, Finn on the ground, wrestling with her shift and her flailing legs, and Peter standing aloft and watching.

I picked up the wing-slane from the end of the stack and turned its blade to the sun. The boys scattered – all but Peter.

'Get out,' I said. 'Get your clothing and go to your father. I don't know you any more.' That's what I said the last time I saw him.

Two children lost. My firstborn. My newborn.

I turned to Sally, but she was gone, running, barefoot, with her skirt falling off her and the strings of her apron flying in the wind. It was nightfall before she came back. I had shark oil burning in a shell. I was watching the wick burn, willing her back before its length gave out; willing Peter to return in her stead.

I sat her on the edge of the bed. In the yellow smoky light, I could see the welts of nettle stings up and down the lengths of her legs. I turned her feet over. Her soles were torn and bleeding. I bathed them in rainwater from the butt outside. I wrapped them in new-washed linen. In bed, I wrapped my arm around her slender waist. I would not let her go. She had cost me too dear.

But, even as I held her, my limbs stiffened with rage. I despised her for her shy crossed eyes; for her bruised side where the cow always hoofed her; for her guileless head that didn't know enough to kick a boy hard in the balls; for that blank-faced look that was all that remained of her family abandoning her.

In the morning, she said, 'Lettuce eaten with salt and oil will cool the blood.' I was bending over the fire, testing the heat of the pot. I threw a handful of flour at its side and watched it turn into a shower of leaping sparks. I loaded the loaves and packed the turf around the pot. Then I turned to examine her face. There was no suggestion in it. Only thoughtfulness.

'We used to grow greens. In Limerick. Not just potatoes and oats and flax. But harty choakes and sparrow grass and lettuces sometimes and succory for the winter. I've got green fingers, that's what people used to say. I'm fertile.'

'Did folk say that as well?'

'Only when they thought I couldn't hear,' she said, and a little smile got the better of her lips.

She was perhaps quicker than I had thought. I had known that her brother had turned Protestant and so shifted his family from their land. I hadn't known that the girl had a skill to speak of. I said, 'It's spring. You can grow me a kitchen garden. Tomorrow, you can walk to Ballinspittle and from there to Kinsale where you can fetch us some seedlings. When you return, we'll dig over a patch in the yard.'

She smiled and, for a moment, I thought her eyes straightened up nicely in her head. I breathed easy all the day.

The next morning, I checked her feet. They had cleaned up well, though we left the linen strips in place for the journey. I loaded a small creel with eggs for barter at the Holy Stone and a jug with buttermilk for her journey. Morning mist still clung to the air, filling in the dip at the bottom of the path that marked the line of my land. I watched her walk into the dip and disappear from sight, like some slim-backed spirit destined for Ballinspittle. Then I picked up the empty slops pail and walked slowly back to the cottage.

In my story, in the one I would rather tell, Sally comes back by sunset with green things spilling over the brim of the creel and seeds in her pockets and the brown of the sun on her face. We eat our mash, and then she takes Eoin on her lap. I throw more dung on the fire. Sean and Michael gather at my feet. Finn listens from the doorway where he watches for the evening star, and Sally chatters about the people in Kinsale. About the ferryman who took her across the Bandon and solemnly warned her not to go near Smugglers' Gate, or the Bailiff would arrest her before she could think twice. About the rope-maker's procession to the Pier with the red-faced piper at the fore. ('They carried a rope between them, thick as my neck, I swear, and so long, I didn't know when I'd see the end of it. It was like some sea monster, Annie, just waiting to spring to life in their grip.') There was a gentleman in high red heels standing in front of the Market House and a lady, coming out of St Multose's, scratching the lice in her wig with a tiny silver claw. At the Holy Stone, there was more mackerel than she'd ever seen in her life, as well as hills of potatoes, and milk and butter to feed 'all of Ireland. Oh, Annie, the butter was beautiful.'

And, though I am listening, I hardly hear, for I am thinking of the day I'll have her married: in a red frieze petticoat and matching waistcoat with green ribbons to catch the breeze.

But my story gets away from me.

The Flower-Pot Test

Sally did not come back with a creel of seedlings and pockets full of seeds. Instead, she came back with two fine people by the name of Mr and Mrs Thomas Manley. He tipped his tricorn to me, but she only stood in the doorway with her nose shoved in a nosegay of dried lavender. I lifted some cakes of horse dung from the wall and mustered the fire to a proper blaze. Then I offered our guests the two chairs by the fire and a cup of china drink. Mr Manley accepted. Mrs Manley told her husband she'd be in the chaise.

'Mrs Fulworth, I must ask you to pardon this intrusion. We met Sally at the market. At the greens-man's stall.'

'Over the cowcumber seedlings,' added Sally, who seemed remarkably composed for a cross-eyed girl who'd just been taken home on the back of a rich man's chaise. 'Mr Manley was buying the making of more vegetables than I'd seen in my lifetime: coarse peas and table peas, scarlet runner beans, French beans and kidney beans, cos lettuce and lamb's lettuce, marrows and musk melons and—'

'You're a planter then?' I interrupted.

'No, no,' he laughed, more heartily than I thought mannerly. 'I am a solicitor by profession and a gentleman-farmer by passion. I follow the natural sciences.'

'We're Catholics,' I said, although it was obvious what we were.

'Sally here happened to overhear my conversation with the huckster—'

'The huckster was saying how Mr Manley would be growing more this season than he and his wife had grown in all their married lives—'

'And I confessed to the man, the way one can to practical strangers, the way I am doing to you now, that it is Mrs Manley's and my great regret.'

I thought it kindest to nod and say nothing, but Sally would go on. 'To which the huckster said to Mr Manley, "Is it your seed, or your wife's bed? The problem. Your seed or her bed?"

'I answered him thus, Mrs Fulworth. "I see you allude to the generative faculty of my spermatozoa and to the procreative propensity of my good woman's uterus. It is kind of you to enquire. However, I can only acknowledge that I know no more on the subject than you yourself, my good greens-man. My seed; her bed. It is, I am afraid, an ineffable mystery."'

'At which I interjected,' said Sally, '"Your nose is a good size." And Mr Manley turned to me, as though seeing me for the first time, and said, "And you're not the first to say so, my dear." Then I said, "If you sneeze when you blow your seed, then all's wasted you know. That's what folk say up home."'

'I thanked Sally for her kind advice, but my wife was waiting, and I said I would have to get along—'

'That's when I asked Mr Manley if he'd tried the flower-pot test, and he turned back.'

'The scientific nature of this test interested me, admittedly.'

Sally took up one of the clay pots that stood in a row beside he fire. 'You'll have to get your wife to piss in this before she goes. And, if you'll pardon me saying so, it can be no mean dribble either.'

He stared abashedly at the pot Sally offered.

'You did want to give it a try, did you not, Mr Manley?'

'I did.' He took the pot, pushed back his chair and strode to the door. 'And she will submit,' he declared, disappearing into the dusk where his wife awaited him.

We heard the clay pot smash.

Then, a timid knock at the door.

I opened it and he poked his head through. 'We will have the two requisite samples sent in the morning complete with glazed pots from my own collection to replace the pot we have clumsily dropped. Good night, Mrs Fulworth. Good night, Sally.'

I let go a sigh of relief, quite sure that was the last we would see of Mr and Mrs Thomas Manley. But the pots were delivered first thing the next morning, labelled with pictures of male and female parts, and still steaming. Sally was pleased.

I said, 'How do you know about this flower-pot test then?'

'I told you, I come from a family that grew more than potatoes and oats and flax. Folk used to come from all over Limerick to find out about growing all manner of things, including children. Sometimes, it's just bodily encouragement that's needed. Quails' eggs, eaten raw, can be good for a barren woman; cock-stones, boiled in a bit of net and then mashed, for a man whose balls want nourishing.

'But none of that's of any use till you find out who's stopping short of the harvest. That's what the flower-pot test's for.' She explained as she worked. 'It's very simple really. You take two handfuls of either barley or corn – in our case corn – and soak them separately in the man and wife's piss. When all's soaked up, you plant each separately in two rows, side by side, so that the sun falls on each the same. Then you water each in equal measures and wait for the answer to be revealed with the season.'

I was impressed, I must say, though I didn't say any such thing to Sally at the time. I wanted things to get back to the way they were before a gentleman had turned up at my door and set my girl's cat-got-her-tongue flapping.

It was not to be. Mr Manley was back before supper. We had just lit the tapers and, even in the dim light, I could see that he wanted something. I did not stand on ceremony. 'What do you want, Mr Manley?'

Sally was turning a pig's head on a spit.

'I should like the corn to be planted in one of my own fields, so as to better observe the results.'

'Fine.' I gathered up the pots where the corn was still standing.

'And there's something else, Mrs Fulworth.' His treble chin trembled slightly on the knot of his neckcloth.

'Yes, I knew there was.'

'I want Sally. That is, Mrs Manley and I do.'

I almost dropped the two pots.

'I was most amazed by the knowledge of vegetative genesis she exhibited at the greens-stall yesterday. I would like her to assist me in my homely pursuits of the natural sciences. And my wife would like to engage her as a domestic. She would be well looked after and paid a tolerable wage, a portion of which we would naturally forward to you on a regular basis to compensate you for the loss of help in the home, *et cetera*.'

My breast was thumping. I wanted to say no, no, she's cost me too dear. My small, dear girl drowned in her tears, my firstborn son turned animal at her innocence.

'Mrs Fulworth?'

Then I remembered Sally's crossed eyes; eyes that were only for me. My future and hers were criss-crossed in those eyes. My old woman's face was in her dreams. I knew she couldn't leave.

I turned to her where she stood turning the spit so evenly, I thought she'd spun herself into a reverie. 'Sally—'

'I know,' she said.

'Well, you're more woman than girl, so you're entitled to speak your own mind. You give Mr Manley his answer.' I stood with my hands on my hips, impatient to get on to the pot that was simmering over on to the fire.

Sally never stopped turning that spit. 'I'll go.'

She'd put on no weight and gathered no baggage since she'd arrived out of the blue the winter before. Only an extra skirt, some hose and a linen shift. I pressed a pat of butter into her hand for the journey and I repeated those words I had spoken so reluctantly to her on that first day. 'I will expect you to visit.'

She nodded. The knot that bound us had not slipped loose.

Chapter Three

Sally was shown into the Great Hall by the footman. Its ceiling was crossed with dark timbers and so high she felt she was standing at the bottom of a wide wood. On its walls were scenes she had hardly permitted herself to imagine: tapestries of Adam and Eve entwined, and the silk-stitched serpent, glossy in the grass between their feet; of Eden, a hundred shades of green, and bright with fruit; and of the Fall in which a creature, half-man and half-beast, stood at the edge of the thistled field where Eve lay, splitting in two with the birthing of Cain.

The footman had told her to stand in the light of the window and had then left, his footsteps resounding behind him. She had never seen a glass window before. She pressed her face close. It was smooth like a sheet of ice on the village pond in the winter, only warm now with the sun. Below her, so close it seemed she could touch him, was Mr Manley, stroking his chins in the Brussels-sprout patch.

'Can you charm bees?'

She turned fast on her heels. She had not noticed Mrs Manley seated in the dim corner by the smouldering fire.

'In the future, you will refrain from pressing your nose to my window. Can you charm bees?'

'No, not that I know of.'

'Warts?'

'No,' said Sally.

'Can you mangle linen? Surely you can mangle?'

'No, I'm sorry. I can use a flat iron though.'

'I am partial to venison pie. Do you make a good venison pie?'

'I'm afraid I've never made anything but oatcakes, stirabout, and boiled mash.'

Mrs Manley turned her gaze towards the roof timbers, in heavenly supplication. Then, 'My small linen must be washed with soap, not lye, is that clear?'

Sally nodded vigorously.

'Have you had the smallpox?'

'No, I've been fortunate.'

'Then you must sign your mark upon a paper agreeing to leave our service if you contract anything of that nature. What is the matter with your eyes?'

'They're lodged at cross-purposes in my head, I'm afraid. That's what my da used to say.'

'Are you simple then?'

'Not that I'm aware.'

'But, of course, if one is simple one is hardly likely to be cognizant of it.'

Sally stared at the floor.

'Can you see properly, to stitch and to mend?'

'Oh yes,' said Sally.

'All right then. They are an ugly sight, but you have not been brought to this house to be looked at.'

'No.'

Mrs Manley unfolded her hands, smoothed her fine woollen skirt and raised herself from her straight-backed chair. 'There is one other thing.' Again, she stared at the roof timbers.

'Yes, Mrs Manley?'

'I do not bed with my husband.'

Sally tried not to blink. 'No, Mrs Manley.'

'Not now. Not before. Not in the life ever after.' With that, she departed the room, leaving Sally unsure whether she could move from the spot or not.

'No potatoes. Can you imagine it? Six acres of fertile earth and not a single potato as far as the eye can see.' Mr Manley had found Sally at the window, some while later. 'Call it revolution. Call it hubris. Call it what you will, but I will not surrender my land to the common concerns of potato scab and potato blight. Each year, I recreate something out there akin to Paradise, though I blaspheme to say it. Apples as pink as a girl's cheeks.

Golden pears, rounded and firm like a woman's hips. Great melons, the delight of which cannot be given expression. Corpulent marrows, rubicund beetroot, thrusting leeks – can you see it all? Can you see the uproar of it all waiting to be in those ploughed-over fields, in those patient and undistinguished rows?'

'Planting-in tomorrow then, Mr Manley?'

'Without fail!' He blew his nose with gusto, then turned swiftly, and disappeared into the dark of the corridor beyond.

The footman did not reappear, nor did Mrs Manley. In time, Sally found her way downstairs and into a small room behind the kitchen. A tallow candle flickered in one corner. A straw paliasse had been laid in another, and there was a pile of bedding which a black tomcat had mounted and claimed for his own. There was no smell of turf on a fire as she tried to sleep. There was no arm clasped round her waist.

She had a restless night, with the tomcat insistent against her belly.

The following day, Sally and Mr Manley sprinkled seed like streams of quicksilver into the ready fields. They made thumb-holes for tender seedlings. They sheltered the frail under bell-cloches Mr Manley had ordered from the Continent. They scattered silt that had been gathered from the Ballinadee Quay on the Bandon River.

Mrs Manley watched all the while from the window in the Great Hall. From time to time, her husband would remember her there and tip his tricorn to her, or perform a deep and generous bow. Sally thought she looked like a woman trapped in a tower; she seemed to watch them at their work, but she did not see them.

Between the planting of the marrows and the sorting of the table peas, Sally saw her raise her fingers to her own reflection in the glass. She watched her trace the features of her own pale face – cheeks and chin, nose, eyes, mouth. She appeared to hesitate at the mouth. When she noticed Sally observing her from below, she retreated from the glass, her lips closing tight as a pact.

Later, as Sally washed Mrs Manley's small linen with lavender soap and cold, cold water, she saw her again in her mind's eye, standing in front of the glass, staring at the ghost of herself while the blood slowly gathered and soaked her crotch. It must have trickled down her thighs in thin, sticky streams, staining her hose and splattering the floorboards. Still she hadn't stirred from the window. She had stood there through the afternoon, watching but not seeing the slow re-birth of spring in the fields below.

There was to be more blood that month, so that Sally's fingers went raw with the scrubbing. And underneath the scent of lavender, in the breeze of Mrs Manley's skirts as she sailed past, Sally could smell her fear. Fear that she was rotting from the inside, like an apple blighted at the core; that her empty womb was the seat of some internal corruption; that judgement had been passed on her perverted womanhood.

In the quiet of the night, by the light of a single candle, Sally would scour the stained floorboards with sand.

On the first of May, she was in the library, balanced on a leather-backed chair and dusting the hundreds of tomes with a prodigious goose-feather. Mrs Manley had given her her instructions before departing, grim-faced, for a 'recuperative visit of indefinite duration' to her mother-in-law's. That was weeks ago now. The very thought of it had made Mr Manley plead openly with his wife to stay, for he knew all too well that Mrs Manley and Mrs Manley invariably saw eye to eye. Sally was fingering a white pigskin binding when he threw open the door and entered the library, weeping.

'Hayfever again, Mr Manley?'

He collapsed at his desk, his bewigged head buried in his arms. 'Sally! Oh Sally!'

'Has Squibb been treading on the leeks again on his way home from The Cockle?'

'It is worse, Sally. I have been outwitted and undone. My efforts toward the greater glory of the natural sciences have been rendered' – he spluttered through his nasal drip – 'impotent!'

'Surely not.' Sally climbed down from the chair.

'I can hardly believe it myself.' Then he looked up unaccount-ably, lurched from his seat and grabbed her hand. 'Come, you must see. Someone must see!' They were running, out of his study, past the Great Hall, down a staircase, through the dark kitchen and out the back. They ran past the dairy, the smoke-house and the brew-house. They ran past fields of tiny sprouts, lettuces and leeks. They ran until they came to a pristine row of bell-cloches. Here, Mr Manley dropped to his knees and, removing his neckcloth, rubbed one cloche clear of the day's mist.

'Marrows, Mr Manley?' enquired Sally.

'Precisely.'

'But it's early days yet. They haven't even come into flower.'

'This one has. A precocious specimen.' He lifted the cloche and lovingly fingered a small, starry-headed blossom. 'Herein lies one of the secrets of the Cosmos, Sally. These fragile yellow petals guard that which inextricably links man to man, man to animal and man to plant. Its fragrant scent is the sweet celebration of the fecundity that is everywhere. This flower is the maker of life, Sally. This flower is nothing less than the reproductive organ of the magnificent marrow, displayed for all to see. Man is a sorry creature, my girl, hiding his god-givens behind the proverbial figleaf.' He struggled for his handkerchief and missed an oncoming sneeze.

'Bless you.'

'And there is still more, Sally. After seasons of scrupulous observation, I have positively identified the he and the she, the sire and the wench, the pater and the mater.'

'Get away with you,' said Sally blushing.

'And not just on the marrow plant, but in melons and cowcumbers, beetroot and carrots, radishes and rhubarb, aspara-gus and spinach – not to mention the orchard and the soft fruits. My studies have been exhaustive.'

Sally was staring at the marrow flowers, squint-eyed. 'So which is which then?'

He raised a flower head between his thumb and forefinger. 'Here we have a male specimen. Note the yellow dust-like substance which clings to my fingers: its spawn. If we peel back this other clasped bud – yes, it is a male – you will note its upright stalk, just here, and the head of the stalk which will shrivel and fall once the spawn has been released.'

'And the she-flower?'

'A gracious receptacle, such as you see here.' His fingers alighted on another flower on the same plant. 'She offers a delicate cleft surface upon which the spawn finds its destined bed, carried on the wind or on the wings of butterflies and bees, for they are the Cupids of the vegetative kingdom.'

Sally's brow wrinkled. 'But surely something's wrong with your thinking here, if you'll forgive me for saying so, for you've got the both sexes on the one plant.'

'Which is exactly as Nature intended it, for the vast majority of plants, according to my research, are happily hermaphrodite.'

'I can't understand you when you don't speak plainly, Mr Manley.'

'They are both, Sally. *Both*. He and she. Him and her. A confounding situation, I will admit, but ours is not to judge, only to admire. Asparagus plants demonstrate a monosexual proclivity, and likewise spinach, but they are not the norm, surprisingly enough. Who knows, Sally? Who knows the greater plan? Who knows what wonders may yet overtake our humble human race, for are we not all – man, animal and plant – related in His eyes? Have I not proven as much?' He let out a great sigh. 'I came so close, Sally. So very close.'

'To what, Mr Manley?'

'To this, to this.' He thrust his hand into his buttoned coat and pulled out a slim booklet. 'I have just received this pamphlet on subscription from the Dublin Philosophical Society.' He pressed it to his breast. 'In short, it notes the findings of a natural scientist – in remote Tubingen – a Mr Rudolph Jacob Camerarius.'

'Mr Camerarius stole your thunder.'

'He did, Sally.' He sighed, bent low and replaced the bell cloche. He picked up his soiled neckcloth and shoved it in a pocket. Then he slid the pamphlet under his coat and walked back to the house, a solitary figure.

Sally could not bring herself to shout to him that he was trampling the tentative results of the flower-pot test.

That night, while Sally slept, Mr Manley crept into her room, crawled on to her paliasse, under her blanket, and evicted the black tomcat from its place on her warm belly. She was sleeping deeply and only half awakened when she felt the soft whiskers of his chin rub against her cheek.

'Go away, Tom. No licking my face.' She shifted on to her stomach.

Mr Manley was both surprised and encouraged by her use of his Christian name. 'No, of course not, Sally. I—I wouldn't presume. I only want comforting.'

Sally was drooling on his arm.

'Say yes, Sally. Please say yes,' he whispered.

From the uncrossable distance of deep sleep, Sally could feel Tom's tail between her thighs.

'I won't invade you, Sally, so help me God. You have but to murmur protest and I shall never come near you again. A single word and I go.' He listened. He listened again, but all was sweet silence.

Until Squibb the footman, tippling home ale in the moonlit kitchen beyond Sally's room, heard a scream that cut through the night.

He walked to the open window and hissed drunkenly into the dark. Then he replenished his mug to steady his nerves. 'Bloody tom's always at it.'

Chapter Four

Sally's scream put the fear of God into Mr Manley, and he fled without a word – out from under the blanket, through the dark kitchen and past the footman. As for Sally, suddenly awake, she lit her bedside candle and shone it about the room, searching, but she found only Tom, rumbling satisfaction at the end of her paliasse. (*Kiss the black cat, stroke its black back. Kiss the black cat and it will make you fat.*)

As soon as light broke, she was off and running, over the fields, down Cork Road, through the Gate, past the Holy Stone, down Fisher Street, and across the Ramparts. She jumped on a cart making for the river on its way to Ballinspittle, and from there she ran over the hill, through the bit of wood, down into the dip and past my slops pail. She was almost sick with running when she landed at my table.

'Annie, oh Lord, Annie, I don't know what I'm going to do!'

'Nor will I till you tell me what's the matter with you.' I was on my knees, sweeping the ash from the hearth into a scuttle.

It took her some time to get it out and make herself clear, and by the time she had finished, I was stirring ash into the soda bread instead of oats. 'And no one else was in that room when you shone the candle around?'

She shook her head. 'Only the tom.'

'And you didn't dream it?'

'Father in Heaven, I wish I had, but his spawn is still spilling from me.'

I was reluctant to believe her at the time, but who knew better what had happened that night than Sally herself? 'Did you feel the thorns of its prick?'

'I thought I was being cut open.'

'A tomcat and a virgin,' I said, collapsing at the table alongside her. 'It's an awful coupling.'

The silence between us was ripe with what couldn't be said. Finally, I found my tongue. 'We must wash you. We've got to swill out whatever there remains to swill.'

'Annie, you don't think—'

'The itch, girl. We don't want you catching the itch, do we?' I was thinking fast. 'Animals are always sucking at their privates.'

'They are.'

'Well, get your clothes off while I fetch a bathful of old piss from the tub.' For, in those days, it wasn't only linen we whitened with stale urine. Most people swore by it.

I found the old iron bath and filled it. Then I lugged it back into the cottage, kindled a good blaze, and set it before the hearth. We did the best we could, Sally and I, given the circumstances. But silently I feared that, if any damage was done, it was done already.

She seemed to be much relieved for the bath though, so that was something. And, me and my foolhardy tongue, I told her that if she remained upright all the day long, she should be all right. She managed to eat a little bread and butter – standing up – and then I sent her on her way home, so I could fret in peace.

The Creator and the Cowcumber

Sally crept in through the back door and into the kitchen. All was quiet. No one in sight. She was grateful she hadn't been missed.

She was just slipping past the kitchen table, when she was startled by the sight of Mr Manley, almost hidden behind a forest of potted fruit and vegetable plants. 'Mr Manley!' she breathed. She tried to think fast. 'There's nothing like a quick walk round the pasture to give one an appetite for the day ahead.'

Her sudden appearance in the kitchen at this hour of the day had sent Mr Manley running behind the narrow trunk of a small flowering cherry tree. Still, he thought, her words were pleasant enough, and there seemed to be no glimmer of accusation in her eyes. 'I've been out myself. To the Holy Stone. My friend the greens-man has provided for me well, as you can see.'

It was her turn. 'So you are not soliciting today.'

He looked up from his bone fertilizer, stammering.

'It's Tuesday, Mr Manley. I thought you had appointments.'

He exhaled heavily. 'No, Sally, cancelled. All cancelled. I have decided I have more important work at hand than sorting out who gets this dead man's blunderbuss and that dead man's hogshead.'

'You're recovered then, from the blow dealt you by Mr Camerarius.'

'Quite, though Cook will undoubtedly have my head for taking over her kitchen. We can get by on oatcakes though, can't we, Sally?'

Since the day when Sally had, in Mrs Manley's words, 'killed' a venison pie, she had been spared the task of the midday dinner. Cook came daily. Now here was Mr Manley willingly dispensing with his dinner, as well as his breakfast. 'Of course we can, Mr Manley.' She paused, taking in the leafy confusion on the table. 'But what are you doing?'

'Come, Sally, pull up a chair and behold.'

'Thank you, but I'd just as soon stand.'

'Fetch me the *Cucumis sativus* from the other end of the table.' He motioned in the general direction of a broad-leafed plant with yellow flowers.

'The cowcumber plant, Mr Manley?'

'None other.'

She did as she was told.

'Now, you shall pass me my instruments as I request them, and for your careful solicitude, you shall have the fortune of witnessing natural history in the making.'

She didn't know what to say.

'Tweezers.'

She searched between clumps of peat, under clay pots and in reams of net mesh. She found them at last in his apron pocket.

'First, we sterilize. Spirit of wine.'

She passed him a jar of colourless fluid.

'Next, we gently emasculate the spawn-filled organ from the centre of the paternal flower.' She heard the metallic click of the tweezers. 'And now, we proceed with it to the mother-to-be, whom I prepared for her great moment shortly before you arrived.'

'You're playing Cupid then, Mr Manley?'

He stopped in his path. 'No, Sally. My role is bigger than that even.' He chose his words with care. 'I am not simply encouraging. I am making. I am *remaking*. I am creating anew.'

'I don't see another cowcumber plant.'

'One needs imagination to create anew, Sally. I am not merely proposing we give birth to more of the same. The destined mother-to-be is this blushing sweet cherry.' He examined an open flower. Then he returned his attention to the spawn organ, slicing it open with the sharp tip of his tweezers. 'Paintbrush, please. And spirit of wine again.'

'But, Mr Manley, think about what you're doing. It's . . . it's blasphemy.'

'I am merely furthering the Almighty's work, so let us not delay.'

Sally retrieved the necessaries. 'But picture it, Mr Manley: a sweet red cherry stretched beyond all knowing in the shape of a cowcumber. You'll be making monsters.'

He dipped the fine-haired brush into the spirit and waited for it to dry. Then he lifted the cowcumber spawn on to the brush and, with great delicacy, stroked the female centre of that cherry blossom with the life-giving substance. Finally, pale with the magnitude of the moment, he slipped a muslin bag over the cherry-cumber-to-be, and let out a vast sigh. 'I may be making monsters, dear Sally, but they shall be beautiful monsters. They will startle and inspire.'

The kitchen door suddenly flew open. Cook entered, and the black tom glided in, past her bulky frame. It went straight for Sally, winding itself round her leg.

Before the month of May was through, she knew she was pregnant. There was no sign of her menses. And the thought of it, of what was growing inside her, turned her world upside down. Her nights were sleepless; her days were dark. Looking through the window in the Great Hall, she no longer saw spring fields of sweet growing greens. Instead, she saw with unbearable clarity the shapes of the impossible: tumoured heads of cauliflower, dangerous spears of asparagus, blighted lettuces, a blasted orchard. And, further still, she saw the dim outline of shapes she could not name: things swelling in the black earth of distant fields, growing as she watched; things part plant, part animal, part human. She'd pull the curtains in the full light of day.

'It's the heat,' she would say to Mr Manley when he found her lingering in the dark. 'The days are growing so warm.'

Some days, at first light, he'd spot her from the small window of his bedchamber, walking half-dressed through the old pasture. She appeared distracted. She seemed to mumble to herself, as if in prayer. (*Tip-toe through the maydew if you will not marry. Tiptoe through the maydew and wait to miscarry.*) He told himself she was lonely for company. Female company. He bundled her into his chaise and drove her to my door himself. He said he'd return for her at nightfall; he'd hope to see her better by then.

I only had to see the empty look in her eyes to know.

'Annie,' she said, drooping like a plant in shadow, 'I can't. I just can't.'

I mumbled something about an infusion of rue, something I'd heard as a girl, but the truth was, I was lost for words.

We sat silently by the fire for most of the day, carding wool and skeining yarn. She held out her arms and I circled them round and round with the newly spun yarn until I was dizzy and her arms could only have been stiff. She hardly moved.

The boys came in at midday for their dinner. I served up tongues and buttered carrots, especially for her, but she scarcely touched her food. I tried to laugh about the day I found her sitting on my slops-pail, sucking butter, but her eyes started to fill. I gave the boys the whole of the suet pudding and told them to head back to the field. Then I turned to Sally and shook her. 'Listen, my girl, what's done is done, and there's no undoing it without undoing yourself as well. Do you hear?'

She buried her face in her hands.

'Now there's only one thing for all this if it's not to end in tears.' I took a deep breath. 'You have to get Mr Manley to lay you.'

She raised her head slowly. She stared at me as if I was mad.

'So the child has a name, Sally. So you're not left entirely on your own. He wouldn't, you know. He might be foolish but he's not mean. He'd help. So long as he believed it was his own child.'

'But what about when he sees it, Annie? What about when he *sees* it?'

'Don't turn fool for what might or might not be. You think about today – about tonight when he takes you home. You get him into that bed of yours and forget about all else.'

'I—I don't know if I can. And what about Mrs Manley?'

'She has never shared his bed. You're not stealing anything she wants for herself. You just think about it.'

She did, all through the afternoon and past supper too, until finally we heard the chaise on the path, and she grabbed my arm. 'But what if he doesn't want me?'

I smiled and led her to the end of the path where Mr Manley was waiting. Then I kissed her and helped her up into the two-seater.

That night, when they arrived back and Squibb the footman had taken the horses, they walked in together through the back entrance, Mr Manley politely enquiring about her day. When they got to the door of Sally's small room, he wished her goodnight and was heading for the stairs when he remarked to himself that he hadn't heard her door shut behind him. He turned and discovered her standing, eyes downcast, holding the door open – waiting.

She was waiting for him. With sudden alacrity, he retraced his steps. 'Oh, Sally! Thank you!' He kissed her chafed hands. 'You do me a great honour!'

Squibb entered the kitchen just as the back of Mr Manley's frockcoat disappeared through Sally's door.

May turned into June and June into July, and Mr Manley was faithful to Sally. Rarely did he miss his nightly visit to her room.

Sometimes he'd want gratifying, but often enough he'd only want babying, and Sally, for her part, grew quite fond of him.

The only wrinkle in her brow was the black tomcat at the bottom of her paliasse. Shift him though she might, he would not let her rest until he was restored to his rightful place. She tried locking him out of her room, but the constant scratching on the door unsettled her. She turned him out of doors, but in the morning it was clear he had worried the hens.

When Mrs Manley returned from her mother-in-law's, looking a sight better for her 'recuperative visit', life for Sally became more difficult. Nothing escaped the attention of Mrs Manley's eye: not the dust on her husband's law books, or the trampled crumbs of earth on the kitchen floor, or the tarnish on the heraldic handles of the cutlery. Sally pleaded with Mr Manley to stay away from her room at nights, for though he and his wife slept in distant wings of the house, she feared Mrs Manley's ears, eyes and nose more than she could express.

It was the frock-coat that gave them away – the black cat hair clinging to the back of Mr Manley's snuff-coloured frock coat. Sally's room had been the long-established den of the family cat. But Sally only made the connection much later. All was still apparently calm when Mrs Manley smiled at her one early morning. 'I should say it's been a good while since you have seen your friend Mrs Fulworth.'

'I don't complain, Mrs Manley.'

'I was not suggesting that you do, Sally. Only that you might wish to visit her today and return, let us say, by midday tomorrow.'

Poor, stupid Sally. 'Oh, Mrs Manley! Are you sure you won't miss me?'

'Not a bit.' She returned to the goose she was plucking. 'You get yourself ready. Squibb will take you, but not a word to Mr Manley. He'll tell me I'm soft.'

That evening, Mrs Manley served her husband a late but hearty dinner of boiled marrowbone and roast goose. 'You spoil me, Mrs Manley. You do indeed.'

She kissed his powdered wig and refilled his mug of nettle wine – for the seventh time. At last, after an indulgent game of two-person Patience, she helped him up the bulging staircase to bed, and she retired to her own chamber.

Not for long. Changing quickly into her nightdress, she quick-footed it down the two flights of stairs and slipped into Sally's vacant room.

Squibb ran when he saw her coming. Standing outside the kitchen window, however, and elevated on the compost heap, he was in a good position to observe Mr Manley's descent. He deposited his candle on the top step and slid down the tail-end of the banister.

Squibb clambered higher on the heap, and promptly sank. By the time he had recovered his hold on the casement, Mr Manley was, once again, disappearing through Sally's door.

By the time the summer was out, there wasn't a person in Kinsale who hadn't heard the story of how Mr Manley had at last bedded his wife – with the exception, that is, of Mr Manley.

In early August, just as the marrows were ripe for the picking, Mrs Manley announced to her husband that she was with child. For an instant, his face lit up at the prospect. Then he remembered he had no cause for joy. 'I see.'

She was steadfast in her silence. She knew he would pay for his infidelity with a memory that would haunt; with a lurking fear that would nip an erection in the bud; with the seeming fact that he had been cuckolded. After years of quiet importuning, he would be left to believe that the lofty heights of his wife's four-poster had been scaled by another.

She folded her smooth, implacable hands across her middle.

He did not let her see him cry.

And so the miracle of the one-time union of his 'seed' and her 'bed' was lost to them both for ever.

Before moving herself permanently to her mother-in-law's, Mrs Manley tied up loose ends. She parcelled up the silver plate and she dismissed Cook and Sally. The house was her family home, and had been for generations. Her father had been one of the savvy Anglo-Irish who had shed his papist skin when he sniffed the Penal Laws in the wind. In so doing, he'd managed to hold on to his family heraldry and to his family motto: 'Eat or be eaten.' Mrs Manley allowed her husband to stay on in the house, for the sake of his professional status, and she permitted him a small allowance for his upkeep or, specifically put, for that of her family home. In short, she left him without a bean. His solicitor's role had only ever maintained appearances.

He wrote a letter of supplication to his mother, the other Mrs Manley, but the letter was not answered, and he could not understand why. He was the injured party. The law made that clear, but he knew only too well how cuckolds were treated in court.

So he lost Sally too. He had not the pocket money to keep her. She returned to my cottage just as she was starting to show, but before she had the good luck to reveal anything to either Mr or Mrs Manley. With her return, Sally lost her hold on the Manley purse strings, for they had suddenly lost all their slack.

My strategy had failed.

Chapter Five

The days grew shorter, the nights longer and Sally's belly bigger. I couldn't reconcile the sight of it with her narrow shoulders, her slim hips and that face as mild as May. At night, she slept in my bed, as she had months before, only now there was the firm round of her belly nestling in the small of my back, growing new life, cosying the unthinkable. I tried not to think.

More to the point, I tried not to let Sally think. So when she asked me, in a voice brimming with hope, with daring even, 'What do you think, Annie, will it be a boy or a girl?', my answer came almost too quickly.

'Well, do you feel the child mostly on your right side or your left?'

Sally tipped herself tentatively from side to side. 'On the right, mostly.'

'All right then, but which of your breasts is most swelled up?'

'My right. Definitely my right.'

'And its nipple?'

'Is darker.'

'Well then,' I said, seeming to relax into the chair by the evening fire.

'Well what?'

'Well, you're carrying your first son, or I'm not a mother of six.'

'Am I?'

'Ask any midwife and she'll tell you the same.'

'But—'

I pretended not to know. 'But what, my girl? Is it a little girl you were wanting? Because, if it is, I fear the time for coaxing is over and done.'

She didn't seem to notice the desperate easiness behind my voice. 'Oh no, Annie. A boy will be fine, just fine.' So I eased her past her demons.

My own were not so easily duped. I let the fire die low that evening. I did not need to see as I knit the tiny lamb's-wool cap. I did not want to be seen. My voice I could trust; my face I could not, for I was remembering scenes long forgotten. A tale that had been told in whispers at the village pond when I was only a girl . . .

'There's those born of too much,' says the old midwife at the water's edge. They call her Mother Midnight.

The women avert their eyes. They don't have to ask. *Excess. Women who lust. Children born covered in coarse black hair; with four legs; with three nipples.* I say nothing. I pretend I am like thin air, so the women do not remember I am there, with my mother's bucket for filling. I stir the surface of the blue pond with my hand. Mud rises from the bottom.

'Then there's those born of a woman's meanness, of a cold heart,' the old woman says. 'Born wanting.'

I hear whispers, lips mouthing the shapes of fear: *children born without arms, legs; without heads.*

Arms and buckets hover in mid-air, under her spell. 'And there's those born of she who's contrary.'

I see some of the women lower their eyes. They do not let themselves imagine. Organs of life that grow the wrong way round: *a spleen for a heart; intestines that curl like a snake in the head; testicles that never drop; a vagina turned inside out like a full-blown flower.* They do not let themselves imagine because they know the seed of the ill-conceived can find its bed in a fertile imagination.

Mother Midnight picks up her yoke and disappears up the road, never spilling a drop.

As the women dip and fill, dip and fill, they remember. Laura with the head of burning red hair whose mother copulated during her menses. Mrs Mullen's niece, the one who spilled red wine on her lap and stained her baby's bonny face. And the Widower Sullivan's son, whom they say he keeps in a cupboard.

His wife rode, bareback, in her fourth month. They say the boy was born with hooves, that she died at the sight of them.

I fill my bucket and run. By the time I get home to my mother, it's more than half empty, and my face is streaming with sweat.

I opened my eyes, searching the dim room for the familiar.

Eoin was standing in front of Sally's chair, laughing. Sally was holding her hands upright between them. Squinting, I could see her fingers, criss-crossed with a teasing web of my yarn. Eoin's brow was wrinkled and earnest. He was lifting one strand, then another, unable to untangle the confusion of strands. They were playing cat's-cradle.

In the morning, Sally said she wanted to go to St Multose's. I was surprised, as she hadn't wanted to go into Kinsale, or even into Ballinspittle, since she had started to show. 'What if word were to get back to Mr Manley, what would he think?' she'd say.

'As I keep telling you, my girl, if there's a merciful God in Heaven, he'd think he was the father of that child in your belly.'

'No, Annie, the time for all that is past. I blush to think I almost deceived him.'

'Well, a poor man he is in all but breeches and frock-coat now, so there's no point in pursuing him, or you know I would.'

But that morning she wanted to visit the church.

'Where have you been, Sally? St Multose's is as Anglican as we are not.'

'I just want to see it. I don't need to go in.'

'Is it someone you know buried there?'

'Something like that,' she said cryptically.

'It's a long walk in your condition.'

'Please, Annie.'

'I'll put the giblets and the pudding on the boil before we leave. The boys will manage the rest.'

We were on our way by mid-morning, taking the path along the edge of my land, down into the dip, over the hill, through the bit of wood, into Ballinspittle and from there to Kinsale. The going was slow with Sally stopping at intervals to rest her weight against a tree or a stone wall or, as chance would have it, an old cow. We approached the church by way of the fields behind the town's north-west wall, skirting the abandoned friary and so avoiding Fisher Street. November drizzle was starting to gather on our heads and wraps, but Sally didn't seem to notice. She was searching the church lintels.

'What on earth are you looking for?' I was nervous. At any moment, we might be chased from the grounds.

She didn't stop to answer me, but only carried on at a keen pace round to the eastern side of the church. Here yew trees crowded, casting green shadows.

'I wanted to see,' she said.

'See what?'

'Something the greens-man told me was here.' Her face was upturned to a frieze that was all but covered by the bower of yew branches.

I was getting impatient. 'Something such as?'

She pointed to a cracked granite shape. 'As her.'

'Oh, Sally.'

I stared at the bulging stone eyes; at the flat line of a mouth that was hardly human; at the splayed, squat legs. The figure's hands were grasping the slit of her sex, pulling it wide with her fingers, like a gibe. Between those forced lips, I could see the exposed bud of an organ – or was it a baby's head?

'Do you think you might be able to lift me, Annie? Just quickly.'

'No, Sally. No.' I knew what she was thinking. Some said that to touch Sheela, especially in pregnancy, was to ward off evil.

'Please, Annie. I'm not too heavy.'

'It's not that,' I said. I looked over my shoulder. The shrill cry of a lapwing made me jump.

'Then please.'

I sighed, bent low, made a stirrup with my hands and hoisted her up, against my better instinct. She got hold of the lintel with the grip of one hand and pushed back a yew bough with another.

She was lighter than I'd expected. 'All right, Sally. Have you touched her yet? Because, if you have, I'd like to go now.'

'There's something – someone – else up here.'

'Never mind, the rain's coming down now, so let's get you down.'

She was struggling with a needled branch. 'It's a him. Can you see, Annie? I think it's Dagda.'

I raised my neck to an unnatural angle, still hump-backed as I was and cupping Sally's foot. I could just make out the pot-bellied figure. He was crawling on all fours towards Sheela, his enormous member rising up to his chest and spurting leafy shoots.

'Have you ever seen such a grin, Annie?'

'You should be ashamed of yourself, my girl,' but she could feel I was starting to laugh despite myself. My hands were starting to go soft. The tower of the two of us began to tremble and rock. Before I could ease Sally firmly back to earth, we had toppled.

My body broke her fall, thank goodness, but nothing broke mine. I arose with a twisted ankle and no way home but to hobble back over field, road, wood and hill. I rested at intervals, leaning against a tree here, a stone wall there and, as chance would have it, the same obliging cow. We arrived back home rain-soaked and shivering; heavy on our feet, both of us, but so light in spirit you'd think we were newly blessed.

That was until we saw Mr Manley's chaise stopped outside the cottage and, more worrying still, Mr Manley sitting before the fire, wrapped only in a homespun blanket. He stood up in a panic as we entered, almost losing the bowl of giblets on his lap, and the blanket as well.

'Mary, Mother of Jesus!' I breathed. Sally ran outside and cowered in the hen house.

'Do forgive this impulsive visit, Mrs Fulworth.'

I stood blinking.

'Your good sons have been most hospitable. When they saw I was besodden and besplashed with mud and rain from my journey, they offered me the heat of your good turf fire here, and a bowl of hearty nourishment to revive me.'

'You *said* we could ride your mare when the weather cleared,' Sean reminded him from the corner of the room.

'Indeed I did.' He cleared his throat and hoisted his blanket forcefully. 'Mrs Fulworth, I have most urgent need to speak to Sally.'

'You must have.'

'I felt I must act at once.'

'Have your circumstances altered then, Mr Manley? Has Mrs Manley taken up residence once more?'

'No—'

'Then you won't be requiring Sally's services again?'

'No, I shan't be, Mrs Fulworth, but—'

'Then why have you come?'

'Please, Mrs Fulworth, permit me a word with your Sally.'

What was in the man's mind? If he couldn't afford to keep her as a domestic, he couldn't afford to keep her as his mistress, consider it though I might. Did he want her to swear in some court before his wife that he had never laid a wandering hand on her? I screwed up my face and studied him hard. And what would be his reaction when he saw Sally's belly? At best, he might plead her case at the Gift House, the new almshouse in town. At worst, he'd run all the way back to Kinsale, clutching his blanket to him. I thought we could do worse. I sent Finn to fetch Sally.

She edged her way warily through the door of the cottage, her eyes downcast and her soaked-through skirts sticking to the round of her belly.

'Sally!'

'Mr Manley.' She did not look up.

'You are well?'

She avoided his question. 'I was thinking of you at harvest time – of the crops, that is.'

'Successful, Sally, and thank you for remembering. The marrows and and cowcumbers were plentiful this year. I very much regret that—'

'Yes,' said Sally, breaking in, wanting to hear no more.

'I regret you were not at my side in the fields, Sally, to share my successes and, yes, my failures too.'

She looked up, her eyes wide with genuine concern.

'The cherry-cumber,' he confessed. 'My efforts miscarried, I am sorry to say.'

'You knew it was not meant to be, Mr Manley. In your heart you knew.'

He sighed. 'It may be.'

I wondered just how long this would carry on. Sally had seemingly forgotten the fact of her stomach; Mr Manley, as of yet, had failed even to notice it. I was on the verge of opening my mouth, for I could bear no more of the shilly-shallying, when Mr Manley opened his first.

'But, oh my sweet, ever sincere Sally, will you do me the honour of marrying me?'

'Just a moment,' I interrupted.

'Oh, Mr Manley!' said Sally, weeping. 'I am afraid you taunt me, and yet, I know you wouldn't.' She was wringing her wet wrap with her hands and a small lake was forming at her feet. 'But you have not yet looked on me.' She stood back and opened her arms wide, exposing her shape.

'But this is marvellous news!'

I kept my mouth shut.

Sally didn't. 'I wish it were, dear Mr Manley. If only it were.' She gazed stoically ahead.

He followed that gaze which seemed to land on Finn, who was lifting a pudding from the pot on the fire. 'I see.' He cleared his throat. 'I have heard this is the tragedy of sleeping so many to a room . . . Sally, dear Sally, let me take you away from all this. Say you will wed me.'

She looked up, amazed. She opened her mouth.

We waited.

She started to speak.

We waited.

'Yes, Mr Manley. Yes. God willing, and Mrs Manley too, I will be your wife.'

'Oh, Sally!' He ran across the room and threw his arms around her – forgetting his blanket. The pot belly and the wide, wide grin looked strangely familiar.

Chapter Six

I thrust his still steaming garments into his hands. 'Tell me, Mr Manley, how are you and Sally to marry, let alone live?'

'It is my plan, Mrs Fulworth, to sever my conjugal bond to Mrs Manley.'

'I know you're no Catholic – and that's another matter all together – but even an Anglican gentleman of your ilk isn't likely to be given the right to marry again, assuming you are granted your divorce.'

He smiled benignly. 'I will explain. I have long believed a certain marital dilemma to be my greatest misfortune, my greatest shame. Now, for the sake of a new life, I will happily proclaim this secret to the world. I will stand at the Old Head of Kinsale and shout it to the Atlantic. I *will* tell the highest court in the land, declaring to all with ears to hear that I NEVER FUTTERED MRS MANLEY!' His face was like that of a man newly delivered from the darkness of a confessional. 'Forgive me my familiarity, but it must be admitted. My wife never consented to share my bed.'

'Now you must forgive me my familiarity, Mr Manley: that is common knowledge. What isn't clear is this: let us say you get your divorce. Say the Court agrees your marriage never happened because it was never consummated.' (Though at the market, you could now hear differently.) 'Would you not lose Mrs Manley's dowry, the house and land that is? Would you not become a gentleman of no means?'

He knit his brow, as though he had missed something early on in that exchange. Then he shrugged. 'My situation has become my servitude. I have closed up all but the Great Hall, the library and the kitchen. It is no longer a home. It is an enclosure.'

'Oh, Mr Manley,' sighed Sally.

'But what if she, Mrs Manley,' I conjectured, 'were to produce some manner of evidence to disprove your case, perhaps fearing she might be judged as a wife who had failed in her conjugal duty and fearing she might lose everything as a result?'

'Are you suggesting she might fabricate details of intimacies never shared?'

'For the sake of our discussion, Mr Manley, let us imagine a still bolder scenario. What if Mrs Manley was to produce an infant in Court and declare it to be yours?'

His face fell. 'Are you suggesting she might present another man's child as my own progeny and so unbalance my case?'

'Something like that,' I said, choosing my words carefully.

'I suppose it must be considered . . .'

I took my seat. Sally poured china drink for the three of us.

At last, he looked up from his meditation, eyes wide and luminous. Then he clapped his hands, frightening young Eoin, who started to cry. 'It matters not. Forget the Court! Forget my wife to whom I gave everything, or would have done! For all I care, dear Sally,' he said, grabbing her unexpectedly by the hand, 'we can exchange rings of plaited wheat! We—we can clasp hands and leap as one over someone's bristle-haired broomstick! We can be led naked as the day we were born into a marital bed bedecked with daisies and forget-me-nots. Do you hear me? Do you hear what I'm saying?'

I sipped my drink. 'We do, Mr Manley. Indeed we do.' I was starting to sniff a man's mid-life upset in the air. Still, one question had to be answered. 'Just tell us how, Mr Manley, *how* then do you plan to provide for you and yours, for you will soon be three, or have you forgotten?'

'I am not so remiss as you would think, Mrs Fulworth. I have a tiny sum from my mother each month. It keeps me in inks and parchment and clean neckcloths. She calls it my professional subsidy. It allows her to remind the ladies at the lending library in Cork, from time to time, that her only son is a solicitor. It is not an amount for even one to live on, but, with a little patience, my monthly stipends should accrue in such a manner as to allow me to abandon my wife's familial home and my solicitor's office – and to make a fair deposit on a local smallholding.'

I set down my cup. 'For what purpose, Mr Manley?'

'I have savoured the novelty of it for weeks in silence, and, now that the time to announce it is at hand, I feel strangely aflutter. Isn't it odd? My dear Sally, my good Mrs Fulworth, I shall grow potatoes!'

I held my tongue. Sally let go a little cry, presumably for the hapless martyrdom of her newly betrothed.

She was, nevertheless, on the edge of a future at last – her own future. In the meantime, the three of us had agreed she would remain with me until her child was out of swaddling. Mr Manley would continue to go about his business, gathering his stipends unto him and quietly fashioning them into a cash deposit for a smallholding on this side of Kinsale. We were on the brink of a new year, of a new century, and Mr Manley, for one, could not wait to be an eighteenth-century man. 'I was born for the new era,' he declared one day, casting another cake of dung on to the fire, for he had grown quite at home with us.

Sally did not appear to be listening. 'Are my feet too small?' she murmured to the room. She was seated, belly-up, on a chair by the fire, trying to mend one of the boys' waistcoats. 'A woman can die of small feet, my mother said.'

I didn't like the wispiness of her voice. I set down my iron, walked over to her, and fixed my hands on my hips. 'All right, Sally, what are you mithering about?'

She looked up, surprised by my sudden appearance. 'There was a woman in Limerick who lived across the valley from us. She had her first child on a still summer's night – that hot, hot summer five or six years ago – and we all lay awake through the long hours, listening to her agony. You could hear it that night like she was just across the road. In the morning, my mother met one of the midwives who told her they'd had to cut the baby free, that the woman hadn't been big enough across. She said you only had to look at the size of the woman's feet to know.'

I slapped her face. 'Do you think you're the first woman to give birth?' My anger ran out of me like an underground spring.

'Do you think you are so special that Death is going to come looking for you — for some cross-eyed girl I found sitting on my slops pail? Do you think, Sally, someone's going to be telling tragic tales about *you* one day?' I stopped for breath. Then I grabbed my wrap and walked out of the cottage, leaving her stunned.

The air was wet and chill, but I hardly felt it with the heat of my blood. I made my way through the black sludge of our field, my feet sinking with every step. I was heading for the coast, for the Old Head. I wanted to yell, not at Sally like I had done, but at myself. I wanted to curse myself aloud, like some Crazy Kate, for being more frightened than I had reason to be. I wanted the crash of the surf to deafen my ears so I'd hear no more of Sally's terrible, gentle sighs. I wanted to curl up like a wave, and break.

The peninsula lay ahead of me like a barren, its few trees twisted and bent by Atlantic squalls. I climbed over the Old Fosse Wall and walked on through sharp-edged grass that bit at my legs under my skirts. I passed the Rock, to which my husband and I had walked countless Sundays to hear the prohibited Mass or to make a confession. I had not gone near it since he'd left, and I skirted it now, pushing on to the narrow isthmus we knew as the Neck. In the distance, I could see the lighthouse, the brazier in its low roof not yet lit for the drawing in of day.

When I reached the top of the Head, when I stood high on that cliff we said looked like the face of our Father on the Day of Judgement (implacable rock face, long outcrop of a nose), I had no sense of how long I'd been walking. I stood at the edge and stared two hundred feet down to the sea.

The tide was out. The shore was empty. All was impossibly calm.

I picked up a stone and flung it.

Then I remembered the game I'd played when I was small. I pulled off my boots and inched my way to the brink of the cliff, gripping the rock with my cold toes and fixing my eyes on the Sovereign Islands in the distance. The two-hundred foot drop tugged at my balance, tempting me to relax, to yield, and for an instant I did.

I got dizzy with the carelessness, with the not caring for and the not thinking about those things I'd been holding out against for so long: against Death that was always nudging me when I was least expecting it; against time slipping so fast away into another century; against the fate that had crossed itself in Sally's two eyes; against the judgement of Nature waiting on an ill-gotten child yet to be born.

I felt my spine ripple. A gull soared past me, chiding. I wanted two arms – someone's arms, anyone's arms – to clasp my waist, suddenly, from behind, to pull me back, to let me drop into the long blades of seagrass.

There wasn't a soul. I prised my toes from the edge. I braced my body. I lifted one leg into mid-air and back, then the other. I'd been doing it all my life.

Sally died on the longest night of the year. Just before Christmas. On the knife-edge of the new century. She bled to death, her body ruptured by the birth.

Chapter Seven

I waited for Mr Manley to come and take the child away. By rights, if not by blood, she was his. He had been Sally's intended. He had laid his hand on her quickening belly in the dim light of our fires. He would have to rear the child.

It was already the first day of the new year when I laid her on the table, on a square of swaddling cloth I'd cut to the length of her. Eoin watched from the end of the table, his eyes peeking over the loaves that were cooling there. It was easy enough to slip the little linen shirt over her head, and even to tie the flannel and clout to her bottom. Then, very gently, I wrapped the hemp-cloth around her and started to gird it with the length of woollen roller, binding her dimpled arms to her sides, swathing her middle and winding my way towards her feet.

For just a moment, I let myself pretend she was my own little girl who'd always been so gentle and shy-eyed. I picked up a fastening pin. I chided Eoin, who had started to pick at the crust of a loaf. I looked back to the child, and saw her face wrinkling, reddening. Then came the rage, sudden as a squall.

'Never mind,' I said to Eoin, who was frightened by her cries, 'she'll rest when she's swaddled. Otherwise, babes do themselves harm. You come round here, there's a good lad, and hold her heels together, like so.' I carried on circling her round with the woollen roller, wrapping her ankles, her feet, and moving back up to her middle. I was binding the loose corners of hemp-cloth at her shoulders when I spotted Eoin smiling behind his fingers.

Her left foot was poking through the woollen bands. I muttered a curse through taut lips and started to unwind my work.

By the time her feet were succesfully bound again, her

shoulder was bursting out from below. It seemed as if she was growing – longer, greater – even as I swaddled her.

I spat out a mouthful of pins. I stripped her of all but her baby-shirt and clout. I lifted her from the table, ready to lay her back in the cradle, wanting to be rid of her, but her fingers got hold of my kercher and pulled it from my head. My hair came tumbling down. She got a fistful and yanked. I could not lower her into the cradle, but I could hardly hold on to her. She twisted and wriggled and kicked, holding fast to the clump of hair near my scalp. My arms stiffened with the strain of her. I wanted to let go – to let her fall on the rush-strewn floor.

Then she did something I had never – have never – heard of a baby doing. *She licked me.* My lower cheek. With the pink end of her baby's tongue. Quickly. So softly. And for a moment, that first day of the new year – of the new century – seemed to undo itself, to unspin like a spool of flaxen thread, rolling away far beyond my grasp.

My arms relaxed. Her hand fell away from my head. I stood with her suddenly asleep in the crook of my arms under the roof-hole of blue sky, and it was as though we'd never been anywhere but there, as though time had moved on without us.

Eoin was pulling at my apron, whimpering.

'I've come for the child, Mrs Fulworth.' Mr Manley was standing at the door. His face was ashen, and his coat, I could see, was buttoned wrong. 'I had hoped to relieve you sooner,' he said slowly, 'but I . . . I was not sure I would be able to look at it after—'

'At *her*, Mr Manley. At her.'

'I also wished to thank you, Mrs Fulworth, for sending your boy, with the message.'

'Yes, Finn said he found you all right.'

We were like two strangers once more, unable to speak naturally with our grief for Sally lodged between us.

'Sit down, please,' I said. We both stared at Sally's baby, asleep in my arms.

'She seems hearty enough,' he said.

'She is that.'

'Such a head of black hair already. Whence comes that, I wonder?'

I avoided his eyes. 'A mug of china drink perhaps, Mr Manley?'

He waived my offer.

'Then I will tell you now. You cannot take the child.' My own words surprised me. 'If you'd come even yesterday – but today's today and I've made up my mind.'

'I don't know what to think, Mrs Fulworth. Your message made everything clear. I even found—' He gave me a weak, embarrassed smile. 'I even found the coral rattle that I myself had played with as an infant . . .' He shook his waist-pocket, and I heard the sound of polished pebbles.

'If she was yours – well, it would be another matter.' I hated my cruelty.

'I see.'

'How would a man like yourself look after a child? Had you considered that?'

'I had thought perhaps Mrs Manley – Mrs Manley, my mother – might lend a hand, providing I gave up my dream of potatoes. And there is the rattle . . . I hadn't really conjectured beyond that.'

'It was thoughtful of you to call, Mr Manley,' I said.

He got to his feet. 'It was no trouble. It was good to see the child. I—' He turned away, lost for words.

'One last thing, then we shall bother you no more. Had you and Sally decided on a name?'

He looked up, his eyes alight at the mention of his beloved's name. 'Yes, we had. I had said I would fancy calling it Thomas, after myself, so I could claim it as my own.'

'But that presents a problem.'

'No, not at all, for the fact is, Sally assured me – she mentioned it not a fortnight ago – that she'd always known the child would be a little girl and that she'd call it Anne, after you if I'm not mistaken.'

I tried not to show my confusion. I simply accepted the coral rattle with thanks.

I stood at the door with Anne in my arms and watched him climb into his chaise. He turned once, waved shyly to us and was off – along the edge of my land, on to the rough-hewn path and down into the dip where he disappeared from sight, travelling slowly forward into the new era, his shoulders slightly stooped.

In later years, who would have thought she had ever had such a thing as a delicate stomach? But, as a babe-in-arms, Anne had enough trapped wind to fill the sails of the ships setting sail from Kinsale Harbour on any given day. Goat's milk, I had to concede, was not mother's milk, and her whimpering was forcing Finn, Michael and Sean into the hen house more and more.

I went into Kinsale and purchased a scuttle of coal. I got a jug of honey as well, and that evening, when our turf fire grew to a blaze, I tossed a few of the costly lumps on to its edges, poking them until they glowed brazen red. Then I lifted one from the fire with the tongs, and dropped it, alive, into a bowl of winter rain.

It steamed and hissed, and Eoin stared at me as if I was exorcising evil itself. I tipped the honey in a golden stream into the bowl of water and sizzling coal. I stirred it round, as the midwife in Ballinspittle had instructed. Then I sieved the lot of it, poured a few mouthfuls into a mug and brought it to Anne's pouting lips. She slurped it with surprising readiness. Then she belched.

After that, I hardly needed to wind her on my shoulder. The fire-in-the-water brew fuelled her digestion like nothing else could. Her cheeks seemed forever ruddy and full-blown, like those cherubim you sometimes see, nestled in the corners of New World maps, puffing at the earth and stirring miniature seas to life.

Later, when she was a little older and sitting on my knee, I would tell her how I had fed her on fire when she was still new to this world; how it would warm her heart as she grew, and her temper too perhaps; how she'd never need fear the dark or the cold or the rain, having eaten fire as a newborn.

As it was, she was ruder than a premature baby had the right to be. Fatter too. I had abandoned the swaddling clothes. She would not be girded. Instead, I cut down to size a pair of Eoin's trous and slipped them over her clout and under her shirt. Still,

I fretted over those baby-legs in the cradle, buffeting the air. I feared she'd never learn to cross her ankles when the time came; that she'd end up walking bow-legged; that she'd grow up wild. But I could not bring myself to try again. *You cannot swaddle a changeling*, Mother Midnight whispered. *It will not be still.*

Our Eoin loved her dearly. By day, he'd wrap his stout self around her, keeping her warm as I churned the milk or carded wool or dug the black eyes out of the newly lifted potatoes. At night, he'd bend over her cradle and coo at her like a wood-pigeon, fingering the black down of her hair, searching for the lice that would bring her to tears in the night.

Sometimes, as she slept in the cradle by my bed, when I knew she was sleeping too deeply to hear, I'd hum those half-forgotten lullabies I'd once sung to my own little girl, mouthing the words to the night, like fragments of a spell that might change her back.

> Dada is riding,
> Mamma is biding,
> Baby is hiding
> at the bottom
>   of the
>   wishing-well . . .

Though I'd let no one have her or hold her or hurt her, I did not want her. (*I do not want you.*) Sleepless and face-up to the night, the darkness seemed ripe with my secret.

Chapter Eight

He raised her, streaming with salt water, from a stone font he had borne in a barrow between turfs. 'Father in Thy Kingdom, we ask Thee to receive this orphan child, Anne, into Thy fold through the power of the Holy Spirit. Keep her free from harm and Evil's way, and deliver her at the Day of Judgement into Thy mercy, Amen.'

'Amen.' The small group of us huddled together for warmth behind the Rock. Behind us, a fishing hooker was making for harbour, tacking towards Kinsale. The wind was out of the south-west and stiff, and Anne was hollering with the wet and the cold.

Father Geary dipped his fingers into the Atlantic water and made the sign of the Cross on her head. 'In the name of the Father, the Son, and the Holy Spirit.'

We blessed ourselves, then I genuflected before the Rock and wrapped Anne to my breast.

She had a name.

Finn saw him first. He was waiting for us on the other side of the Old Fosse Wall.

'Pay no mind,' I said, determined he wouldn't worry them. Sean and Michael climbed to the top of the wall and peered over. 'Sean, help Eoin over. Michael, get going or our dinner will be boiled to a mush by the time we get home.'

They gave up their positions reluctantly. I clambered over, glancing at him warily. He was leaning against the stonework, his arms folded casually across his chest. He didn't even look up.

We went back across the fields, the same as we came. I would not hurry our progress.

'Sean, if you stop looking behind you, you'll stop tripping over your feet.'

'He's behind us.'

'If he chooses to skulk behind us,' I said in a loud and careless voice, 'that's his business.'

Finn had pushed on ahead of us, walking at an angry pace, eyes fixed on the ground. Watching the back of him slowly dissolve into the black of the fields, it struck me. He had his father's gait.

A year and a half on, and you'd think he'd just walked in after a day's labour in the field. He doused his head in the water butt. He stroked the side of the cow. He walked into the cottage, took a seat on the bench and loosened the laces of his boots. Then he stood up, peeled a dry pat of dung from the wall and threw it on to the already healthy blaze in the hearth. He took his seat on the bench again, and I could tell from the slope of his back that he was waiting for his mackerel and potatoes.

I told the boys to bring the bowls, and slowly I filled one after another from the pot on the hearth, stealing glimpses of that back of his between servings. I tried to read it like some would a face. I tried to see if those shoulders, more rounded now, said *humbled* or if the curve in that muscle of a neck said *I will bend*, but I could tell nothing.

When we'd eaten our meal, and no longer had the excuse of food in our mouths, I risked speech. 'Peter. Where's Peter?'

He looked up, surprised. 'You told him to go, that's where he is.'

'To you. I told him to go to you.'

'Well, he's gone. Hardly stopped. He went over the water, and I haven't heard a by-your-leave from him since.'

I jumped to my feet, my hands smacking the tabletop. The boys turned. He leaned back on the bench and waited, daring me. 'There's more,' I said. 'Pass me your bowls.'

That evening, when the fire was low and the wick in the lamp was almost at its end, I climbed into my bed next to my husband, and we, all of us, listened to the clenched silence of that one-room cottage. The bed seemed smaller now than it had once been. He and I had little choice but to sleep, back against back. I could feel the cage of his ribs and the uneven rhythm of his breathing.

I did not fear him, though I could still smell the violence in his sweat. I didn't care that he'd been in the bed of another. I could only think, over and over to myself, *there isn't the room, in my bed, in my home, at my table, in my heart, there just isn't the room.*

I could not remember how we had begun, all those years ago. Only that, once, he had clasped his strong hands around my waist, as if they were a belt he was fitting, and when his fingertips had met at the small of my back, we had smiled.

Come morning, he was up before any of us and gone, and for a moment I almost wanted to thank him for turning round on his heels and righting the wrong of coming in the first place.

Only later did Michael and Sean find him at the far end of the field, stooped over the crop, checking the leaves for wireworm, potato scab and the black mark of blight. I watched him from the shadow of the cottage as he walked up and down those rows, fingering the leaves, taking up handfuls of soil here and there, pulling out the misfits. All the while, my two boys trailed behind, trying to keep up. Michael was thirteen now and Sean ten, and I knew they were falling in love with his long, long stride.

Finn was watching too from behind a heap of peat we'd dumped next to the hen-house. He was slicing it into blocks of twenty pounds or more apiece, and wielding the wing-slane with a vengeance. I walked over to him and stood, just watching, my arms folded over my breast. 'Those are mighty turfs you're cutting.'

He wiped his face with his sleeve.

'There'll be the drying still, of course,' I started. 'Eoin and I can manage that. But you and Sean and Michael will need to look to the rickling and the clamping this year. I've got too much on with a new baby about the place again.'

He nodded, patient of the interruption.

My words were idle. I was standing there for no other reason than to stand close to someone, to Finn who was more gentle and more angry than any other I've ever known.

He watched the progress of a teal in the sky overhead, avoiding my eyes. 'Do you want me to kill him?'

The bird dipped out of sight. I tried to laugh. 'Get away with you.' Then I reached up and tousled his hair which was sometimes red and sometimes yellow, depending on how you looked at it and which way the sun was shining. You could never fix Finn one way or the other.

A smile crept over his face, though still he wouldn't look at me. 'Get away yourself.'

Eoin was afraid of his father and had, since he'd returned, been clinging to my skirts more than usual. His da laughed at him, not unkindly either, but it made our youngest all the more wary. So I thought nothing of it that rainy afternoon when Eoin tugged plaintively at my sleeve.

'Not now, lad.' I was bending over the fire, testing the heat of Anne's goat's milk.

He started to whimper, as he hadn't done since he was a toddler stumbling around on new legs. I turned my head and glanced over my shoulder.

My husband, his father, had lifted Anne from the cradle. He had her at arm's length over his head, mollycoddling her in mid-air. It was the first notice he had taken of her. I turned back to the fire.

'Isn't she on proper food yet?'

I prodded the turf with the tongs. 'No. There's time.'

He started bouncing her on his lap, so vigorously she began to cry. 'Hush,' he said, suddenly tender. 'Hush now.' She went quiet, and that's when it came to me. He thought Anne, large for her months as she was, was our own little dear girl, our daughter who had not lived to have a name. 'What did you call her then?' he said, almost an afterthought.

I straightened, like something had been shot up my back. 'Where are your eyes, man? She's not yours.' My words tumbled out too fast.

'No?' His face reddened.

'No, she – your girl – our girl is gone. Dead.' I couldn't explain fast enough. About Sally, a girl out of nowhere, in whose tears my little one drowned; a girl who was with us, then gone, leaving nothing behind but this orphan's orphan. About Mr Manley and the tomcat. It all seemed impossible at that moment, unreal in that room that smelled of burning milk and his sweat. 'She – her name is Anne.'

'Her mother's daughter,' he said, returning her to the cradle. 'How dear.'

'No, she's—'

Eoin was in a fit of tears in the corner behind my bed.

'Get out,' he said.

My mouth went dry.

'Get out and take your bastard with you.'

'You're mad,' I breathed, backing away.

'You heard me, Annie.'

'I did, but I cannot believe what I'm hearing.'

'Believe it.'

'But I, I am the one who has kept this farm going, or have you forgotten? I said nothing when you up and left for the cunt of Lord-knows-who but it's *me, me,*' I said, thumping my breast, 'who sowed and harvested and reaped and fed our five sons—'

'My five sons. Take what you need and get out.'

My senses reeled. *'Yours?'*

'The boys are mine by law, and so's the worthless lease for the land you're standing on. Get out.'

'Mary, Mother of Jesus.' I stood, breathing hard, trying to think fast. Wondering when Finn would return for his dinner. Wishing him home. Wanting him and Michael and Sean to stay far away. I slid down the length of the wall behind me, as though my legs were giving way, as though I might faint. Then I lifted a handful of rushes from the floor and shoved their tips into the fire where Anne's milk was boiling over.

My hand burst into flame. 'How dare you come back into this home and tell me to leave it? How dare you come back here and tell me what's mine?' I brought my blazing torches close to his face, so close I could see his features, details I had almost forgotten – the downward curl of his bottom lip, the straight line of his nose, the stubble that was always red though his head was black – and I tried to hate that face as the flames wavered there like a threat between us.

I expected to hear his voice lower to a growl, to feel his fist in my face, but he only turned away. He walked over to the bench and sat down. 'You'll burn your hand in a moment. Just get your things together and go. You have no place here any longer.' It was his terrible, terrible calm that winded me.

I found myself dropping the rushes on to the fire and moving, as if in a trance, about the room. I folded my shift that I'd rinsed out only an hour earlier. I found my hose (one in the cupboard, the other behind the bed). I knotted my second skirt around that morning's batch of oatcakes. I took my wrap down from the peg and pulled a piece of cord from the turf stack to bundle it all. Then I cursed myself, pulling my wrap out of the bundle, remembering suddenly that I'd need it. Evening was coming on, I'd need to tie Anne to my breast with the length of it. I gathered her to me, and at the last minute, lifted the cradle cloth, remembering the dried petal of her caul. I pulled a single stocking out of the bundle and slipped it in the toe. 'You'll never drown,' I mumbled, girding us round with my wrap. Already, the rain was beating on the roof.

In that uncanny scene I couldn't shake myself free from, I turned and was making for the door, shuffling toward it, when the sight of Eoin, crumpled in the corner, jarred me to my senses. I turned on my heels and retraced my steps to the corner, getting hold of his hand. 'Get up,' I said. 'Come on now, on your feet.' He did as I told him, but his face had such fear in it I almost sank to my knees. 'Hold my hand. Do you hear? Just hold my hand.'

We walked, not proudly, but unhurriedly out of the cottage, past the sight of my husband's back.

I might have waited behind the hen house or under a tree for Finn to come and find us. Later, he'd look. He'd search the mud-churned path and the patch of black wood and the caverns in the cliff-face along the shore. There was no point in letting him find us. There was no home to return us to, and knowing it would break him.

The going was slow with the mud and the rain and night coming on. Eoin was still too small to walk much of a distance at once, and what with Anne at my breast I couldn't carry him at all. As we neared Ballinspittle, I had it in my head to knock on the door of a well-lit home and ask for a place for the night. I eyed each as we went, swallowing hard, trying to shape my story in my head as I walked.

I couldn't.

We approached the walls of Kinsale late in the evening. I knew that the Gift House was to the south. I headed north. I told myself some suitable shelter would soon appear. I went up Fisher Street, past St Multose's and the Holy Stone. The marketplace was abandoned. The day's slops had amassed into a dam in the gutters; the rainfall was mounting to a flood underfoot. More houses on Cork Street, many of them now dark. I studied each and kept walking.

I hardly know what I was thinking. Maybe that, at last, when the town had run out, the darkness of the fields ahead might frighten me enough to quell my pride.

Fog had blown in out of nowhere. Ahead, only a few lights persisted. Eoin was trembling in his rain-sodden clothes and Anne, who'd not had her milk, was wailing. I'd brought the oatcakes and was trying to reach one in the bundle on my back when I remembered she could not yet take whole foods.

There was a house in the distance. I turned off the road and crossed over a field, my back curling with the weight of Anne at my breast and Eoin on one arm.

As we drew near, I saw it was a bigger place than it had looked from the road. I comforted myself, remembering I'd have no story to tell; no pride to contend with. Finer people seemed to accept the misfortune of the resident poor with little explanation.

I steered us round to the back door and knocked firmly. I waited. Nothing. I knocked again, drumming my knuckles against its oaken panels. Then bolts sliding back and the door opening to us and someone muttering. The face of a manservant came slowly into view behind a flickering taper.

'Pardon the hour,' I said, 'I have with me an infant and a small child, and no place to go. Could you send word that we are in need of a roof for the night and a bit of nourishment?

'Already retired,' he said, wasting no words on us. 'To bed.'

'Oh.' Even as I stood there, I was fixing my thoughts on the chicken-house which would surely, if I could just find it, harbour the three of us for the night. I was ready to turn when he spoke again.

'This way.'

I hovered on the doorstep, hardly believing.

'Be quick about it.'

I sallied through the door into a darkened room. I could see nothing, but I felt the flags solid below my feet. They made a change from mud.

We followed his faint light through the room, into another, and through an open door which he closed promptly behind us. I could make out a straw mattress on the floor, a welcome sight. I decided against reminding our friend about food that night. Instead, I settled Eoin on the mattress, fed him an oatcake and tucked him in, under my second skirt. Then I unwrapped Anne, laid her next to Eoin and waited for her tears to give way to sleep.

Come first light, I was already awake, flat on my back and wondering just how long we might loiter. I turned on to my side and checked Anne, then Eoin. I was feeling their foreheads for chill or fever when I saw it: curled up in the middle of the mattress and licking the soles of Anne's feet. A black tom.

It was like waking into a dream.

Chapter Nine

Shoo the cat, shoo the cat,
a child is asleep.
Shoo the cat, shoo the cat
before it can creep,
into the cradle and over the lace,
drawing the breath from the wee sleeping face.

It was Sally's tomcat, and the sight of it had set old rhymes reeling in my head. I chased it into a corner, gathered Anne to me and bound her again to my chest with my wrap. She was starting to whimper for a feeding, but I didn't stop. I slapped Eoin's cheeks till he woke with a cry. I spat on the hem of my skirt and wiped his eyes of sleep. I stuffed his shirt with the straw that was spilling from a corner of the paliasse. At last, I pulled on my boots, picked up my bundle, and got us through the door. I can still see that animal as I pulled the door to, licking its fur into a ruffle. Provoking a storm, a fisherman would say. I shut the door fast.

'Mrs Fulworth! Good day!'

I fell back against it.

Mr Manley stood before me, at the bottom of a bulging staircase, dressed only in a nightdress and a pair of leather mules. 'I have it on report from Squibb that you arrived somewhat later than might have been hoped for last night. I am afraid I have only just now heard you were here.'

I blinked, dazed by the siege of his words.

'But all this is piffle, for I have not yet thanked you for your swift response. I did not hope you might reply in person. In fact, I feared you might not reply at all. I take it you will breakfast with me this morning, you and the offspring.'

'Thank you, Mr Manley. We will.' I could hardly believe my own composure. Moments before I'd been planning to steal as many eggs from his hens as we could carry.

He showed us to the kitchen table and mustered porridge and buttermilk.

'And for the little one, Mr Manley?'

He lifted a milk pail from its nail on the kitchen panel and thrust it at the footman, who loitered by the fire. 'Squibb, duty calls.'

'Not the goat, Mr Manley.'

He nodded solemnly. I unwrapped Anne and cradled her in my arms, worrying about her clothes, still damp with last night's weather, and the cord belt at her waist which was chafing her belly. Eoin was, it seemed, more content; he followed Squibb out to the barn to watch the ritual contest between goat and man. For my own part, I was wondering just how much Mr Manley might explain before I found myself obliged to.

'Squibb isn't a bad sort,' he chattered as he spooned the porridge up. 'He enjoys his hops more than Mrs Manley thought seemly, and for a footman, he drags his feet more than is to be desired.' He cudgelled an oaty lump with the back of his spoon. 'Indeed, I thought he would never get round to delivering my missive to you.'

I accepted my porridge and smiled weakly.

'He knew its contents, you see.'

'I see.' But I didn't.

'The truth is, Mrs Fulworth, I might have borne my message to you myself, but I feared . . .'

'Yes?'

'I feared your reply.'

'I came, didn't I?' I surprised myself with my own daring. 'There is no harm in discussion.'

He looked up, relieved. 'Well, don't fret that you'll be sleeping on that paliasse again. That was merely Squibb's ignorance.'

I studied his face, trying to fathom just what it was that lay in his mind, but for once he mystified me. Nor was there any time for conjecture. We had hardly finished our porridge when he was up again. 'Would you permit me to show you your chamber?'

'But Anne's milk . . .' I said lamely.

He smiled. 'All will be hers by and by, Mrs Fulworth, I do assure you.'

I had little choice but to follow Mr Manley up the groaning stair, past the library, past the Great Hall, which was strangely familiar to me from Sally's tales, and up yet another twisting staircase, at the top of which lay the unknown. As I climbed, Anne grew into a hefty weight against my shoulder, one which reminded me that, above all, I must tread carefully.

The bed was worryingly tall.

'Try it, Mrs Fulworth. Please do. It was formerly my mother's bed, on those occasions when she came hither, though usually it was myself who went thither, so it has had but little use.'

I did not want to seem ungrateful, so I passed the wriggling bulk of Anne to Mr Manley, who was pleasantly surprised. I approached the brocade height warily, considering as I went the best means of mounting it. I turned myself round, facing Mr Manley and Anne. Then I got hold of the soft edge of the mattress and hoisted myself up and back. My feet were left dangling over the side like a child's, but at least the bed had not embarrassed me as I'd feared it might. It had not loomed up like some white-capped wave and lost me in its goosedown swell. Could I sleep on it though? The paliasse below stairs beckoned.

'You must roll, Mrs Fulworth. To test it, you see.'

'Test it for what?' I wanted to get off.

'For give. For stability. You see, this bed has been exceedingly well stuffed. Especially made for comforting a difficult mother. Do roll, Mrs Fulworth, I beg you.'

With misgivings, I lay back, gripped the edge and swayed to and fro a little. I managed to produce a sizeable dimple in the mattress, but I did not let go.

'No, no. Allow me.' He returned Anne to my arms, excusing me from my exertions. I slid off the bed as he mounted it. Then, in one robust move, he threw himself into the very middle where the life of the thing launched him into flight. He rolled back and forth, buoyant on the brocade spread. 'Forgive me my saying so,' he said, 'but this is a jolly good bed.'

I changed the subject. 'About your message, Mr Manley.'

'There is time, indeed there is. You are here and that is what matters. Once again, I thank you, Mrs Fulworth.'

'And I you, Mr Manley, for . . .' My words were going astray. I could not discover what I needed to know. I could only make good my bluff. 'For the bed, naturally. But we must—'

'And do you like the looking-glass? It is Venetian, and gives quite a good likeness. Do have a peek, Mrs Fulworth, I exhort you.'

I shook my head like a shy-faced girl. I'd hardly seen my own image before. Only in puddles and in the bowls of pewter spoons – and in the clear blue pools of Sally's eyes on that day, a lifetime ago, when I found her outside my door.

Down below, someone was beating a tattoo on an iron kettle.

'That'll be Squibb. At last,' he declared triumphant, 'the goat has submitted.'

He looked considerably more cowed when I confronted him the following day in the field.

'We must speak, Mr Manley.'

'I see.' He dropped his hoe. 'Shall we adjourn to my library?'

'If you prefer.'

'The children?'

'Are with Mr Squibb.'

'Good of him,' he said, frustrated.

'Yes.'

'Will you walk this way?'

We passed field after barren field, sidestepping a rusty pair of pruning clippers, an abandoned trowel, and an almost toothless rake. 'The weeds are getting the better of your land, Mr Manley.'

'Indeed,' he sighed. 'We are surely fools in the eyes of Nature, Mrs Fulworth, for that which one tenderly cultivates cannot live out a season, while that which is crossed with the random, with Chaos itself, will thrive. The hybrid plant, the shoot of the perverse crossing, has an indomitable vigour.'

In the library, I refused to take the only seat. Mr Manley seemed in greater need.

'I did not explain myself in full in my recent epistle, Mrs Fulworth. I had hoped to test the waters so to speak, in the first instance.'

'Go on.'

'I expressed my sincere wish to adopt Anne as my own, as I'd engaged to do after Sally's death – only this time with the, I hope, more acceptable proviso that you might raise her here in my home.'

I swallowed.

'Since Mrs Manley's death . . .'

His wife? His mother?

'. . . my estranged wife has, as I endeavoured to explain, made known to me her wish to return from Cork to this, her family home. You see, my mother's home, my wife's residence of late, is now to be sold.'

'I see.'

'This home is my entitlement by marriage. It is also the place, in my most recent misfortune, which I have come to cherish. I am no potato farmer, Mrs Fulworth, and never have been. This is all I know.'

'Well, surely she cannot return,' I said, though even as I spoke, I remembered what it was to have your home taken out from under you.

'No, on the contrary, our marriage still exists in the eyes of the law, so she is free to come and go with . . .'

'With?'

His eyes narrowed. He seemed to change his mind. 'Impunity.'

I called his bluff. 'Funny name for a child, Mr Manley.'

His face went blank.

'Sally guessed as much,' I lied. 'She had the Sight, it cannot be denied,' as did everyone whom Squibb had told.

'And she never said! All that time and she never said she knew!'

'I expected she wanted to spare you.'

I'd taken a risk, but not so great a one as I might have taken. As far as I knew, Mr Manley still suspected another of fathering his own child. Squibb, that drunken witness to Mrs Manley's deception, had of course made the facts known to most of

Kinsale, but never to Mr Manley himself. I held on to the secret like a bead on a rosary.

'Well, the difficulty is this, Mrs Fulworth,' he said. 'Mrs Manley will surely be back in this home before the year is out *with* her merrybegot in tow, a child she will declare as heir no less.'

'It would be the sensible thing to do, given her situation.'

'But don't you see, Mrs Fulworth? I could not go on. Not here. Not in my home as I know it. I could not endure the deceit, and yet, not only would I have to endure it, I would have little choice but to confirm it to the eyes of the world. Unless . . .'

'Unless?'

'Unless I were to produce an heir myself.'

I remembered yesterday's familiar romp on the bed upstairs and blanched.

'Oh no, dear Mrs Fulworth. Forgive me my coarse phraseology. No, I mean Anne. Sally's Anne. I mean Anne to be my heir.'

He offered me his seat, which I now gratefully accepted. 'Is Mrs Manley's Impunity a girl then?'

'Yes. A girl.'

'How would the law decide in such a matter: one girl bastard over another girl bastard?'

'I said in my missive, I had a plan, Mrs Fulworth.'

'You did.' I didn't miss a beat.

'I am proposing, with deference to your sound judgement, that we raise Anne as . . .' He straightened his neckcloth. '. . . as the recently orphaned child of a distant Manley cousin, for the sake of a legitimate claim. My mother, may she sleep forever, is gone. There is no one else to assert that Anne is not a Manley.'

'Anne Manley.' I shaped the name in my mouth, trying to make it real. 'Would your legitimate "niece", let us say, then have the advantage over – I crossed two fingers – Mrs Manley's illegitimate heir?'

'No, Mrs Fulworth. Not a niece . . .'

'No?'

'Not a niece, but – to put it delicately – a nephew.'

The word lingered between us like a shameful intimacy.

'The name Anson,' he quietly explained, 'is in fact an old

63

family name, traditionally passed from one generation to the subsequent. It was,' he cleared his tightening throat, 'my father's name. It is my own middle name. I . . . I thought it might suit our purposes.'

I couldn't speak. I understood his meaning too well.

'I am painfully aware that I ask a great deal, Mrs Fulworth. Too much, many would say. Yet I know not what else to do, or to whom I might turn. In offering me your consent, you would be doing me the most humane of services, for which I should count myself fortunate simply to be able to provide for you, Anne, and your lads.'

I was stunned. 'But Sally. What about Sally? She died birthing that child, and now we are to pretend she never existed. How dare you suggest a thing? How dare I even consider it?'

He turned to the window, too ashamed to speak.

'It is wrong, Mr Manley.'

'Is it, Mrs Fulworth? I honestly do not know any more. I am a man adrift in his fears and may well have turned foolish with hoping. Even as I speak, my better self tells me that it was base of me even to think I could barter with Sally's child for my own sorry purpose. Forgive me, I beg you. You should leave me now, before I once more take leave of my senses. Go now please, Mrs Fulworth, and return to your own home where I shall endeavour not to bother you again.'

'It is now my turn to confess, Mr Manley.'

He turned to me.

'Anne, Eoin and I, we have no home to return to.'

'But—'

I shook my head.

His eyes were wide with concern. 'I am sorry to hear it, Mrs Fulworth. Truly I am.'

'Yet should your wife and her child turn up again, you would have no home to offer us.'

'I wish it were not the case.'

'Never mind. It was not meant to be. Anyway, how could you have provided, in this plan of yours? I admire your ever hopeful heart, but I have not forgotten, and I mean no offence, your reduction of circumstances.'

64

'You forget my mother, Mrs Fulworth. There was no one else to whom she could bequeath her, albeit modest, estate.'

'I see.' I was at a loss again. I could submit to the deceit of his plan and live out a lie with a roof over our heads. Or I could do right by the man. I could inform him there and then that his wife's child was none other than his own, at which news husband and wife would surely reconcile. I would turn inevitably to the almshouse and so render our three lives as uncertain as the wind.

It was no option. 'We will try your plan, Mr Manley.' I searched for the words. 'We will, the four of us, together, try.'

For once, he simply nodded. His own desperation had left him a chastened man.

Upstairs, this is what I found laid out on my bed:

two stiffened waistcoats of flannel, one red and one yellow,
three caps of linen edged with lace,
six pairs of knit stockings,
two long bibs and one bib collar,
and one pair of kid leather pumps.

But no coats. No trous. Instead I found diverse items, the sight of which left me wondering whether I had understood anything Mr Manley had said that day. There were

two linen shifts,
two white cotton aprons,
four canvas underskirts,
and two skirts, one in a purple baize, the other in a popinjay taffeta.

I fingered each skirt as if it had been conjured from air. I marvelled at the matching bodices: whalebone stays, silver buttons on the one, velvet ties on the other and – I could only stare – the taffeta bodice nearly afloat with ballooning sleeves. Even Anne seemed awed by the richness of colour and cloth on the bed.

I laid her on her back, untied the cord at her middle, eased her out of her over-sized trous, pulled the linen shirt over her head and changed her clout. Then I made her anew.

Her idle fingers were poking at the taffeta sleeves when Mr Manley popped his head through my open door.

'He likes the virago sleeves, does he not, Mrs Fulworth?'

I nearly dropped her.

'Short-coated, you said, Mr Manley. There was no coat. I found no coat.'

'*Coat*, Mrs Fulworth. Petticoat, that is to say, skirt. Short-coated or, otherwise said, a short petticoat. It should reach only the tops of a child's feet. I understand that one's nephew should be in coats by the age of six weeks.'

I'd forgotten the ways of gentle people, if indeed I'd ever known them at all.

Ahead of me, in the looking-glass in which my world wobbled, I caught sight of Mr Manley with Anne in his arms, and was again confounded. Her disguise that was no disguise unsettled me more than I could reason. There was nothing to disbelieve in, no deceit through which to see. Anson was a breathing illusion with a head of black hair and the ruddiest of cheeks.

Then I saw. 'Mr Manley! Turn away from that glass!' I cried out, but not soon enough.

Every mother knows – *what* had I been thinking? – no babe should see its reflection before it has lived out a year, or the young soul will be lost forever to the likeness. 'What have we done, Mr Manley? What *have* we done?'

He only tut-tutted, but I couldn't shake off my sense of dread. Anne's new soul had escaped us – had escaped *her* – when I wasn't looking.

Chapter Ten

Anne was Eoin's wonder, as she had been from the first, but the remaking of the wee baby girl in his hand-me-down trous into the little lad in skirts had left him not a little mystified. And, once she discovered her feet, there was no holding her back. I stitched leading-strings to the armholes of her bodices and waistcoats, but it was no good. In those early years, she was always hiding – in the wheelbarrow, under the goat, in the crab-apple tree – and Eoin was always seeking. 'Anson will disappear one day,' he said to me once.

'Aye. Into thin air,' I replied with a wink.

'And I'll cry,' he whispered.

Mr Manley was like a new man since the coming of his nephew. He had seen off the threat of Mrs Manley and her heir-to-be. He had managed to piece together the remains of his solicitor's practice, so that it was, if not successful, then at least faithful to its erstwhile tradition of almost getting along – 'And tradition carries weight with people of substance, Mrs Fulworth.' His beloved home was not only secure, but more alive than he had ever known it to be, and Anne was very nearly the son he never had.

It was early November, near the end of her sixth year, when I sensed something was afoot. I had most of the season's pickings potted, pickled or preserved. The flesh for the coming winter – mostly mutton and pork – was nearly cured, and the children were stitched into their clothing before the first real frost. It was a morning much like any other when Mr Manley gathered us together in the Great Hall and announced he was off to Cork.

'Right then,' I said, 'you'll be wanting some victuals and a flask of something hot.' I started for the kitchen.

'I'll hitch up the mare, sir, if that's all then,' said Squibb, already dreaming of lethargy at the Cockle.

'Well—'

Squibb lifted his cap and made for the door.

'Are we to go with you, Uncle?' asked Anne, pushing herself and Eoin forward.

'No, I—'

'Shall we go bother the goat then?' she said, turning to Eoin.

'A moment everybody!' he shouted, reining us all in. 'Is nobody at all curious as to the purpose of my mission?'

I wiped my oat-sticky hands on my apron. 'Why are you going to Cork, Mr Manley?'

He was several times on the verge of speech. Then, 'No, I shall not tell you,' and he beamed with his secret.

Squibb glared. I folded my arms impatiently. Below stairs, I fretted, my bread was baking to stone.

Then he started shouting directives. 'Mrs Fulworth, some victuals, if you please, and a toddy in a flask too. Squibb, make ready the chaise! Why do you dally? Eoin, fetch me my muff and spatterdashes! Anson, my greatcoat and sword! Come, come!' he clamoured, clapping his hands at the lot of us.

I thought he would never be on his way, what with his indecision about which wig, and the mislaid carriage blanket, and the pebble that seemed to have lodged itself in the toe of his long boot. At last, Squibb, seizing the moment, slapped the horse's rump and Mr Manley was off, evidently a little sooner than he had expected.

O'Daley Agin Dooley

On the Sabbath, it was not expected that Squibb or I should accompany Anne to St Multose's. We agreed instead to take her and Eoin to the Harbour to look at the fishing hookers moving in and out under sail.

We never got there. We had hardly made it as far as the Holy Stone when we heard a clamour so great it seemed to be coming from everywhere at once. Squibb sniffed the air. 'It's coming from the ring, but that's no cock fight.'

The ring was on the other side of the town wall. We double-backed along Fisher Street and nipped through Blind Gate. Soon we were travelling along a footpath that had already been churned into mud by countless feet. At last we arrived at the outskirts of the ring, only to meet up with a wall of like-minded bodies. 'What is it?' I said to Squibb, who was ungainly tall and therein had an advantage.

'A match, I believe.'

'Who can you see?'

'There's Jumping Jack O'Hennessy in the centre of the ring. He's already stamping about, and there's two fierce somebodies up there, sitting on hay bales with their backs to one another.'

'Anyone we know?'

'I couldn't say.'

'I want to see,' whimpered Anne. 'Pick me up, Squibb.'

'Me too,' pleaded Eoin.

'Now lads, you're too great for the gangly likes of me to bolster.'

Still they whined.

'All right. Listen here. When Squibb gives the word, we all make a dash for the front. Understood?'

They nodded, and me with them.

Squibb checked his left shoulder. He checked his right. Then he disappeared into the thick of the throng. 'WOLF!' came the awful, crowd-sundering cry. 'WOLF! In yonder field, by Jesus!'

Anne, Eoin and I dug our heels into the fresh sawdust at the edge of the ring, and Squibb came off not so very badly trampled. The crowd slowly drifted back.

'Didn't think I had it in me, did you, Mrs Fulworth?'

'No,' I smiled.

'Can't take all the due,' he told me, spitting out a scrap of sawdust. 'Got the idea from a tale my mother used to tell me, though I'm damned if I can remember its particulars.'

'Best to let it lie, Squibb.'

The ringside was peopled once again, and adrenalin was high after the wild wolf chase. Jumping Jack O'Hennessy looked like a pot about to boil. 'Crier, cry out the challenge!'

The Crier stepped fastidiously into the ring and puffed up his chest like a windy bagpipe. The whole ring went as quiet as a church. 'Hearken ye here gathered to the challenge I shall repeat to you. "I, Moira Dooley, of Ballintubber, having had words with Katie O'Daley, and requiring satisfaction, do invite her to face me in the ring with a crown in her right hand to match the crown in my own. The first woman to lose her crown – or her balls – to admit defeat."'

The crowd of us cheered lustily.

'Now the Reply,' declared the Crier. '"I, Katie O'Daley, of Ballymartle, hearing the Challenge, will not fail, Justice willing, to give her more blows than words, desiring only an eager opponent – and from her no favour – so that, in this respect, she might be true to my knowledge of her if to nothing else!"'

We hollered again.

Moira and Katie seized the hems of their skirts, stuffed them up through the waistbands of their aprons, and tied the bulk into great knots at their sides. Moira was the more sturdy of the two, I could see that. The girth of her legs was big with muscle. Katie, though, was lean and sinewy. 'She'll be quick, that one,' I confided to Squibb.

'Aye, but Moira has the look of the sorely wronged. I'm for her.'

Jack motioned the two of them to centre ring. 'Secure your crown!' he shouted, and each woman dipped a hand into her apron front, making a fist round the coin. 'Take your stand!' Katie's arms curled into two raw-knuckled fists, while Moira raised a powerful thigh.

When the call came, Moira's boot landed square on Katie's face. Blood coursed like the Bandon River from her nose and, for a moment, she lost her footing, but only for a moment. When the boot came again, swinging high into the air, Katie got hold of it, and Moira toppled fast on to her tailbone.

Anne ballyhooed with delight.

But Katie was down again, flattened under Moira's bulk, and pummelling her back with the hand that grasped the coin. 'She's down and out,' said Squibb, but he was wrong. Flat on her back, she forced up her legs, resurrecting her two knees with a surprising force. The suddenness of it threw Moira, head first, into a beauteous somersault and she landed, winded, at the feet of Jumping Jack. But she hadn't lost her coin.

'I love you, Moira!' shouted Squibb, who didn't know the woman from Eve. 'Come on. On your feet now!'

'You're a beauty, Katie O'Daley!' shouted Anne, who had, it seemed, been spending too much time with Squibb.

Moira stumbled to her feet and started back again across the ring, falling into stride as she went. Then came the move that would leave us breathless.

In a surge of marvellous strength, she grabbed Katie by her narrow waist and hoisted her skyward. Both coins rolled away, but nobody cared. The two of them were spinning round and round like some terrible windstorm, spinning like they'd never stop. Moira's cheeks were bright with the rush of blood; Katie's were as white as Easter snow. High over our heads she was poised, resolute as a sacrifice in Moira's grasp, as potent as an offering to some angry old heathen god.

Moira slowed almost to a halt. She seemed to breathe in all the air in that crowded ring. Nobody moved. Anne squeezed my hand so tight my fingers went cold. At last, bending her knees low, Moira made one fiercesome thrust and sent Katie revolving high into the air, twisting against that blue Sabbath sky like the Spirit was moving through her.

When she landed again in Moira's firm hold, her eyes were shining. I could see them bright as day. Anne saw them too. 'I love you,' I saw her mouth to the woman high overhead.

Then Katie was descending to earth. Moira lowered her to her feet and dusted her off.

'Who won, Squibb?' Anne asked as we walked away.

'Hard to say. Nobody, not even Jumping Jack, could say which coin hit ground first.'

'What did they have words about in the first place?' asked Eoin.

'I don't know, son,' I said. 'The best way to make a pot of broth? Or to milk a cow? Or to murder a husband? There's no telling.'

We walked back into town and through the hushed streets, all strangely still except for the sound of two crowns jingling in Squibb's waist-pocket.

Mr Manley arrived back when expected, with a wooden crate strapped to the rear of the carriage, and boxes and parcels besides. The bulk of this baggage was foisted upon a protesting Squibb, but the crate, Mr Manley insisted, would be borne by himself.

'What's in it, Uncle?' asked Anne, searching the crate for cracks.

'You must guess. You must all guess,' he declared, slowly recovering his breath.

'Spirits!' said Squibb.

'A wee beast,' said Anne.

'Gold!' said Eoin.

Mr Manley turned to me. 'Well, Mrs Fulworth?'

'Well, it's weighty, that's for sure.'

'Yes.'

'Must be you've discovered the philosopher's stone,' I said, giving him a wry smile.

Saying not a word, he prised open the lid of the crate and threw it back to reveal – we weren't sure what. From where I was standing, it looked like dirt. Black, potato-making dirt.

'Terra Nova,' he proclaimed.

We blinked.

'The New World itself!' he declared. Then, lowering his head to the open crate, he kissed an earthen clump.

Chapter Eleven

'Mr Manley,' I said, 'would you explain the difference between New World earth and Old World earth?'

'Aye,' said Squibb joining in, 'for if it is used dirt, sir, and not new dirt, I must warn you that you have possibly been had.'

Eoin giggled, but Anne was in a world all her own, pushing her hands through the rich brown soil. 'I've found something!' she called out and we choked on our laughter. She was clutching a waxy paper packet. 'It looks like seeds.'

'It is, my boy. In this instance, the seeds of a New World wonder known as the pump-kin: a relative of the marrow, I do believe, but of a corpulence and colour hitherto unknown to us in Ireland.'

'There's more in here, Uncle.'

'There surely is. The seeds of that most poetically named of the cowcumber family, the acorn squash. And . . .' He was ransacking the crate now, heedless of his riding gloves. 'And here, Mrs Fulworth, a bit of martagon root, esteemed a culinary delight by the pagans of the land. For you, Eoin, the starchy tuber of the yam, more commonly known as the sweet potato, but most uncommon in its taste I am assured. And these black seeds, Squibb, if memory serves me well, are the tender beginnings of a marvellous fruit known locally as the watery melon – generous in its proportions with, I understand, a lurid red pulp that will excite all but the most hardened of fruit fanciers.'

Squibb accepted the packet with a new-found respect.

'Come spring, I will sprinkle this rich, virgin earth across my land in a rite of renewal that will befit the season. I will plant each tiny seed, every humble tuber with the greatest solicitude.

I will fashion out of this weary Old World plot of land my own New World beginnings, and come harvest, we shall gather together – we, this little family – and give thanks around our horn of plenty.'

It had to be said, for his own sake as much as anyone's. 'But, Mr Manley, what if these seeds don't take to our soil? What if they should drown in our Irish rain?'

His eyes narrowed. 'I'll say this but the once, and I'll say it to you all. A new world can tolerate anything save the Unbeliever.'

We clutched our tubers and seed packets to our breasts and nodded.

Mr Manley's New World in County Cork was never to be. Events in that month of December were to set our lives on a new course, one that was uncharted and, I feared, unnavigable.

'What think you of the galleon, Mrs Fulworth?' he shouted to me. We were standing in the Great Hall, at distant ends of a vast banquet table. I stared, trying to make sense of what I told myself must be a festive centrepiece. Yet it was no bowl of decorative fruits. It was no jug of yellow day lilies. It was not even a great, gaudy candelabra.

It was a galleon. A broad-beamed, ocean-going galleon, solidly sculpted from pure confection and becalmed at the centre of an otherwise bare table.

'Mrs Fulworth?'

I had never seen such a thing. Its sugar-white masts bore flags of bright silk that fluttered in the draught of the room. Its sparkling deck was lined with miniature cast-iron carronades, and its hull was buoyed up on the frozen crests of indigo waves.

'I'm not sure I know, Mr Manley,' I shouted back, still struggling.

'Overwhelmed?' he queried, cupping his hands to his mouth.

'I must be,' I yelled.

'What was that?'

'I said, aye, Mr Manley, it does take one's breath away.' I was coming round now. 'Especially when one realizes one has a galleon on a banquet table but no banquet to go with it.'

'It is a difficulty, admittedly, but I so wanted this birthday, Anson's seventh no less, to be memorable.'

'It will be that,' I called.

'I am so relieved you think so, for there is another reason as well . . .'

'I am listening,' I said, one hand to my ear.

He glanced stealthily about the place. 'He is tomorrow to be b——ed.'

'Birched?' I said, frowning. 'Has he caused offence?'

'No, no, b——ed, I said.' He worked his lips purposefully.

'Beached? Thank goodness for that, for he cannot swim. But I am not sure I understand why he is to be set afloat in the first place.'

'BREECHED!' he shouted to the rafters.

'Ah, you mean, tomorrow he will don breeches?'

He nodded vigorously.

'He will put away petticoats for good?'

He nodded again, pressing a finger to his lips.

'And he will be a proper little man, is that it?'

He felt the sting of my words and blushed.

Never had any bride that was to be dressed upon her wedding night more hands about her. The morning of Anne's seventh birthday found the local tailor, at the top of the house, adjusting the crimson breeches that had been fashioned and parcelled in Cork. Mr Manley was in attendance, fiddling with the brass-moulded buttons on Anne's new coat. Eoin was there too, earnestly exhorting the roll-up stockings to roll up, while Squibb stood at the ready with periwig in one hand and rapier in the other. When I at last poked my head through the chamber door, trying to glean a bit of the mystery, I was assured by all that it was no place for a woman.

Down below, I prepared the Breeching Day banquet. Otherwise put, I stirred the stirabout and I mashed the mash, again. I'd suggested to Mr Manley that we slaughter and stuff with edibles a few of our roosting hens, but he would hear none of it. 'It is only one day of the year, Mrs Fulworth. Let us not get carried away.'

I did not mention the velvet breeches. I did not remind him of the sugar galleon. I only said, 'I will not fuss, Mr Manley, for you, at least, can eat your words on the day.'

I was drumming my fingers against the beeswax polish of the banquet table when Squibb threw open the door to the Great Hall with a footmanly flourish. 'Master Anson Manley!' he announced to the single personage of me gathered there.

In she marched, parading crimson breeches, silk-ribbon garters and brightly buckled shoes. In one hand, she carried a cocked hat edged with silver braid. Her other hand rested on a glinting rapier. She bowed to me, and her powdered periwig slipped askew.

'Well!' boomed Mr Manley with Squibb, Eoin, and even the old tomcat in formation behind, 'is my nephew not a genuine gallant?'

My smile tightened. 'Certainly no one could say otherwise, Mr Manley.'

'No, indeed. Tell me, is that stirabout I smell, perchance? Is that a robust mash I spy? But lo, what wonder do I behold upon our banquet table?' He winked at me from across the room.

'It's a ship, sir,' said Eoin point-blank, trying to be of service.

'No, lad, no. That is no ordinary ship. That it is a galleon. A veritable vessel of war, of battle on the high seas, of sea dogs' drama, of—'

'It's made of sugar, Uncle.' Anne had already drawn up alongside and was licking the hull.

'Aye,' agreed Mr Manley, reluctantly relinquishing his prepared speech.

'Are we to eat it then?'

He muttered his way to his seat and viciously stuffed his napkin into his shirtneck. 'No, you are not to eat it!' he shouted at all of us. 'It is with such thinking as yours that the Spanish lost the Armada. Now eat your mash, one and all!'

We ate in silence, quieted not so much by Mr Manley's words as by the polished expanses of table that separated us from one another: Mr Manley at the distant end, me at the other, Anson and Eoin on either side, and Squibb, standing officiously at the doors of the Great Hall, affecting to be a manservant. As for the old tom, he strolled up and down the length of the table, lording it over us all.

The last of the stirabout had been scraped from the pot and the day was looking like doom when Mr Manley suddenly pushed back his chair. 'Squibb,' he shouted, 'fetch the flint and tinder! I very nearly forgot.'

'Forgot what, Uncle?' asked Anne hopefully.

'The salute, of course!'

Squibb quick-stepped it to the kitchen for the tinder box while I cleared the table. He was back in no time. Mr Manley positioned himself above the bow of the galleon, loaded a carronade with a tiny powder sack and struck the flint. 'Stand back and scoff no more, for these are no confectionary carronades. These are the very tools of war.'

The recoil of the first gun seemed to take him by surprise, but the little boom resonated wonderfully in the lofty rafters, and our applause encouraged him. 'Take cover!' he shouted. 'No mercy shall be given!'

Another carronade exploded, followed in turn by its neighbour. 'Here, Squibb,' he ordered, 'you man the guns at port. Here's the flint. I'll hold off the enemy from starboard.'

'Right you are, sir!' Squibb dropped his cocked hat and pushed up his coatsleeves.

We counted seven carronades on each side of the galleon, the repeated firing of which was now mounting into all-out war. Eoin and Anne were falling down dead all over the Great Hall, while the galleon's sugary gunwales were beginning to melt with the flames that leaped from the mouth of each miniature bore.

'Squibb,' bellowed Mr Manley, wiping his brow, 'why have you ceased firing? I shall give no quarter to mutineers!'

Squibb's jaw had fallen slack.

I saw Eoin and Anne scurry to their feet.

I turned, following Squibb's glazed stare, to the portal of the Great Hall.

Mr Manley was impatiently trying to unstick a silk pennant from a sugary mast. 'Squibb, what foe has struck such terror to thine heart, man?'

Squibb dropped his tinder box, proceeded to the door, and donned his cocked hat once more. 'Mrs Manley, sir!' he announced. 'And child!'

She stood at the entrance to the Great Hall, her hands folded forbearingly below her narrow waist, her gaze steadfast. Terrible moments passed as Mr Manley struggled for speech behind his guns. Meanwhile, I anxiously watched as the black tom, the old family cat, crept under the hem of her grey silk skirt and eased himself past her underskirts, a greeting to which she neither objected nor warmed.

Instead, she began to remove her travelling gloves, briskly releasing each finger in turn. 'Thank you for the ten-gun salute, husband. I was not aware you were expecting me.'

'I . . . I was not aware that I was either,' tried Mr Manley as he offered the new arrivals each a chair. 'Do join us.'

Mrs Manley accepted. The girl stared fixedly at the floor. 'Allow me to present Thomasina.'

Mr Manley winced.

Thomasina curtsied awkwardly and hastily retreated behind Mrs Manley's high-backed chair.

Mr Manley gargled discreetly with ale, then swallowed. 'And I should like you to make the acquaintance of Anson, my nephew, who is seven years today. You will remember the good Mrs Fulworth, now his . . . nanny, and Mrs Fulworth's own lad, Eoin.'

'You may approach,' she said, beckoning Anne.

Anne crossed the Hall without ado and stood before her.

'You are a very pretty lad in your velvet breeches.'

'My uncle had them made for me in Cork.'

'Did you know, Anson, that your uncle is in fact my husband, which thus does make me your aunt, and yet you'll think me a fool, for I know nothing of your good parents.'

'Nor do I, ma'am.'

The arrow-head of her chin raised itself.

'Yes, both deceased,' interjected Mr Manley. 'Perhaps my mother, bless her, had cause to mention an elderly cousin of my belated father, one Hargrave Manley?'

'She had not.'

'I am not surprised, for it is ancient lore now, but the two sides of the clan fell out, over what cause no one can remember. Hargrave had six offspring, two of whom I last met in my distant boyhood and have never come upon since, and four of whom I never met at all. Now of those four' – I dared not so much as glance at Mr Manley for fear I should make him think twice – 'the first died of rickets, the second took up an army commission, the third married a peripatetic preaching man, and the youngest, a schoolteacher, married a local girl and set up home in his father's house. However,' he took a deep breath, 'Hargrave, being of an advanced age, died soon after this marriage was made, and it was only latterly discovered that he was most sorely in debt. The rest is the making of tragedy. The young couple lost their home, the lass fell pregnant, delivered the child but was set upon with a hellish fever and died. He had little recourse, what with neither wife nor means nor home, but to thrust the child upon the parish. Soon after, he disappeared – gone it was thought to London to lose himself in that city. The local cleric, stumbling upon my connection quite inadvertently, addressed me post-haste, not long after my mother's death, and pleaded my charity on the babe's behalf.'

Anne was weeping at her new tragical history.

Mrs Manley seemed unimpressed.

'Where do you come from, child?' she enquired.

'I do not know,' Anne replied, wiping her nose with her muslin cravat.

'A draught of ale, Mrs Manley?' offered Mr Manley.

'I am not staying.'

'No?' His face brightened noticeably.

'I have seen what I came to see.' She stood, replaced her gloves and straightened Thomasina's cap.

I could see Mr Manley searching his mind. 'What you came to see?' he repeated, smiling too courteously.

'I have seen my familial home once more,' she answered.

'Ah,' he said, smelling danger.

'And, more to the point, I have ascertained to my satisfaction that this child Anson is indeed your long-lost cousin's child, your "nephew" so to speak, so I shall trouble you no more except to say—'

'I am all ears, Mrs Manley.' He was like a man on the edge of the Promised Land.

'Except to say that we, Thomasina and I, shall take up residence at a mutually convenient date within the new year.'

We were dumbfounded.

'But how?' stammered Mr Manley. 'Why?'

'It is simply this, Mr Manley,' she said, coaxing her daughter out from behind her chair. 'I have decided that Thomasina has been too long without her papa.'

'But surely you do not now claim . . .'

'Dear Mr Manley, I have no need to make claims.'

And it was true, for beholding Thomasina – all of us for the first time – it could not be denied: she was Mr Manley's daughter, right down to the little chins that trembled as we stared.

'You, you never said the child was mine!' railed Mr Manley.

'I never said she wasn't,' replied Mrs Manley, smoothing her silken skirts.

'But it's utterly and entirely impossible!'

Mrs Manley smiled indulgently. 'You forget yourself. Nettle wine was ever your undoing.'

Mr Manley's eyes started to fill. Behind him, the galleon was listing on its sugary keel.

Squibb, who had stood stoically silent at the doorway till now, approached. 'A word, sir.'

'Not now, Squibb.'

'It is vital, sir.'

'I have things on my mind, Squibb.'

'The child is not your nephew, sir.'

'Squibb!' I shouted, even before Mr Manley could.

Mrs Manley tried to restrain a smile.

'Is it true, Uncle?' said Anne, weeping again. 'Am I not your nephew?'

Mr Manley's hands gripped the back of a chair. 'You are dismissed, Squibb.'

But there was no stopping him. 'The child—'

'Dismissed!'

'—is your own bastard, sir, if you will pardon me saying so.'

Mr Manley turned to him, amazed.

'The child is Mr Manley's own,' he repeated, addressing his former mistress, 'and as genuine a bastard as any. I myself bore witness from the adjacent kitchen to the events leading to that fateful conception. It is, as you once told me, madam, the skill of a good manservant to be neither seen nor heard.'

I was glad to be breathing again. Squibb hadn't made matters worse, and perhaps, I thought to myself, his revelation had indeed mended our situation a little. Anne was a boy with a bloodline again, even if Mr Manley's reputation had been besmirched in the process. And I, for my part, no longer had to look at that old tomcat twice.

'I do not doubt what you say, Squibb, impertinent as you are. Nor do I in any way doubt my husband's evident ignorance. That does not alter the fact that Thomasina is Mr Manley's legitimate heir. You only have to look at her to know.'

Mr Manley lowered himself into a chair, defeated.

Squibb weighed her words. 'Purely coincidental, Mrs Manley, if I may speak so boldly.' He turned to his employer. 'Mr Manley, answer me this: did you ever, to your knowledge, bed your wife?'

'No,' he desperately replied, 'I have been wracking my brains but I cannot even recall the evening in question.'

'Mrs Fulworth, did Sally, during her employment in this house, ever comment to you on the circumstances attending Mr and Mrs Manley's marriage?'

'Aye, perhaps she shouldn't have, but she did.'

'What precisely did she tell you?'

'That Mrs Manley had told her on her first day here that she did not and would never share a bed with her husband.'

Squibb turned to Mrs Manley, bowed punctiliously, and returned to his position at the door.

Mrs Manley walked to the window where she stood, hands clenched into fists at her side. She made a lonely figure, framed against that window pane, and for a moment, I pitied her despite myself.

The children had scattered. Eoin I finally discovered on the dark stairwell, where he had trapped a tearful Thomasina. Taking a candle, I mounted the stairs and searched each of the bed-chambers for Anne. I descended and searched the kitchen. Then I climbed again to the second floor and opened the library door. 'Anson?' I had returned to the Hall, ready to enlist Squibb's help, when I spotted her, underneath the far end of the banquet table, stripping herself of her new garments.

I got down on my hands and knees. 'Anson?'

'Go away!' She flung her coat and shirt out from under the table.

'What's the matter, child?' I hoped against hope she might merely be weary of the day.

'Everyone's saying things about me.' She cast out her buckled shoes and her white silken stockings. Mr and Mrs Manley, their faces still dazed by all that had passed, turned slowly round from their separate corners to watch us. Squibb watched from the door. Eoin and Thomasina peered in from the landing.

'Aye,' I said. 'I know. It's not fair. Come out now. Come out and I'll tuck you into your truckle-bed, just like always.'

'No,' she said, crawling out warily, her naked shoulders shivering in the cold. 'I don't want you to. You say things just like all the others.'

In the dark shadow under the banquet table, I could just see the inside-out crimson breeches and the crumpled linen drawers lying in the heap where she'd abandoned them. 'Anne . . .' I tried, squeezing her small soft hand. I wanted to embrace her, to warm her. But she pushed past me, walking silent and naked across the Great Hall and through its vast portal, as though she were entirely alone.

Chapter Twelve

Mrs Manley was to take up residence in the new year.

Mr Manley's last days, as I remember them, were spent dismantling his library.

I stood at the foot of his ladder, shouting, 'Where are we to go? Tell me that.'

'I am sorry, Mrs Fulworth. I cannot say.'

'Why can't we remain here? You and Mrs Manley could live separately, as you did once.'

'Things are changed. There is Anson—'

'Anne,' I reminded him.

'And the girl Thomasina. And there has been too much said too late in the day.'

'Almost seven years ago, you promised us a roof, Mr Manley. There is no going back. You have a daughter now.'

'Do you speak of one in particular?'

'Your words don't become you. You know I mean Anne, the child your Sally died for; the same child who is now in need of your protection.'

'I have none to give, Mrs Fulworth. What do you wish me to say? My home is gone. My reputation will soon be destroyed and, with it, my practice. Mrs Manley will see to that. My private means are scant.'

I would have been glad of tears, of remonstrations, of woebegone speeches – of anything except this reason which came like a foreign speech from his mouth. 'Are we done for then, Mr Manley? Is that what you are trying to tell me?'

'To be frank, Mrs Fulworth, I have not thought as far ahead as your fatalism would imply. I expect there will be lodgings to be had. In Cork, perhaps.' He sighed, weary of me.

I wanted to knock him from his ladder, to shake him till he came to his old self again, but I only said, 'Anne does not believe you are her father. You must tell her.'

He eased himself slowly down the ladder, one arm crooked under a stack of books.

'Mr Manley?'

He walked to the hearth where a fire burned. He seemed to stare into the flames, gathering his reply. He seemed to. Before I could shout, he had jettisoned the arm-load of books on to the fire.

I ran to the hearth and saved a few with the poker, shielding my face from the sudden roar of heat. Pages curled. Bindings crackled and split. Words flew into ashes. We saw delicate engravings take on a terrible new life as flames licked at them and raised them up. I watched a fat apple blossom shrivel on the branch.

He spoke as though hardly a moment had passed. 'She is better off, Mrs Fulworth, not believing.'

The days yielded begrudgingly to the new year, for, though our time left in the house was short, the atmosphere was heavy and the hours long. I wanted us out. Gone. Then I could rail. I could double-talk. I could beg. For the moment, I could do nothing but worry for us.

It was a day dead with the bite of winter when he found me in the field, bending low, digging for late turnips. I turned, expecting Squibb.

'Finn?' I breathed.

'Who else?' he said, smiling shyly.

He was twenty if he was a day. 'But I never said . . .'

'I knew. My da knew. The whole of Kinsale knew. House-keeper to a gentleman. It's not so big a town.'

I wrapped my arms around him, and he let me as the fourteen-year old boy never would have. 'But why now?'

He looked at the sky, at the line of poplars ahead. 'You had a life here. We would only have unsettled it.'

'No, Finn,' I said, grasping his hands in my mucky pair, 'why *now*?'

'Your husband is dead, Ma.' He toed a bare patch of earth.

There was something more, I knew there was. A gulf grew up between us, a flat, grey sea. 'Did you do it, Finn?'

'Ma, I . . .' His eyes met mine and frightened me. 'I . . .'

'Out with it, Finn!'

'Didn't kill him.' He laid his hand on mine. 'But it's good of you to spare him a thought.'

I flung his hand away. 'Oh, go away with you! A dead man is no joke.'

'And he wasn't too comical in life either!' he shouted to the field.

'Ssshhhht. You'll go to Hell for this, my boy, you will.' I pressed my fingers against a smile.

'I hope not, as I don't expect a priest-in-the-making would get too warm a welcome.'

I nearly lost my footing. 'Jesus, Mary and Joseph!'

'More oath than blessing, but it will do for the moment.'

'Oh, Finn!' This is what he'd come to say. I blessed myself quickly, as if it was a charm that would undo his words.

'A deal.' He winked. 'You call me Father and I'll call you Mother.'

I slapped his cheek. 'There are still priest-catchers everywhere, or haven't you heard?'

'I've heard.'

I looked at the stranger before me. The red-gold of his hair had darkened to brown, except in the stubble of his face. And his nose was different, as if he'd broken it and it had mended badly. Most of all, the brooding was gone from his eyes; the angry colour from his cheeks. He lifted the creel of turnips from my arms, and we walked slowly toward the house.

'So how then?' I said, trying not to think. 'How did your da go?'

'Last year, his chest started to rattle like something had come loose. Three nights ago, in his sleep, it just stopped.'

'So it was like that then.'

'Like what?'

'Peaceful. I never pictured him dying . . . so peacefully.'

'What did you picture then?'

I snatched up a Christmas rose from the tangle on the old

pasture wall and passed it to him. 'I am not likely to tell a priest, now am I, Finn?'

It was he who changed the subject this time. 'So I don't imagine you'll be returning to the cottage, not after this,' he said, eyeing the lie of the land that surrounded us.

'No, I don't imagine,' I said, suddenly too proud to say anything more.

'You wouldn't recognize Sean and Michael.' He tried to make light of it.

'Nor they me, I expect.'

'They run that farm on their own now.' We walked on, the crunch of our footsteps across the frozen pasture marking our silence. 'And what about my little brother Eoin?'

'He's inside,' I said, easing my arm from the link of his. 'Let me fetch him.'

'Don't.' He got hold of my hand. 'I'm off, Ma, to Kerry.'

I would not see him again.

Or Sean.

Or Michael.

Or Peter, my firstborn.

Or my little dead girl who never had a name.

I walked him as far as the first bend in the road. When I turned back for home, my gait gave way to a run, to a mud-splashing sprint back up the road as far as the side door.

Eoin was there, chopping kindling on an old tree stump in the yard. I gathered him to me, pressing my face, clammy with sweat, to his fresh cheeks. He wriggled out of my arms.

'What's the matter?' for he'd never been strange with me.

'Anson's gone.'

'Gone where? Hiding again?'

'Vanished. I said he would.'

I got him by the shoulders. 'Where? Into town?'

'No!' he said, his face darkening. 'He's disappeared. I told you he would. You made him leave.'

I looked away, thinking I would have to call Squibb, for the day was dull and already the light was draining from the sky.

Then I saw her, standing next to the water butt, watching us.

'There she is! Have you been there all the while?'

She stood, her arms folded, resolute as a keep. She was wearing a pair of new woollen breeches and a linen shirt she'd left untucked. Her breeching-day rapier hung at her side.

'You must be cold, child. Why do you stand there?' The day's freezing mist had gathered in the unkempt thickness of her hair. 'Look, Eoin. Anne is here after all.'

He threw down his axe and pushed me aside. 'Turncoat!' he shouted, at which of us I didn't know, and ran into the house.

Anne stared at me like the ghost of herself.

I said, 'He'll be back.'

She hardly blinked.

'All will be put right in the end, Anne.' I took a step towards her.

She backed away.

'You have been wronged, child, it's true—'

'Aye,' she said with a suddenness that surprised me.

'Anne—'

'Is that my name?

'It is. Your mother's choice.'

'I had no mother.'

'Don't talk so foolishly!' I said, suddenly exasperated. 'Do you think you gave birth to yourself?'

'Maybe.'

'You're a wicked child for saying so.'

'I'll say what I like. You always do!'

'I'm saying, trust me. Please.'

'Are you my mother?'

'I'm not but—' I took another step, touched her arm.

'Then I don't know you.' She shook my hand from her. 'And you don't know me!'

'Let's go talk to your father.'

'I have no father!' and she ran from me, disappearing in the old pasture amid the dead stalks of summer.

The fog was thick as a winding-sheet at the Old Head. I stood two hundred feet up, alone at the top of the cliff with the face like our Lord on the Day of Judgement, and I listened. I could hear the almighty crash of the tide on the shingle below, but I couldn't see it. I could hear the muffled cries of seabirds as they swooped and dived headlong into the dense mist, but I couldn't spot them. I could hear the sound of my own weeping, but I couldn't feel it on my face. I sat down and pulled off my boots and stockings, my skin a rash of goose pimples.

Then I got to my feet again and inched my way towards the edge of the cliff. The seagrass and rock were slippery with bird shite and the salty wet of the air, but the soles of my feet were hard-worn. At the crumbled edge, my toes curled round a rough ledge of rock. My body stiffened against the slight breeze. I pressed my fingertips into my hands, cutting crescent moons into my palms. I closed my eyes and felt once more like the girl I once was, standing on this cliff face, willing herself to stand upright despite the wind and the pull of the beach below.

Somewhere below, footsteps were crunching on the shingle. Children were gathering kelp, I imagined, or weed for the fields. Beyond, just off shore, I could hear the shouts of fishermen in Holeopen Bay, shouting to one another, their voices echoing oddly in the fog. 'Pull in out of the wind,' said one. 'We'll fire up the kettle!' said the other. They sounded so close.

I opened my eyes. My head was light from gulping sea air. My toes were as white as lime against the rock ledge. I couldn't feel them. I couldn't lift them either. Not one foot, then the other, as I always had. I stood there like a woman who had been changed to stone.

I would not let myself shout. I would have to fall back. I would damage my backbone and bruise myself on the rubble behind, but I would have only myself to blame: a woman of a good age and certainly a girl no longer.

From nowhere, arms flew about my waist, cutting my breath in two. I was hauled in, before I could even blink, upon the paunch of Mr Manley. He broke my fall. 'Forgive me, Mrs Fulworth!' He clung to the middle of me. 'Forgive me my hard heart.'

'I'm afraid I . . . I got myself stranded there on the edge,' I stammered, red-faced. 'I don't know what got into me.'

He passed me a wet stocking, which I accepted gratefully. 'I should never have forgiven myself, Mrs Fulworth.'

'It would have served me right if I'd fallen.' I found my other stocking. 'Please, let's say no more about it. How did you find me here?'

'Eoin saw you leave for town. "When will she be back?" I said, surprised at the news, for you hadn't mentioned a jaunt. He didn't reply, but only turned away in a peculiar attitude. Then I remembered the library, this morning, and I knew something was wrong. I took the chaise into town and discovered you had been spotted at the piers, heading on to the coastal path. I have been searching most of this afternoon, not only to find you, Mrs Fulworth, and to right my wrong, but also to tell you I have had a letter. From a Mr Biggins. A timely letter and one which requires your reply.'

'My reply?'

'Yes. Your urgent reply.'

Mr Manley seated himself at the head of the banquet table in the Great Hall. Squibb stood above him with the vital taper in one hand, all the better to read with over his master's shoulder. I pulled up a chair. Eoin skulked by the low coal fire. Anne, who had come in at last from the pasture, sat by herself under the corner window.

'What does he say, Mr Manley?'

'Mr Biggins, my apothecary in Cork, himself says little, which I must confess makes a change from our previous correspondence, for there is nothing so irksome as long-windedness. However, he has sent me a notice which he has obtained from one of his enviable connections in that city.'

'It says——' started Squibb.

Mr Manley whipped the notice out from under Squibb's nose. 'It is entitled as follows: "A Brief Description of the Province of Carolina, on the Coasts of Florida, Wherein is set forth the Healthfulness of the Air; the Fertility of the Earth, and the

Waters; and the Great Pleasure and Profit which will accrue to those that shall go Thither to Enjoy the same. Together with a most accurate Map of the whole Province."' He breathed again.

'Now, speak not until you have heard all, Mrs Fulworth, I beseech you. "Carolina is a fair and spacious province on the continent of America and doubtless there is no plantation that ever the English went upon, in all respects as good as this. In the midst of this fertile province, there is a colony of English seated, who have overcome all the difficulties that attend the first attempts, and have cleared the way for those that come after, who will find good houses to be in whilst their own are in building; good forts to secure them from their enemies; and many things brought from other parts there, increasing the no small advantage of the place." What, Mrs Fulworth, is there left to say?'

'It sounds—'

'No, no. You promised not a word, remember. "The whole Country consists of stately woods, groves, marshes and meadows. It abounds with a variety of brave oaks, a panoply of fruit trees including medlars, peach, wild cherries, mulberry-trees, as well as vines. The woods are stored with deer and wild turkeys, of a greater magnitude and a more pleasant taste than in England, being in their proper climate. Here too are as brave rivers as any in the world, stored with great abundance of sturgeon, salmon, bass, plaice and trout. The summer is not too hot, and the winter is very short and moderate, best agreeing with English constitutions."'

'And what about Irish ones?' interrupted Squibb.

'Pray, your patience,' Mr Manley admonished, 'for now we arrive at the meat of the matter: "Is there any Brother born whose spirit is elevated above the common sort, and yet the hard usage of our Country hath not allowed suitable fortune?"' A significant nod from Mr Manley. '"He will not surely be afraid to leave his native soil to advance his fortunes equal to his blood and spirit. Here, with a few servants and a small stock, a great estate may be raised, although his birth have not entitled him to any of the land of his ancestors, yet his industry may supply him so, as to make him the head of as famous a family."' His face was flushed in the candlelight.

'Now, Squibb, hearken to this: "Such as are here tormented with much care that with their labour can hardly get a comfortable subsistence, shall do well to go to this place, where any man whatever, that is but willing to take moderate pains—"'

'I'm sorry, sir, but that rules me out,' said Squibb.

Mr Manley turned to me. 'Mrs Fulworth, listen to this: "If any maid or single woman have a desire to go over, they will think themselves in the Golden Age, when men paid a dowry for their wives; for if they be but civil, and under fifty years of age, some honest man or other, will purchase them for wives."'

I understood I was now permitted to speak. 'I believe I am a civil woman, mostly, and I am still a good stone's throw from fifty years, but I'll be damned if I'll be saddled with another husband.'

He judged it meet to conclude. '"If therefore any industrious and ingenious persons shall be willing to partake of the felicities of this Country, let them embrace the first opportunity so offered by the aforenamed steerage company, that they may obtain the greater advantage." So, Mrs Fulworth? Squibb? May I assume that you too are excited by these prospects?'

I looked at Squibb. He looked at me. 'No,' we said in one voice.

We were to leave in a fortnight, our passages already booked.

'Mrs Fulworth,' called Mr Manley, as I rushed past the door of his erstwhile library, 'come share with us this New World vision!'

I could see he had persuaded Anne and Eoin into the library to study the map that lay rolled out upon the now bare floorboards. Neither child had said much on the subject of going, at least not to Mr Manley or me. I settled down on my hands and knees alongside them.

The map was a wonder, I had to admit. Its border was composed of small windows, each with its own strange view: in one, two naked primitives with hairy groins fought with spears; in the next, a goddess, with heavy breasts, tamed a wild boar; in another, a fat-faced child stumbled under the weight of a great creel of diverse fruits; in the bottom corner, two men in armour and capes of mail clasped hands. The green seas were alive with a flotilla of galleons, with beasts of the sea and Neptune's race of mer-maids and men.

'Where is Carolina?' asked Eoin.

Mr Manley's finger traced a wriggling coastline. 'This is our destination, lad, and our destiny.'

The land was a rich coppery brown. Tiny figures stood atop it: folk tilling the fields and standing at the water's edge. Un-imaginable animals stood among stick trees, animals I couldn't name.

Mr Manley could. 'Notice the pol-cat, the creature with the broad white stripe running down its back. In self-preservation, it neither bites nor claws nor mauls. Instead, it emits a perfidious perfume from its nether regions and, in so doing, poisons the very air which its predator breathes! Here, the buffalo with its distinguishing hump, a vast brute, many times the size of a cow, and here the black-snake which can, I am told, whip the rattle-snake to a certain death. This beast is the bear, the flesh of which they say is tastier than beef, pork or mutton.'

'Are we going right across the ocean?' said Anne, staring at it.

'Indeed. We shall commence our crossing here on the right side of the map, and we shall . . .' – he struggled for accuracy – '. . . cross to the left.'

Every night thereafter, Anne cried herself to sleep, gently so I might not hear.

'Anne,' I'd say to her quietly in the darkness of our chamber, 'why are you crying?'

'I am not crying,' she'd reply, turning herself over, pushing her face into the pillow. Each night the same.

'Are you afraid of something?' I'd say.

'I am not crying,' she'd protest.

I'd lie awake until the labour of her own sobs carried her off to sleep.

On our last night together in that chamber, she crept out of her truckle-bed and climbed into mine, sheltering under my bedding. I gathered her to me. She was cold and her face was wet with her tears.

'You've not been not crying again?' I said, stroking her hair in the dark.

'Aye,' she said.

'Because you're not frightened?'

'Of the water,' she said.

'Ah, of crossing the big sea.'

'With it so big and me so small.'

'It might swallow you.'

'Like the great mouth of a sea beast.'

'And you'd drown.'

'Aye,' she said, sniffling.

'No,' I said.

'No?'

'I have something to give you.'

'What is it, Annie?'

'In the morning,' I said. 'We must sleep now.'

'But—'

'Trust me,' I said. Then I slipped my arm round her middle and she slept.

In the morning, I opened my trunk that sat at the door of my chamber, ready for Squibb to load. I took out a tiny velvet bag that I had stitched a long time ago. It had a golden pullstring.

'What's in it?' she asked.

I smiled.

She pulled the drawstring and peered inside. 'I don't see anything.' She shook the open mouth of the sack into the cup of her hand. 'What is it?'

She turned it over in her hand: the shape of a wind-shot petal, the colour of mother's-blood.

'It's your caul,' I said, 'the hood you were born with when I pulled you from your mother's womb. Seamen would pay gold for it.'

'Why?'

'It's your mother's gift to you, Anne. Do you see? Never lose it and you'll never drown.'

We tied the golden pullstring to another piece of cord and I knotted it round her neck, firmly so it wouldn't slip loose.

Later, in those nights at sea, I would try to unfasten that cord at her neck, suddenly frightened it might choke her in her sleep, or mark her soft neck. But I couldn't undo the knot I'd tied, nor could I lift the cord over her head. She wouldn't allow it.

Book Two

Chapter Thirteen

I can still see her that day, walking through her father's fruit grove, in among the lemon and pomegranate trees. In the distance, beyond the rice fields, the Yamasees were burning tracts of woodland, driving the wild hogs out for the kill, and the afternoon sky seemed to shake with the heat. I was cleaning the big window in the entry hall – the tang of vinegar bit the air – and, as I worked, I watched her, plucking waxy leaves from the trees overhead.

She was threading her way along the serpentine walk which wound through the grove in slow, showy curves. She was not wearing the stays for which her father paid £2 8s. I could tell by the way she jumped for those branches. Whole trees stirred.

I had not wanted to catch her eye, but suddenly I found myself rapping the glass. I wanted to shout, Be still! Be still! You'll drive yourself to distraction, walking alone on that twisting walk, jumping after leaves. I waited. I knocked again, more boldly, and she turned, but it wasn't her face that looked back at me. It was hardly a face at all: two cut-out slits for eyes in an oval of dark satin.

It was the fashion: to protect the complexion from the fierceness of the sun, or the sting of the sea breeze.

I remember bending for the pail, almost slipping in a puddle of water – and I remember the sight of my own frightened face.

One memory mends the last. There was no window in Mr Manley's entry hall. There was only a large framed mirror. I used to clean it with vinegar.

Charles Town, Carolina, as I remember it, was poised on the very edge of America, a bright spit of land that poked out into the

Atlantic like a dare. Its light seemed endless, its streets impossibly wide and its population like none I had imagined. Free and easy talkers idled alongside silent slaves. Gentleman planters spat tobacco with sharp-faced traders. There were white-faced society women, and Yamasee squaws who wore sashes spun from buffalo hair. There were also more churches than I could put a name to, including one, just upriver from us, which was entirely round. Its congregation boasted an absence of corners in which Satan might hide.

Yet there were vast tracts of wilderness where snakes with rattling tails charmed squirrels and hares into their jaws, where wolves in packs devoured stray horses, and wildcats caterwauled in the night. Even the wood-pigeons were not as we'd known them. In their seasonal flights, they were known to lay waste whole forests, stripping them of all that was edible, even snapping oak branches with the weight of their roosting.

New plantations, however, were always pushing back the horizon. They were of a length and breadth I'd never thought possible, and yet they seemed, at the same time, to be no more than make-believe. We were children here, so small, so earnest as this patch of wood was felled, as another boundary was measured out in careful strides.

Mr Manley's plantation, like many, was founded on low-lying swampland that hugged the Ashley River. Rice seed, it transpired, had only to meet this boggy soil to come to harvest. Cultivation was little more than the digging of a shallow trough with a hoe. After his first success, Mr Manley would often ascend his Observation Tower, specially built, and linger there as if he was viewing Creation itself.

I could not believe. Even years on, I lay awake in the night, frightened that the house was sinking into the swamp, that the ground would not hold.

We had Indians in the early years, usually bought from other Indians, but as he prospered Mr Manley purchased Negroes, some at £60 a head because it was known they were better workers and not so likely to stray. I hardly spoke to one in those years, unless you count the little Negress who worked in the house. She was only four feet tall in her stockinged feet, though on making the purchase Mr Manley had been assured she had at least another foot in her. If she had, she never let it show. We called her Black-Eyed Susan, like the flower, and I only had cause to beat her the once. It was the day I found Anne, not yet ten, fingering the dark fullness of her lips and Susan simply standing there, letting her.

It seemed to me I had swallowed a dangerous secret, just knowing there were many more of them in Charles Town than us; that we were safe because we could count and they could not; that it was only an act of will that put us in the houses and them in the fields in bent-backed rows. Sometimes, walking past, I'd meet a man's eyes, just visible over the towering rice crop, and I'd have to look away.

Downriver, Charles Town grew more and more lively by the day. Giddy even. With each new season, there were more clubs, societies and entertainments. Merchants stocked Dutch linens, French cambrics, East India silks, luxuriant furs, Hyson tea, demerara rum, ivory-handled pistols and long-range muskets for the turkey season. Plantations were growing with a vengeance, gardens blazed with azaleas, and I'd never before smelt such fear in the air.

Every July and August, the twin rivers, the Ashley and the Cooper, swelled to flooding, and whole plantations disappeared under water. It suited the rice crop well, but the mosquitoes too as it happened, so most families escaped to town dwellings for a respite from nature. Summer was therefore the Season in Charles Town, the fresh sea breezes encouraging perpetual minuets, and more. Palmetto leaves fanned hot cheeks. Dowries coupled with inheritances. Idle chaperones sucked on lemon halves to quench their thirst.

It was often said that the youth of this city grew faster to maturity than anywhere else in the American colonies. It was, I was told, all down to the heat. At the age of thirteen, Anne, however, did not crave the pleasures of society. The summer rains were already driving at the window panes when she announced to me that she did not 'intend' to go to town for the Season. 'Why doesn't he take me to the market and trade me for an ox, for Lord's sake? It's been done before, and I wouldn't complain if I were at least permitted, publicly, to snuffle and snort and fart as much as an ox.' She was rocking to and fro on the walnut rocker at a great speed.

'I'll tell you why he doesn't trade you for an ox.' I didn't look up from my needlework. 'Your father doesn't need an ox. It's that simple.'

She jumped to her feet, nearly upsetting the rocker. 'I've told you, Annie, don't call him that! I won't have it!'

I grabbed her arm and pricked it with my needle. 'It's not for you to pick and choose, my girl. He is indeed your father and that is that.'

'Only he's never been too sure himself.'

I boxed her ears. 'You'll show some respect if you're a Christian girl.'

'And you should show some sense if you're as old as you look, Annie. His true daughter is in Ireland, and you know it!'

I grabbed a fistful of hair, pulled her head back, and forced a bar of lye into her protesting mouth. 'You'll not be so free with your talk, not while I have to listen to it!' I had her back almost flat on the table, but it didn't stop there. She was kicking me, bruising my ankles with a vengeance, when Mr Manley ambled through the door. He stopped in mid-stride and clasped his hands to his breast, as if he were seeing, in his own kitchen, Jacob wrestling with the Angel.

The vision ended the moment her bodice burst. Snap went the laces and the stomacher flew from her like a thing possessed. Thank the Lord for the shift, for she wore no stays.

Mr Manley's impassioned hands fell to his sides.

I released Anne's head.

She spat out the bar of lye and hacked.

'Did you want something in particular, Mr Manley?' I said, smoothing my hair.

'I'm afraid someone has arrived.'

'Is this person afraid as well?' I was not yet recovered from my distemper.

He fiddled with his cravat.

I sighed noisily. 'Did you succeed in discovering his name or must we call for Squibb?'

'Beau Blakely Esquire,' he pronounced tentatively, 'but he says we are to call him "Buck".'

'Does he say anything else?'

'Not a great deal, though he seems well-mannered enough. He lives upriver on the Cooper. I know the place. A vast spread, if memory serves.'

'And do you know what Master Beau Blakely wants?'

Mr Manley cleared his throat. 'My daughter, it would seem.'

'What? All at once?'

'No, no. He'd like to press his suit. Court her attentions, I believe.' He confronted Anne's glowering face. 'He has apparently seen you at Sunday worship. His family's pew is but three ahead of our own.'

Anne had recovered her voice, and you'd think she'd never lost it. 'Does he wish to make love to me?'

Mr Manley flushed. 'In due course, I expect, but he should first like to make your acquaintance, which seems to me the rightful order of things.'

'Tell him it is mortally sinful to look at a girl that way in church. I'm surprised he should look round for shame.'

He was at a loss, hovering in the doorway like a soul in Purgatory.

'Tell him,' I said, 'that he may call again tomorrow when Anne will be, come Hell or high water, more disposed to receive him.'

Beau Blakely Esquire was not as I'd expected. Seated on the edge of the chaise-longue, he looked irrefutably short. Worse still, one look at his teeth and I knew why the poor boy went by Buck.

Anne would be merciless.

I loitered just outside while Mr Manley paced the drawing room, ransacking the library of his mind for suitable subjects of conversation. 'So, young Buck,' he said, turning somewhat too swiftly on the polished floorboards, 'a native lad such as yourself, I expect you've shot your share of wild turkeys.'

'Yes, sir,' said Buck, whistling an inadvertent tune on his teeth, 'a twenty-five-pounder last autumn, sir.'

'And a fifty pounder this autumn, I dare say!'

'I don't believe they make them that big, sir.'

'Cynicism does not suit a youth such as yourself, young Buck.'

'No, sir,' Buck reluctantly agreed.

Mr Manley was floundering fast. I made my entrance.

'Mrs Fulworth! Beau Blakely Esquire, allow me to present the good Mrs Fulworth, a faithful friend to my family and the keeper of this house.'

Buck was on his feet now, though I discerned little measurable improvement in his stature. As I accepted his hand, I wondered if, for his sake, I shouldn't send him on his way; if it wouldn't be somehow kinder. My hesitation forfeited the moment. Anne appeared at the door.

I do not exaggerate when I tell you I scarcely knew her, so complete was her transformation. It was her hips that first overwhelmed me, miraculously full in their hooped surrounds; her waist, winsomely whittled by costly stays; and finally her girlish breasts, also harnessed to tremendous effect. And this was only the scaffolding.

To every eye, she was a picture in red and white silks. The sheen of her skirts seemed to draw all the light to her. Her dark hair was combed and glossy, prettily tied back to show her smooth white forehead and dainty ears. She had even gathered a spree of false curls into ringlets at either side of her head to frame her face – the lower part now hidden, incidentally, behind a painted palmetto-leaf fan. The effect couldn't have been more beguiling. Only her modesty-piece, tucked at her cleavage, was slightly askew.

I spotted Squibb and Eoin, under the magnolia tree outside the corner window, with awestruck noses pressed to the pane. Susan, who had helped Anne to dress in secret, now beheld her work from the cover of the nearby coat-tree. As for Mr Manley, he hurried across the drawing room and offered his daughter his arm. Buck just plain whistled, whether with unrestrained admiration or laboured exhalation, we were not sure.

'Beau Blakely Esquire, I present to you my dear daughter, Miss Anne Manley.'

'It is an honour, Miss Manley.'

She peeked demurely over the edge of her fan. I bit my lip and waited.

We took our seats. Anne arranged herself on the chaise-longue, occupying almost the whole of it with the spread of her hoop. Buck managed a seat at the far end.

She did not come out from behind her fan as she spoke her first words. 'Master Beau Blakely?'

'Yes, Miss Manley?' He leaned her way.

'Do I not indeed have fine child-bearing hips?' She put the question to him, shamelessly patting the girth of her hoop.

Poor Buck. I could tell he wasn't even sure, in the way that men aren't, just how much was Anne and how much construction. That aside, a reply in the negative could only have given offence to the one he sought to woo, while an unqualified affirmative might have been misconstrued by her father as an improper advance. 'To me, Miss Manley, you look just fine. Very fine indeed.'

I had to give him his due.

'Shall your family be going to Charles Town for the Season, Buck?' I enquired from across the room.

'Yes, ma'am. Mother looks forward to it, though Father only goes willingly when the 'squitoes drive him out.'

'And you?' queried Anne sweetly from behind her fan.

'Well, I hadn't thought much about it, till lately that is.' He made cow eyes at her.

She averted hers, strangely shy all of a sudden. For a moment, everyone was lost for words, even Anne herself it seemed. Could she possibly, just possibly, be falling in love with him loving her? I couldn't credit her with more.

'The Cooper, Buck. The Cooper,' said Mr Manley, lurching into conversation once more.

'Sir?'

'Your river, so to speak.'

'You could say that, sir. I've grown up on it, that's for sure, what with our place sitting alongside so much of it.'

'And how does it compare? The Cooper, that is, to the Ashley. The Ashley to the Cooper? *Et cetera.*'

'I'm not entirely sure, sir, as I've really only known the Cooper.'

'And I the Ashley.'

'Aye, sir.'

'No, *I*, Buck. I the Ashley. You the Cooper. Do you vacillate?'

'I hope not, sir.'

Our audience at the corner window had not yet grown bored. Eoin, I could see, was still transfixed by the wonder of Anne, but Squibb had recovered himself sufficiently to be pulling faces. Donkey-toothed faces. Once again, the conversation was on the wane. At any moment, Buck might catch a glimpse of that toothy view.

I was about to make a move when Anne suddenly did, crossing the room and drawing the blind. 'I hope no one minds,' she explained, 'but the late afternoon sun is surprisingly strong.' I'd never heard such tact from her lips, and she was convincing too as she waved the fan before her face.

'Perhaps you need a little air, Miss Manley,' offered Buck.

'Indeed, I think I do.'

'Shall I accompany you to the verandah?'

'Would you?' He extended his arm, she her hand, and they sailed out of the room, a gallant pair.

'You look bemused, Mrs Fulworth,' said Mr Manley, smiling like he was already a grandfather.

'I am, quite frankly.'

'Nature will take its course.'

I made no reply, and for once I was content not to. I was happy simply to reflect on the spectacle of the impossible made possible. Or was until I saw Buck leaving the place in a hurry not a quarter of an hour later.

I found Anne, sitting on the porch swing. I couldn't read her face, for still she hid behind her big palmetto leaf. Her eyes, though, were guilty enough, that I could see. 'What have you said now?'

'Nothing.'

'Nothing?'

'Not that I'm aware.'

'I see.'

'No, you don't as it happens, Annie.'

'Well, perhaps you will show me then?'

Slowly, she lowered her fan. I wished she hadn't. A glossy beard of false curls covered her chin.

Chapter Fourteen

We did not go to Charles Town for the Season. Modesty forbade it. Worse still, Anne turned moody, Squibb turned evangelical, Eoin was love-sick, Mr Manley had dry bellyache, and the floodwaters were creeping up on us like despair.

'Deliver us! Deliver us!' I can still hear Squibb shouting to the heavens, thigh-high in water.

'Yea, deliver us!' I shouted back from the verandah. I was already weary of his new-found faith, of him trying to baptize any passing body outside my kitchen window. It was no small mercy when the sky opened up, the rain drove down, and Squibb lost his footing. He didn't surface again for the better part of a day. Turned up at last with a turtle under either arm for soup.

Eoin moped. He'd taken a fancy to Anne, or rather, to the vision of her he'd seen in the drawing room. I said, 'Put her out of your mind, lad. She's not the one for you. Think of her as you would your sister.'

'Aye,' said Squibb solemnly, 'and if that doesn't do the trick, then think of her as you would your brother.' It was a point of some awkwardness that Squibb would still fondly remember Anne as 'a bonny little lad'.

Anne was more worrisome. For most of July, I could not budge her from the window-seat where she sat huddled, watching the floodwaters rise. I cajoled, urged and upbraided her, but she seemed hardly to hear a word I said. Black-Eyed Susan whispered, 'It's them mosquitoes. The infernal humming in the ears. I seen people give in to it before now.'

In August, she took to drifting on her father's rice barge, dressed in Eoin's cast-away clothing. Day after day, she floated over the sunken crop, like a body stranded after the Great Flood.

Sometimes I'd watch her from an upstairs window, barge-poling herself along, circling the Observation Tower, sometimes sticking lurid swamp flowers behind one ear or in a boot. More often than not, though, she simply lay belly-up on the barge, letting the breeze blow her where it would.

It blew her, one evening, into the cypress swamp, which was as far as I could see from the little balcony at the top of the house. 'That's badlands,' said Black-Eyed Susan, who stood watching with me.

'Trees to shelter the dead,' I mumbled, as the tiny shape of her barge disappeared around the bent shape of a cypress; more shadow than tree with the sun going down. We squinted for sight of her.

'No need to send a boy,' Susan said, like her voice was in my head.

'No,' I heard myself say, 'for the dead won't have her.' A strange lament was whispering its way through the two of us.

'She's got no soul to have,' said Susan.

'Lost it to her looking-glass likeness when she was just a babe . . .'

'And won't be at peace till she finds her like again.'

Anne didn't come back that night, or the next morning. I assumed she'd spent the night stretched out again on the floor of the Observation Tower. I was about to send Eoin to fetch her when Susan slammed down two empty water pails.

'That well is growling, Mrs Fulworth. I'm not fetching water, not so long as it growls at me like that. I've already had Mr Squibb yelling at me this morning, and Mr Manley howling upstairs, and I'll be damned if I'm going to be growled at besides.'

The well was on a rise at the back of the house. I picked up the pails myself and headed that way. Halfway there, I studied the thing. Nothing unusual. On I went, creeping towards it in stealth, still thinking I might surprise a skulking coyote or maybe a small wildcat. I had one hand on the crank when I heard it. Not so much a growl as a ground-shaking rumble, as if there was terrible wind in the belly of the earth.

I picked up the buckets and started back for the house.

The sun was wrong that day. I was thinking as much as I walked back, pausing to check the linens on the line. It sat low in the sky, red as a sore.

The sheets were still wet. There was not so much as a breath of wind, which was strange, for I could smell the sea, and the harbour was more than three miles away. I remember too wondering whether I should take in the wash anyway, for it was not fresh sea air, but strong-smelling, briny as rotting fish.

Half of me was fretting over the sheets and half of me was thinking I wouldn't let Anne out of my sight again if I could help it when I saw the ocean wave – a rolling, white-crested wall of water – rise out of the Ashley and burst its banks.

I'd seen storms in our seven years, I'd smelt the blue fire of lightning burning the ground in front of me, but I'd never seen the Atlantic raging in a river. Before I could reach the verandah, we were at sea.

Eoin and Squibb got me to the fruit cellar before the roof came off the house. The foundation let go a terrible shudder, and for a moment, we thought we'd be buried alive. I remember Susan clinging to me and me clinging to her, and all of us praying, the Negroes too, and Mr Manley trying to stretch his arms around the poor shaking huddle of us.

Outside, the rain was thrashing the land. Trees were being torn from the ground and driven into the air like stubble. We were hours in that cellar, feeling the water level rise over our knees, our thighs, our stomachs, listening for the quiet that wouldn't come.

'She's dead, Mr Manley.' I spoke faintly to the dark. I could no longer bear the terror of those words in my head.

'No,' he whispered.

'Drowned.' I thought of the caul in its little velvet bag, upstairs in my top dresser drawer. She wouldn't wear it any more; said she didn't believe in charms now that she was old enough to know better, that it was just a bit of blood in a sack. I gave way to tears.

'Hush. Hush now.'

'I should have sent someone to find her long ago,' I sobbed. I waited – longed – for him to say it.

'She was never one to be stopped.' In the dark, he managed to find my hand and take it in his own, squeezing it hard. 'Anne is, as you and I know, a force of Nature in herself. Pity the hurricane, Mrs Fulworth. Pity the hurricane.'

When the violence had at last spent itself, we climbed up a step-ladder into Chaos.

Sturdy walls were blown through, ceilings had collapsed, doors of solid oak had disappeared and the wrecks of small trees lay submerged in what had been the drawing room. In the kitchen, a library of books drifted in the flood. From a blown-out window, I watched the chaise-longue float by, carried on a rushing current.

Shards of glass were everywhere, and Mr Manley's hand, I suddenly noticed, was awash with blood. He was sucking it like a distracted child. I turned, without thinking, to the kitchen table behind me (still there) and pulled the linen runner from its top (still in place) to press to his injured hand. Even as I did so, I upset that morning's jug of milk. The hurricane had left it standing, full to the brim, a ridiculous miracle. Not twenty feet away from me, the verandah had been ripped from the side of the house.

The stairwell was also still strangely intact. Mr Manley and I mounted it together, his hand grasping mine. As we neared the upper floor, the whole sky appeared overhead, brazenly blue, and at the top, from what had been Anne's room, we surveyed the plantation.

A salty tide had drowned even the summer's flood. The fields were at sea, and the golden harvest of rice crop ruined. Seaweed clung to the branches of the few surviving fruit trees in the grove below, and over by the herb garden, we watched porpoises surface, two by two, the sun glinting off their coppery backs.

His hand was cold in mine. 'Where is she?'

*

He assembled a search party, which sailed over the ocean swell on rafts made from pine clapboards, torn from the house by the hurricane or by the force of their own hands.

Mr Manley stood unsteadily aloft, pressing his spyglass to his eye, searching the east, the west, the north, the south. Yet everything was strange. The landmarks were gone: the river disappeared; the Observation Tower levelled; the boundary of woodland blown through; the horizon suddenly too near. All around them, freshwater fish floated belly-up, poisoned on the brine. Bloated ground fowl drifted past, their hapless wings oddly skewed. Drowned livestock twisted in the current.

They looked for her in a passing barrel, in the floating fragments of the Tower, in the watery space where the hen house had been, in the remnants of the slave quarters, under the collapsed tool shed, in the broken-down buttery, and in the branches of the remaining trees. Now and again, those who could swim took deep breaths and dived into the tide, searching a submerged copper cylinder or a corn trough, pushing their bodies through the sheaves of the drowned crop.

Near to nightfall, at the watery edge of the plantation, Squibb told Mr Manley that they could only turn back. At first light, they would start out again, and silently he reminded himself that they would need to bring nets.

Mr Manley didn't reply, but only stared in the direction of the cypress wood. 'We'll search the swamp.'

Squibb opened his mouth to protest, but spat into the flood instead. Beyond the swamp was another plantation, and another. Farmland would eventually give way to woodland; woodland to the savannah, the savannah to the foothills; and the foothills, to the Blue Ridge Mountains. Mr Manley might never be at peace again.

As the moon rose, they paddled into the swamp's evergreen darkness. The trees here, densely grown, had mostly held their own against the gales, but they made the going for the rafts almost impossible.

'We can't see a thing, sir!' shouted Squibb from his raft.

'Mr Manley, sir,' called Eoin from a distance, 'I think I'm lost.'

'As are we all, son.' It was his raft that crashed first – then another and another – each coming from its own direction, each hitting something that suddenly seemed larger than the swamp itself.

'What in God's name is it?' yelled Mr Manley.

There were sounds of kicking and knocking and banging in the dark. 'It's made of wood,' someone ventured, 'but it's no blown-down shed.'

Another voice called from what seemed to be the other side. 'God, it's a house! Do you think anyone's inside?'

'You're wrong,' bellowed another. 'It's curved on this side. And those are planks, not clapboards.'

'It's the round church from upriver!'

'A sign!' shouted Squibb.

The words seemed to come from on high, ringing out across the swamp. 'It's no SIGN!'

'Did you say that, Eoin?' called Squibb.

Nobody moved.

This time, more terrible still: 'Who do you think it is? Good Queen Anne?'

'Daughter?' cried Mr Manley. 'Can this be?'

'It can and it is,' came back her impatient voice.

'PRECISELY – WHERE – ARE – YOU – NOW?' he yelled, taking charge.

'At a gunport. On the starboard side, I think.'

'A SHIP?'

'A ship once, a shipwreck now. She's wedged between a pair of trees. The keel alone must be twelve feet off the bottom.'

'LISTEN CAREFULLY: WE CANNOT SEE YOU FOR THE NIGHT. DISEMBARK AS YOU EMBARKED AND WE SHALL JOYOUSLY RETRIEVE YOU.'

'I can't. The Jacob's ladder is long gone.'

He turned to his men. 'We need a plan of action.'

'I *have* a plan of action,' she called.

'Your attention, everyone. WHAT – IS – IT?'

'Only this: that you come back in the morning when you won't be like blind men at sea. I'll spend the night in a cabin in the stern, which isn't badly askew.'

'ARE – YOU – CERTAIN – DAUGHTER?'

'I am.'

'AND – YOU – WILL – STAY – WHERE – YOU – ARE?'

Her silence spoke volumes.

Mr Manley had us up long before first light, not that we slept much. Such was the turmoil of the house that I claimed the kitchen table for a bed. Mr Manley took the dining table. Eoin stretched himself out on the porch swing, which we had recovered from the fruit grove. Squibb curled up in the copper bathtub, and most of the Negroes slept upstairs, under an open sky.

'Canvas!' was the call I awoke to. 'And rope, and block and tackle, I want plenty of rope. And Squibb, you must go into town and find us a ship's carpenter. We might require expert advice.'

Squibb went off only to return with a surly-faced deckhand. 'It was the best I could do,' he confessed to me. 'The town's in uproar. The sea wall is down. Entire houses have been swept into the Atlantic, families and all.'

Mr Manley stepped into the kitchen and greeted the stranger. 'My daughter is marooned on a ship that has been driven over land and wedged at some height between two stubborn trees. What do you propose?'

'That you get her out, sir.'

Mr Manley huffed not a little. 'What I mean to say is, what do you advise, given the circumstances?'

'Tell her to jump ship.'

'What sort of advice is this?'

'The sort, sir,' said the sulky deckhand, 'that you get for less than a crown.'

'I'm sorry, sir,' said Squibb at last, under duress. 'He said he could tie knots.'

Mr Manley did not hide his distaste. 'Bring him along, Squibb. He's another pair of hands if nothing else.'

Ahead of us, I could see bare masts rising out of the swamp like a new forest. The going was slow. A stiff wind had blown up making the paddling hard, but I had flatly refused to be left behind. At long last, we were pushing through evergreen boughs, peering past twisted trunks for a glimpse of the vessel, when it came, unbelievably, into view. *The Conception* was a shipwreck like no other. Its massive barnacle-crusted hull sparkled with a life all its own, and high above the cutwater a fat golden child with wings hovered between the treetops.

'What kind of a vessel is it?' I asked.

'A snow,' said Eoin knowledgeably.

'No, son, she's a brig,' said Squibb.

Anne's head appeared at a gunport. 'Does it matter just now? Hello, Annie.'

'A snow,' insisted Eoin.

'A brig,' maintained Squibb.

'Neither,' said the no-good deckhand. He seemed to have come to life at the sight of Anne. 'And both.'

'You're talking in riddles, man,' said Squibb. 'I suggest you stick to knots.'

He was undeterred. 'She has two mainsails. A square mainsail when a snow and a boom mainsail when a brig.' He looked up to Anne. 'Goes both ways,' and I saw him wink at her in a low-down manner.

So did her father. 'Anne! The tackle is ready. You need to catch the end and haul it up. DO – YOU – UNDERSTAND?' He threw the rope high, but it came short of her reach.

She looked down at the canvas sheeting that we now held taut between the four rafts, in case she should fall. 'Never mind that,' she shouted. 'JUST LOOK OUT BELOW!' With that, she pushed herself through the gunport – feet first like a wrong-way-up newborn – and landed with a triumphant whoosh.

We were, all of us, launched into the water.

Chapter Fifteen

She was drawn, inexplicably, to the calamity the hurricane had left behind.

In the weeks that followed, she drifted no more, but navigated a raft across the receding floodwaters, down the swollen Ashley and over a route of black-water creeks that took her, not to the bustling harbourfront, but instead to a remote corner of Charles Town. There, in the shadow of an oak, she'd loosen her hair, let it fall to her shoulders and pull a battered tricorn from a sack. Then she'd make her way, head down, into town, dressed in the russet jacket and leather breeches Eoin had outgrown two years before.

I had Eoin follow her. With every outing, he watched her edge closer and closer to the waterfront, until finally she was making her way along the tumbled ruins of the sea wall. He saw her peeking under rubble in the exposed foundation of a small family dwelling that had slid into the sea. He watched her pocket a child's wooden spoon she found sticking out of a drift of sand. She chased after what looked to him like someone's monogrammed handkerchief, fluttering in the wind.

Sand was everywhere and, with it, tiny white-boned skeletons, bleached shells and dry seaweed that crunched underfoot. The dunes had been ravaged by the gales, and their buried remains cast into the wide city streets. Around one such find, a crowd had gathered at the steps of St Mark's. Someone was holding up a kind of bone Anne had never seen. He was fingering its sharp point.

'Elephant's tooth,' said a Negro in the crowd. 'From Africa.'

The crowd turned to him.

'A beast,' he went on, his hands drawing them a picture, 'greater than a buffalo, with ears like palmetto leaves and a nose . . . a nose like a mighty swaying man-part.'

They looked at that tooth again and nobody spoke for staring.

'Shipwrecked,' someone said at last.

'What cargo,' breathed another.

'And the sea,' said Anne, almost to herself, 'big enough to swallow it.'

The Negro looked at her. 'Aye,' he said. 'And more. Much more.'

Later, down at the waterfront, she stood just shy of the morning hubbub at the docks. A Dutch West India merchant ship was in harbour, a three-masted square-rigger. Great, full-bellied vessel that it was, it had only just weathered the rage of the hurricane at sea.

She watched as they rolled hogsheads of rum down gangways, as they hauled sacks of sweet demerara sugar and crates of foreign spices: nutmeg, ground cinnamon bark, dark cocoa. Then came the human cargo: black bodies, some shuffling on two chained feet; most carried from the hold, already stiff.

'Why are you offloading here, for Christ's sake?' shouted the harbour master. 'Why not at sea?'

'Needed the weight,' said the Captain, rubbing his face with weariness. 'Ballast in the storm.'

Anne knew that Eoin followed her, and she let him, just as she had let him traipse after her in the days when they were small. They had an unspoken understanding, Eoin pledging never to let her catch sight of him, and Anne promising never to turn around. But I knew that he gathered oysters for her from the cool, muddy beds of the creeks. I knew that he wrapped them in white muslin and left them for her to discover as she returned to her raft. Sometimes too, he left her sprigs of sweet grapes, plucked from the vines that grew wild in the woods. I worried for my youngest son.

One day, he didn't go after her.

'Are you weary of her then?'

'No,' he said, his voice, throaty.

'I suppose she's cursed you at last for following her.'

He sighed as if I were a dumb beast in the field.

What Eoin Saw

He had followed her along the waterfront the day before, past the market and the mission, past the docks and the Customs House, past the ships' chandler and the repairs-yard where, for a time, she had stood in a crowd of seamen and surveyed the careening of a ketch. Some of them were smoking, some spitting, but no one was speaking, and she had established her right to be there, in the company of men, precisely by saying nothing. In time, she was off and moving again, disappearing into the shadow of the big goods warehouse, heading for, of all places, the grog house at the remote end of the front.

It was, everyone knew, more shack than establishment, knocked down in every storm and righted again before even a Sabbath would pass. It teetered on slimy stilt-legs at the water's edge, and its frequenters did likewise. Spew gathered like sea-scum on the tide.

('And you left her there!' I shouted at Eoin. 'On her own!'

'Let me finish!')

As she'd neared the place, it had seemed to Eoin that she was about to turn back, for she hesitated at the sight of an Indian, tall in stature, who was trying to trade at the door. He wore no breeches, only two pieces of canvas hanging at his groin, a girdle of wampum at his waist, and a linen shirt with an immense ruffle. She watched as a drunken Scotsman tried to tempt him with a feeble collection of small farming tools, but the Indian only grabbed the man's noggin of rum, swilled it once round in his mouth and spat it in his face. Then he paddled away in a pirogue laden with furs.

Anne pulled down the brim of her hat, almost covering her eyes, walked up to the front stoop and peered inside. With the bright light of outdoors, it must have been like staring into a cave as dark as pitch, and the air more foul still. There was the stink of piss on the back wall, a press of bodies and a cloud of cheap tobacco smoke.

'Are you coming or going?' a disembodied voice shouted at her.

She moved inside without a word, as Eoin, in turn, sidled up to the stoop.

When he spotted her again, she was seated at the end of a long bench, looking shyly about her. Most in that crowd were throwing back the rum-and-gunpowder mix the place was notorious for. Across from her, a young seaman was tossing his glass eye to friends. At the back, a fight was going on, while to her left an old man was pissing into his boot. She leaned back against the wall, spread her legs and for a moment seemed to breathe easy.

Then a rough, whiskery cheek against her own made her jump.

'A boyish cheek,' the old man sighed. He took up her hand. 'And a strong hand. Broad and firm. I should like to sip rum from the sweet cup of your hand, boy.'

She pulled it from him, and Eoin edged his way inside the door.

Someone dipped a dusty noggin into a barrel up front and thrust it into her hands. 'There you go, lad. That'll put a beard on your face.' His laughter was not unfriendly.

'Not so fast,' shouted another, as she sniffed the stuff. 'You'll take off your hat first, my boy, to show a little respect for the demon drink.' A hand snatched her hat and sent it flying round the room.

She lowered her face to her drink. In one go, she downed the lot.

They waited for her to choke, to bluster, to retch, but she only sat there, eyeing those who had circled around her.

'Now there's a right one,' said the Scots trader.

'A self-made man,' nodded another.

'I'll have my hat,' Anne said.

Somebody tossed it into her lap, a body that stood in front of her now, blocking her way. She looked up at the face, at the surly smile, and retreated under her hat. It was the deckhand, the one Squibb had employed at the scene of the *Conception*, the one who had winked at her from a raft below.

She got to her feet, ready to run.

He pushed her back on to the bench and remained where he was.

'What are you staring at?' she tried.

Their audience roared at the boldness of her voice.

'At a loose cannon I once saw breaking free from the gunport of a grounded ship.'

'Do you know him, Bonny?' asked a seaman with a flapping sleeve for an arm.

Anne looked at the floor.

'Aye,' he said, 'and I know he's not to be trusted.'

Eoin tried to push his way through the crowd, but the wall of bodies would not give way.

'You see, he's not what he seems.'

'What is he then, Jim?'

'A rich plantation pup, which I'll do well to remind his father of just as soon as I can. Get up,' he said, kicking Anne's shins. 'Your papa had better think you're worth my trouble.' Then he pushed her out the door of the shack. Eoin followed.

As they rounded the corner of the warehouse, he shoved her up against a wall.

'Kiss me,' he said.

Anne walloped him.

'I could have let them at you, you know.'

She was moving at a pace up the street, past the repairs-yard and the chandler's, past the docks and Customs House. He caught up with her finally at the market.

'A peace offering,' he said, snatching a codfish from a stall. It was a good size, nearly a foot from head to scaly tail.

She stopped and looked at him, bemused.

'Don't you see?' he said to her, and his face was earnest.

She folded her arms.

'It's your codpiece,' he said, and thrust the fish down the front of her breeches.

Eoin saw her smile.

She turned round, seeking his face in the crowd. 'Go home,' she mouthed to him. 'Go home.'

'She turned round,' he muttered. 'She was never supposed to turn around.'

Chapter Sixteen

I had let things go too far. Now, by day, I did not let her stray from my sight.

There was a roof over our heads again, no more canvas tacking, so I was able to keep her by my side. I put her to making the morning loaves, watching as her fist punched the newly risen dough with a vengeance. I made her catch and kill a goose for dinner. From the window, I saw the long white neck trapped under a pole, held down with her feet; the desperate beating of wings in her arms; then the crack of wood and the sudden slump of the bird's neck. I made her beat all the carpets, bolsters and quilts in the house. We hung them from a line in the herb garden, and I set her on them with a mighty walnut branch until clouds of dust choked the two of us.

She protested. 'I've done enough. This isn't my work, and you know it.'

'If you won't sit for your lessons, I am obliged to find you useful occupation.'

'I'm going to speak to my father.'

'Your father now, is he?'

She scowled.

'Fine,' I said. 'We will speak to your father.'

'He's not my father.'

I sighed and pushed her the broom. She thrust it back at me.

I called for Susan. We got her by an arm each, hauled her upstairs, and into her room. I closed the door behind us and turned the little key. 'Only wild things need to be caged, Anne,' I said through the door. 'You think about that.'

Something smashed on the hardwood floor.

The next morning, I turned the key, but she would not come

out. She remained entrenched behind the closed door of her shuttered room.

'Is Anne ill, Mrs Fulworth?' Mr Manley enquired with concern.

'Fevered,' I told him. 'But in need of no physician.'

He nodded sagely to me. Female delicacy, he'd decided. I left him safe with his happy illusion.

Her fourteenth birthday passed, and still she would hardly venture out. Except at nights. By the window. Down the clematis plant that grew in a tangle up the eastern wall of the house. He waited for her there, like some nocturnal animal. I knew he did. By day, Susan would find salt stains on her skirts, on the toes of her boots.

'Did I kill my mother?' she said to me one day. The year was aching towards spring. She was at the drawing room window, emptying a vase of its stagnant water.

'Of course you didn't.'

'She died when I was born.' Her voice was flat, unnerving.

'She did, when she was not much older than you are now, but it was the strain of birth. You didn't kill her. A child can't help being born.'

'Sometimes,' she said, not really listening to me, 'thinking about it, it makes me feel dead myself.'

'Don't talk like that, Anne.'

'Anyway, if death wasn't all around us, life would be ... bloodless, wouldn't it?'

'Life is just living, Anne. That's all it is. With a little luck, it's neither bloodless nor bloody.'

'I'm bleeding,' she said, her voice almost hoarse.

A kind of peace settled over the house that spring. Walls stood sturdily again, the rice fields were newly planted, and the outbuildings restored. Even Mr Manley's Observation Tower was resurrected like a testimony to his New World faith. Only the grounded *Conception* sat steadfast in the cypress swamp, a weighty memorial to the day when the world was blown inside out.

'We have come through, Mrs Fulworth,' Mr Manley opined one day.

'We have.'

Life began anew for us. Mr Manley spent long days in his fruit grove, grafting new combinations: lemon on to apricot, apricot on to peach. Squibb had abandoned his faith almost as quickly as he'd found it. 'I've said it once and I'll say it again, Mrs Fulworth. Demon spirits or no demon spirits, nobody exorcises Squibb.' Instead, he took up with a wild girl named Letty who lived in a backwoods hut. He'd have me know that she could grip a buffalo's hump barefoot and hold her own.

Eoin had set his sights on the Charles Town militia. That spring, he shouted himself through the drill, armed with a pitchfork in the vegetable patch. Soon, he was eyeing up Mr Manley's rifle and powder horn which hung over the fireplace in the drawing room. He hummed and hawed a bit, then all at once, he came out with it. 'Muster Day's in June, Mr Manley.'

'Oh, I see, I see,' he mumbled, and for once, he did. 'You have your eye on the Weapon.' He made an elaborate gesture toward the fireplace. 'I mounted the thing, it being my understanding that it was one of those things one did mount.'

'Rest assured,' said Eoin, 'it was made for gunfire as well.'

'I take it the militia is in need of more men?'

'Indeed, sir, why it wasn't ten miles from here that a man was tortured to death "à petit feu" by the Indians.' Eoin leaned confidentially toward him. 'It's a heathen method, sir. They stick a man's body full of pitch-pine splinters and light him up, piece by piece, till he's blazing like a human torch.'

Mr Manley fell into a fireside chair, waving his hand at the rifle. 'Take it,' he said. 'Take it.'

Anne announced unexpectedly that she was keen for us to move into her father's town dwelling for the Season. Her father was overjoyed at her change of heart. 'You shall have no equal at the assemblies, my dear! Mr Dallymore, your dance master, tells me your minuet is coming along splendidly now.'

We ordered damasked, brocaded and Persian silks; printed calicoes and cambric muslins; scarlet, mauve and turquoise stockings; caps, gloves and fans, and shoes of embroidered linen. And she stood still for the fittings. She did not twitch. She did not wriggle. She did not threaten to swallow the pins she gripped between her lips.

'You've grown into a fine young lady,' I dared to say.

I looked at her reflection in the oval glass. Her face revealed nothing.

Misgivings tugged at me when I was least expecting them. Sometimes, I'd think I could see a shadow – behind the magnolia tree, by the well, behind the porch swing. Sometimes I feared Jim Bonny was lurking about the place – about Anne – like a stray cur we couldn't shake.

Initially, I was glad to get to Charles Town again, to leave the plantation behind, yet no sooner had we arrived than I wanted us home again. Anne was not like other girls her age. She was awkward in their company.

'Do you not powder your hair?' enquired Miss Verity Browne over a game of whist one afternoon.

'No,' Anne replied, 'as you can see, I do not.'

'Is it because you do not know that you should powder your hair? Or is it because you wilfully choose not to powder your hair?'

'Or is it,' interrupted Miss Rose Deerford, trying to help, 'that the powder makes you sneeze as it always does me?'

'I do not powder my hair,' said Anne, laying her cards on the table, 'because lice thrive on powder and I, for one' – she flicked something from Miss Verity's coif – 'like not lice.'

'You are ill-mannered,' Verity announced.

'And you are ugly,' countered Anne.

'And you are both hurtful,' said Rose, beginning to cry.

So the afternoon drew to a close.

Anne fared no better at the summer assemblies. While the city's youth danced on through the evening, Anne could not get herself past the opening pitter-patter.

'I believe you dropped this,' said Master Ridley Taylor, passing her a white handkerchief.

I held my breath.

'Thank you, but I didn't. Mine is tucked just here in my—'

'No, no, Miss Manley. You don't quite understand. *I believe you dropped this*. That's what I say, if you take my meaning.'

'I don't.'

He laughed. 'You are endearingly perverse. Let us begin again. I say, I believe you dropped this. Then I pass it to you. You thank me, and I ask you for the next dance. Well?'

'Well, I hope you have more handkerchiefs than sense, Master Taylor. Good evening.'

The summer was slow to pass.

I worried more with each passing day. Too often, Anne asked her father if he would allow her to visit the sights of the city by sedan-chair.

'Again, Daughter?'

'There's much to see here, Father.'

He'd pass her a few coins. 'Well, mind the chairmen look respectable.'

'Why don't we hire a chaise instead, Anne,' I'd try, 'so I can keep you company?'

'Don't fret, Annie. I'll see you anon,' and she'd be gone.

The days were hot, airless. For the first time, I found myself craving the damp, bone-cold chill of Ireland; of the Atlantic wind skidding over the Old Head of Kinsale. I walked to the sitting-room window and opened it wide. I leaned out over the busy city street. I breathed deep for air, but I couldn't catch my own breath for thinking. I knew she was going to the city's waterfront. I knew she waited there for him. Outside, the air above the sun-baked street trembled with the heat.

Nothing happened. Not that summer, or that autumn, or that winter either. Our days seemed to slip away in the gentle routine of plantation life until we discovered the body, face down in the river, jammed on the rocks.

It was spring, 1715. Eoin waded in, grabbed him by his shirtneck and rolled him over. The sight of him didn't make sense, that was my first thought. He had no face. No cheeks or chin with whiskers. No smooth brow. No lean line of a mouth.

Only a shock of white teeth. His entire face had been pared away, like apple peel from his head.

In the early years, it had been so easy. Glass beads and bracelets. Small looking-glasses with silver rims. Spinning tops. Linen. Dyed cottons. Rum and sugar. A few rifles and a pouchful of shot. A pewter knife and spoon. In return, deerskins, enough for Carolina and beyond, and slaves from remote tribes for export to West Indian sugar planters. And land, always land, more than we could see. They'd retreated without force.

The traders had been warned. There had been prohibitions against wrongdoings. Cheating. Beatings. The taking of Indian women. But there was also talk of Indian debt. £10,000 sterling. £50,000. 100,000 deerskins.

Some said the Spanish were behind it. Others said it was the French. Nor was it just the Yamasees. There were more names than I could remember. The Euchees. The Creeks. The Abikaws. The Talliboosees. The Chickesaws. The Congarees. Traders were hunted down like beasts of the wood.

The Carolina Assembly sent a peace-making delegation. No one returned. Then, on the horizon, a storm of smoke. Plantations were burning.

Anne and I sat on the porch swing across from one another. I can still hear the back-and-forth creak of that swing, even and familiar. Better than a lullaby, I thought, better than a prayer. I wanted it to go on for ever.

Anne broke the quiet. 'They won't stop till they get to Charles Town, you know. Why should they? There's no one to stop them.'

'There's the militia,' I said hopelessly, 'and Governor Craven at the fore.'

'Is that why they're arming slaves, Annie? Because the militia is such a force to reckon with?'

I could not bear to think beyond the porch and the swing creaking. Eoin was there, in that storm of smoke.

'I'd rather be there than here,' she said, as if reading my thoughts.

'You're a liar for saying so.'

'You wait,' she said.

'None of us will be waiting long.' My temper flared. 'For very soon *there* will be *here* and we'll all be in the thick of it. So forbear a little longer.'

I left the porch. I walked past the herb garden, through the fruit grove and on through the plantation, stepping on new shoots without care. At the bottom of the Observation Tower, I took a deep breath and started the spiralling climb to the top. The way was narrow. The walls stank of fresh pitch.

He did not hear me enter the round chamber at the top. He was leaning against the casement of the glassless window, his back to me. Here, above the treeline, there was already a smell of burning on the breeze. I joined him at the window and we stared together at the black horizon.

'I am a poor semblance of a father, Mrs Fulworth.'

'You are her father, and she is your daughter. Nothing can alter that.'

'I should not have brought us to this place. It is Chaos here.' He followed the flight of a bright kingfisher with his eye. 'She may die, Mrs Fulworth.'

'I know.'

'And I may have no means of preventing it. Do you see? A man is helpless here.'

I had no words.

'So I hide in this tower. I cannot face her.'

'You have nothing to hide.'

'A long time ago, Mrs Fulworth, in Ireland, when I feared I would lose all, you implored me to gather Anne to me, to make her believe in the fact of her father. I never did, and she never believed. Quite rightly, she has scorned me.'

'No,' I said. 'That isn't so.'

'You are kind. I see more than I allow.'

'And Anne sees less than she might.'

'I am a fool.'

'And your daughter is a wilderness. Given time, she will see her way through.'

'Given time.'

Beyond us, it was June. The air was gentle, the leaves on the trees in the wood beyond, still a tender green. The day was too bright.

Back at the house, we didn't find her on the porch or in the drawing room. She was in the kitchen with Squibb and Black-Eyed Susan. 'What are you three up to?' I asked.

Squibb and Susan looked at the floor. Anne had the face of a cat who had swallowed a bird.

'Good day, Mrs Fulworth. Mr Manley.' It was Jim Bonny. He was leaning up against the far wall.

Mr Manley searched his memory. 'The deckhand? Why, I ordered you never to—'

'And I don't take orders from you, sir.'

'On your way,' said Squibb, getting hold of his arm.

He shook Squibb off with ease. 'Thank you for your send-off, old man. I will be on my way, just as soon as Miss Manley has gathered a few essentials.'

'I want Annie to come with us,' she said, ignoring our incredulous faces.

'She'll lumber us.'

'No one's going anywhere, Anne.' The tone of my voice was one she knew not to challenge.

'We are. We're going to the West Indies. Come with us, Annie. You'll die here. They're getting closer by the hour.'

'He's lying to you. Can't you see that, girl? Governor Craven has laid an embargo on all vessels up and down the coast. No ship is sailing anywhere.'

'A ship leaves the eastern shore of Folly Island tonight,' he said.

'Those channels aren't navigable, and you know it,' shouted Squibb. 'You run while the running's good, or I'll have a few of our Negroes remind you what those legs are for. Our Anne's not yet sixteen!'

'I'm going to marry him,' she announced. 'When we get there. Come with us, Annie.'

I was dumbfounded. I looked to Mr Manley. 'Tell her,' I said. 'Make her listen. *You are her father*. Stop her.'

He crossed the room and faced her. She crossed her arms and leaned nonchalantly against the sideboard.

'Go,' he said. 'Go now. Go safely.'

'Mr Manley!'

'You won't give your daughter to the likes of him!' shouted Squibb.

Anne stiffened. 'I'm no one's to give!'

'Go all the same,' her father said in a quiet voice. 'Take whatever you need.' He made to kiss her forehead, but she pulled away.

When she turned to me, I could see she was crying. 'Annie?'

'You are a wicked girl,' I said.

'I need you, Annie.'

'You need no one but yourself.'

'You're wrong.'

'When have I ever been wrong about you?'

'Now. You're wrong now!'

I sighed.

'Please come.'

'Why?'

'Please.'

'I hardly have a choice, do I? I've hardly had any since the day you were born.'

'Mrs Fulworth,' said Squibb, 'you're no longer a young woman. Think about it. This is your home.'

'No, Squibb. I lost my home a long time ago.'

'And Eoin?' said Mr Manley, taking my hand in his.

'He's grown now. He has outgrown me. May the Lord help him.'

We left as the ash started to fall like a soundless rain. It blew in through windows, through the open doors.

'I fear this New World is dying, Mrs Fulworth.' Mr Manley kissed my cheek. 'God bless.'

It was dark by the time we made it downriver. In Charles Town, the harbourfront was lifeless. Ships sat on low waves. A lone mongrel trotted up and down one of the piers, anxious for its master. Somewhere, a church bell was ringing.

Anne and I wandered down to a narrow beach. 'Jim has to

find his mate,' she explained. 'He's the one with the rowboat. He'll take us out to Folly Island, and we'll meet the ship there.'

I sat down on a pile of netting. Anne rolled up the legs of her trous – for Bonny had outfitted her once more – and paddled in the ebbing tide.

'Ooh, it's cold for June,' she called to me, like a child who knew only that moment. She was little more than a shadow in the dark, a disturbance on the water's calm surface. 'Come here, Annie! Look!'

'What is it?' I shouted, not moving from my spot. I was stiff now and cold.

'*Come see.*'

I heaved myself off the beach and wandered down to the water's edge. She was kicking and splashing. Water sprayed my face.

'Can you see it?'

'See what?'

'Look!'

Then I saw, where her limbs had stirred the tide. Bright flecks of silver flashing in the black water. Motes of light, like I'd never seen. 'How do you do that?' I looked at her suspiciously.

'Jim says they're alive, like fireflies in the night. Thousands of them.'

She spun herself round, whooshing her arms through the water. Light streaked the darkness again and again. Then she extended her hands to me. 'Come in, Annie,' she called.

'No,' I said. 'My joints are already stiff.'

'I know you want to. Please.'

I sat down, pulled off my boots, hauled my skirts high, and waded into the sea. The cold shot through me. 'I'm going back in,' I called.

'No, you're not.' She came and got hold of my hand, raising my arm high. 'Now turn, Annie. Spin. That's right, spin!'

Light streamed around me like some kind of uncanny magic. I laughed, giddy, and nearly fell over with all the spinning and the sand shifting under my feet. She caught me though. Her arms were sturdy. Her balance was sure. She held me there in that glimmering tide, and I wept.

Chapter Seventeen

It was as if, that night, she reached into the darkness around us and pulled the world inside out with one hand. Nothing would be the same again.

Above us, the ship's timbers were groaning and so was Captain Cain. 'Women,' he was telling Jim Bonny, 'are bad luck at sea.' We four – Bonny, his mate with the dory, Anne and myself – were stranded on a tar-black sea. There were no stars. The moon was just a chewed-off sliver of fingernail.

'You've been paid,' said Bonny. 'Let us board.'

'They're all milk and blood and tears,' he grumbled. 'The sea doesn't need to fucking drown you with the runny likes of them on board. I'm not having it.' A small sack of coins crashed into the puddle of water at our feet. Behind us, the line of the horizon was glowing red like a brand.

'What woman are you talking about?' Anne demanded.

The lamp in his hand seemed to swell in the night, as two eyes we couldn't see searched our shapes. 'She might be old,' he said, meaning me, 'but that's still a woman.'

'No,' Anne shouted back. 'You're wrong. A woman once, but a woman no longer.'

'What are you on about?' Yes, I wanted to say, what are you on about, girl? But I held my tongue.

'I had hoped it wouldn't have to be said, but I have no choice. You're looking at the unhappy ghost of my own dead mother.'

'Fetch off!'

'I wish to God it wasn't so. She died not speaking to me, her only son, and now' – Anne sighed heavily – 'she's trapped between this world and the next, mouthing messages I'll never hear.'

Above us, we heard snorting. 'Since when is a ghost on the run for her life?'

'Throw me down your cutlass,' Anne said.

Laughing, he obliged.

'Now hold your lamp steady and you'll see she's no more solid than water. Stand up, Ma.'

'She can hear you then,' he scoffed.

'Aye,' said she, my new-found son, 'that's her tragedy. She can hear every word we speak, but she can't say so much as "Forgive me, my child."'

'For the love of Jesus, Anne,' I whispered, 'I'm not going to let you kill me with that cutlass.'

'Hold still,' she muttered, hardly moving her lips, 'and stand like this, side on to him, that's right. Now move your arm away from your other side just a crack, like that.'

'I told you she'd hold us back,' Jim complained.

'Are you watching up there?' she called.

'Aye, though I've never known a son to kill his mother and ask for witnesses before.'

With that, she drew her arm back and thrust the blade into my ghostly heart. For an instant, I felt the edge of it, rigid against my ribcage, and almost cried out. Then she pulled the cutlass back once more, and I was left, standing.

'Well?' Anne demanded.

'It came out the back of her . . .'

She threw the cutlass overhead, and we heard it clatter on the ship's deck. 'Then let's say no more about it, for these are indignities no dead mother should have to bear.'

'One question,' said the voice in the dark. 'Why wouldn't she speak to you before she . . . passed over?'

'Her last words were, 'I'll die before I see you run away to sea, Anson,' and plead though I did, I could neither get her to open her lips or nod me a blessing. True to her word, she haunts me now, here at sea.'

'No second thoughts then?' ventured Captain Cain unsteadily.

'Why? A ghost is no bad thing at sea.'

'Isn't it?'

'No. It's like people say, Death has no bones to pick with the dead. It will leave us be.'

'What people?'

'Are you taking us or not, Captain?'

'Can she climb up,' he enquired, 'or does she more or less have to float?'

'While in this world,' said Bonny, between his teeth, 'she climbs like the rest of us.'

It was a stinking vessel, fretted with worm-rot and swimming with bilge. Pans of burning brimstone fouled the air in the fo'c's'le to keep back the vermin, and an ancient pump screamed like a sinner all day and all night.

Not unreasonably, I expected to die in the dark water of Charles Town's harbour that first night. I was sure we'd break up on the rocks in those inhospitable channels and, if truth is told, I was not a little disappointed that we did not end it all there. At the time, it seemed to me a more reliable fate than any I could imagine for us with Jim Bonny. I said nothing. I could no longer shout or whisper. Wittingly or unwittingly, Anne had talked away my voice.

I became a veritable dumb-show for Captain Cain's tiny crew, obliged every now and then to pace the deck and worriedly work the sea air with my lips. They were rare moments when I found myself alone with her and able to speak.

'Sshht, Annie! Keep your voice down, will you.' We were bent low in the dark of the hold.

'You didn't have to kill me.'

'Don't exaggerate. It was the only way of getting you to safety, and you know it.'

I grabbed her shirt and hauled it up. She had bound her breasts with a piece of stolen canvas. 'Flatten yourself like this, and you'll never give suck. I can tell you that now.'

'It's not my first concern, believe it or not,' and she grabbed the end of her shirt and stuffed it back into her breeches.

'Well, my voice is my voice, and I'll do as I please with it.'

'No, Annie, you won't,' she said, turning strangely solemn. 'I forbid it. Is that clear?' She walked to the ladder.

I ran to my hammock and rooted in the hemp sack I had hurriedly stuffed with a few belongings. All but her ankles had disappeared by the time I reached the bottom of the ladder. I grabbed one.

She lowered herself, slowly. 'What is it now?'

I unclenched my fist and pushed my hand up to her face. Light spilled through the hatch, brightening the crumpled velvet bag that sat on my palm. I stuffed it under her shirt, forcing it between her breasts and the canvas. 'From your dead mother,' I said.

Captain Cain's jacket was made of sailcloth and buttoned with bits of old yellow cheese you could break a tooth on. His trous were newly tarred and noisy, snapping in the westerly as he came up alongside me one day. 'Choppy,' he called, nodding to the waves.

I nodded and we both looked out to sea again, our faces flattened in the gust. I was about to go, for there was something too familiar in the sharing of sea air, when he clapped his hands to his mouth and shouted over the wind. 'My Molly's long gone.'

I managed a quick but kindly smile.

'And yourself?' he enquired, turning to me.

I shrugged and looked about for Anne.

'Can't be easy,' he called.

I was able to feign distraction, for at that moment three seasick and squealing hogs – our nourishment for the journey – went rolling past the poop rail. He took no notice. 'You must get a little world-weary now and then. Am I right?'

I pulled my wrap closer to me.

'Truth is,' he said, giving me the once-over, 'if you weren't deceased, I might get it into my head to wed you, for I'm a man of few words and you're a woman of even fewer, which is a rare thing.' He cleared his throat. 'Still, if you're feeling up to it, I'm the broad-minded sort . . .'

I looked him square in his rheumy eye and hissed. I hissed until his sea-legs gave way. I hissed until he was stumbling past the poop rail. I hissed until he was reeling alongside those three downcast hogs.

I became the ghost of myself on that journey. The silence in my mouth left me empty. Loneliness turned me shadowy, and fear of the future set me adrift in memories: of my little one drowned in Sally's tears and Sally dead and my boys lost to me and the soul of Anne fled, and my homeland, unreal as memory.

I haunted the vessel.

Even as I did, day by day, week by week, Anne was changing too. Even as I faded, she was growing – ruder, heartier, comelier, longer, broader, more brazen; growing fleet of foot and flint-eyed, single-minded and hot-headed; growing larger than life itself. One moment, she'd be airborne in the rigging of the mizzen mast, and the next, she'd be tying knots like sleights of hand: diamond knots and Flemish eyes, goose necks and cats-paws, butterfly knots and Spanish bows. Look again, and you'd find her on her back, dreaming new constellations into the night sky: the Four-Breasted Woman, Satan's Horns, the Little Dog Who Forgot His Hind Leg, the Seven Waves, the Pair of Crossed Eyes. The crew too would be flat out and face up on the unscrubbed salty deck, while Captain Cain altered his charts like a lost man.

We had put to sea and our bearings were gone.

Jim Bonny got hold of the Captain by a cheesy button. 'If we don't make New Providence in seven days,' he threatened, 'you'll make a tough chew for some fish.' On the following day, as though the four winds were in no mind to be hurried, we were becalmed. The topsails drooped like an old man's gut, the face of the sea was as untroubled as a virgin's, and we were down to our last hog.

Even worse than a seasick hog is a hog that will not be caught. Now that all was still, the said hog had suddenly recovered its porcine energies, charging up the larboard and down the starboard with the ship's cook grasping after its trotters. The crew had it cornered in the stern, then at the bow. A man went overboard, but the hog ran free. Captain Cain tried to sweet-talk it. Jim Bonny tried to stare it down. Anne leaped from the main mast on to its bristling back, but to no avail. It bolted and she landed, brained on the binnacle box. Finally, in one running leap, like a hell-ridden swine driven over the cliff by Christ Himself, our hog sailed over the gunwale and sank without a trace.

It did not bode well. We were marooned on a windless sea with only maggoty biscuits, one leaking cask of ale, another of stale water, and the fish we could hook to preserve us. There was no calm on that becalmed ship.

After the first week, Captain Cain slept tied at his middle to the mizzen mast, wrinkling his nose for a hint of a breeze.

After a fortnight, Bonny was stealing food. Anne knew it, and I knew it.

'Who are you staring at?' he growled at me one day.

I could say nothing. The crew sat slumped against the sides of the deck, all of them listless with hunger.

'I've been thinking about you, Dead Annie, mourning your passing, of course, and suddenly it came to me. A ghost does not need nourishment.'

Anne raised her head. 'Shut your mouth, Jim.'

'But surely it's true. It's the living who need to eat. If we don't want to join her in the afterlife, I suggest we make the most of your dead mother's rations from here on in.' The crew were coming to life, nodding their assent. Anne jumped to her feet and grabbed Bonny by the collar.

'Anson,' he said, smiling broadly, 'you're an honourable fellow, if not an honest one, but we both know you're no match for a man.' He flung her against a heap of tackle. 'A dead woman does not need to eat. It's that simple.'

One night, in the dark of the fo'c's'le, I heard them.

'Cain was right,' I heard him whisper, 'women are bad luck at sea. You're bad luck at sea.' I could hear his breathing, louder than his words. Her hammock creaked with his weight.

I waited for her voice.

It didn't come.

I turned over, buried my head in my arms, and slept the sleep of the dead.

Time itself was becalmed. We no longer knew the day or even the week with any certainty. Eels swarmed beneath the hull.

Captain Cain was still wrapped in the ratlines one morning as I passed. I did not stop. I found Anne, alone at the head of the ship, crouching over a pot.

'Annie,' she said, glad to see me, glad that we were, for a moment, alone.

I could not find my voice. Only a faint smile.

'You don't look well.'

I shrugged.

Her face was straining. 'My gut is badly bound,' she explained. 'Little wonder.'

I sat down on the deck. Already it was warm with the morning heat. I looked up. Not a speck of cloud. Not a breath of wind.

We were together like that – with me silent and Anne hushed and straining, and what could we say anyhow that we didn't already know? – we were together like that for what seemed like hours or maybe even days because time had stopped, and there was no telling a moment from for ever.

That's how it seemed when Anne, out of the blue, passed wind. It erupted from her backside with a force that blew her off the pot, with a force that sent me reeling along the sunny deck, with a force that seemed to blow Captain Cain back to the helm. 'All hands on!' he shouted.

His crew emerged from the hold blinking in the brightness, rubbing their eyes.

Anne rumbled once more.

'Fine on the starboard bow!' ordered Captain Cain.

The crew moved with spirit, hoisting the sails, tuning them to the gathering breeze. And it was true, I could feel a cool breeze on my sun-burned cheek. I could see it lifting strands of Anne's dark hair, blowing it across her eyes. I could hear the rise of waves against the ship's hull.

'Bear away before the wind!' came the call.

We were moving once more.

Later, some would say that Anne's wind could fill a ship's sails, that she could blow up a storm if she got it into her head. I, for one, was tongue-tied. The old wives' tale had swallowed the old wife. Only the ghost of her remained.

Chapter Eighteen

A breeze was blowing off shore, and we smelled New Providence before we saw it. It was the stink of wood rot and foot rot, of heavy breathing and unclean living. Below us, the ebb tide was drowning in the dross of the God-forsaken. 'Smell that!' Anne shouted from the rigging, as if you needed to make an effort. 'Liberty!' she declared to Captain and crew, to fish and to gulls. 'The smell of liberty!' Of the libertine more like, but I managed something like a smile, for here, for the first time, I could see Mr Manley's daughter, his natural heir who saw only the compost and not the shite.

The harbour was afloat with all manner of craft – sloops and snows, dories and pirogues, rafts and drifting washtubs – and life ran rampant aboard it all.

A series of dangerous salutes volleyed between two friendly vessels. A wash line swayed between the main masts of another pair. Not far from us, a raft was breaking up, and its family of six were suddenly log-rolling like they'd been born to it. Closer to shore, a fiddler on a sloop, a drummer on a schooner and a piper on a hag's-boat were cobbling together a tune, even as a string of people on the beach hauled in a bloated body in a fishing net.

The shoreline seethed. Children, white, black and mulatto, were crawling in and out of tents fashioned from driftwood and palm fronds. Seamen cosied fancy-women in homes made only of sailcloth and tilting spars. Pale faces peered out from the hulks of beached wrecks. Cockerels fine-stepped it through rubbish. A mangy cow was mounting a donkey, and under the cover of trees a still was rumbling, loud on three shaking legs.

It was a community of outcasts.

I wanted to go back. I wanted to be gone. But even as my thoughts doubled back, I heard the anchor's chain, slipping free of the windlass, and the dead splash of a hundredweight of iron.

Blinking into the sun, I searched the rigging for Anne. She was gone. They were dropping the boat for shore when she finally emerged like a stowaway from the hold, with Bonny behind her.

The boatswain dropped his tackle. Captain Cain dropped his jaw.

Anne was standing before us in mildewed skirts and a bodice.

She crossed the deck to where I stood, amazed. Studying her new shape, I could see she had not yet loosened her breasts from the canvas, but she had, much to my wonder, tied back her unruly hair.

'Jim's idea,' she said, 'for life ashore.'

Captain Cain was in earshot, and before we knew it, he was jumping over the binnacle box and grabbing her by the shoulders. 'For the sake of your poor dead silent mother, I must speak.'

We waited.

'I don't know what to say except this.' He tugged at her skirts. 'This is not the way, lad! Aye, we now abide in the Torrid Zone. Aye, it is a lawless place, but I urge you, do not yield to the polluted wishes of men who have been too long at sea. Now, go down below and right yourself, or you will not leave this ship.'

Anne looked from me to the Captain and from the Captain to the crew who waited, mouths agog. Then in one swift move, she hoisted her skirts, disappeared over the rail, down the step and into the empty boat.

Bonny had gone after her, but it was a while before we could get anyone to ferry the lot of us to shore, for a small but heated war seemed to have broken out among the locals. Gunfire was ringing out everywhere, and somewhere, a ship was on fire. 'You'll grow accustomed,' Captain Cain comforted me as we crouched on all fours under the boom. 'They're temperamental in these parts, but no one bears a grudge.'

That evening, I recognized the log-rolling mother of the family of six. She was seated under a coconut palm, darning what she claimed were bullet holes in the day's washing.

'Did you see that ship coming into harbour this afternoon?'

I shook my head, perhaps too vigorously.

She had watched our ship sail in from her vantage point on the log, she told me. 'And who would have guessed?' she said, patting the sand where she sat, drawing me in, a gullible stranger on the beach.

I settled down wearily against the trunk of the coconut palm. I was afraid to listen and afraid not to listen. Since leaving Charles Town, truth had turned willy-nilly on me and, like a sailor's sea-legs, always unsteady on land once he's lived at sea, I no longer stood sure on what I'd once known to be so.

How One Thing Led to Another

Well, the first thing I know is this. There's a ship coming into harbour, and I say to myself, Peg, that's no Spanish enemy for we'd as soon laugh at it as fight it. It's no pirate catch either for no respectable pirate I know would risk sailing home in such an eyesore. So, I conclude to myself that it can only be more mope-faced colonists clamouring after the good life in our little haven. (A coconut at that moment fell from the tree, almost killing Peg, but she wasn't distracted.)

Now the fact is, I'm willing to share and share alike, but we're already over a thousand bodies on this island as you well know, and as many in harbour again, and sometimes I think to myself, one more body and we're going to bloody sink. You see what I'm saying? An island's no better off than a boat at sea when everyone and his mother's jumping aboard. The plan is for me and mine to sneak up on the newcomers unaware, board their vessel and put the fright into them, so they turn around and sail back to wherever the hell it is they came from. Are you with me?

(I gave her a sheepish nod.)

Only thing is, my man can hardly tie his bootlaces let alone knots that will bind a raft and, before I know it, we're breaking up. I go under and surface again just as one of our logs goes crashing into the back of my head. I'm down again, then up again, and finally I'm just holding on to that log for dear life, drifting in towards shore – not far behind a girl who's all by herself in a boat and paddling like she was born to it. The tide's going with us, not against us, and it's not long before she's standing in the tide, hauling her boat up to the beach. I have, by this time, recovered my strength and I'm now right behind her. Close enough, in fact, to see saucy Dick Turnley sauntering her way. As she turns quickly round from the head of the boat, he walks right into her, deliberately.

'Out of my way!' she says, seeing right through him.

'Can't hear you,' he says, smiling. 'You see, I've only got the one ear.' It's true. He lost one of his jug ears in a brawl the year before last. 'But I've still got mouth enough,' he says, 'to tell you that you're coming to share a drink with me.'

'Like hell I am,' she says.

'Can't hear you,' he says again, playing pig-ignorant. 'Must be I'm going deaf in my good ear.'

'Listen,' she says, her voice low like a threat, 'I am not drinking with you. Not now. Not ever.' Meanwhile, that fellow from her vessel is swimming up behind, and he's looking none too neighbourly.

'Come again?' Dick shouts, shaking his head and fingering the plug-hole where his ear used to be, as though he might just catch her reply, if she gives him the one he's waiting for, and whichever way the girl makes to turn, he blocks her path.

Now, her hand was quicker than anyone's eye. When I blinked, his pistol was in her grip. 'WELL, CAN YOU HEAR THIS?' she bellows, and without so much as stopping for breath she blasts off his other ear.

People stop what they're doing and gather round, dumbstruck. The mean-looking fellow heaves himself out of the water and stands fast behind her.

But she's not daunted. 'By God!' she shouts, looking Dick dead in the eye. 'Is that a head? I thought I was shooting the handle off a mug!' Then she spits on the smoking pistol and returns it to his shaking hand.

But, you see, it didn't end there. No, that shot which rang out clear across shore and harbour blew the Brunty brothers straight out of their hammocks. Ever since the day Joseph Brunty tried to cheat his brother Bill out of a foot of the sand that blows between them, each man's fingers have always slept clenching a loaded musket.

So it's no surprise to anyone that the one is now accusing the other of trying to murder him in his sleep, and soon each man is dodging shot from behind their respective palm trees. It's one of their bullets that ricochets off the senile Admiral's flagstaff and soon the old man's shooting up a storm, rousing all with ears to hear, and shouting, 'Get the moustachioed bastards!' Now he might be senile, but he wasn't an admiral for nothing, and soon every man is reaching for his weapon, and that's what started that storm of gunfire here on the beach today. It wasn't the Spanish or the French like everyone's saying. It was just one flat-chested girl.

Of course, it was all those guns going off on shore and all those birds falling from the sky that got the old twelve-pounders in the harbour fired-up too. That's how that brig burned to the keel. It was a misfire, not a Spanish curse. You see? And all this while, do you know where she is? Strolling up the beach with her surly-faced fellow, as if neither of them had a care in this world.

Peg concluded. 'Ten dead. Dozens with bits blown off, and do you know what's more?' she asked, with eyes wide and crows' feet straining.

I shook my head, turned my face.

'They say . . .' She edged closer to my ear. 'They say she killed her own mother.'

The sun was dropping from the sky so fast it seemed it would fall over the edge of the world. Overhead, the fronds of the palm tree were flapping in the night breeze like dark wings. I didn't want to hear any more. I got to my feet, stiff now from sitting.

'Mind how you go,' says Peg, a little put out as I walked away.

At my feet, white claws vanished into wet holes with every step I took. Ghost crabs were everywhere.

In the dark of our makeshift lean-to, a whisper. Anne's voice. 'Annie?'

I pretended I was asleep, dead to the world on the other side of the sackcloth curtain.

'Annie, I didn't . . . did I?'

She took away my voice.

'What they're saying. You said I wasn't to blame. Annie?'

I didn't know. I didn't know her any more.

'Tell me the story of how you found her sucking butter on your slops-pail.'

Hush. Hush. Let me lie in peace, girl.

At last, I heard her turn over. Then just the sound of the tide breaking on the beach below us.

In the morning, I was awakened by shouting. Anne and Jim Bonny were yelling on the other side of the curtain.

'Another day,' he said.

'No. Today,' she insisted.

'Why so all of a bloody sudden?'

'Are you going to marry me or not?'

'Well, where's the need? Now that we're here, I'm not going anywhere, am I?'

'It was the plan.'

'You won't find a man of the cloth in this lot, let me tell you.'

Somebody kicked the side of the lean-to, and the roof nearly collapsed on top of us.

'Is it the dowry then?' she demanded. 'Is that what you're waiting for?'

What was she saying? There was no dowry. There was no time, even if Mr Manley had given his blessing.

Jim paused. 'It might ease our way into wedded bliss.'

'Fine,' she said. I could hear her hauling on her clothes.

'Fine what? Where are you going?'

'To fetch it. I buried it after we landed, for safekeeping.' She stamped her foot into a boot. 'But don't forget what you said. I've got a witness this time.'

'Who?' he shouted.

'Her,' she said. She flung back the curtain and exposed me.

I wanted to shake her. I wanted to shout, *why wed yourself to the likes of him? Look at him! Listen to him, girl! Are you so desperate to show me a thing or two that you'll cut off your own head to spite your face? For the love of Christ!*

My face was burning. My voice was rearing in my throat. I opened my mouth to shout, to storm when she lifted her hand to my face, so that only I could see, and unfolded her fingers like a conjuror who had pulled something from behind my ear.

On her palm, a velvet bag. In the bag, a caul. Hood of mother's blood. *Seamen would pay gold.*

My words never came.

I stood on the shore the morning they stole a dory and paddled it across the harbour, Anne's back to me all the way. It wasn't even first light yet, and the harbour was so still. Hardly a wave as they climbed aboard Captain Cain's vessel. Not a ripple as Bonny tickled the sleeping man's armpit with the mouth of his pistol. Not a crying gull as they roused two bewildered crew to bear witness, as they repeated the words after a frightened old man who could only think of his Molly long gone. Not a hoarse whisper of wind as their oars dipped and twisted once more, pulling them back to land, to light breaking and to me walking away.

Chapter Nineteen

There was a kind of lizard in those parts. It was small but plump, and it would creep up and down the walls at night. If you were quick, very quick, you could snatch it. You'd feel its tail, alive in your grip, and maybe you'd forget to breathe. By the time you opened your hands to look again though, the creature itself would be long gone. Only the tail would be left, wriggling lizard-less on your palm.

In their dreams,

Peg peeked under Anne's petticoat, and took bets.

Bill Brunty rolled with her in his hammock on top of a wave.

Joseph Brunty buried his blushing face in her breast and took suck.

The Admiral duelled with her, swordfish at dawn.

And Unconscionable Nan, perhaps the fanciest of fancy women in New Providence, bore Anne's children.

In reality though, it went more like this.

The Admiral got Anne into the hammock, no one knew how (and Jim Bonny didn't care).

Bill Brunty was discovered peeking up her petticoat.

Peg clasped Joe Brunty unexpectedly to her matronly breast.

And Unconscionable Nan, who had made her fortune by *not* blushing, went pink as passion fruit whenever Anne passed.

Anne herself seemed hardly to notice the hubbub she left in her wake. As toasts were swigged in her honour in front of the local still, she tickled the beards of roaming nanny-goats. As sea-thieves laid their booty at her feet – rolls of fresh tobacco, bags of sweet-smelling pimento, jars of old-world brandy – she'd step over it, spotting a big conch shell or maybe a washed-up starfish on the shore. She liked her pleasures the same as the next person, out Anne had a perverse faith in serendipity over endeavour; in the ephemeral find over the sought-after Spanish doubloon, and our crooked lean-to was leaning ever more 'to' with the unstoppable spread of her discoveries.

I remember a rusting astrolabe; a monstrous gold-lacquered fish, the figurehead of some wrecked vessel; sea fans that she had gathered from the tide after the last storm; a clutch of decaying frangipani blossom; a dead bat; a silver place setting; and a corked bottle with a rolled-up message inside that read, 'MIND YOUR OWN BUSINESS'.

'Oh, that,' said Peg, seeing the bottled note. 'That's the third this month alone. Wish the poor bastard would change his tune.'

'Is it someone marooned then?' asked Anne. We'd heard about such cases from Captain Cain, tales of men who'd been abandoned on some sandy island that was falling into the sea.

'No,' said Peg. 'It's only the Governor at it again.'

Anne's was crestfallen. 'I thought there was no governor here. I thought it was a lawless place.'

'It is,' replied Peg, scrubbing out a cooking pot with sand.

'Doesn't he govern then?'

'What do you mean?'

'Doesn't he make proclamations?'

'You're holding one,' said Peg.

Anne looked at the crumpled note with new interest. 'But no hangings?'

'No, not in ten years or more.'

'Any statuary?'

'Not that I've seen.'

'Does he walk among the people?'

'Never.'

'Then how do you actually know you have a governor, Peg?'

'*Because*,' she said, staring at Anne as if she was simple, 'he *told* us so, just like a bloody governor. A damp note in a leaky pickling jar, if I remember rightly.'

Unconscionable Nan discovered the next bottle a fortnight later. She was bathing at high tide, swilling water over her milk-white shoulders and swishing her downy armpits with sea foam, heedless of the onlookers who watched from ship and shore.

'You're a well-rigged woman, Nan!' shouted one from a skiff.

She wasn't bothered. She'd been ashamed of some things in her lifetime, but her body had never been one of them. She was watching a glittering shoal of minnows coursing through her cleavage when she noticed an ink bottle, circumnavigating her right thigh.

She plucked it from the sea and unplugged it. 'I'LL SEE HER,' read the tiny missive.

Nan was unimpressed. 'Her-who, you old coot?'

A second smaller bottle insisted at her buttocks. She reached round and lifted it from the water. Anticipating a timely reply to her own query, Nan was to be disappointed. 'NOW,' was all it said.

The Governor resided in the mouldy ruins of Fort Nassau, a defence that the English, in their day, had fashioned, pallisade-style, from palmetto logs and lime. Once upon a time it had sat, quite respectably, on a low hillside overlooking the harbour's western point of entry, armed with half a dozen nine-pounders.

After one rainy season though, the bulk of it lay at the bottom of the harbour. After two, the Lord Proprietors had abandoned the irksome island, fort and all. No one knew when the present incumbent took up his role in the ramshackle fort. Not even Peg could say for sure where he came from. 'I once heard that he came to New Providence as a Christian missionary, if you'll believe it, and that the Archfiend appeared to him on the hillside in the shape of a mockingbird. He knew it was the Archfiend because the bird spoke to him in his own voice and said, 'What will you have?' He replied oh-so-proudly, thinking himself too strong to be tempted, 'Nothing. I'll have nothing from you.' 'So be it,' said the mockingbird, and the next thing he knows, he wakes in the old rotting hut in Fort Nassau, surrounded by ruins.'

'Why didn't he just leave?' said Unconscionable Nan.

'Couldn't find his way out. Never has been able to. Once he even employed a native guide. They walked in circles for three days, ended up back at the hut, then the guide took off. That's how the story got out. He's got one old Negro slave up there who does his bidding, launching the bottles and such. Apart from him, he never sees a soul. Professes himself a hermit just to save face.' She spat on her youngest's forehead and wiped it with a bit of flannel. 'Mind you, I also heard he was just a disgruntled cotton picker from Little Cayman, so you just never know.'

'Why me?'

'You can't refuse the Governor,' replied Peg.

We were standing at the start of the overgrown path that twisted westward towards Nassau.

'But what about disobedience and disorder, for God's sake? What about riot and uproar?' Anne looked from face to face appealingly. 'What about New Providence, the free-for-all?'

'Bring us back some gossip on the old loony, won't you,' said Nan.

'And don't let him interfere with you,' said Bill.

'Jim?' pleaded Anne, more desperate than we'd realized.

Jim Bonny shrugged. 'Watch out for swamp.'

So it was settled.

Anne Meets the Hermit Governor, as Recounted by Anne Herself
I headed off down that path, as you know, armed with only my machete and hacking away as I went. Vines and razor grass were everywhere, and strangler fig choked most of the trees. It wasn't long before the shore disappeared behind me, and I was left just trying to sort out north from south and east from west.

After a time, I finally climbed free of all that green tangle only to find myself nowhere. Barrens as far as my eye could see: stretches of sand, mosquitoey marshes, bloody great drooping pine trees, and no path anywhere. I was beginning to think, right, they're having one over on me, when I spotted a mocking-bird in a stunted pine, devouring some pigeon's eggs.

('Did it speak to you?' said Peg.)

Of course it didn't, but it did bring the mother pigeon back in a hurry. There was a big flap in a tree up ahead as she took flight, and that's when I saw the wave of black pine in the distance: the hillside of the Governor's fort. I made the crest of it in no time and suddenly there was the shore again – bits of blue between the pines – and the sound of the tide on the rocks just below. I could even pick out the Admiral's flag.

('It's nothing,' said the Admiral, overcome.)

But when I turned inland again, I couldn't see anything but trees and a broken-down palisade. I would have come straight back again if I hadn't tripped over a certain plank. It was streaming with termites, but I could see it was some sort of sign. GOVERNMENT PROPERTY, it said. BUGGER OFF. STAY AWAY.

Well, bugger you, I thought, and I carried right on till I came to an old waterlogged hut. I called, but no one answered. I went around the other side and called again, but no one. Finally, I pressed my face to one of the old gun slits, and this voice like the devil's boomed out of the dark at me. 'Do you READ? Do you know what a bloody BOUNDARY is, or do I have to draw one down the middle of you with the point of my cutlass?'

It stopped me in my tracks. 'It's me, from the shore!' I shouted into the darkness. 'We got your message, both parts, in those old bottles of yours.'

'You have no PLACE here.'

'They thought you wanted to see me.'

'I did,' he whispered.

'Well here I am.'

'Listen and listen well: you have no PLACE here.'

'Right, I'm going,' I said. I'd had enough.

A long arm shot out of the gun slit. A hand, white as gristle, caught hold of my shoulder. My right arm froze. The machete fell out of my hand.

'DINNER TIME!' he commanded, and an old slave came up from behind with a shot of spirit on a tatty pillow. A second arm slid out of the gun slit, grabbed the noggin and disappeared again, like an earthworm into a hole. 'Bitch!' he whispered. 'Bitch!' Then he spat at me.

'I've done nothing to you!' I said, but my knees were starting to tremble. His fingers were still locked on my shoulder.

'You've ruined the Census,' he hissed at me.

'What Census?' I said. 'I don't know what you're talking about!'

'Shut your mouth, you toothy cunt!'

I pleaded with him to just let me go. The old slave had picked up my machete and now he was right behind me with it poised between my shoulder-blades.

'There is no PLACE for you. Do you understand? No column means no place in the Census. No place in the Census means you do not exist in the eyes of this Government.'

I took a deep breath and prised his hand from my shoulder. 'I'm going now.'

'If you put one foot over this Government's boundary, my civil servant will cleave you in two.'

I started to walk away, my heart kicking in my chest. His slave followed, at arm's length. I could hear his feet in the undergrowth, but I wouldn't let myself turn around. I had one foot over that termite-eaten sign when I heard what sounded like someone crying. I turned. It wasn't the slave with my machete. It was a pale old man. His back was as bent as a banana, and the rest of him was all knees and elbows.

'Don't go,' he said. The glassy whites of his eyes were bloodshot.

I just stood there, staring. This was the man who had threatened me with his cutlass. This was the man who had spat in my face. This was the Hermit Governor. I could feel the blood rising to my head.

'Wait a little . . .' he said.

I didn't. I got him by one arm and twisted it behind his back. Then I hauled him, quaking, past his favourite sign and down to the edge of the hillside. Below us, we could see the harbour battering the rocks. 'Where's your boundary now, Governor?' That's what I said to him.

'And?' said Peg, planting her hands on her hips.

'And what?' said Anne, sipping from a mug of rum.

'Then what?'

She tipped her head back, spurting a little fountain of white rum from her lips. 'The Governor resigned.'

Chapter Twenty

The following morning, a mussel-digger found him smashed on the rocks below Fort Nassau.

There was no time for talk. People from the beach followed the breathless man back, wanting to see the Hermit Governor for themselves before high tide carried him away.

'He wasn't very big,' said Joe, as we all gathered round.

Everyone stared, silenced by the sight of the dead man's back, skewed on the jagged rock, and the mangled neck where the sand flies were jumping. 'I didn't turn him right side up,' said the mussel-digger apologetically, 'because the birds would go for him.' The Admiral clambered awkwardly over the rocks and covered the wrecked body with his flag, weighing it down at the edges with little stones.

By nightfall, the air was humming with cicadas, and with talk of Anne.

Got him where she wanted him.
Maybe he jumped, or just plain fell.
While she was there or not?
That's between her and the devil. We'll never know.
Well, she's got the reek of death on her, that much I know.

I found her by evening, sitting on a branch of an old seagrape tree at the far end of the beach, staring out over a dark sea. 'I've been thinking about Squibb and Eoin,' she said, 'and my father.'

I sat down between the massive roots of the old tree and sighed.

'I'm sixteen today, you know.'

I didn't. I'd forgotten about days and months. Time seemed as stagnant as still water.

'I'd be on the move again if I could, but no one among the lot of them here will have a girl on board. I've tried. And Jim, well, he said we'd have a boat of our own by now, but I'll be beached for ever if it's down to him.'

I shifted my weight on a twisted root.

Her voice was cold. 'I didn't kill him if that's what you've come here for, Annie. A breeze could have blown him over the edge.'

I didn't know what to say, even had I been able to say it.

'The day before yesterday, Jim was eavesdropping on a New Englander captain. It so happened that this captain had stopped in Charles Town not a fortnight ago, and he was telling some first mate type about the Ashley River Plantations – about them being burned to the ground.'

I turned to her.

'Jim got to his feet and said to the Captain, "I'm married to the daughter of one of those planters, a Thomas Manley." And the first mate asked him if he was sure because he had heard it was *her*, "that Manley girl", and not the Yamasees at all, who had set light to the river land. "Sheer spite as she ran off," he told Jim.'

She hesitated. 'It's funny, not because I did it – well, you were there – but because I once dreamed I did, a long time before the war even. I was standing at the foot of the Observation Tower, and it was a white-hot day, like you get in the dead of summer, only the land was dry, not flooded like it should have been. I was standing there, breathing heavy, as if I'd been running a long way, and I was swallowing the hot air and the heat was in my head, teasing out my thoughts, and I could feel it in my fingertips too. Then, before I knew it, I was striking a metal join on the side of the Tower, just with my little finger, and sparks were leaping out.

'The Tower started to burn like a piece of straw and I had to back away from the heat. I tried to raise my hands to shield my face, but I couldn't lift them. And that's when I saw: they weren't flesh and bone any more. They were flint. I tried to make a fist but couldn't. I tried to wipe the sweat that was streaming down my face but I couldn't do that either. So I just ran from the place.

'Since hearing that story about me torching the plantation, I've been turning my head inside out thinking about it.' She tore a handful of leaves from a branch. 'I know it's only a story like my dream is only a dream, but each keeps getting around me somehow. And if I let it, Annie, his tale makes an omen of my dream, and then my omen dream turns his tale into something like Fate, and I start remembering an oil-soaked torch in my hand, and Jim coaxing you on ahead, and the smell of earth burning . . .'

I got to my feet and reached into the darkness of the tree until I felt an arm, then a hand. I tugged on it and she slid off the branch.

'Say something, Annie,' she said, her voice almost a whisper.

She was too young to know that once you've lost your voice you may never find it again. I led her back up the deserted beach in silence, her hand cold as stone in mine.

They say it was in 1718. They say July, though it might have been November, so implausible were days and weeks and months in that place. Nevertheless, it was that clear, still morning when all talk (of Anne, of pirating, of trade winds, of booty and battle wounds) died. Coming into harbour, scooping the wind in its sails, was a 360-ton man-of-war.

Its three masts loomed over the community of spars in the harbour. Its gilded stern flashed in the light between sea and sky. The Admiral lowered his spyglass. 'The end of an era,' he pronounced. No one needed to see the red blazon of St George. After more than a dozen years as true republicans, the people of New Providence knew: the British were back. It was an end to the Hermit Governor's legacy of hands-off government. It was an end to the dream democracy of mob law. A new governor had arrived.

'We've sent governors running back to Albion before,' said Bill. 'We'll do it again!'

'Thirty-four guns,' said Joe, squinting into the distance, 'and a crew of two hundred, I'd say.'

'It's no good,' declared the Admiral, waving his spyglass wearily on the air. 'Not this time.' He leaned against his flagless flagpole. 'It's Woodes Rogers.'

'Not the old privateer?' said Homer, who operated the still up the beach.

'A privateer! Pmmph!' said Peg. 'A wartime pirate, more like. No different than half the men here, except he couldn't stick with the work. Everyone knows the pickings get leaner in peace time – and us and all. Since the last bloody treaty, my man's found little more than salt water at sea, and you can't feed a family on that. I'm with Bill. Let's blast him.'

'It's a lost cause, I tell you,' the Admiral insisted.

'Why?' demanded Peg.

'The man's a convert, sea thief to thief trapper, and if there's one thing I know it's this: Heaven hath no zeal like a man converted. Buff your boots while ye may, gentlemen, and don't give him cause to look at you twice.'

There must have been well over a hundred men who marched to the water's edge, grasping loaded muskets as Rogers – accompanied by son, daughter and eager spaniel pup – approached in a skiff rowed by two ship's underlings. Standing there, appearing and disappearing behind the ocean swell, the men of New Providence must have looked a strange and dark assemblage to Rogers as he drew near to shore. Here were barefoot, barrel-chested youths shouldering the one-legged remains of ageing seamen. Here were the grizzled faces of the murderous next to the haunted faces of the nearly murdered. And here were devil-may-care slubberdegullions alongside men who'd cut off their own hands to put an end to the shakes.

The skiff hit the bottom, and its crew hauled it in. For a moment, Woodes Rogers did not rise from his place, but merely surveyed his new subjects – with second thoughts, some suggested. Others would remember the cool, unblinking eye of a man of business. Instructing his son and daughter to remain in the skiff, he stepped on to shore in one long stride. Not even his boots got wet, I remember.

But on the beach there were long glances. The new Governor had arrived unarmed, with not so much as a dirk in his stocking.

Without a word, the hundred suddenly moved into formation. A corridor, a double file of pirates took shape up the beach, with muskets rigid as splints against arms.

It looked like a guard of honour.

In the boat, the little spaniel was yapping as Rogers removed his hat and proceeded into the narrow passage of half-dressed bodies. From up the beach, we watched as his wigged head moved along the length of it, for he stood taller than most. He walked slowly, solemnly. Governors did not hurry.

On the shore, some feral dogs had taken up the spaniel's call and were now howling like a storm was coming. Not a word as Rogers approached the end of the island's guard, not a breath until at last he emerged into the full light of morning.

The call came before he had a chance to turn around. 'Fire!' A deafening fusillade of musket fire charged the still air.

I expect Woodes Rogers thought he was dead.

As it happened, all muskets had been skyward aimed. To all intents and purposes, it was a salute.

Governor Rogers replaced his hat and turned to his new subjects, his face surely belying a drumming heart. 'On behalf of myself and my children, I thank you.' He spoke slowly. (Governors did not hurry.) 'I am most grateful for this ... welcome to the shores of New Providence. May I serve you' – he extended his arm to the guard of honour – 'as well as you have served me here this fine morning.'

The guard wobbled slightly. The ranks started to break. Some were making a run for it.

'Tarry, gentlemen.' It was no request.

Each man stopped where he was.

'Firstly, a happy message from our Parliament and King.' There was no sour edge to his voice. He withdrew a packet of parchment from his greatcoat and unfolded it. '"Be it declared and enacted by the King's most Excellent Majesty, by and with the advice and consent of the Lords spiritual and temporal, that all piracies, felonies and robberies committed in or upon the sea, or in any haven, river, creek or place where the Admiralty has power, may be examined, enquired of, tried, heard and determined, and adjudged in any place at Sea, or upon the land."'

The Governor looked up. 'Gather round,' he said, shouting up the beach at the reluctant lot of us.

I followed Peg down to the scummy tide mark. I looked about for Anne. She was nowhere.

'"And whereas several evil-disposed persons in the plantations and elsewhere,"' continued the Governor with a straight face, '"have contributed very much towards the increase and encouragement of pirates, be it enacted by the authority aforesaid, that all and every person and persons shall be deemed and adjudged to be accessory to such piracy."'

'Does that mean spouses too?' shouted Peg shamelessly.

'In theory,' said Rogers pointedly, 'it does. However, my message is one of hope. I carry upon me King George's own words, and they read thus: "Whereas We have received information that several persons, subjects of Great Britain, have committed diverse piracies and robberies upon the high seas, in the West Indies or adjoining to our Plantations; and though We have appointed such a force as We judge sufficient for suppressing the said pirates, yet the more effectually to put an end to the same, We do hereby promise and declare, that in case any of the said pirates shall surrender him or themselves, *every such pirate shall have Our gracious pardon*."'

Someone, behind him, tapped the Governor on the shoulder. He turned, surprised that his person had been touched. At first, I could see nobody, for his frame was large. 'That's fine for some,' said a petulant voice.

Anne. It was Anne.

'But there are *others* who haven't even had a chance to try their fortune in the first place; to get what they can as best they can before settling down under a nice palm tree with pieces of eight and a King's Pardon for comfort. What hope, Governor, do you offer them?'

The Governor looked down on this raging girl whose hair was flying in the stiff breeze. Then he looked to his daughter, Flora, who sat forbearingly in the skiff, petting the little pup he'd had as a gift from the King.

'What hope?' she persisted.

'This,' replied the Governor. 'The sum of £100 for the man – or woman – who leads me to a commander of any pirate vessel. The sum of £40 for the discovery of any pirate-serving lieutenant, master, boatswain or gunner. For every inferior officer, £30. For every private man, £20.'

Anne spat at his feet. They said she did. I didn't see it, and I didn't dare believe it.

'Otherwise,' said the Governor, in the same even tone, 'I can offer these unhappy individuals of whom you speak nothing but this: one, a speedy trial; two, a free scaffold and gibbet, value £40; and three, a suit of iron, value £9, also on me.'

By the end of September, three hundred reprobates on the island had recanted. The Governor had, at the same time, found the garrison he was after: humiliated men who were glad of the work, if more glad than ever of their drink. England was again at war with Spain, and Woodes Rogers dreamed of the day he would repel the Don. By the end of December, after the seafront hangings of nine men who had taken the Pardon and reneged on their oaths, the pirate pestilence was almost beaten.

Then, early one May morning, Bill Brunty spotted – not the black banner of King Death snapping in the wind among the harbour's spars – but a bright array of calico underwear flapping from the forestay of a newly arrived ketch. 'It's Jack Rackham!' he shouted to all and sundry.

People crawled out from under their sailcloth and palm fronds. They rubbed their salt-sticky faces. They hacked gobs of spit and worse on to the sands. Then they squinted at the ketch in the distance, trying to make sense of all that merry underwear.

'It's been almost four years,' sighed Unconscionable Nan.

'He'll find us changed,' said Peg.

'Aye,' muttered Joe, 'what with the Hermit Governor dead and the public-spirited Rogers now in his place, we are not the sturdy citizens we once were.'

'Could he possibly not know?'

'Whether he knows or not, he should make off while his neck is still his own to break.'

It was too late. Not an hour later, Calico Jack had landed on shore in plain view of all. He stepped smartly out of the skiff, for it was laden with goods and liable to roll. Then he stood on the beach, searching the group of us for familiar faces as, all the while, we stared. I, for one, who had seen many a dandy in Charles Town, had never seen his like.

Where to begin? A tricorn, trimmed in ostrich feathers, sat jauntily on his tie-wigged head, and the wig was itself a marvel – glossy black, spiral-curled, and harnessed by a vast velvet ribbon, but that wasn't all. His coat was double-breasted, full-skirted and wide-cuffed. His cravat was a splash of gold lace. His waistcoat was the colour of Jamaican plums. At his hip, a sword with a gold-lacquered hilt. Small children were fingering it and also his silk-stockinged calves, which were artfully padded.

I glanced at Anne. She was sniffing the air unabashedly, for there was, rolling off him, the unmistakable scent of lavender water.

'Nan!' he suddenly shouted with genuine fondness. 'Dear Nan, pretty as ever.'

'Though never so pretty as you, Jack, I must say! You're keeping well.'

'I am,' he said and kissed her full on the lips. 'We were three entire days looting *The Madeira* and, better still, those Spaniards gave us no cause to be ill-mannered about it.'

'You were always a civilized sort, Jack.'

'I wish I were, Nan,' he said, going quiet, 'but let's not dwell on it till I've a drink in my hand.'

'Jack, forget your speechifying. It might work on Nan, but it does nothing for me!'

'Salt Beef Peg!'

'In the flesh.'

'And such a wonderful lot of it too!'

'Go 'way!'

'I will if you wait where you are.' He backed away, one finger poised in the air, then turned to the skiff and foraged in its cargo. He returned with both hands behind his back. 'Choose a hand, Peg. Any hand.'

She touched his right arm.

'For you, Dame Peg . . .' He revealed his smooth-gloved hand. 'A golden goblet. May it never be empty.'

'Which church did you have this out of, Jack?' she enquired, scrutinizing its base.

He smiled. 'Your turn, Nan. Right or left?'

'Left, I should think.'

'Well answered. For you, Nan, a bracelet of silver filigree, the only setting for such a singular gem.' The ruby blinked, bright as blood.

'Jack?'

'Yes, Nan.'

'You didn't have to . . .'

'What?'

'Chop off her hand to get it, did you?'

He frowned with mock displeasure. 'I certainly did not. The senorita even asked if I might help her with the clasp.'

'Ballocks, she did,' murmured Anne.

'You said?' queried Jack, straightening his cravat.

'I said, ballocks. I have nothing against what you do – I'd do it myself given half a chance – but there's no point in dressing it up. Speaking of which, is that your perfume I smell?'

'It is. Lavender.'

'And am I right in thinking you've painted your lips?'

'And eyebrows,' confirmed Jack.

Anne snorted, but Jack held his ground. 'I would like very much to give you a small token as well. Would you do me the honour of telling me your name?'

'Anne Bonny, but I'm not interested in your jewels. They're difficult to sell these days without drawing attention.'

'Something you'll not wish to sell then. Something invaluable. Wait here.'

'I might.'

Calico Jack returned to his skiff, opened a large hemp sack and jettisoned its contents, little by little, on to the beach: three eggs, a loaf of leavened bread, four avocados, guava fruit, two large yams, a bag of what might have been ground coffee, and a tub of oats. Then he pulled something from the very toe of the sack.

'For you, Anne.'

'A tomato,' she said flatly.

'A tomato elsewhere,' he smiled, 'but here, in this earthly paradise, a *love-apple*.' He wiped it clean with his linen handkerchief. 'Bite it.'

'No, it's all bruised.'

'Have you ever eaten one?'

'No,' she confessed.

'Bite it,' he said, holding it out to her. 'Please. You'll like it.'

The crowd was growing. Everyone waited. Salt Beef Peg, Unconscionable Nan and I. Dick Turnley. Bill and Joe Brunty. The Admiral and Homer, who had abandoned the still for a moment. Even Jim Bonny prowled at the edge of the crowd, watching.

Anne stared at the love apple and Calico Jack stared at Anne. Whether the moment trembled with the force of a charm or a dare, no one knew. Only this was for sure.

Anne bit the tomato.

Chapter Twenty-One

That same day, Calico Jack strolled up the beach, hawking the remains of *The Madeira*'s fabulous booty: gold-threaded vestments, a gentleman's muff; precious rings; a fox-hair wig; a gold-tipped cane; a pair of gentleman's pumps; a few pieces of silver plate. He spent most of the afternoon manoeuvring in and out, round and about the shabby shantytown that covered the beach like the muck after a gale. Yet he showed no sign of sweat or strain when at last he arrived, empty-handed and with not a fly on him, at the Governor's own encampment.

He stood face to face, tricorn to tricorn, with Woodes Rogers. 'Captain Jack Rackham,' he said, announcing himself.

The Governor sniffed the air at the sudden scent of a flower he could not quite remember.

'A contrite Captain Rackham,' emphasized Jack, 'for after much sombre reflection, sir, I have come before you to renounce my felonious ways. Yea, I am here to beg the King's most gracious Pardon – for the unpardonable.' He removed his hat. 'I am here to swear upon the Holy Book. I am here to take the Oath.'

Woodes Rogers had heard all manner of confessions since he had arrived, almost five hundred in all. Some of the shaking miscreants had wept openly before him. Others had felt compelled to narrate in terrible detail every blow they had ever dealt, every plunge of their cutlasses into soft flesh. Still others had bemoaned their criminal parentage, their bad blood. Now here was a man who removed his hat with humility, a man whose speech was simple but affecting in design. Yet never had the Governor been less affected.

'Rise,' intoned Woodes Rogers.

Jack straightened himself.

The Governor studied him, noting everything from the lavish wig to the plumpened calves. 'Your repentance is sincere?'

'It is,' replied Jack.

'And you will, I presume, be joining the island garrison?'

'No, sir,' he said, 'for I believe I would do best to avoid the company of other reformed men – for fear I might fall into old ways.'

'How would you make your way then?'

'Fishing,' said Jack. 'Nothing ambitious at first. A simple dory.'

'You think you are suited to the work?' asked the Governor, eyeing the ostrich-feather trim of Jack's tricorn.

'Perhaps not, but it is an honest living.'

'You are earnest?'

'I am.'

'I am glad to hear it.' The Governor's notary appeared with the Holy Book. 'Lay your hand upon the Book of our Lord and repeat after me.'

Jack solemnly swore, then he followed Governor and notary to a small mahogany writing desk that teetered on the sand. 'You will sign here, Captain Rackham.' The Governor's index finger tapped a parchment that lay on the desk under a massive conch.

He signed. The notary replaced the conch. Woodes Rogers shook Jack's hand. 'You are given a second chance at life today, Captain. Do not make us regret it.'

'No, sir.'

'I shall send a crew to man the ketch in the morning. Please ensure all your personal belongings and crew are removed.'

'The ketch?'

'Aye, Captain, as you only just now agreed by signature.'

He went pale.

'Do not tell me, Captain, that you are not willing to support this colony as every reformed man pledges to do, either in service or in goods?'

'Naturally I am willing but—'

'You desire a simple life. You said as much yourself. This government will provide you with a fishing dory.' He looked Jack in the eye. 'I think it is a generous offer.'

Jack replaced his hat, yet seemed not so tall as before. 'Thank you, sir.' That was how Jack Rackham unwittingly marooned himself on New Providence.

Many wondered why he'd bothered with the Pardon in the first place. Why hadn't he just freebooted it after renewing old ties and offloading his chattels?

Some said he was buying time so his crew could careen the ketch in one of the coves and be off again before the Governor looked twice. Only now the ketch was gone.

Others said, no, he's almost thirty. He's after a quiet life with only a small fortune to tend.

There were those who disagreed. He's lost his pirating nerve, they claimed. Everyone knows the challenge to the *Madeira* was really down to his crew.

A few of us knew better than all of them put together. Peg, Nan, and I. Dick Turnley too. Jack Rackham wanted Anne.

'You make a sad fisherman,' she shouted to him one day from shore. He sat, chin in gloved hand, miserable in his new dory which bobbed on the ebb tide. 'I'll bet you don't know a porcupinefish from a pufferfish.'

'Do you always mock a man when he is down and out?'

'Do you always go fishing in your wig?'

'I never *go* fishing. That is the unfortunate point. I am bound to a bluff I cannot find my way out of.'

'You're not as quick on your feet as people say you are then.'

'And you, I can see, are every bit as dangerous as people say.'

'When are you coming into shore?'

'When the high tide brings me in,' he sulked.

'Determined to get in a full day's fishing then?'

'No,' he replied morosely. 'I dropped my bloody oar.'

Anne started to walk down the shore, leaving him stranded.

'You'll help me drown my sorrows come evening,' he called to her. 'You've just made them a sight worse. The still at sunset, do you hear?'

'I certainly do,' she shouted back, but that's all she said.

She didn't need to say anything more. Seeing was enough for earless Dick Turnley who stood watching them from the shadow of a manchineel tree; who did not move even as the noxious sap dripped from the stems of the dark, waxy leaves. It fell on his head and bare arms, blistering his skin like a burn.

Nothing happened. Not at first. By day, Jack fished, meaning that he passed his hours 'improving himself'. Feet up on a warped sea locker, he tried to teach himself Spanish from a gold-lettered tome he'd lifted from *The Madeira*. Sometimes, he invited Homer, the landlord of the local still, on to his dory for discussions of a metaphysical nature; a fortnight 'flew by' on Original Sin, he said. He obtained a water-glass (a replacement oar as well) and, leaning over the edge of the dory, his cravat dangling in the sea, he studied the strange fish and coral growths that abounded under the turquoise waters of that reefy isle.

By night though, Jack was true to himself. He spent money. On old friends. On the ketch's unhappy crew. On fancy-women. On the Governor's odd little notary. On children who stuck to him like bees to honey. On sea-crazy, sun-struck old seamen who skittered across the beach yelling at nobody. He spent money on any flea-bitten feral dog that thumped its tail in front of his feet, and it wasn't just food and drink. It was donkeys, cows and cart horses. It was a porcelain bathtub for Nan. It was a new gold-braid coat for the Admiral. It was a costly pair of black crape stays, whaleboned and all, for Salt Beef Peg.

Only Anne would have nothing from him. She was not so much proud as uninterested, which frustrated Jack all the more.

'You are a hard one,' he told her.

'You mean I'm not easily bought. And if you're trying to charm me, give up now. I do not want to be charmed.'

'Oooh,' said the crowd at the old still. The sun had not yet set and already she was giving him what-for.

'I think you do,' he said.

'Think what you like.'

'I will for it's only a question of time.'

163

She rolled her eyes.

'I'm the determined sort. Ask anyone here. No one – nothing – has ever resisted my quiet charms.'

'You're all mouth, Fisherman Jack.'

The crowd sniggered and, for a moment, he chewed on a gloved finger. 'Come with me into the wood.'

It was a while before she could speak above the whistling and thigh-slapping. 'This must be evidence of your quiet charm at work.'

'You're stalling,' he said. 'You're wary.'

'Of a man who's all gold lace? It would be a first.'

'Then you'll come.'

Reluctantly, she followed him past the still, through the clearing where the cold spring bubbled, and past the big flame-of-the-forest tree. Then they disappeared from view.

I stared hard at Jim Bonny who was seated on a tree stump, quietly sipping his rum. He looked up at me, an expression of mild surprise on his sour countenance. 'She does as she pleases. I don't have to tell you that.'

I turned away, helpless. It was then that I spotted the hunched, narrow shape of Dick Turnley's back. He was standing alone in the clearing, his gaze fixed on the dark space where Anne had disappeared into the wood. *Go home, Dick*, I silently pleaded to the back of him, and the deaf man, hearing a mute woman's words, turned suddenly and unaccountably around.

Even from a distance, I could see his face and his lips were badly blistered from the manchineel's sap.

Go home, Dick.

But the poison of that tree – poison that the Caribs had once used on the tips of fatal arrowheads – was under his skin. He shook his head.

> *A Tale Whispered through a Sack-Cloth Curtain*
> *Or (as Homer would entitle it years later),*
> *The Story of Rackham's Achilles' Hand*

First, Annie, he got down on those buff-breeched knees of his. I thought he was going to make a speech, but he didn't say a word. Instead, he started combing through the grass for something. I was already getting bored. 'I'm going back,' I told him. 'I need a drink.'

'So you don't want to see, I suppose,' he said, all high-minded.

I got down in the grass. 'See what?'

He pointed to a delicate green fern, no bigger than my finger. Something you'd step on without a second thought. 'A bet,' he said, 'that I can charm even this tiniest of living things.'

'How are we to know that it's charmed? Or are you going to make it speak as well?'

'It is for you to judge,' he said. 'But if I charm it, you owe me a kiss.'

'And if you don't,' I countered, 'you'll stop plying my husband with drink.'

'Agreed.'

He removed his coat, though not his gloves. He stretched out his arms. He flexed his fingers. He cracked his knuckles. Then, bending low once more, he extended one kid-leather hand and tickled the little fern. 'Oh, my sweet, sweet nothing,' he cooed ridiculously. 'Oh, my little wild one. Are you playing coy again?'

But when he lifted his hand, something *was* different. The little fern had folded in upon itself; its twin fringe of tiny leaves had closed like two hands over a blushing face. He tickled it again, and it just drooped, fainting dead away.

He puckered his lips at me.

'One question first,' I said.

'We did not agree to questions,' he said, fearing I'd try to unravel his charm.

'Why do you never take off your gloves?' I stared at the smooth leather that reached over his wrists and under his buttoned shirt sleeves.

'I do.' He pulled one off. 'Happy?'

'And the other?'

'A wound,' he said, and for once, I believed him.

'Is it ugly?'

He nodded. 'A wild Dutchman once tore almost the whole of my thumb off with his teeth. We had only the ship's boatswain for surgeon on that journey. He sewed it back on with a sail needle. I wouldn't let him cut it off.'

'It can't be comfortable in that glove in this heat,' I said. And I told him there were so many eyesores around here anyway that one unsightly hand was not going to stand out in the crowd.

We were face to face, crouched in the grass.

'There's more,' he confessed.

'Pus?' I asked.

He shook his head, distraught.

'Ingrown nails?' I tried, for he's a man, Annie, who might worry about his manicure, and I couldn't think of anything else.

'The Dutchman was not only foul of deed,' he admitted, sighing, 'but, sadly, foul of breath as well.' He couldn't look me in the eye. 'My hand smells.'

'Of his mouth?'

'Aye.'

'That's impossible,' I said.

'I regret to say it isn't.' He said he'd taken advice, that he'd bathed it in everything from cold fennel tea to warm piss of pig. 'But as I am sure my foe could himself tell us were he here, there is no cure for . . . halitosis.' He'd said it.

I swallowed my giggle. Then I asked him if I could have just a little sniff.

He winced. 'No, you cannot.'

'Well then, you'd better kiss me before our bet expires.'

'The desire is gone,' he said, moping in the grass. 'Pity does not arouse me.'

'Shame,' I said, leaping up and walking away. 'Because' (in our little lean-to, Anne listened for the staccato rhythm of Jim's snoring), 'because I was in half a mind to let you tickle me like you did that fern.'

It was all the encouragement he needed. In the morning, before any of us were up and about, Calico Jack was outside our lean-to.

'What do you bloody want?' grumbled Jim, who stumbled into the morning, thick-headed again.

'I'd like to speak to you and your wife,' said Jack, treading carefully.

'Anne!' he shouted.

She appeared in a dirty shift.

'He wants you.'

'Both of you,' said Jack. 'I would like to speak to both of you.'

I clambered out of the lean-to myself at this point and discovered Anne, smiling broadly at the scene of Jack's ceremony and Jim's indifference.

'Forgive me, Anne,' Jack implored her, 'for what I am about to say. It is not as it might seem, I promise you.' He turned to Jim and removed his hat. 'Mr Bonny, I would like to buy your wife.'

Jim pulled on his shirt and scoffed. 'Why pay for what comes easy to you anyway?'

'I am a heartsick fool, I confess.'

'More fool than you know. She's trouble. Ask anyone. I sleep with her on my right side and a machete on my left.'

'Well then, allow me to make you a free man. Two signatures and a handshake makes common law where I come from. What do you say?'

'How much?' He was splashing his face in the last of the rainwater. 'And I don't mean a few casks of spirits.'

'Two hundred pounds.'

Jim lifted his head slowly from the butt.

'Providing Anne herself agrees,' Jack added.

'Well, thank you for remembering me at last!' she yelled, her arms indignant against her breast.

'Now don't get het up,' urged Jack, 'not before you give it due consideration.'

'Why should I be any better off with the fishy likes of you than with him?' she stormed.

'Anne, think about it, please. This man is pus. You've said so yourself countless times. He's a low-life, a lay-about and—'

'And worse,' added Jim.

'And you are?' she demanded.

'An undeserving wretch, I know. A cocksure fool with only a tidy fortune to his credit. A—'

'Swallow the shite, Jack,' she said, losing patience.

He shifted the sand with his boot. 'I am a man with only a stinking hand to offer you in marriage.'

Anne unlocked her arms and scratched her armpit. She looked at Jim. Then she looked at Jack. 'Fine. I accept.'

Jack grabbed the first person he saw to witness the agreement. It was deaf Dick Turnley. He'd been standing under a nearby tree all the while.

I had never seen the Governor close up before. Anne had. She'd tapped his person. She'd spat at his feet. But now Woodes Rogers sat before us, not ten paces away, in a magnificent chair. His hand rested purposefully on a golden arm. His back, upright as ever, was cushioned by magenta velvet. The whole effect was balanced by four clawed feet of gold on the sandy beach.

'Your name,' he instructed.

'Anne Bonny,' said Anne.

'And yours,' he said, not looking at me, but rather shifting some silken drapery that spilled over his knees like a train.

'My mother,' said Anne, quick-tongued as ever. 'My poor dumb Irish mother. My moral support. My Christian example.'

'A name would suffice, but never mind. Jeremy!' the Governor shouted. 'Have you found that insipid spaniel yet?'

'Aye, Father,' said Jeremy, returning to the scene and supporting the little spaniel at arm's length, 'but I fear it has been rolling in something yet again.'

'Forget that. Return it to Flora's lap – feet rather. Make it sit.'

'I shall try, but if there is a cur on heat nearby, a firm hand will not avail us.'

'Shall I hold my shoe upon its lively tail, Father?' tried Flora, who was seated in her own chair, though we could hardly see it for her hoop.

The Governor ignored her and turned irritably towards Anne. 'Do you know why you are come here today?'

'No, sir. I do not.'

'Is there nothing you would like to confess to me?'

'Not that I'm aware . . .'

'Jeremy!' yelled the Governor, leaping out of his chair and disturbing his drapery. 'The dog nearly emptied its bladder on the map! You are supposed to be standing here, like so. You are *supposed* to be holding the map. Do I ask too much?'

'No, Father.' Jeremy, humbled, took his position between his father's chair and his sister's, and dutifully unrolled the map. It showed New Providence looking as if it occupied most of an ocean.

'It has reached my ears,' resumed the Governor, 'that you are unhappy with your lot.'

'Unhappier than some, I suppose. Happier than others.'

I tried to smile on her behalf.

'Let me speak plainly, Mrs Bonny.' Behind him stood a single wall of brick, the grit of which was still wet between its rows. I could not, for the life of me, understand how it stood in the sand on its own like that. 'I have it from one Richard Turnley—'

'Dick Turnley?'

'I have it from one Richard Turnley that you are attempting to sever your legal bond to your husband, one Jim Bonny; that you have, furthermore, unlawfully engaged yourself to re-marry, one fisherman by the name of Rackham; and moreover, that you are presently implicated in a loose and unseemly relationship with this same man.'

Anne lowered her head and drilled the sand with the toe of her boot.

'Is it true then?'

'More or less.' Her face was reddening. Her back stiffened.

Over by Miss Flora's chair, there was loud whispering. 'Flora!' shouted her father. 'What is it now?'

'Begging your pardon, Father, but Mary isn't sure where she is wanted with the fruit bowl and I'm afraid I do not know myself.'

'Behind you, Daughter, two paces behind you.'

'Should I perhaps hold a papaya? I am never sure what to do with my hands, you see.'

The brick wall was starting to tremble. Behind it, someone was trying to suppress a laugh.

'Silence!' shouted the Governor.

The wall was still.

'There is something I should dearly like everyone to read. You, Flora. You, Jeremy. You, Mrs Bonny. Your mute mother too. And Mary. And the two brick-layers. Yea, even the cursed royal spaniel.' He pointed with a single finger to the cartouche prominent on the wall above his white-wigged head. 'My heraldic arms. My family motto. *Dum spiro spero.* While I breathe . . .' His hands were white-knuckled on the arms of his chair. 'I hope.

'I *hope* – Jeremy – that you will, some distant day, give me cause to be proud. I *hope* – Flora – that you will perchance grow wiser than your mother who was a goose of a girl till the day she died a middle-aged woman, may she rest in peace. And I *hope*, Mrs Bonny, you will understand that, if I ever – ever – hear of such ambitions again, I will not hesitate to have you publicly horsewhipped, and it will be Rackham himself who is made to wield the whip!' He exhaled heavily and leaned back into his chair.

'Now kindly remove yourselves from this portrait.'

Chapter Twenty-Two

I can see them still in my mind's eye, in the dory, sitting in the shallows where the reef rises up like some ancient and slippery underworld. Jack is coiling a line around his bare arm. The air is humid, the sky all rolling cloud and shafts of light. Anne is bending over the dory's edge, peering into the green lagoon.

'Here,' I can hear him say, years on, leagues away, 'have a look.' He reaches across and lays the water-glass beside her. It's a smooth, glass-bottomed cylinder of wood, rolling now in the dory's wide bottom. She picks it up and holds it to one eye, closing the other. His shape dissolves into the white cotton blank of his shirt, his eyes, into two dark splashes. He might be anything.

'It doesn't work on the air,' he is telling her. 'You have to hold it to the water if you want to see anything.'

The water is so clear, even now without the glass, she can make out the dark ridges and valleys of the reef ahead. She toys with the glass in her hand, stalling.

Old words and watery images collide in the listing boat of her memory. A soft velvet sack hanging from her neck like a lucky rabbit's foot. Sails, like sheets on the line, snapping in the wind, and the New World so big that the ship she travels on must soon crash into it. She is too small to see over its rails, so she peers through the gunports instead, squinting for whiskery sea beasts and the drowned bodies of men lost at sea. But this is an ocean as dark as a secret, as turbid as winter soup. 'Has anyone ever seen its bottom, Annie?' Fin whales rise by the hull, fleeting arcs of silver. 'No, Anne, it's not for us to see.' She twists the little bag's silken cord until it pinches her throat, wonders what would happen if she should tumble, head over heels from deck, before any hand could catch her. At night while the timbers groan, she sleeps in a cradle of ribs on a dark seabed and dreams of an ocean as deep as a dead mother's womb.

'Go on,' Jack seems to say, smiling at her. 'It's another world down there.' He waves to me on the shore where I loiter, a guilty look-out.

In my memory, I watch Anne lean over the side once more, lowering Jack's glass to the water, and her eye to the glass.

Huge fans wave back and forth on the invisible current. Old divers who hover about wrecks like scavenger fish tell new men, young men, be wary: sea fans can lull a man to sleep, and when he wakes it's to the sound of his own lungs bursting. Up ahead, yellow fire coral is burning on the reef; touch it and your hand burns too. It's a dangerous place, this old and crusty underworld. There are sudden drops in the seabed, rocks at impossible angles. Below her, she watches the black flailing spines of a sea urchin. (I know the names, have listened for them. I have been remaking this moment slowly, carefully.)

She has seen enough – is about to lift the glass from the water – when she glimpses, there by the head of the dory, bright towers rising out of the sandy bottom like a watery illusion. She shifts on her knees for a closer look. Wide-eyed fish with yellow tails skirt the towers, grazing on clumps of bushy coral. She sees something else, something strangely familiar: pale, bending digits – she counts five – growing out of the sandy bottom like a buried hand. Deadman's-fingers.

She turns back to Jack, laying the water-glass down. The water is calm, hardly a ripple. The trees on shore are still, the close weather about to break.

'I could kill Dick Turnley,' she says, slowly.

From the shore where I gather driftwood, I watch Jack take out his handkerchief and wipe the water-glass with care. Then, with nimble fingers, he returns it to its leather case; touches her cheek.

In those parts, fishermen used to talk of she-fish that defied Creation. They'd discover them sometimes after a gale or a squall: females that had willed sudden colours out of scaly skins, that had forced startling dimensions from a filigree of white bone; unnatural organs from delicate flesh. Cleaved in two, it was sticky spawn, not clusters of eggs, that spilled from their innards, but they were neither he-fish by nature nor she-fish as hatched. The fishermen called them fatal-fish. They were born in the wake of violence at sea; born, it was said, after the loss of too many natural males. They were also a bad portent: hauls would be meagre in the months ahead.

'It hasn't been easy gathering a crew,' she was telling me. It was evening. The sun had almost dropped from the sky, but Anne was taking off her shoes and pulling on her boots.

I leaned up against the crooked lean-to wall. *Do not leave me.*

'Not surprising,' she continued, 'considering the scaffolds on the beach haven't yet rotted. They're enough to turn anyone to prayer, and anyone who isn't praying these days seems to be in Woodes Rogers' bloody garrison. So we have no choice. Do you understand, Annie? He and I have to try to lay our hands on a ship. We can't stay here. Turnley's seen to that.'

And you will see to him. He has not even the ears to hear you coming.

'But no one can know, not even Jim. Especially not Jim. He's still in a temper about that £200 he never had off Jack.'

Still, after four years, she would pretend that I might, at any moment, speak; that I might turn to her and say, 'Is it not close?' Or, 'We can do with this rain.' She'd imagine that something was always on the tip of my tongue; that I'd never lost my voice that night in Charles Town harbour when she made me into the ghost of myself.

I watched as she slipped into a baggy pair of canvas trous and a stiff fearnought jacket.

'You needn't be looking through me like that. There's no trembling soul in here waiting to be saved, you know.'

I know. I do. It was lost to your looking-glass likeness when you were just a small babe — and you in my care. And I weaned you on water strained from glowing red coals. And I let your unswaddled baby feet buffet the air. Forgive me, my raging girl.

I watched her go. I squinted until she disappeared into the shore's stretch of darkness, until she was only a red lantern swinging low on the night. I did not know where she was going.

I didn't know if she'd come back to me. I had not the voice to ask.

She did not return that night or the following day, or the day after that. I was alone. Not even Jim Bonny's shadow slid about the place. Someone said – was it Anne or Salt Beef Peg? I couldn't remember – that he was off somewhere clearing mangrove trees, a picture which seemed to me so unlikely I felt sure I must have got it wrong – and maybe more besides. Suddenly, on my own, I no longer trusted myself. My memory was betraying me.

Salt Beef Peg visited me with a string of flying fish in her hand, but I think I hardly knew her. I spent another entire day emptying the lean-to of Anne's rubbish, almost overturning its four shingled walls in a vain attempt to find the little velvet bag with the caul, small as a petal. What had she done with it?

There was a long night too when I lay sobbing, for I could not remember the name of my little baby girl who'd drowned in Sally's tears all those years ago. I could not find her name on my lips.

I do not remember rising from my hammock. I remember only the sweat on my face going chill in the draught, and the narrow cracks of light between the shingles, and the ha-ha ha-ha of laughing-gulls throbbing in my head.

Virginia Lazarus at One Hundred and Four

When I awoke, I no longer lay slack in the dip of my hammock, but flat on a thin paliasse. Reaching out, I felt the rough-hewn surface of a table beneath me.

'Eat dis,' someone was saying. Fingers and softened vegetable found their way between my two dry lips.

I spat it out like a wilful child. I did not want to be fed. I did not want to be flat on my back on somebody's eating table. I did not want to open my eyes.

'I cun see yu eyeballs movin under yu sneakin lids,' the voice said. It had the strange music of a bow gliding across a heat-warped fiddle. 'Come back ta life, womun, and tek what I give yu.'

I opened my eyes a crack. A sinewy black arm loomed over my face.

'Eat,' it seemed to say.

I opened my mouth.

'Good.'

I sniffed the air. There was a hint of lavender.

'Gone. Jack an her, her an him, I pay no mind. Plenty trouble, I don know what. Tings, I don know where. Some folk talkin, an some sea-tieves itchin ta go, an still no ship ta board. An de taste o money too, sweet like sugar on dey lips, I cun tell, but I jes cluck me tongue an promise datJack I see ta yu. I have a bright cloth on dis table an all, only he has me cut it up in a hurry for underwear. Him ever on de run and me ever coverin he arse wit me calico.'

Anne. I mouthed her name to the mud roof above me.

'Staystay. I come ta de girl-boy. Dey get yu on a donkey, don ask me how, an bring yu here. She vex datJack for yu, and a good ting too. Everyone know wit shore folk it's each man for herself, which is why I live in de wood. Salt water creep into dey lungs at night like obeah and mek dem crazy. Look, dere it is even now, splashin down yu whitey cheeks. Yu has a whole sea inside yu by now, womun. Could be yu never be calm.'

I turned my head and wrenched the back of my neck.

'What yu see, eh, troo yu tears? A ol-ol woman wit a face black an fuzzy as a coco-nut shell. Yes, so old, she should be long-gone dead. An what don yu see? Sit up on dose God-given elbows. Go on.'

Tears blurred my sight, but I did as she told me. Trembling on my elbows, I beheld an ancient woman in a bright red calico print. She sat, propped up in a bamboo chair, with a blanket over her lap.

'What don yu see?' She waited.

I shook my head.

'I tell yu den. Me two legs. Dey disappear one day under de sugarcanecrusher when I am half de age I am now – an me along wit em almost. But I am lifted up, free of de mighty wheel, an sweet mercy, dey ghosts is wit me still. When it rain, I feel de old stiffness in me knees an ankles. When I am restless, I hum a hymn an I cun hear me foot keepin time on de ground. An on a good day, I cun even reach de little gourd o sugar up dere' – she nodded to a shelf behind her – 'on de tips o me gonetaJesus toes.'

Oh Anne, why did you never come back to me?

Fingers in my mouth, food on my tongue. 'Yu wan ta say someting, yu say it, Anniewomun! May be I cun not read a book but I cun read a face. Swallow yu words jes one more time, and dat's yu dead, hear.' She sat resolute with the gourd of food in her legless lap.

I lay back down on the table.

'Don say it den. Go ahead an weep for yu own passin. Yu is already laid out fine. Dead, yu no trouble for me. I always eat on me lap.'

I was seeing double through my tears. On the mud wall behind her, I blinked back the sight of two black wooden crucifixes. Crudely cut. One Christ, a stick man with a wooden mound for a groin. The other Christ, the same dark mound, but two others on his chest. Breasts.

'Mek yu confession den ta me himanher Africun Christ. I not deny no dyin' woman.'

My face was streaming, my sides heaving. I was sucking the air for breath, stoking cold words in my lungs.

'I am—' *afraid   alone   the ghost of the woman I was.*

'*Breathe,*' she said. 'Yu flamin' ta speak.'

'I am—'

She wiped my raw face, got hold of my hand. 'Yu *is*. Yu jes is. It is enough, eh?' Her free hand dipped into the gourd. 'Ssshtnow an eat.'

Even as I talked in my sleep that night, a ship's watchman was waking to the touch of her pistol, steady on his lean cheek, and to the cool metal of her blade, rubbing the hairs on the back of his neck. Even as I drifted into dream, the crew of eight were heaving *The Seahorse*'s cables, weighing anchor and driving her down harbour in darkness.

Word had it that the sloop answered a call from the fort, and from the guardship as well; that a man who could only have been

Jack shouted something about a split cable and no grappling irons with which to hold fast. It was all the time they needed.

They put out a shy sail, enough to give them steerage-way to the harbour's mouth. Then they hoisted all the canvas they had, and stood to sea.

Chapter Twenty-Three

I had found my voice but lost my girl. She had disappeared into a story that everyone was telling before long. I heard it first from Virginia Lazarus' calico man.

The Buoyant

Anne and Calico Jack went after Dick Turnley with a vengeance, haunting the turtling spots off New Providence. They sighted his sloop at last about a league off Piss-A-Bed Cay, little more than a sand bar but named all the same for a shrub that flourished there in its patch of wood. Like other cays in those parts, it was always losing ground to the Atlantic, shrinking with every wave. Whole islets disappeared in a lifetime, making sea charts as fickle as sea stories.

Why bother with the likes of Dick Turnley? Why sneak up on a man who had opened his mouth only to avenge his mean pride, who went to the Governor only to thwart a match he envied too keenly? Anne Bonny, Hosea informed me knowledgeably, hated to be crossed.

So when Turnley's sloop came into view, *The Seahorse* dropped anchor, and half its crew – George Fetherton, Noah Harwood, Patrick Carty, 'Anson Bonn' plus the Captain – manned the ship's boat and sidled up alongside *The Buoyant*.

They found only four hands on board, all of them with feet up on the gunwales and fishing from deck. 'He's not here,' said an old seaman with his line clutched between his knees to spare his hands for the jug at his side.

Jack turned to shore. A single figure moved about on the beach. 'Patrick, Noah and George, you hold on here and gather what you can of the tackle. Anson, you can help me with the rowing.'

But the surf was high. They couldn't bring the boat ashore. 'I'm not turning back,' she told him. They studied Dick on the beach, patiently salting flanks of wild hog on a bamboo rack. He observed them but didn't move, not even as they waded up to their armpits through the tide, their weapons held high above the waves.

On the beach, they stood, streaming. 'You should have at least tried to run, Turnley,' said Jack.

Dick only lifted a strip of raw meat and turned it over on the rack.

'He's deaf,' said Anne. 'But he can read lips.'

Her kiss was an attack. Her hand was rigid at the nape of his neck. When he finally managed to throw her off, he was struggling for breath, for balance. He wiped his mouth with the back of his hand and spat on the beach.

'Isn't that what you wanted, Dick? Isn't that what you've been after me for?'

He looked up amazed, recognizing her only now in the shape of the young seaman who stood before him. He started to back away.

Something at his neck caught her eye. A silver chain – a locket. Her caul, she knew it. 'Give it back, Dick, and I'll say we've settled.' He had discarded the little velvet sack when she'd sold it to him years ago.

'Anne?' Jack, behind her, didn't understand.

'No, I paid gold.' Dick's voice was too loud, now that he could no longer hear it, and his words were oddly slack. He wrapped his fist around the locket.

'I can get more for it again. These are worrying days for pirates who can't swim a stroke. You know that. The Admiralty's guns lurk behind every wave.'

'I paid gold,' he repeated helplessly. 'It's mine.'

'You owe me dearly. The Governor did not invite me over to his camp for a glass of port.'

'I don't know what you're talking about.'

'I think you do.'

Behind them, Jack was kicking sand. 'What is it, Anne? Whatever it's worth, we'll have to divide it eight ways. It's not worth the bother.'

She didn't care about the money. But how could she say that the reappearance of that ancient charm had unsettled her like nothing else could? 'We could have it off you in a trice, but give me the locket and we won't touch you.'

He shook his head. Tears stood in his eyes. 'You said I could have it. I paid. Years ago.'

'Fine.'

They got him into the tide and into the boat. A conch shell lay in its bottom, a blow-horn for times when fog closed in without warning. Anne picked it up and pressed it to the raw hole where his ear had once been. 'Listen, Dick,' she whispered, looking at him. 'Ssshhh now. If you're quiet, you can hear the sea still rolling in the shell . . .'

They rowed back to *The Buoyant* and took away the sails, the sail tools, the lanyards and dead-eyes. They invited three of the hands aboard their own vessel and put the fourth one, the old man, in a boat to fend for himself.

Then they tied Dick Turnley to the mainmast.

When the last clove knot was hitched, George Fetherton, one of the hands, was about to rip the locket from the man's neck, but she stopped his hand. 'No, George. It's bad luck to steal it from a drowning man.' George looked from Anne to Dick, dropped it, and walked away. 'There,' she whispered, 'I didn't let him take it, did I?'

She clambered down to the boat that waited. They hoisted their booty on to *The Seahorse* and set the sails. Then they towed *The Buoyant* out to sea and sank her.

Now by night in the rocking fo'c's'le, the old fear would no longer surface in the dark of her. The dead weight of Dick Turnley would anchor it firmly at an unfathomable depth. *Hood of mother's blood.*

She did not sneak a small conch down her trous.

She did not shave the soft down of her face into stubble.

And though she kept her fearnought jacket well fastened, she did not batten down her breasts with stiff sailcloth. Not this time.

For Anne had mastered the swagger and the wink.

While every other pair of legs on that rolling deck rose and sank like a set of burdened scales, she strutted, in apparent defiance of the ship's sway. While some, early on in that rainy season, clutched their bellies and held fast to the poop rail, she breezed up seventy feet of main mast and crowed from the crow's-nest.

She'd swab the deck, then down the vinegar-water for a dare. She'd holystone the planks, then skid down the stretch of them in her stockinged feet. She'd caulk *The Seahorse's* seams and chew on lumps of tar like some did spruce gum. On calm days (some swore), when the wind was low and the sea was flat, she'd launch a silver reale off the tip of her thumb and skip it all the way to the horizon. (Others claimed it was only sunbeams on water; that the coin, usually offered by someone keen to see, skipped nowhere but down the length of Anson Bonn's shirtsleeve. People would see what they wanted to see.)

Not surprisingly, it was Anson Bonn who put this question to the crew's Piratical Council: 'Why wage war when we could bluff instead?' *The Seahorse* was skirting the Berry Islands, on the lookout for vessels to bolster its stores and manpower.

'What do you know, Bonn?' countered George Fetherton. 'You're as green as a banana at all this.'

'Aye,' said Patrick Carty, who'd lost another reale only that day, 'no prey, no pay. It's no good us just shouting about it.'

'And it's no good,' she said, as if she was speaking to the afflicted, 'losing five men at a go when we're only eight to start off with. Seven, forgetting Bones.' Bones was the Cook.

'It can't be denied,' intoned Noah in his Chief Justice's voice.

'It can't be helped,' argued George.

Captain Rackham took a seat on the binnacle box and crossed his plumpened calves. John the Younger started counting crew on his fingers, forgetting, as he invariably did, the thumb he'd lost last year, rolling casks. John the Elder nodded off. The Council was nearing its usual stalemate when Tom Earl hollered from the crow's-nest, and everyone jumped.

Calico Jack got hold of his spyglass. 'A schooner. English. A coastal trader with eight cannon to our fourteen. Maybe four swivel guns. Tacking north-east.'

'Away from us,' said John the Younger.

'That's right,' said Jack. 'They haven't seen us.'

'Or better still,' said Anne, 'they have.'

'All the more reason to give them our all and take our due,' rallied George.

'All the more reason to vapour, to dissemble, to coax their fear and save our measly shot,' she answered him.

'Time for a vote,' called Noah. 'Those who are in a mind to be buggered by Death this day, say "Aye".' Noah had been elected for his voice, not for his even-handedness. 'And those who are not so disposed, say "Nay".' Only George abstained.

'Usually, I stay in the galley.'

'Not today, Bones.'

'I cannot *play* the trumpet,' he protested.

'So much the better,' she said, slinging its harness round his neck.

'Or the drum,' he added, beholding the sudden circumference of his normally concave middle.

'We don't want music, Bones.' She gripped an earlobe and spoke directly to his brain. 'We want terror.'

The Seahorse shadowed the schooner for hours. Then, out of the blue of the day, the scream of a trumpet. The hammering of a drum. And a ship in a storm of smoking sulphur.

On deck, they raged with the heads of devils – with ribbons of live fuses tied to their hair. They clashed cutlasses. Stoked muskets. Fired wild volleys at the sun. Danced a stomping jig of no deliverance.

Not even stopping when the schooner raised its white flag.

Or when that vessel drew alongside so they could board.

Not stopping until four of the traders were shot dead with their arms rigid in the air.

'Bags of pimento ... nine,' said Noah. 'Rolls of tobacco ... twenty.'

'Twenty?' shouted John the Elder. He was recording the figures in the ledger.

'Aye! Diverse women's apparel, new: THREE chests. Did you get that?'

'I did,' he called.

'And of what remains,' concluded Noah, 'only ballast.'

In the stern, Bones was still screaming.

Chapter Twenty-Four

One evening, a long time ago (I can still see the rush of bats in her angel-trumpet tree), I said to Virginia Lazarus, 'Virginia, why did you ever take up with him?'

And nodding, she said, 'Wit dat Jack yu mean.' Sometimes, we had no need of words between us.

'He's a mercenary – and worse. You can't know.'

'I do know.'

'Then you should know better.'

'What should I know, Anniewomun? Dat he tek yu girl away from yu? All me life I know folk who tek away. Dat only mek him white.'

'I don't know what you see in him.'

'Nothing but a joy for colour. For me dyes. For me calico. It's enough.'

'Not in my view, it isn't.'

'Den yu blind.'

'I see fine, Virginia.'

'May be not as good as yu tink.'

I turned to the doorway, my back to her. She drummed her fingers on the table. Then she shouted at my back. 'Cun yu see de ghosts o me legs? Cun yu see dat much?'

I turned round; faced her. 'No.'

She slapped her invisible thighs. 'Jes like I tink. Lame vision, but dis time I have no cure,' and she sat back in her chair, righteous as a woman of one hundred and four years.

'Maybe, Virginia,' I said, trying to hold back my temper, 'maybe you see what you want to see.'

'Oh-ho! Yu tink me soft in de head – an not jes in de heart wit teking yu in.'

'I didn't say—'

'No, but what yu mean is someting again.' She had cornered my thoughts. 'Listen here. Yu ears mus mek up for yu bad eyes. One sense for de other, yu wit me? Now open yu ears and hear dis. I wear one joyful red dress. I have two ris-again legs. I am one ol woman wit two lifetime inside o her. All plain ta de eye.'

'With cataracts,' I muttered.

She was shaking her old head. 'Sometime, Anniewomun, I jes don know why I fed yu back yu voice.'

The Seahorse quit the Berry Islands, putting the Bahamas at its stern. Its crew plied south-west, slipping between New Providence and the island of Andros, through the Tongue of the Ocean, and into the channels off Cuba's north coast. There, Spanish men-of-war gathered way, heavy with Peruvian silver and gold.

The sloop dropped anchor in the shelter of a cove just down coast from the harbour at Puerto Santo, and loitered there for several days. 'I once heard', said John the Elder, labouring pork gristle between his gums, 'that every Spanish seaman is given, as pension, a full set of gold teeth, and that if they're knocked loose by an enemy fist in some battle, he'll swallow the whole lot rather than spit them out.'

'Shit,' murmured Richard Corner.

'Precisely, which is as wiley a strategy as I've ever heard.'

The crew were sitting in the dark of the galley, below the shut hatch. Typically, they made a point of eating their food without a light to see it by.

Anne slipped away and found Jack on deck, keeping watch. 'How long are we going to sit here then?' she demanded.

He looked up, a little bemused. 'Until your captain has taken care to see us adequately stocked.'

'When are you sending the boats to Puerto Santo?'

'I'll send the boats,' he said, his eyes narrowing, 'when I send the boats.'

She unbuttoned her jacket, lifted the tail of her shirt and loosened its ties. Then she leaned into the breeze, letting it cool her breast. She measured her words. 'And just how long do you think we have, Jack?'

He pulled off a glove. His ruined hand travelled under the tail of her shirt and up the groove of her back, burrowing in its warmth. His breath was hot on the back of her ear. 'I'll plunder Time for us.'

She sighed. 'Where's the ship, Jack? On what sea?'

His head was heavy against her shoulder. 'Just ahead of us,' he whispered, 'always just ahead.'

'No, Jack, that's where you fool yourself. If it's anywhere, it's beating against the wind, fast behind us.' She shook herself free of his weight. 'We can't afford to lie to or shorten our sails. If we do, I'm off.'

In Puerto Santo, rations. Powder and shot. Long-barrelled muskets. Canoes. And over forty itinerant seamen eager to be earning again.

They pushed into the Windward Passage, hovering between Cuba and Hispaniola, and waited. On the first day, they sighted only a herd of porpoises, skimming the sloop's flanks. 'That's a gale coming,' declared Noah. 'A sure sign.'

'It's always a sure sign, Noah,' Anne shouted from the rigging.

On the second day, no gale, but no Spaniards either. That night, as the moon climbed into the sky, the crew watched a star rise after and follow it. They turned to Noah. 'Aye, lads, I'm afraid so. A storm, if I'm not mistaken. If we're wise, we'll make for shore.'

Anne looked to Jack.

'We won't head for shore,' he ruled. 'We'll hold our bearings.'

On the third day, no storm, but a ring around the sun, and a crew restless for danger. They hung on to Noah's every ominous word. 'I don't know what to say.'

'What is it, Noah?' asked John the Younger.

'Tell us,' insisted George.

'A noose strangling the sun means only one thing: bad luck for the crew that sights it and bad luck for the vessel that sails under it.'

On the fourth day, perversity triumphed over fate. They saw gold. The Don came into sight at last, homeward bound for Seville: a squadron of seven men-of-war.

*

They did not stuff their cannon with powder and shot. They didn't steal a helpless fishing vessel and sacrifice it as decoy. Nor did they tease the flagship from the squadron and lure it into sudden shallows.

That night, they lowered ten canoes into the water and five musket-bearing men into each canoe. Without a chart or a compass, they dead-reckoned their way through the star-jagged dark of sea and sky, and paddled to windward of the Spanish flagship. The wind was faint. The vessel's sails were lank, but its decks were bright with lanterns.

In the distance, the broken sounds of voices carried over the water: the watch changing hands on the neighbouring vessel. Over half a league away.

The canoes bobbed, silent as driftwood, under the flagship's massive flank. The crew that paddled them wore the night like a mask; were faceless even to themselves.

The helmsman was an easy mark. A single shot.

Then, the crew on deck and in the rigging, working the sails. A steady volley and bodies fell out of the night. The canvas flapped. The 350-ton ship lurched on its side.

A marksman took aim from below the stern, blasting the mainsheet and brace, and toppling the mainsail. Another blind fusillade, and not a man aboard was even able to discharge a loaded cannon.

Anne heard something knocking against her canoe – a log, not a body this time. A makeshift wedge for the mighty rudder. Within a quarter of an hour, the flagship was crippled.

More than half the crew were dead by the time they boarded. Of those remaining, few resisted, and they did so in vain. Then the marauding crew smashed cask after cask of spirit, setting the hold awash and celebrating.

A Spaniard's raging tongue was hacked from his head. (Boast or truth, I do not know.) Another made to eat it. The cabin boy fed as well, on cockroaches found drowning in the hold, his lips iron-bolted shut.

A report of a captive man – the Captain? – stripped naked,

his belly slit open, the end of his innards pulled out and nailed to the mainmast. Then a shanty song and dance. Sail needles, spikes, swords and dirks, compasses and penknives piercing his fleeing backside while, with every desperate quick-step, the length of his gut unwound.

Ashore again, life was unreal. In the little cove near Puerto Santo, they caroused. There was money, flasks, and Cuban women for everyone.

'Blowzabella!' called Jack. 'Come raid my pockets and see what you find!'

'Isabella!' she admonished.

'Take no offence, my sweet-legged girl—'

'Wife!' she chided.

Only now did Jack observe Anne, in jacket and trous, sitting on a nearby stump, whittling a bit of wood. 'Translation is so ticklish!' he called to her.

'She seems in no doubt,' said Anne, turning her blade over in her hand.

He cleared his throat. 'Blowzabella . . .'

'Isabella!'

'It is – allow me to explain – a term of endearment.'

'Endearment?' she repeated.

'Aye, affection . . .'

She frowned.

'Love!' shouted Anne.

'Ah!' said Isabella. 'How?'

'How? How is it a term of affection?' stammered Jack.

'Of love,' she reminded him.

'Well, Blowzabella is the heroine of an English song.'

'True?' she said, turning to the sailor on the tree stump.

'Yes,' said Anne. (Jack braced himself.) '"Blowzabella the Bouncing Doxie". A right knee-slapper.'

Isabella folded her arms and turned back to Jack. 'Sing.'

'I'm afraid I haven't committed it to heart, my dear one.'

She drew the loaded pistol from his side.

'"Blowzabella, my bouncing doxie,"' he chirped, '"Come, let's trudge it to Kirkham Fair, there I'll liquor enough to fox thee, and young maids at which to stare." I should really have a bagpipe to accompany me for the refrain . . .'

She fired a shot between his legs.

'"May the drone of my bag never hum, if I fail to remember my Blowze!"' He flashed a hopeful smile, took a deep breath and ran with it. '"May her buttocks be everyone's drum, if she thinks I will pay her a souse."'

Without a word, she emptied the two pockets tied to his waist and walked over to Anne who sat, whittling still. 'You like hold wood better than me?'

Anne looked at Isabella, then to Jack. She patted her thighs.

Isabella seated herself, fanning her skirts out over the sailor's tarred trous.

'Isabella is a pretty name,' Anne flirted.

'*Bella!*' she corrected. 'Beautiful!' But she tugged playfully at Anne's dark locks, rubbing a long curl over her lips.

'Aye, beautiful,' murmured Anne, so low that Jack had to strain to hear from the rock where he sulked.

'Kiss me,' said Isabella.

Anne circled her waist with her arms, drew her towards her and kissed her, slowly. Jack left in a huff.

'Don't worry,' said Isabella, nibbling Anne's neck, 'he only jealous.'

'I know.'

Captain Rackham called an end to the celebrations earlier than usual. 'We have a ship to careen, men, or have you forgotten?' he barked.

At high tide, they ran *The Seahorse* close in and beached her. The cannon and stores were removed, the topmast taken down and the vessel tilted over on to wooden supports. Tom Earl was the ship's carpenter. 'A good few inches of barnacles, sir,' he said, scrutinizing the keel, 'and that's once we see our way clear through the weed.'

'And the planking? Any telling?'

'The innermost layer is sound enough. I've assured myself of that from within. As for the outermost, well, where there's sea, there's sea-worm, sir.'

'I am aware of that, Earl.'

'Do you know when she was last tallowed and tarred, Captain?'

'I didn't enquire when we made away with her, Earl.'

'I'm with you, sir. We can do nothing but scrape her bottom and see. That planking may still be sound.'

'You think so?'

'Aye.'

'Well, that's something.'

'On the other hand, it could be a honeycomb of holes.'

In the end, it was only a carpenter's enthusiasm. *The Seahorse* was upright in less than a fortnight, her keel scraped and waxed, her sails in good repair. Speed was again her advantage. Confined space was Jack's. He'd woo Anne again in stealth.

The crew was once more diminished though. Most of the forty-odd who had joined in Puerto Santo were too intoxicated with drink and lechery to abandon the easy life overnight. They'd stay behind, they told Jack, and pray humbly for wrecks when the tide of their wealth ran low.

The Seahorse was barely past Puerto Santo when a vessel under a swank of sail came between it and the horizon. 'French!' shouted Patrick Carty from the crow's-nest. 'Maybe out of Hispaniola. Friendly this time round, aren't they, Captain?'

Jack took up his spyglass and saw a sloop, the twin of his own: a large 100-tonner, fourteen cannon, and a bowsprit sharp as a needle. 'If they are French . . . Drop some ropes!'

'What for?' Anne shouted. 'They'll only slow us down.'

'Do it!' he yelled.

The ropes were thrown.

'Should I drop some sail too?' offered John the Elder.

'Do that and I'll drop you too. I want them to think this is all the speed we can manage.' He turned to the crew. 'It could be they're just shipping coffee, but it might be that they've been waiting for the English sloop with the Seville gold on board. Whatever it is, I want us to look like an easy mark.'

Somebody protested, but Jack didn't stop to listen. 'A merchant ship, stiff in the water with cargo, and passengers. That's our disguise, all right?'

'But, Captain, as soon as they draw close enough, they'll see we've no passengers,' countered John the Elder.

'Gather arms, tackle and shot, and don't anyone interfere with those ropes.' Then he descended into the hold.

When he emerged at last, they couldn't see him under his load: women's skirts and underskirts, wrapping gowns and shawls, mantles, caps and one large hoop. The neglected contents of the three chests they'd lifted from the trading schooner, months ago. 'Drape your ugly bodies as best you can, but don't restrain your limbs.'

Anne was uneasy. 'They'll see through this, Captain.'

'Will they indeed, Anson?', and he threw her a mob cap.

When the two sloops stood within half a league of each other, the French colours came down and the black banner went up. Pirates.

'Cower!' ordered Jack from under a shawl. His crew threw their arms about one another and trembled. Under her hoop, Anne felt for the scabbard at her hip. Meanwhile, Noah – whose fulsome beard rendered disguise unlikely – played the Captain and hoisted the white flag.

In no time, the challenging vessel's crew were pulling to, grappling on and making ready to spring.

'Arms!' came Jack's timely call. Loaded muskets were swept up from the deck, and half the enemy crew were lost in the first volley. But others came after with hurtling cutlasses and pistols stashed in roll-up stockings. They pushed down the decks, slicing full-blown sails and silken mantles alike.

The Seahorse's men had the advantage though, for surprise still strained the faces of their attackers. Jack flew out from under his shawl and pierced his opponent's middle. George tossed his pinner cap into one man's eyes and seized his arms. And at one point, when John the Elder was grabbed by the waist of his wrapping gown, he loosed the tie and gave his captor the slip.

Only Anne seemed trapped behind the point of her sword, gaining no ground, if not giving any either. The hoop was her bulwark, holding her opponent at the edge of its circumference, while she moved freely to cut and to thrust. Her challenger, however, was the better swordsman. He fenced with a deft arm, he feinted with an agile mind, and he was light on his feet too, dancing Anne, before she knew it, into the corner of the stern.

Suddenly, the hoop seemed to overtake all her sense of space. It was a wobbling cage, threatening to trip any misjudged foot, but she didn't dare watch her feet. Her opponent was no longer at arm's length, but so close she could see the sunburned pink of his neck, the pitted skin of his cheek, the glimmer of blond hair above his lip.

She parried but was tiring fast. Her forearm was starting to tremble. Sweat was streaming into her eyes.

The point of his blade pricked her breast, under her collar bone, within a heartbeat of her life.

She answered with a blind thrust, almost losing her footing even as he evaded her sword and cut the air again with his own.

Hot edge of metal. Under her ear. Against her neck's cordon of muscle.

Never drown.

The sword hilts were dazzling her with sunlight, and the sky itself was drawing her eye: so white, so bright it seemed opalescent with colour. The clashing of metal rang in her ears. It sounded in the marrow of her shoulder bone the moment before she dropped her sword.

He hesitated. For a fraction of an instant, he hesitated. Anne looked at his face. She had decided she liked it – the shy eyes, the strong cheekbones – by the time she saw the gloved hand curl fast round his neck and grip his jugular. She watched him fall back   slowly slowly

saw his sword float free of his hand
and the blade crash soundlessly to the deck
then two bodies sinking   and slowly
the leather hand   (she knew that hand)
straining towards her enemy's face,
clapping itself over his gasping mouth.

She fell, dizzy in the wobbling wreck of her hoop. Dizzy with the brightness of her own near-death. And dizzy with emotion for her opponent who lay sprawled in the stern.

Book Three

Chapter Twenty-Five

Days after, they were still finding blood: dark, sticky puddles in the hollows of warped planking, smeared corners on sail canvas, ridges of it under their fingernails. By night, as their hammocks rocked in the dark, they nursed private wounds – lost fingers, sliced ears, smashed ribs, a cheek almost cleaved from the bone – and they fished in the black swell of their dreams for the part that would make them whole again. Only Anne had escaped real injury. Her breast had been pricked by the tip of a blade. Her neck had been bitten by its keen edge. She dreamed she was pregnant.

'It's not possible,' Jack was declaring to all. The crew stared at her jutting belly.

'Remember the seahorse, Captain,' intoned Chief Justice Noah. The ship's figurehead gleamed high over their heads. 'It's the male that grows big with the offspring.'

'But I never touched the lad.'

Where was he? Where had her partner gone? She wanted to turn, to run, to search the decks. 'Stand still!' ordered Noah, but even as he spoke, she was crashing dizzily to the deck.

When she came to, she was alone in a pool of bright blood. The deck was awash with it, and her belly was gone.

He was there, sprawled before her, unconscious. She remembered the sunburned pink of his neck, the fair hair that tumbled in his eyes, but she couldn't remember her lover's name. 'It's all right,' she whispered to him, as the tide of her blood lapped at her thighs. 'I'm not pregnant after all.'

Mark Read was the only survivor of his twelve-man crew. As his ship was set adrift, he came round to the sound of bodies hitting the water, and someone kicking his side.

'Still alive,' the boot seemed to say. 'Throw him or stow him?'

'Stow him. He's good with a sword.'

They tied him in the galley with only Bones for company. At mealtime, they pelted him with fish bones and stale biscuits. That night, they offered him a hammock, then wound him in it. They carried him to the sloop's rails, suspended him at arm's length, and let him listen to the sound of the surf below. When they unrolled him at last, he could hardly stand on his legs, but he said nothing.

So they dipped him from the yardarm to see how long he could hold his breath. They got him by the scalp and tipped rum that could strip paint down his throat. They tattooed his forearm with sail needles and gunpowder. A sinking ship. Three slow, tall masts.

Calico Jack did not dissuade his crew.

'It isn't necessary,' Anne insisted in the quiet of his cabin.

His hands ran down the smooth of her back and over her buttocks. 'No,' he said, 'it isn't.'

They hovered off the coast of Cuba, stranded at sea. Heavy rains had come, swallowing the shoreline, while the sails swelled with a violence they could hardly contain. The crew wanted to put in to land, but Jack wouldn't have it. In the height of the rainy season, the slow but sturdy ships of the *guarda costa* combed the inlets for enemy craft that couldn't weather the winds. The crew urged him to make for French Hispaniola, but he refused. They'd roll long before they found safe haven.

Rations were low: boiled marrow-bone and the pieces of dried fruit they could sieve from the flood in the hold. They slept in wet clothing and woke in wet clothing, and when they weren't wrestling with the sails they were living in the hunched darkness of the fo'c's'le like animals underground.

In time, small talk and tall tales gave way to silence. Only a few sounds remained, enforced intimacies: Patrick Carty cursing the urine that burned through him before it hit the pot; Noah softly moaning and John the Younger's hammock creaking with their double weight; George whimpering in his sleep like a dog when it's kicked; and Calico Jack, drunk and raging. His mood had swung.

'Which is worse,' he yelled down the galley table one night, 'to be possessed, or to be fucking dispossessed?' His eyes flared in the smoking lamplight.

'Shut up, Jack,' said Anne under her breath.

'Would you rather stink with evil – ' he pushed his face in Tom Earl's ' – or live like the dead? Assuming we don't already.'

'Why don't you go rant on deck, Captain?' Tom got to his feet.

Jack laughed quietly, then he caught Mark Read's neck in the crook of his arm. 'You tell us, Read. God knows, my crew's sick of your patient silences.' They saw him reach for the dirk; watched him press its warm blade to Read's rigid throat. 'Your forbearance doesn't flatter us much.' A surface cut. A bright stripe of blood. 'The fact is, you butcher with the best of us, Read. A moment more and my deckhand's heart would have been twirling on your sword.'

Anne tried again. 'Leave him alone, Captain.'

'Anson, there's as much evil in this man as there is in any one of us here. I'll show you.' He bent his head low, so that his cheek nestled against Mark's own. Then, pressing his lips to the small wound he'd made, he started to suck, as though he would print the younger man's throat with a dark love bite.

Anne was on her feet by the time Mark's fist landed deep in Jack's gut, and he retched.

Anne and Mark were alone, staring at opposite ends of the table, when the oil in the lamp finally ran low. Neither had spoken. She was on her feet and heading for the fo'c's'le when she was surprised by his voice.

'I was touched for Evil, you know.'

She turned.

'When I was a boy.'

'He's been drinking for three days now. He didn't mean anything by all that.'

'Just like I didn't mean anything by almost killing you.' He looked up, his face a challenge.

Touched for Evil, a Tale Told in the Dark

We lived for years on the Isle of Dogs. My mother worked in the kitchen of a big farmhouse there, which is almost all there was in those days: the farm, a few abandoned smallholdings, a chapel, two broken-down windmills, and the Kennels. Whenever the wind was out of the east, we'd get the barking and howling, and my mother always said there was nothing like it to put your nerves on edge.

When I was about twelve, I asked her where my father was. She said he was a bargeman on the Thames, so most days I'd spend just sitting on the mud flats, thinking he'd have to pass eventually – not that I would have known him if he had. Then, one day when the river was choppy, a barge drew up next to one of the jetties.

There were four men working the poles, not the usual one or two, and at its centre was a small woman seated on a tall chair steadied by guy-ropes. Her hands were locked on its arms, as if she expected it to rear up and throw her at any moment.

They tied the barge to the jetty, then two of the men lowered themselves and a sedan-chair into the river, while the other two offered her their arms. I could tell by her face she'd been seasick, and her balance wasn't good as she got to her feet. I think she was worried the barge was going to give way too quickly.

I ran back, slipping over the flats, over the fields, hurdling torn-up tree trunks, and stormed into the kitchen at the farm. It was the end of November and we'd had nothing but rain and gusts all month. The winds of contagion, the Curate said. A lot of the house staff were down with scrofula. Of those left in the kitchen, at least four or five were either crippled up with swollen joints or weak with fever. When I shouted that a barge had drawn up with four bargemen, no one took any notice. 'Be a good boy, Mark,' my mother said, and she kissed me.

But later that day the Caretaker sent a message. Everyone from the farm, in bed or not, was to make their way immediately to the Kennels. It was an order. We were led out of the house by the Overseer in a long bent-backed line and taken over the fields, pushing against the wind all the way.

We shuffled at last into a long, dim room that smelled of wet dog, and the Caretaker appeared, wearing a stiff collar and his official chain. One of the labourers whispered he'd only assembled us to show off the young bitch he'd reared for the New Year Hunt in Epping Forest. But he hadn't. 'Her Majesty the Queen will see the boy first,' he said to the amazement of us all.

We sank to our knees. In the far distance, Queen Anne herself sat in the same tall chair, with the guy ropes still hanging from it.

Some of the fevered women from the dairy started to cry. My mother squeezed my hand so tight it hurt, as we watched the Caretaker's boots approach. Then a hand reached out, hoisted me up by my shirtneck, and led me down the length of the room.

As we drew near, I found myself staring at the Queen's leg. It was stretched out on a cushioned stool and wrapped up in a yellowish poultice.

'Closer,' she said.

I felt the Caretaker's hand on the small of my back, pushing me forward, and was terrified. I was sure she'd seen me staring at her bad leg. And I could see small scabs on her face.

'Your name,' she said. I managed to whisper it, but I wanted to turn and run. She wasn't anything like the miniature I'd seen on the Curate's writing table. Her hair was lank and wind-blown, and I could smell vomit on her breath.

'You are, I am told, the only child on the Isle of Dogs.'

'The flooding, Ma'am,' the Caretaker informed her. 'The farmers would not persist.'

Her eyes studied me, not unkindly, but I feared she was going to take me away with her like the little terrier in the cage behind her chair. Everyone in London knew she wanted a child; she'd miscarried more times than you could count on both hands. 'Do you not grow very lonely, Mark, being the only child?' she asked me.

'You are the only Queen,' I whispered.

'That is true, and do you love your Queen?'

I didn't know what I was supposed to say. 'Once', I said, 'I kissed your miniature on the Curate's writing table.'

She took my head in her hands, and I flinched. They were cold, damp. She moved her palms slowly over my brow, over my hot cheeks and down the length of my throat, as if she was going to steal the heat out of me. I could feel the beat of my blood under her fingers. I was about to break away when her hands just fell into her lap again. Then she leaned back in her chair and shifted her leg on the stool a little.

The Caretaker's chain was knocking against the back of my head before I knew it. 'Withdraw now in a backward fashion,' he told me. I didn't know what he meant, but as soon as the Queen motioned for one of the old farmhands, whose neck had swollen to the size of a gatepost, I just ran.

'So?' Anne said, across the galley table.

'So?' Mark said.

'So do a sad woman's cold hands leave you holier-than-thou or originally sinning like the rest of us?'

'What are you getting at?'

'Did she purge the Evil?'

''Well, I never came down with scrofula, if that's what you mean,' he mumbled. 'Apart from that, I don't believe much in good and evil.'

'What do you believe in?'

'Just Fate getting the better of us all in the end.'

'Fate's only chance pretending to be something better and people like you willing to believe.'

'So it was only chance my sword came just short of your life. You weren't meant to live?'

'I wasn't *meant* for anything, which is why I can do as I like.'

'Freedom's bleaker than I thought then.'

'So's a tidy life.'

The squall hit them in minutes, before the crew could even haul in the patch of half sail. Noah got hold of the wheel as the first wave crashed over the deck, but he couldn't hold it for long. It went spinning through his hands until George grabbed on as well, and the two managed to turn the ship round to larboard and drive her into the swell.

The Seahorse shuddered atop the first twenty-foot crest, and every man shuddered with it, thinking things could get no worse until the moment of that stomach-lurching drop when she plummeted into a valley so narrow they feared she'd never climb out again. On deck and still drunk, Jack ordered Noah, George and the rest of the crew below deck to pump while he lashed himself to the wheel. When they protested, he bared his cutlass.

The sudden glimpse of Mark Read then, still clutching the gunwales minutes later, annoyed him. The sight of Anne in the crow's nest, somewhere between black sky and black wave, enraged him. 'You bloody fool!' he yelled. She'd harnessed herself to the mainmast with a piece of broken rigging.

'More the fool to be trapped in the hold when we founder!' she shouted back, but her words never reached him on the gusts.

He looked back over his shoulder. 'What are you staring at, Read?' he shouted. 'Never seen a captain at the helm before?' The rain drove between them. Mark said nothing but only studied Jack's hands on the wheel as the sloop dipped headlong into the yawning deep, and the sky above narrowed again to the breadth of a finger.

Time was only the movement of each new wave before the bow; the slow dread that the next one would rear up and bare the ocean bed itself. So no one could say how long it was before Jack and Mark heard Anne at last, hurling words from the crow's-nest. 'Fine on the starboard bow!' she cried. They sank into another dark chasm – held their breath – then glimpsed it from the top of a curling wave. A single light, swaying on the distant shore.

'Get all hands on!' Jack ordered Mark. 'Open the hatch!'

'You're more drunk than I thought!' he shouted back. 'We'll be lucky to hold our position, let alone make for that light!'

'The wind's out of the south. We'll hold it in our sails. Open the hatch!'

'Sometimes it's out of the south. Then it smacks us from the east!'

'Take orders!'

'Those are wrecking communities on that coast. It's all reef. Why do you think they're signalling now?'

'Because we're not the only ones adrift! They've got their own men trapped in this. Now open the hatch, or we'll be rolling before I can tell you again!'

Their first attempt at sail almost toppled them. The gusts grabbed the boom, caught hold of the mainsail's slack and ran with it as *The Seahorse* shook like a small creature seized in the jaw of another.

'Trim that sail!' yelled Noah. 'The gaff's about to snap from the mast, for God's sake!'

Jack heaved on the wheel, easing the sloop round to leeward. Waves shattered over the decks, stunning the crew, pitching them against the boards like baubles.

'Keep her shy to the wind!' called John the Elder. 'It's going to rip the canvas clear through!'

'It's a sail, John!' he boomed. 'Not a fucking white flag!'

It took six men to haul in the runaway sail and tame it in the squall. As the next wave swelled to breaking point, they clung – to blocks, lanyards and cleats – with hands that had been stripped raw by the running ropes.

Overhead, Anne was shouting again from the crow's-nest. They couldn't catch a word, but in a moment they saw for themselves. The coast had jutted into sudden view off the starboard side, but their guiding light was suddenly gone.

'We're going to wreck!' cried John the Younger. Jack was driving the sloop at speed towards the nearest point, a craggy spit of land, as if it was some familiar anchorage.

'He's going to run us aground. He's going to run us aground.' Flat on the deck, Noah embraced the mainmast with both his arms, while John the Younger grasped the older man's ankles like a drowning man grasps at wreckage. They heard snatches of words blowing with a fury from overhead. '. . . even know this bit of the coast! This is . . . drunken idea of spite! You can't . . . ten lives because you're . . .' It was Anson Bonn twenty-five feet up in the crow's-nest and raging at the Captain. Noah and John listened for some kind of reply – for a wavering of his resolve – but heard nothing over the shrieking gale. They pressed their faces to *The Seahorse*'s deck and waited for the keel to smash.

It never happened. Instead, the squall shrank to a breeze, and they raised their heads to the sound of Jack calling for more sail. 'Spread that canvas!' he yelled. 'I'd like to drop anchor before nightfall if anyone's up to it!' His crew stumbled to their feet and stared at the scene as if they'd been tricked. *The Seahorse* sat in a small inlet, safe between a wooded shoreline on the one side and a long, sheltering spit of land on the other.

Jack cut himself free from the wheel and stumbled towards a rail. He couldn't trust his legs. They trembled now with a mind all their own. Grasping the rail, he looked up to the crow's-nest, eager for the relief on her face – for a wave of her hand – but saw only the back of her: she was searching the decks from above, looking for the body she feared lost. He saw her back straighten, knew she was ready to call out for all to hear, when she swallowed her cry. She'd found him, somewhere in the bow.

While everyone else gathered by the wheel, dazed by the unbelievable view, Mark Read leaned against the distant main-rail, staring past the bowsprit and up the narrow corridor of water. And even as Jack stared at Anne, willing her to turn around, she stared at Mark and silently pleaded the same.

Chapter Twenty-Six

'I almost killed us,' he said. They were in his cabin. The door was shut, the air close.

'I know you did.'

'No, listen to me, Anne. I almost *killed* us. I almost drove her on to the reef.'

She pulled her face away from his hand. 'I'm going up for air.'

On deck, the whole world was blue. Jackets, shirts and trous were hanging from the rails and yard-arms, blowing in the late afternoon light. Noah and John the Elder were mending the sails, both naked as the day they were born. Some of the crew had taken one of the boats to shore. George and Richard were sitting on the narrow shingle, fishing with two lines apiece; Tom was shooting at wood pigeons in the distance. Even Bones had come up from the galley. He stood in the stern, squinting in the sudden light. 'You just never know, do you, Anson?'

'No, Bones, you never do.'

She found Mark swabbing down the larboard deck. For a moment, she stood behind him, watching as his mop repeatedly missed the bucket. He was studying the crook of land, searching the trees. 'You're still thinking about that swaying light we saw from sea.'

He turned, and she looked at him, as if seeing him for the first time. He was short – a little shorter than she was – but he had a burly build, wide across the shoulders with strong arms. 'I'm trying to work out where it came from.'

'One man with a lantern, I'd say. Whether he was trying to wreck us or guide us, I don't know. And it doesn't matter now. We're in the clear.'

'But there's no settlement for miles. There's not even a clearing.'

'Then he was on his own.'

'So where's his camp then?'

She shrugged. 'Maybe he had second thoughts when he caught sight of us.' She nodded to the view behind her shoulder. Behind her Noah and John were spreading the mainsail in the bow, bending low and scrutinizing it for damage. Their buttocks rose like pale moons against the blue sky; their testicles bobbed up and down like buoys in a harbour.

Mark smiled. It was a shy smile, but it gave her courage all the same. She picked up his bucket and emptied it over the side. 'Forget the decks. Teach me how to outfence you.'

He hesitated. 'We should have more space.'

'Then we'll go ashore.'

'It'll be dark soon.'

'I'm the one who needs excuses. Just be glad I don't hold a grudge for our last encounter and help me drop the boat.' Suddenly, she was confident. He was looking at her; for the first time, his eyes were unguarded. She knew he wanted her.

They never reached the shore. As the sun disappeared behind the treeline, a Spanish man-of-war loomed into view at the mouth of the channel and gagged it with its tonnage.

John the Younger was screaming from the crow's-nest when a dozen tongues of gunfire scorched the twilight. No shot that time, only an unmistakable message. Come morning, *The Seahorse* would be turned into a sitting target. Already the guard ship towed an English schooner in its wake, the flank of which the sloop's crew could see was undamaged. There had been no contest.

George kicked a gun carriage. 'We'll be lucky if they let us surrender.'

'We should have held our bearings and weathered the bloody storm,' muttered Noah.

'Hindsight's a fine thing, Noah,' said Jack, lowering his spyglass. 'Only you could be mumbling to yourself now from the bottom of the fucking Windward Passage.'

Anne stood at the taffrail, staring at the rising tide. 'There's no way round them. We're like some ship trapped in a bottle.'

Jack turned, ready to shout, to curse his crew into life. Then he saw Mark, arms folded and staring at the deck. 'Haven't you bloody jumped yet?'

Mark met his glare.

'Well, that's our only hope, men. Isn't it? Swim for shore and run for the woods. So what if you never find your way out again. So what if you can't swim a stroke.'

'There are the boats,' whispered John the Younger.

'And this is the River Styx. Go to Hell, the lot of you.'

'Where are you going, Captain?' Noah demanded.

'I'm retiring to my cabin for the night. Call me when the first thirty-two-pounder blows a hole in the hull.' He was halfway to the hatch when he turned lightly on his heels, as if he'd forgotten something — a word to the watch or his tricorn on the heap of tackle. 'Anson, my boy.' She didn't turn round from the rail. 'What do you say to one last fuck?' He saw her back and shoulders tense, and smiled. 'Well then, I'll say goodnight.'

They sat in the darkness on deck and listened to the water lapping at the hull. The night was starless. There was only the light of a distant lantern, swinging in the breeze at the rear of the Spanish stern — the light that had guided them into shore.

'He's right. There's no point just sitting here, thinking about it.' Tom got to his feet.

'You're not going anywhere. Sit down.'

He did as John the Elder told him.

'I always thought it would be my foot slipping on wet rigging,' said Noah, 'or someone's blade whistling through my ribcage.'

'Shut up for once, Noah,' said George.

'I was just saying that—'

John the Younger kicked a fiddle block across the deck. 'Why don't the whole lot of you shut up!'

George laughed. 'Since when do you give us orders?'

'Since this time tomorrow we'll all be bloody well dead.'

'Don't start blubbering, John,' said Noah. 'Nobody pressed you aboard.'

'Easy for you to say. This is your seventh ship, not your first.'

'It's bad luck,' said Anne. 'No one's saying it isn't.'

'It's more than bad luck, Anson. Jesus, I haven't even lived out fifteen years!' He buried his face in his lap.

'For Christ's sake, stop your mewling!' shouted George.

Anne joined Mark at the taffrail. 'What are you thinking?' She could feel his arm, warm against her own, and she wanted to stop time.

'Nothing. I'm just looking,' he said. From where they stood, they could just see the schooner, moored to the man-of-war's far side. All but its stern rested behind the frigate's bulk.

'I wish there was something to see,' she said. 'Just a clear view would suit me.'

He spoke slowly, shaping his words, studying the channel. 'I think I might see something . . .'

She searched the view. 'What? What, tell me.'

'A possibility. Maybe.'

She let the rail take her weight. 'I liked it better when you believed in Fate.'

The crew waited impatiently for the tide to ebb. Finally, when there was only an hour to first light, they eased the two boats down the slide. Without a word, they loaded them with every musket, pistol, boarding axe, sword, cutlass and dirk they could find on board. They strung themselves with powder horns and shoved pouches of shot down their hose. What remained of the Seville gold had to be abandoned. They couldn't afford the weight. Then they muffled the oars with strips of sailcloth and climbed into the laden craft, one by one.

Jack was the last to board. 'It won't work, you know.'

'Just get in,' Anne whispered. 'When we're all dead you can say, "I told you so."'

'Read's the one who's been burning to say it.'

'Keep your voice down.'

'He warned me to stay away from this coast.'

'You knew as much yourself. He didn't need to warn you. You took a chance and were unlucky. Now get in and pick up an oar.'

They pushed off into the darkness, guiding the boats by the

light in the Spanish stern, steering their way between the shoreline and the long arm of land that pinned them. The tide was still, but there was a strong wind blowing off shore. It kept blowing them into the shallows near the spit.

'What if it gets light before we make it?' whispered John the Younger to Mark.

'Then we die a little sooner. Now be quiet.'

A crashing noise broke over the water. All oars hovered in mid-air.

'Just a wild hog,' whispered Noah, 'on the shingle.'

They pushed on through the clamped darkness, drawing slowly closer to the man-of-war. They could hear voices now, the sleepy exchange of the watch. And closer. High above them, dice were rattling across a polished deck. When they came upon the vessel at last, the two boats nipped in close and hugged the vast midriff of its starboard. Each small crew lifted all but two of the oars from the water. It was like nestling alongside a sleeping beast.

As they neared the stern and its pool of lantern light, they lifted the last of the oars, buried their heads in the dark of their clothing, and let each boat drift with the wind – past the towering stern, past the watch, and through the fleeting brightness that lit the schooner's smaller stern. They ended up on its larboard side, just beyond the channel's mouth, and out of sight of each ship's watch; the *guarda costa* were watching the channel, not the sea behind them.

The Spanish watchmen never heard them approach. There were no boots on planks. There were no shouted threats or cries. There was only, in the end, the sound of four bodies slumping over the schooner's rails. Anne, Tom and Patrick eased them gently on to deck.

Even as the watch fell, Mark and George were slicing the cables that moored the schooner, freeing her from the man-of-war's tug. The rest of the crew were lifting the weaponry on to deck. The tide had slowly started to change. If they'd timed it right, the schooner would begin to drift with the outgoing tide. The wind was strong, but sail was impossible. One swing of the boom and the Spanish crew would be on top of them with twenty men for every one they had just killed.

Jack unstrapped the wheel and eased the rudder round. It was all anyone could do – that and hope the tide would soon catch them in its flow. Mark paced the larboard deck. Anne hovered, rigid in the rigging. Jack stood hunched over the wheel, holding it fast.

The sky was just breaking with first light when – slowly, soundlessly – the schooner started to drift round to larboard and nudge its way into the open sea. The wind fell in behind, and soon, they were inching past the reef.

As the topsails spread out against the widening sky, they heard the first volley thunder in the distance. The *guarda costa* had opened fire on *The Seahorse*.

Anne found him, alone at the bowsprit, watching their new vessel, *The Harbinger*, cleave the waves. The day was clear, the wind fresh.

'It's like there's no one else in the whole rollicking world,' she said.

'Aye, it's good.'

She rested her hand next to his on the mainrail. 'Your hands don't look like a seaman's.'

'I've got all my fingers, you mean.'

'No, they're finer.'

She lifted her hand and placed it over his. From below deck, there was a burst of voices and song. Mark turned to her, but couldn't find his words. He watched her unbutton her jacket with her free hand; saw her loosen her shirt-tie; felt her take his hand and push it under her shirt and press it to her.

His fingertips glanced over the firm rise of her breast. The rough skin of his thumb brushed her hard nipple. She saw the blood rise to his cheeks.

He pulled his hand away, slowly.

'You knew,' she said.

'I didn't,' he stumbled.

'You did. I could tell by the way you looked at me. Jack saw it too. Why do you think he's been such a bastard?'

He stuffed his hands under his armpits.

She tried again. 'A part of you knew – wanted—'

'No.' He looked her in the eye. 'No, I didn't.'

They turned towards the sea, trying to catch their breath in the stiffening breeze.

'I *saw* you look at me.'

He turned, and she watched him make for the hatch, then disappear below.

Chapter Twenty-Seven

Once Virginia Lazarus said to me, 'I can't sleep right since yu cum to me home, Anniewomun. Yu toss an yu turn, like yu can't mek up yu mind which is best.' Bamboo trees were clacking in the darkness behind the hut. I said nothing.

'What yu tinking bout?'

'A baby.'

'Dead or grown?'

Still, after all these years, I couldn't say it.

'What is de child's name?'

'She never had a name.'

'No wonder she keep yu awake.'

'The priest wouldn't christen her.'

'How she die?'

'Drowned.' *In the tears of a cross-eyed girl.*

'Well, how bout we jes let her cry herself ta sleep?'

'Aye.'

As *The Harbinger* neared the tip of Hispaniola, fog closed in. Suddenly, the spars seemed to float in mid-air, and the ship's bow disappeared from its stern. The crew paced her decks, moving in and out of the pressing cloud like the ghosts of her last crew.

When the wind dropped, she slowed to a complete halt. There was nothing for them to do but bide their time and drift. Already the euphoria of their recent escape was giving way to a muffled quiet. No one dared say he wanted to turn back for New Providence. Everyone knew it was hopeless; a man would never be pardoned twice.

Anne found Jack, leaning over the wheel, working the cold

out of his bad hand. 'Are you holding that wheel or is the wheel holding you?'

'Both.'

'So where do we go from here?'

'Hispaniola, it seems.'

'Why Hispaniola?'

'Why not Hispaniola?'

'There's nothing there for us.'

He shrugged. 'Enough coffee and sugar to last a lifetime. Mango groves that go on forever. The odd Spanish flotilla passing off coast.'

'A pleasant view, you're saying.'

'We could recruit again in Tortuga. It's just off shore.'

'From a bunch of planters and slaves? The French purged the place of our sort years ago, and you know it.'

He flexed his fist. 'Maybe Jamaica then.'

It was getting her nowhere. 'Have you said anything to Mark yet?'

'No, but I'm sure you have.'

'We don't need bad feeling aboard.'

'Speaking of that – of bad feeling, I mean – do you lust after him very much?'

'That's enough, Jack.'

'I'm interested.'

'You surprise me.'

'He's plain, you know.'

'Then there's nothing more to say, is there?' She turned and walked away.

Sluggishness had descended with the fog, and, by the third day, most of the men had taken to their hammocks. 'If the world was still bloody flat,' said Noah, 'at least we could sail over the edge. It's no good for a man to think he can go on forever, let me tell you.'

'Tell who, Noah? No one's listening.' Patrick was slumped in his hammock, trying to remember the feeling of Newfoundland rock under his feet. Richard was playing noughts-and-crosses by himself. Tom lay flat on his back, counting the deck planks overhead.

That night, Anne was awakened by the sound of Mark rising suddenly from his hammock. She rolled on to her side, pulling the thin blanket over her head, thinking he would feel his way through the dark to the corner where the piss-pot sat. He didn't. He headed for the hatchway instead. She heard him mount the ladder, one rung at a time. Then he was pushing on the hatch door with his shoulder and climbing barefoot on to deck.

A clammy breeze blew in after him, stirring the close air; he hadn't closed the hatch. Anne heaved herself to her feet and went to close it. From the top of the ladder, she glanced over the decks. No sign. If he'd wanted to retch over the side, he wouldn't have walked far.

She clambered on to deck and lowered the door. The fog was still dense. She couldn't see more than a foot in front of her. 'Mark!' Her call echoed strangely.

No answer. She started down the deck. The planks were slippery, and overhead the rigging creaked with the damp. For a moment, Tom appeared like a sleeping illusion in the look-out only to disappear again behind a bank of mist.

She cupped her hands to her mouth. 'Mark!'

She found him just before she stumbled into him. He stood near the bowsprit, hunched over the rail. 'What's the matter?' He clutched his blanket in both hands. 'Are you sick?'

He didn't look at her. He only raised the blanket slowly up, as if he would drop it over the rail.

She grabbed hold. It was sticky with blood. 'Mark? What's the matter? Did Jack come after you?'

Still he didn't speak. He didn't even seem to hear. He only tugged the blanket away from her and dropped it into the sea below. She watched him walk back down the deck. She heard the hatch door fall shut. By the time she'd returned to her hammock, he was breathing deeply again, fast asleep.

'Where's your blanket?' she asked. It was morning. She was

folding her own away in her chest, to keep the damp off it. 'You must have been cold last night.' She tried to sound careless.

He looked around for it, suddenly perturbed. 'Not as cold as someone else was, I guess.' He thought someone had stolen it from him in the night.

Another day and more fog, erasing *The Harbinger*'s bevelled edges, smudging its taut rigging. Oblivion spread like damp, and as it did the reports of each consecutive watch grew more and more uncertain. No longer did the ship's log fill with news of trade winds and tidal movements. No longer did it note the knots on the log-line and the landmarks on shore.

The first trick of the fog was a disappearing gun carriage. One moment, it stood ready at the gunport; the next, it was gone, leaving its cannon afloat in mid-air. 'A man could have rolled right under it' (John the Elder).

On the middle watch, the following was recorded: a coil of rope lifted its uppermost end and shook itself, 'like the rattler on a snake' (Richard Corner and John the Younger).

Jack scoffed. 'What will it be next? A blind harpist thrumming the ship's rigging?' But the reports didn't stop.

Tom Earl saw the shape of Mark Read walking the deck when Mark Read swore he'd never left his hammock.

Noah Harwood reported that the *Harbinger*'s figurehead – a half-woman with a mouth that streamed with each wave's flood – had shut that same mouth and raised a finger to her lips as he passed. '"Ssshhh," she said, just like I'm talking to you now.'

Anson Bonn recorded a floating mangrove tree. It had drifted past the bow, upright on a mass of muddy roots with 'a horde of oysters sheltering there'. And that wasn't all. A sea-cow, with 'the breasts of a mermaid and the face of a fatling', swam after it, feeding on the oysters.

Jack didn't know whether she was mocking him or not. He was even less sure what to believe when, late one night, taking his turn at the watch, he thought he saw her and Mark Read through his night-glass, pulling stunts in the rigging. A blanket of fog billowed overhead, and there was Anne – or the shape of Anne – fifty feet up at the cross-trees. Read was some twenty feet below her, hanging upside down, it seemed, with his knees pushed through the ratlines. Jack held his lantern high and watched with mute fear. The fog rolled in again. He could just see a pair of hands grabbing the timber, then two legs swinging high into the night. When she slipped into the fog like a body into a lake, and plummeted, he knew he'd lost her. He was waiting for the terrible thwack of her body on the deck when she emerged at last, on the tips of Mark Read's fingers.

When John the Younger appeared on deck to relieve the watch, he found Jack bent over the water pail, swilling his eyes.

So when the merchant ship appeared out of nowhere, the crew would have stood blinking if it hadn't crashed into the schooner's skids.

'God, she's drifting,' said Noah. 'Who lets a merchant ship just float away?'

Jack cupped his hands to his mouth and called out. They waited. No reply came back through the dark. 'Clap on,' he commanded.

'It's a trick,' said John the Elder. 'They're waiting for us below deck.'

'Merchant ships don't go after us, John. We go after them. Besides, who could have seen us in this fog?'

'There's something not right about it,' said Anne.

'Aye, there's something not right about it, and the poor bastard who let her drift away is kicking himself now, you can be sure. So clap on.'

George threw the grappling irons high over the merchant ship's rails, then heaved. In a minute, he was climbing up into its stern, swinging a lantern in one hand. 'No bodies, Captain!'

'Tie her on then!'

'You mean, tie us on, don't you?' said Anne. The drifting vessel outweighed the schooner by at least a hundred tons.

The crew armed themselves and climbed, two by two, up a pair of heaving lines. On board, all was quiet. At the helm, the wheel turned by itself.

They moved up and down the decks like wary thieves, searching behind the masts and kicking piles of mouldering sailcloth. There was no sign of life on deck – only a clay pipe that had rolled out from under a gun carriage. There could be none below: all three hatchways were firmly battened.

They regathered at the main hatch, their lanterns burning in the fog. 'Someone must have been towing her to the Cap-Français when the lines snapped. She's probably some French prize.'

'Where's the damage then?'

'Maybe her crew surrendered.'

'No, the boats are gone. They must have abandoned ship.'

'Who abandons a ship stiff with cargo?'

'Maybe that last squall made them think twice. Maybe they feared it was going to land them on a reef.'

'Just open the hatch,' said Jack. Suddenly, he was as nervous as a grave-robber.

Tom pushed the timbers through the bars. Noah pulled away the canvas sheeting and grasped the hatchway handle. 'It's stuck, sir. The planks must be swollen with the damp.'

'Here,' said George, 'let me try.' He grabbed fast, almost stumbling backwards with the effort, but the door remained shut.

John the Younger went back to *The Harbinger* for a crowbar. They waited, fidgeting at the hatch, uncomfortably close to one another. 'You know, a man can just slip overboard in weather like this,' said Noah. 'Usually, no one hears the splash.'

'They'll be looking for this ship,' said Anne. 'Someone doesn't just lose a three-masted square rigger and put it down to experience.'

Over the light of his lantern, George's head seemed to float in mid-air. 'Our ship comes in and Bonn here wants to sail away.'

'Maybe I'm wary of an easy haul, Fetherton. Maybe I like a challenge.'

'Like Mark Read, you mean.'

'Shut up, Fetherton.' Mark's voice was low.

'I saw Anson follow you up on to deck the other night. Find a nice quiet corner somewhere?'

'You're bloody seeing things, George,' he said.

John was back with the bar. He passed it to Tom who forced

it under the hatch door and wrenched it open. Both stood back. 'Captain?'

Jack took a lantern and turned, lowering himself into the hatchway. He went slowly, feeling for each rung of the ladder – another and another – fearing the stench that was so strong he could taste it.

From above, they heard his boots hit water. They saw a broad arc of lantern light swing through the steerage. Then they heard him retch at the bottom of the ladder.

It was a cargo of slaves: four hundred Negroes, manacled one to the other by the wrists; lying shoulder to shoulder on raised boards that served as bunks; one hundred bodies to a tier, two tiers to each side of the hull; the ankles of every fifth man or woman clamped to a supporting post.

Anne stumbled down the ladder after Jack. She picked up the lantern he'd dropped and shone it round the steerage. She saw fevered bodies bound to corpses. She saw the swollen stomachs of pregnant women next to the heaving ribcages of the dying. At the waterline, the hull was holed, and the sea trickled through, lapping now at the lower bunks. When she saw a newborn face-down in the flood, she turned fast on the last rung and scrabbled up the ladder like an animal from a hole. But halfway up, she lost her footing, and tumbled backwards into the water.

It was a tide of brine, blood and vomit; of piss and excrement; of bilge and dead vermin. It was the stagnant sea of an underworld.

Annie, can the Devil swim?

Nay, he is frightened of water, the same as a cat.

So drowned seamen are taken by the Lord.

Always.

And the sea is Holy Water?

Aye, you were baptized in it.

'For Christ's sake, Anne, get up!' Jack was pulling on her.

How strong is an undertow, Annie?

As strong as sleep, my girl.

'I've got her arms! You get her feet!'

She heard Jack behind her. Saw Mark before her as the water streamed over her face. 'I'm all right.'

'Then get up the bloody ladder.'

On deck, a clatter of voices.

'We could tow the ship into harbour at the Cap and sell the lot of them there.'

'Christ, Tom, half of them are already stiff. There's no telling how long they've been cooped up.'

'Eight weeks from West Africa.'

'More.'

'Tom's right. The other half just need air. We get them on deck, say fifty at a go, and by the time we make shore, they'll be ready for market.'

'Are you crazy, Fetherton? This is probably a Crown vessel. No one merchant could have shipped in this quantity.'

'So?'

'So, are you recommending we just pull up outside the Customs House and offload there?'

'No.'

'This isn't a cargo of Irish linen and lace. It's not something we can just sneak round the back way.'

'We can pull into Tortuga and smuggle them from there by the dozen into town.'

'Now that won't take long, will it?' smirked Noah.

'Nooo,' said John the Elder, 'we should be able to shift them before the *rigor mortis* gets really bad.'

'Well does anyone have a better idea?'

'No, but they'll need watering if there's going to be any livestock left to shift.'

Bones had followed them across the decks. His voice was a whisper. '*The Harbinger*'s got lots of water.'

'We'll take it in turns starting with the night watch.'

'Can't we wait till first light?'

'No, we can't. It's all the same in this fog anyway.'

Anne was on the middle watch with Patrick. Tom passed them a bucket and a ladle each. 'You can squeeze round the back of the bunks to reach their heads, but when you do the top row you just have to reach up and tip the ladle twice over their faces. There's no head room, and they can't manage the ladle themselves.'

She could smell the stench on his clothes. 'How far did you get?'

'Read and I covered the larboard lower rows and half of the one above.'

'Where is he?'

'Trying to get warm over there by the wheel, under that pile of canvas, but I think he's fallen asleep, so don't fall over him.'

They filled the buckets at the barrel on deck and went below. Lanterns burned at the bunk posts. They stepped off the ladder and waded into the flood.

'They're going to die,' Anne mumbled. 'They're all going to die.'

'It's got nothing to do with us,' said Patrick. 'We just found them. You take the starboard lower.'

She fixed her eyes on each open mouth and tried to look no further. When a mouth didn't open, she moved on, scooping stale water in her ladle, waiting for the line of bodies to end. She didn't look at the eyes, open or shut, or at the flesh rubbed raw by iron, or at the baby wriggling between its mother's breasts – not until the woman had spat the water back into her face, and Anne saw what she'd wanted her to see: the birth cord still binding her to her child.

She put her bucket down, took the dirk from her side, and cut it. Then she offered more water and started to move on. 'Yu. Yu,' the woman tried. Anne shook her head. 'Yu!' She pointed with her chin to the child on her chest.

Anne concentrated on the ladle. What could she do with a newborn baby? What could she possibly do?

She moved away, spilling water as she went. She found the next mouth. And the next. It opened. She filled it. Another. The lips were full, beautifully shaped, and suddenly, she remembered her young fingers on Black-Eyed Susan's mouth – tracing the strong curves of her lips as if they were lines on a strange, new map.

When she felt the mouth tremble below her fingers, she reached quickly again for the ladle and shied away from the lantern light.

Patrick went back to find George and Noah, who were late relieving them. Anne leaned on the deck rail, trying to clear her head, grateful even for the foggy air. Then she remembered Mark, asleep by the wheel, and turned. The sailcloth had been thrown aside. He'd gone back to the schooner for the night, but had forgotten his stockings and boots on the slaver's deck. She picked them up. They'd never dry out there in the open air.

She settled back against the rail and waited for the next watch to arrive. Noah, for one, was always sleeping through his turn. Tonight, she was more impatient than ever for her hammock and for sleep.

She only heard him when he tripped over a block a few yards behind her. He was shuffling up from the deck. Behind him, the hatchway door was shut. She and Patrick had left it open.

'Mark!' She shone a lantern his way.

He blinked at the light, but he didn't wake up.

'I've got your boots,' she said, trying to be matter-of-fact. 'I thought I'd take them back before George claimed they were his.'

He didn't reply as he neared the rail. Once again, his back was stooped, and she could see he was clutching something. 'Not another blanket, Mark. What did you do? Steal it from one of the slaves?'

'Ssssh,' he said to the deck. 'Ssssh . . .'

It wasn't a blanket. 'For Christ's sake, Mark!'

He let go before she could grab it from him; the tiny body hit water before she could see if it was dead or alive.

Chapter Twenty-Eight

As the sun burned through the fog, *The Harbinger*'s crew were leaning on the rails, watching fins the colour of gunmetal plough through the swell. The waters off Tortuga were shark-infested. Already in the distance, small fishing smacks were setting out from the Cap, making their way towards the island. Shark oil fetched a good price at market. Moreover, many a shark's belly in those days had been slit open to reveal a fisherman's fortune. Among the rusting grapeshot and the bent pewter spoons were Spanish dollars, pieces of gold plate, and severed hands, encrusted with rings.

'This is our chance,' said George. 'We recruit every smack we can to smuggle the Negroes into coves up and down the coast. That way, we're not sitting here for more than two days, and no one notices the sudden arrival of four hundred slaves.'

'And what makes you think these fishermen won't sell news of us to the French governor?' asked Noah.

'The cut they'll get of whatever deal they do with the planters.'

'It wouldn't take much,' added John the Younger, 'to beat the price of a day's shark oil.'

'And it wouldn't take much,' Anne concluded, 'for them to sell our Negroes and never put to sea again.'

Jack wasn't listening. 'I want seven of those fishermen on this deck within the hour. Take the two boats and divide up. Bonn, Fetherton and Carty in the one. Read, Corner and John the Elder in the other. Earl, you stay behind and plug that hole in the slaver's hull. The rest of you can man the pump below her decks. If that water level rises any higher, they'll be drowning in their sleep.'

*

Hiding behind an outcrop of rock, Anne, George and Patrick watched a smack approach its buoys. When it drew up alongside and its three men bent low, straining to raise the net of bait-fish, they paddled out of the shoals and attacked from behind. George was first to board. Anne was close behind. There was a skirmish, which later she'd only dimly remember, for even as she wrenched her victim's arm behind his back and laid her blade over his lips, she was watching the net. It was sliding over the side, running back into the deep – so fast, she'd never be sure whether she had seen a Negro baby caught in its confusion of cord.

Seven wary fishermen climbed up the Jacob's ladder and on to the schooner's deck. From the one smack, there were two twin brothers and an ageing father; from the other, three men – their hands still sticky with shark's gore – and a mulatto youth, who helped with the nets.

'He's all we need with four hundred Negroes on board,' George complained.

'Tom, search the lot of them for knives,' ordered Jack. 'No one keeps so much as a fish hook on his person.'

'George is right,' said Noah. 'With the lad half and half, how do we know which half we can trust?'

'Whichever one suits,' said Jack. 'I've got 350 tons to sail with a schooner in tow, and I need every hand I can get.'

'Then we should have taken more than two smacks,' George persisted.

'And we'd soon be well outnumbered. Forget the talk. I want us in Jamaica in three days' time.'

'But that means we'll have to sail by night,' said Noah.

'It does, and when any man is not on deck he's below deck, feeding and watering the Negroes. Nobody sleeps till we drop anchor, is that clear? Noah, I want you at the helm of *The Harbinger* as we tow her through the Passage. In the meantime, all hands on the slaver, and be quick about it. I want all the sails loosed and set, ready to scoop the wind.'

'They don't even speak bloody English,' said George, nodding at the seven.

Jack ignored him. 'What did you find on them, Tom?'

'Just a couple of gutting-blades, a half-whittled fish, and this.'
Jack reached out a hand to catch it as it flew through the air, a
flash of silver. 'It was on the mulatto lad.'

He eyed it, then weighed it in his palm as if it was some kind
of charm. He turned to Anne and let a long chain and locket slip
out of his hand and dangle from his fingertips.

'I think they found it in a shark's gut,' Tom explained, 'but
the clasp's bust. I've tried getting it open myself, but it's
clamped tight as an oyster.'

Jack watched Anne's face; saw her mesmerized by the sway of
the locket on the air.

'Throw it over,' she said slowly.

'Why would I do that?' he said, smiling.

'It's worthless.' It was as if there was only one locket in the
world. All over again, she could see Dick Turnley bound to
the *Buoyant*'s mainmast and the glint of silver against his
neck.

So could Jack. 'Quite likely,' he teased. 'I'd say it's not even
silver.'

'Throw it over, Jack.'

'Now that seems hard.'

'Aye,' said Mark, speaking up, 'the lad's got little enough as
it is.'

Jack drew the locket back into the cup of his hand and closed
his fist round it. He saw Anne blink as it disappeared, like
someone surfacing from water. Then he tossed the locket across
the deck – not to the net-boy, but to Mark Read himself. 'You've
got the soft spot for the lad. You give it to him.'

The crew, taking no interest in a worthless locket, were
already making for the bow, preparing to board the slaver. But
Anne loitered behind the mainmast, long enough to see Mark
Read call the mulatto boy back to him; close enough to see him
press the locket into the smooth of the boy's palm; close enough
to hear him speak gently to the boy in words she couldn't
understand.

Aloft in the rigging, the crew were jumping between the yards
and foot-ropes, balancing themselves along the furled length of

mainsail while they waited for John the Elder's call from below. Anne was poised behind the bunt, watching the net-boy as he leaned forward and gripped the distant yard-arm. She could see the helpless trembling of his leg. She could see the locket, dangling from his neck like a silent threat.

It had surfaced again. That membrane of blood she had trawled from her mother's dead body. That good omen. Fate's all-too-ready offering. *Never drown.* She wouldn't have it.

The wind up high was beating her cheeks, clearing her head like a cold snap in the spring. She'd only have to unhitch the sail-knots in front of her – one by one, eyes innocent on the horizon – and loose the bunt first. There'd be a wild flapping of canvas. The mainsail would fly out of control like the giant wing of a panicking bird, and the net-boy would be knocked from his perch at the yard-arm before he could even blink.

She looked down to deck; imagined his body broken on the planking; saw in her mind's eye Noah's needle darting in and out of the hammock's weave; saw the seam close over the brown neck where the locket still glinted; waited for the final stitch through the smashed nostrils. 'Not a twitch!' he yelled to the Captain. Jack nodded, and the body was thrown over the rails into a sea so clear she could see the blood that stained the hammock's hemp-cloth, and the smooth muscle of a shark's back gliding towards it in the deep.

'Let fall!' It was John the Elder, far below. She was a moment behind the others, but the mainsail unrolled like thunder as the crew released it – first at the yard-arms, then at the bunt. Its great belly dropped and swelled with the growing wind.

'Set the pins!'

She watched Mark below, winding ropes in tight figures-of-eight around the mast pins. She saw him look up, hand to his eyes, and survey the angle of sail. She saw his fair hair as pale as corn silk in the sun; felt the strength in his hands as he hauled a rope in, calming the sail below her. Then he saw her watching him, and turned away, pretending to check the knots.

They were under way, heading south-east through the Windward Passage, making for the Jamaica Channel, while below deck Negroes were still dying. 'We have to drop some of the bodies,

Captain,' said John the Elder. 'The ones still alive down there are starting to die from so much death.'

'Three days, I said. If we start to break those chains now, it'll be Chaos.'

On that first day, she said to Mark, 'Where did you learn French?' She loved the words in her mouth. They were sweet with the taste of intimacy. They intruded on his past. They interrupted the private language he shared with the beautiful net-boy.

His throat went pink, but his voice strained to be matter-of-fact. 'When I was thirteen, I left the Isle of Dogs, gladly, and went into service. I was a footboy to a French lady in London. She called me her little Dog-Boy and said she would civilize me by teaching me French.'

'She gave you lessons?'

'If you can call them that. I attended her at her daily *toilette*. I had to comb the lice from her wigs and run after the cat when it got hold of her mouseskin eyebrows, and hold up her gowns when she needed to shit in the fireplace with the blocked flue. But in the quieter moments, when she painted her face or rolled up her stockings, I had to repeat parts of French speech after her – and bark whenever I got it wrong.'

'You learned fast.'

'Aye, and lived to regret it. After a few months, she set me to writing her courtly letters. She called it La Dictée. *Ma chère Madame Lefour* . . . or worse still, *Chère maîtresse de ma coeur* . . . She devised each, and I tried my best to write what she said as she said it. Then she'd have me seal it with red wax and drop it into the post bag. She'd make a great show of it when it was delivered, officially, into her hand. After a while, she got it into her head to make me read selections at her fortnightly salon. She'd open the latest letter, place it in my trembling right hand and make me hold a little riding crop in my left.'

'You had to read it out loud?'

'Aye, while my arse burned in front of the fire. I'd stammer through it miserably, then dodge behind the virginal while the guests clapped and fanned their cleavages. After six months, I couldn't bear it any more, so I ran away and almost threw myself in the path of a press gang one night at the London docks. What are you thinking?'

'Poor Madame Lefour.'

On the second day, they counted another fourteen dead bodies below deck.

'If we lose another Negro,' Jack warned them, 'I'm going to start throwing crew overboard.'

They nurtured their cargo on stale water and rum, lifting each head so it could swallow. They dug maggots and weevils from the rations of biscuits with the tips of their dirks. They threw fish into the galley sacks to coax the vermin out of the foodstuffs and into the dead flesh. They flushed contagion from the hold, burning brimstone and vinegar. They rinsed the sores of each slave in salt water, and sometimes, they left the hatch open – a bright square of light to distract them from their pain.

Armand, the net-boy, could not be persuaded below deck. 'They sing to me in the tongue of my mother.' He struggled for the words. 'I hear them.'

'They're groaning,' said Patrick. 'Not singing.'

'Non. Ils savent que je suis ici, en haut. Ils savent que je peux entendre.' He crouched above the hatch, listening. '"Hele mue plene." – Ecoutez mes cris, je pleure.'

Mark translated. 'Listen to my cries, I am weeping.'

'"Lamo sala bule." La mort de celui-là me brûle.'

'The death of that one burns.'

'"La baba mwe ki pli bule ete." Mais la mort de mon bébé m'enflamme.'

Mark's voice dropped to a whisper. 'But my baby's death inflames me.' Anne saw his shoulders curl under a weight he couldn't name.

Later that night, she found him bent over the rails, searching the dark sea for the wake of a memory. He didn't move as she lifted up the tail of blond hair and pressed her lips to the back of his neck. Dry kisses. Shy as the paper wings of a moth. He didn't say a word as she rubbed the back of his arms where, still, he felt the strain of a burden he couldn't remember.

They didn't hear Jack on the deck behind them. Later though, she'd watch, in her mind's eye, the nervous flexing of his bad hand. She'd hear the creaking of the salt-stained glove over the hilt of his sword. She'd feel the surge of his instinct to skewer them, as one body, on its thin blade.

It was the smack of his glove on the deck at their feet that made them turn.

'Go on, Read,' he threatened. 'Pick it up.'

'There's no need,' said Mark.

'Pick – it – up.'

Mark kicked it back across the deck. 'I'm not interested in your challenges.'

Jack glared at him, then turned, leaving his glove behind.

At first light, as the Blue Mountains of Jamaica reared into view, Mark found Armand below deck, tied between the bodies of two dead Negro men and stripped naked except for the broken locket. '*Plene mue, plene mue.*' He mumbled like someone caught in a fever. '*Hele hele hele mu nu ale, nous sommes disparus.*'

By the time Anne was halfway down the ladder, Mark had cut the ropes and lifted the boy to his breast. '*Ssshhh,*' she heard him whisper. '*Sssshhh, c'est moi. C'est toujours moi.*'

Chapter Twenty-Nine

She said, 'I want you to sell him with the others.'

'The net-boy, you mean.'

'No planter's going to care whether he's brown or black.'

'True.' Jack looked up from a curling map of Jamaica. 'But I'm not selling to planters.'

'What?'

'I'm not about to bolster the lot of King and country with cheap slaves.'

'Are you mad? Who else is going to buy a ship-load of sick Negroes?'

'Somebody,' he replied, 'without an acre of plantation or a stick of sugar cane.'

In the Jamaican District that came to be known as Look-Behind, the first British surveyors rode back to back in pairs on one horse, travelling over highland ground pitted with sinkholes and trip-ropes. They clung to tracks choked by razor grass, screw pine and ferns twice the height of a man. *But only the wiss-wiss breathes*, the saying went: the leafy camouflage of the runaway slaves who lay in wait.

On horseback, they studied the green darkness for the whites of eyes or the sudden flash of teeth. They passed through hamlets they never saw: Quick Step, Me Ear Hear, Wait-a-Bit, Me No Sen Yu No Come; settlements that disappeared at the blow of a bull horn into a chain of underground caves. The surveyors dreamed of England in black ink and vellum. Newmarket. Devon. Ipswich. Windsor. They eased swollen rivers with the fine points of their nibs. They mapped ranges of isosceles triangles.

Beyond the District of Look-Behind, at the foot of one triangle known as Blue Mountain Peak, there was no such place called Nanny Town. There was no renegade community of Negroes readying itself for war with the British. There was no amassed wealth in any mountain cavern. Nor was there any British trader, in Kingston or Spanish Town, so low he would sell weaponry to a Negro with money. And the white birds that roosted in the island's trees at twilight were not the ghosts of slaves, though old black women might whisper as much to children at bedtime.

There was, however, a Negro River which flowed down Blue Mountain Peak and through the mountain-bound interior. You could find it on any map, rushing over land towards the Caribbean Sea, emptying into the lonely arc of Morant Bay on Jamaica's south-east coast. Jack had found it on his curling map and measured it now, pressing the infected length of his thumb against its charted bends.

She would have to come to them. If the surveyors hadn't made it past Blue Mountain Peak, his crew never would. They'd drop anchor and wait in the waters of Morant Bay.

'I want you to sell him with the others,' she insisted. 'Do you hear me, Jack?'

'I do.' He rolled the map into a tight scroll. 'But Queen Nanny, I understand, likes her Negroes pure.'

Queen Nanny. The Right Excellent Nanny. Warrior Priestess of the outlawed Maroons, it was said she could heal her warriors by touch alone; that she could give suck to a babe at will; that she could summon the dead with a whisper. What's more, it was claimed, and not only by her own, that she could repel British gunfire with the mighty bulwark of her buttocks.

His crew wouldn't have it. 'Since when does anyone sell Negroes to Negroes?' Noah protested.

'Since rumour has it that Queen Nanny is wealthier than Governor Lawes himself,' said Jack. 'Since Lawes and his like would as soon hang us as trade with us. Since we can breed trouble at a profit by swelling the numbers of Nanny Town.'

'It's an evil plan,' whispered John the Elder.

'You think so, do you? Go ask the poor brutes below deck

which is the greater evil: to sell them to the planters or to take money for returning them to their own.'

'Jack Rackham, the philanthropist.'

'What do you suggest then, Read, in all your Negro-loving wisdom?'

'That you count me out. I'll not trade in half-dead bodies.'

'I counted you out long ago.'

By midday, the crew were leaning on the ship's larboard rails, watching the mouth of the Negro River for any tremor of life. Their seven-cannon salute had been noted; all day, the strange grammar of the bull horn had drifted up and down the river. Yet, by sunset, nothing.

'They could be just ten yards from the shore with canoes, waiting to ambush us in the night,' whispered John the Younger.

'Quiet, lad,' Noah told him. 'Your ears are of more use than your mouth just now.'

Time was slow to pass. Patrick Carty set himself up on the poop deck, fishing with maggots and a line. Pairs of gaming ten-bones rattled across the planking in petty bets. The twin brothers they had pressed into service off Hispaniola mended their only clothes with patches of hemp-cloth and hot pitch. Bones tried to remember the punchline of a joke he'd once heard.

Nobody opened the hatch. Nobody went below. Nobody noticed Armand, who sat quietly against a heap of tackle, unclasp the locket at his neck and wrap it in his fist. Anson Bonn was high overhead in the crow's-nest. Mark Read was spitting tobacco in the stern. Jack was drinking by himself at the prow.

On board, silence as the evening drew in and a flock of white birds settled on the slaver's bare spars. Silence as Armand choked Jack's shout with a twist of a chain; as his throat was cut by the slow bite of metal.

By the time Anne had slid down the ratline and made it to the prow, Armand had dropped the locket and run. She found Jack, bent double and retching air.

'Can you breathe?' she said, crouching by his side.

She heard a hoarse word.

'Let me see your neck.'

He waved her off.

'Let me see, Jack.'

She pulled him under the light of a hanging lantern. Found a ring of bruised flesh. A swollen jugular. Saw his lips were blue at the edges.

'You're crying,' she said.

'Drunk,' he whispered.

'Tell me.'

He bent down and picked up the broken locket and chain. 'For you.' Each word, a labour. 'For you.'

'What's the matter?'

'I told you.'

'You're ashamed.'

He sucked the sea air, wiped his eyes with the back of his bad hand. For a moment, he seemed surprised by its nakedness – its glove, lost to a challenge he could hardly remember. 'Infected again,' he said, showing her the hand, trying to distract her.

'You're ashamed because he's only a boy.'

He struggled to put breath behind his words. 'I'm ashamed because I couldn't move.'

She took his hand in her own two. She could smell its stink. She could feel the rucked stitches that ran through the flesh below the dead thumb. And she could feel the locket, sweating between their palms, like blood money.

'Sell him, Jack.'

'No.'

'We'll say he ran off.'

'I said, no.'

'He has to go.'

'Aye. I'm all too aware.'

Council law said forty lashes for any man who had assailed another. The next morning, however, Jack told no one. He gargled with salt water. He wrapped a linen cravat around his bruised throat. Then he found Armand asleep on deck, head on Mark Read's shoulder, and laid sword, pistol, shot pouch and powder horn at his feet.

Mark woke first. 'What's this about?'

'Arms for the net-boy. We have a quarrel to settle. Tell him we'll row to shore within the hour.'

'What quarrel? He doesn't have the words or the weapons to do you injury.'

'He'll understand.'

'But he's probably never drawn a sword in his life.'

'Then he'll have to aim his pistol well.'

'It's murder.'

'No,' said Jack pointedly. 'It's a duel.'

Armand was awake now. Others were gathering round, but Anne hung back.

Mark got to his feet. 'You bastard.'

'This isn't your quarrel, Read.' Jack turned to go, but stopped short when he felt the cold tip of a sword slip under the tail of his wig. 'What are you doing?'

'Quarrelling with you. With witnesses to boot.'

'Leave off, Read.'

Anne dropped the rope she was pretending to splice and pushed past the others. 'Mark, drop the blade.'

'I'll drop it if the Captain agrees to row to shore with me now, to settle this quarrel before he duels with the boy.'

'And if he doesn't?' asked Anne.

'I think he will.'

'That's no challenge,' said Noah. 'It's a threat.'

'Then it clearly wants redress.'

Jack felt the eyes of his crew. He thought of Anne behind him; remembered the warmth of her hands on his; remembered the sight of her, bending over Read, burying her face in his neck.

The bull horn sounded again in the distance, louder now.

'Drop one of the boats,' he said.

The End of Mark Read

It should be a familiar tale.

Six in the boat. Hardly a word spoken. A shovel, wrapped in a hammock, lying in the bottom between their feet. (Better to be buried than to be dropped at sea.) The scrape of the keel on sand. The removal of coats. The loading of pistols – all thumbs. Back against back. Then twenty paces along the tidemark where the beach is reliably flat. Even footing. Each boot sinking in damp sand. Turn. Draw. Take aim.

Jack's pistol misfired. Mark's bullet grazed the trunk of a palm tree.

There was a panic of wood-pigeons in the distance. An awkward moment. The slow realization that the other was still standing. Then, a second time, the bluff of measured paces. The unnatural movement towards danger. The hand moving towards the hilt.

Jack tried to breathe deeply as he walked, harbouring each lungful of air. When the scent of lavender water blew back at him on the breeze, he was comforted. It reminded him of the small, fluted bottle on his nightstand which needed to be replenished. It transformed the predictability of routine into the surety of fate. In a few days' time, he'd visit the perfumery in Spanish Town. He'd purchase two phials. He'd find the local tannery and choose a pair of new deerskin gloves. In the privacy of his cabin, he'd take a sheet of writing paper and roll it into a wide-lipped funnel, pouring it into his bottle with a steady hand. With the surplus of scent – normally, a little less than half a phial – he'd sprinkle his handkerchiefs, his wigs and his underwear. Finally, he'd pour the last inches into a pewter bowl and lay his bad hand in its shallow bath. He'd wait for the sting of alcohol in his wound, then bury the hand, lavender-soaked, in new leather.

Mark smelled only the tang of his own sweat. His shirt was starting to stick to his back and chest, but he wouldn't unbutton his shirtneck. He felt the churn of his bowels. He remembered his grandmother, still sealed in brocade and whale-bone, yielding to a rush of rank fluids at the moment of her death. He remembered the stink of her dead body; the wads of hemp-cloth his mother had rolled into soft plugs; the indelible stains on the mattress, and he feared his body's betrayal more than death.

The two men came to a halt within a sword's length of each other. They stood, feeling slightly ridiculous now in the pinch of ceremony. Jack flexed his bad thumb over his sword's hilt – it could stiffen to grip even if it could hardly feel. Mark straightened his shoulders. Worried about the sand in his boot. Then, the call from Noah to cross blades, and the bone-juddering crash of metal.

The beach turned to mud under their heels. The sword-hilts grew hot in their hands. A cloud of sand flies passed between them like a doubt. But again the swoop of blades, the desperate clatter and drive toward flesh.

Anne stood with Noah, George and John the Elder in an uneasy huddle up the beach. They made reluctant witnesses. 'It shouldn't have happened,' said Noah.

'You'd think we had men to spare,' said John.

Yet no one shouted them to a halt. No one ran down the beach and pulled them apart. They told themselves there was no stopping it now. Death was in the air, they said, and they shook their heads, straining to hear it in the cicadas' frantic hum; smelling it in the rotting weed; watching for it in the breeze that shook the green blades of palms. They folded solemn arms across their chests and waited for Death. They narrowed their eyes and squinted for it.

Anne knew there was no hearing or smelling or seeing it, but she said nothing, not even to herself. Least of all to herself. She didn't want to hear what she was afraid she was thinking – willing. She bent down, picked up the piece of bladderwrack at her feet, and started bursting its dark blisters with her thumb, one by one. Another moment, and it would be over.

'Jack's got the advantage,' said John. 'He's got more power behind him.'

'Aye, but Read's got strategy. He knows how to feint.'

She looked up – saw Jack nearly stumble – and looked away again.

'It shouldn't have happened,' Noah repeated.

'Not like this,' said George.

Silence except for the ringing of blades.

'Read needs to get that hair of his out of his eyes.'

'He needs to straighten up. What's the matter with him?'

She dropped the seaweed and looked up. Saw Mark's shoulders bending under their old invisible burden.

'I've heard it said,' said Noah, so quietly, they were afraid to listen, 'that Death climbs on a man's back at the end and rides him.'

No. Mark was the better swordsman. Mark was the one who had to live.

'He's lost his nerve,' whispered John.

It was true. Jack was almost on top of him. He could do nothing more than bar Jack's strikes.

'All for a mulatto net-boy.'

No.

'Anson?'

She was walking down the beach. She wouldn't allow it to happen. She'd appeal to Jack. She would let him love her.

'Christ, Bonn, get back here!'

Later, no one would agree on what happened next. Noah said Jack saw Anson coming down the beach and was, for an instant, distracted. John said, one word from Anson and Jack pulled back. George said Anson startled Jack with a knife at his back.

Whatever the case, there was a still instant. Not enough time to draw breath. Not enough time to recover a stance, but time enough for Mark Read to reach for his shirtneck and rip.

Buttons punctuated the air. Jack floundered. Something was wrong. He was lifting his sword once more, but his arm was slow-moving, mechanical almost. They saw Read grasp his own sword with both hands. They saw it sink into Jack's wrist.

Jack's sword and hand fell to the beach.

Mark Read dropped his weapon. Crossed his arms over his chest.

But no. Not so. *Mary Read*, as she would be known, dropped her weapon. Crossed her arms over the shame of her breasts. Watched, speechless, as a Negro woman walked out of the forest – bare-breasted, full-hipped – and laughed at her.

By the time she could persuade the crew to turn away, to look behind them, they were surrounded.

Chapter Thirty

'It's true,' said Virginia Lazarus. 'De soul is a flighty ting.'

I was dipping buckets in the waterhole behind her hut. The rains had been steady, and the hole itself had disappeared under a calm stretch of water. Virginia was seated beside me in her bamboo chair.

'I don't know what I could have been thinking, letting her see herself in the glass like that,' I said. 'She wasn't yet six months old.'

'So it fly away wit she likeness, is dat what yu tell me?'

'Aye.'

'Den she be lookin still. Yu say, where is she, where is she? Dat's where she be. Lookin.'

On the shore of Morant Bay, the tide rushed in over her boots, almost unbalancing her with each breaking wave, but she made no move. For the first time she could remember, she was at a loss. From the corner of her eye, she could see Jack, handless, and she knew he'd rather be dead. What wheel would he grip now? What swank could he risk with an arm staunched in tar? She watched the woman she'd known as Mark slip out of her shirt and wrap it around the stump of his arm. She watched those sudden breasts almost disappear, flattening into muscle as this stranger raised her arms to wind the shirt around the damaged limb. In the distance, she could hear the one they called Queen Nanny still laughing to herself, and she wanted to run, before she too was discovered.

The tide eddied around her ankles. She felt her boots sink into the sand.

When she looked again, Queen Nanny was gone. (Into the

wood? The air?) But her laughter seemed to carry on laughing without her – stopping only for breath and the occasional, 'O my, o me o my' – as the circle of lances tightened around them.

Anne tried to catch the eye of the warrior who stood before her, solid as a mangrove tree. 'Tell your Queen Nanny that we've brought her a ship of Negroes, that we're not selling them to the British. We're giving them to her.'

'We know yu are,' he said quietly. 'We tek dis ship. Already. Yu give wit not a very good fight.'

'We found it adrift off Hispaniola,' she tried. 'We've been trying to feed and water those slaves for days now.'

'An is it hard ta get de starving ta eat, eh? De dead ta lie still?'

'Let us go,' she pleaded. 'Our captain will bleed to death if we don't get him back to our ship.'

'Fine,' he said.

'We can go?'

'No. He cun go. Put him in de boat and lessee how well he row.'

The six of them were tied one to the other and led into the dense wood that stifled the shore. They moved like the near-blind, unaccustomed to the dim light, to the suddenness of roots, to the earth that turned to clay under their feet. There were no trails. Their four captors navigated by the sound of the river without seeing the river, just as they walked without watching the ground at their feet. The crew of six stumbled after like one misshapen body.

'Where are we going?' Anne shouted ahead.

'De place has no name,' said the one who led the way. He wore a bamboo breastplate and a priest's collar around his neck.

'But how far?'

'Till we stop.'

'Our captain is losing blood.'

'Hush-hush,' ordered the leader. 'Yu speak wen spoke to. Remember dat.'

'An yu don talk back,' said a second.

'Yu tell no lies,' instructed the third.

'She know wen yu lie,' added the fourth.

'She cun see a black mark on yu tongue.'

'May be she tek she Quichua-knife an cut out de rotten bit.'

'An yu mus wash yu hans in de river first, hear? Yu mek sure dey clean.'

'Yea, under de nails an all.'

A litany of warnings, a path that closed up behind them faster than a wake at sea.

Going to Nanny

When they came to the place where the Negro River slowed to a hush, they bent over its bank, at lance-point, and washed their hands in its cool flow. A bamboo raft idled alongside, moored to a boarwood tree. Its seat was decked with water hyacinth and cushioned with variously monogrammed, mildewed pillows.

'For de Right Excellent backside,' announced the upright Maroon in the collar and breastplate.

Anne saw they were being watched. From under the cover of trees, other Maroons – men, women and children – were pointing at Jack's bloody arm; at his plumpened calves; at the pink patch of Noah's bald head; at the bare-chested seaman who was half woman. Some of the children giggled. A young mother blew Anne a mock kiss.

They were led to the low entrance of a cave. 'On yu knees,' their captor ordered. 'Yu mus crawl troo. We all children before Nanny.' When they hesitated, he kicked the back of Noah's knees, and they sank as one to the ground, shuffling along in a defeated line while the children clapped their hands and sang.

At the dark edge of the cave, Anne stopped, bringing the six of them to a halt. 'I can't go in,' she said. George and John the Elder loitered just inside. The others waited nervously behind her.

'I'm right behind you.' It was Mark Read's voice – still, his voice.

Anne turned. 'And who are you?'

The tip of a lance pierced her jacket and shirt. She felt blood trickle between her shoulder blades. 'Yu speak wen spoke to. Now go.'

They crawled into the narrow tunnel. Anne raised a hand and found clammy stone only inches above her head. 'I can't breathe,' she whispered.

'Yes, you can, Anson,' said John. 'Count to three and breathe, then three again and let it out.'

They eased their way around a bend, and daylight was lost. They crawled, grateful now for the rope that joined them. 'Is he still behind us?' George whispered to John. The question was relayed down the line. They stopped. Listened. 'No,' said Noah at last. 'We're alone.'

'Christ,' muttered Jack, 'that means it's a trap.'

'And there's not even the room to turn round,' said George.

'We can back out.'

'What for? They'll have blocked it at the river end.'

'There's not enough air,' said Anne. 'I know there's not enough air.'

In the dark, Mark Read's voice again, so familiar. 'We all go on. If even one of us stops, that's it.'

They moved on, inching through pools of stale water, searching for any threshold in the stone. They came to a slope. A widening. A bend. A ledge. Another bend. A fissure of light. They pressed their fingers to it. They shouted through it. Then they pushed on again into the darkness while bat wings fluttered between them like palpitations in the blood.

'Rise.' A single word out of nowhere, and two lean legs blocking George's path.

They struggled like the lame to their feet and discovered space in which to straighten, a draught of fresh air to breathe. They were standing in a long, dim chamber with their captor once more. The starched white of his priest's collar was bright in the shadows. They waited for his command, but he only folded his hands behind his back and lowered his head.

Her voice, when it came, was as slow and deep as distant thunder. 'Yea, come ta Nanny.'

No one moved.

'Yu. Yu wit de breasts of a fat boy, come.'

Their guard cut the rope and nodded at the stranger they knew as Mark. She stepped warily forward and followed him across the chamber. Halfway there, she beheld Queen Nanny, seated on a vast stone, under a small hole of light. She was tall, even when seated, and powerfully built. At her breast, she cradled an infant. Another child bounced on her outstretched leg, gripping the hem of her black petticoat like a rein.

'Stand tall,' Nanny ordered.

She straightened her back and pushed out her chest.

'Yu called what?'

A hesitant pause. Then, 'Mary Read.'

'Yu dugs are little.'

She nodded.

'Yu goose-pimples are greater dan yu paps, but no mind.' She breathed in deeply and exhaled. 'Yu bring me a ship o four hundred, stiff in de water wit de weight o so many dead.'

'Aye.'

'But one babe is lost. No one leave till he is found. Because yu are de only she, I ask yu: where is dis child?'

'I don't know.' A black wave rising, a weight dropping out of her hands.

'Tell Nanny.'

'I don't know.'

'Yu lie.'

'No, I—.'

'Stand straight!'

She tried to pull her shoulders into line again.

'What yu got on yu back? I see no sack o wood. I see no sack o coconut. I see no sack o hog's bone for soup. What yu got on yu back?'

She shook her head.

'Tree babies on yu back. Dat's wat I see. One white, one black, one brown. One long dead, one new dead, one may be yet ta die.' She studied Mary's frightened face. 'Where is de lost child?'

Behind her, Mary could hear the crew shuffling nervously. 'I didn't know what I was doing,' she whispered.

'I ask yu, where?'

A cloud passed over the hole of light and, for a moment, Mary disappeared even from herself. 'At the bottom of the sea.'

Queen Nanny rocked the child at her breast. She kissed the

soft spot on its head. She wiped a dribble of milk from its lips. When she spoke at last, her voice had lost its thunder. 'So he ghostbabyself cling to yu now.'

'Aye,' she breathed, 'like strangler fig.'

'Come.'

Mary took a step forward.

'Closer.' Queen Nanny passed the babe at her breast to the silent guard. Then she brushed the bouncing child off her leg like a fly from her knee. She stood and took Mary's head in her hands. 'He is de babe new dead. Who is de babe long dead? De white child on yu back.'

'I don't know.'

She massaged Mary's temples, brushed her warm palms over her cold cheeks. 'Yu own little one?'

'No.'

'He look like yu.' Queen Nanny's hands ran down the back of her neck, easing stiff muscle. 'Whose child den?'

Mary felt her throat tighten. 'My mother's.'

'Den why he sit on yu shoulders?'

'I don't know.'

'I say yu do.'

'He died in the womb.' She wanted to run. 'Curled at my back.'

'Ah. An wen yu born? Den what?'

'My mother . . .' She lowered her face. 'She brought him back to life.' Milk leaking from Nanny's breast.

'An she bury yu.'

'No one ever knew.'

'Not yu?'

'Not till I was grown.'

'What he called?'

She shaped a name on her lips.

'Louder, woman.'

'Mark. He was called Mark Read.'

'An who name yu Mary?'

'Me.' She looked up. 'Just now.'

Nanny laid her hands on her bare shoulders. 'Mary, two dead babies on yu back and one may be yet ta die. One white. One

241

black. One brown. De first is de second is de tird. An de tird is de second is de first, hear? Yu mus teach dat child ta walk or it get so heavy, it kill you.'

The stone chamber gave way to a smaller chamber, and the smaller chamber gave way to a wide doorway of stone. They emerged only yards away from the hole through which they'd crawled on their hands and knees. On the riverbank, the scene was unchanged. Queen Nanny's raft nudged the muddy bank. Children giggled at them. They'd travelled a fool's circle.

In a small clearing, Nanny unwound Jack's bloody sling and studied his wound. 'Dat'll teach yu not ta be starin at womin's bosoms, eh?' She shook her head and laughed. 'O me o my, forget de crab-face, Captain-man. Yu live.' She washed his handless arm in a bath of river water, salt and cotton-leaf juice. Then she dipped its stump in cooling molasses. 'Sweeter dan tar,' she said, 'if not so good in de rain.'

He stared at his pollarded limb.

'Yu an yu lot free ta go. Nanny scuse yu.'

Jack nodded humbly and was turning to go when she grabbed him. He thought his ear would come off in her hand.

'But if I ever – ever – find yu trying ta sell me children agin, I slit yu wit me own knife from head ta toe an I wear yu hide on cold mountain nights. Hear?'

'Aye, I hear.'

'Now leave us be.'

The Harbinger's crew drifted towards the river bank, knowing only that it would lead them eventually to shore. They were seamen, inland and lost. Anne stayed behind.

'Yu still here? Nanny say, on yu way.'

She didn't move.

'What yu after?'

She reached into her jacket and lifted the locket over her head. She'd worn it like a weight round her neck since Jack had passed it to her the night before. She'd tried, over the years, to lose it, to sell it, to sink it; to undo the force of its charm. That morning though, before the duel, she'd made up her mind: she would bury it with Jack's body on the shore of Morant Bay. 'Take this, from us,' she said. 'It's good luck.'

Nanny took the locket and chain in her hand and weighed it. 'It's not silver.' She tried to pry it open and couldn't. 'An it keeps a dark secret. What is dat secret?'

'Only that the person who wears it will never drown.'

'Who tell yu dis?'

'My nanny, a long time ago.'

'Now yu wan ta give it back ta Nanny. Why?'

'A gift to you.'

'Yu lie.'

'No. I don't like anything at my neck. It gets in my way. But it's worth a great deal.'

'I know yu don like anyting at yu neck. Funny dat. Not birth-rope or chain-rope – or hemp rope.' Nanny lowered the locket over Anne's head once more.

'What do you mean?'

'Never drown don mean never die.' She gathered up her black petticoat and started to head for the river bank. 'Now on yu way ta where yu goin.'

She stood, like an abandoned child, watching the figure of Nanny disappear through the wood and called out despite herself. But it was my name that slipped through her lips like a trip of the tongue.

By the time she caught up with the others, she was in a foul mood. For a while, the six walked along in silence, ashamed to have been taken by a group of runaway slaves – and shamed by the sight of the rafts now pushing upriver, slow with the half-dead cargo of the slaver's hold. When a woman came to, crying with the pain of sunlight in her eyes, they retreated wordlessly from the open bank to disappear in thickets of bulrush and wild cane.

Anne watched Mary, pushing through the chest-high growth ahead of her. Over the green stalks of cane, she studied the blonde of her head (pale as cornsilk), the square shoulders, the sunburned pink of her neck, and she remembered again the fine down at the nape of that neck brushing her own cheek; she remembered the salt taste of Mark's skin on her lips. She remembered stealing his hand (fine hands, not a seaman's hands at all) and pushing it under her shirt. His fingers had glanced over her warm breast. His thumb had read the rise of her nipple. *His hand, his fingers, his thumb.*

Anne was just behind her now, matching her stride, walking soundlessly along the path she cleared through the cane. (Once, Anne told herself, their swords had charged the air with the brightness of steel. Once, her breast had been pricked with the tip of Mark's blade. Her neck had been bitten by its keen edge.)

Anne got her by the waist, driving the breath from her lungs.

'What the hell are you doing?' Mary struggled against the deadlock of her arms.

'Embracing you. Holding you close. Forcing myself upon you.'

'I'm sorry. I couldn't—'

'I would have let Jack die.'

'I never asked you to.'

Anne kicked her feet out from under her and they fell, rolling over ground sticky with the juice of crushed cane. Finally, she pinned Mary under her weight. 'You – he – never had to ask.' She studied the face she knew so well. She brushed the hair out of the eyes she'd loved. And even as she remembered the softness of breasts below her own, she felt the stiff rise of manhood beneath her. 'Jesus . . .' She rolled off and stumbled to her feet.

Mary reached into her breeches and slowly pulled out a wool-wrapped, sawn-off stag's horn. She smiled.

Chapter Thirty-One

Virginia Lazarus remained one hundred and four. Sometimes, I'd put it to her and say, 'Surely by now?', but she'd only shake her head and make me regret the question. 'I wen under de sugarcanecrusher at de age o fifty-two, wen I was haf de womun I am now. Twice de womun I was mek me one hundred an four. Even an ol black womun can reckon her years, Annie-womun. Even an ol slave knows de sum o her life.'

Time was steadfast in her grass-and-mud hut. The sun set at the same hour each day. The wet season was sometimes dry and the dry season, sometimes wet. Hosea, her calico-man, would appear when we least expected with a donkey's load of unbleached cloth, and entire weeks would slip away as we concentrated on the business of whitening.

We'd steep the cotton in a solution of boiled ash. We'd lay it to dry over bushes in the bright sunlight. We'd wash it, then steep it again – wash and steep – sometimes five or six times over. Then we'd soak it in a trough of sour goat's milk, spread it in the sunlight once more, and rinse it through. At last, we'd stretch it out on the eating table. I'd wash my feet, climb up and stamp the cloth out flat, dancing alone on that tabletop while Virginia kept time below, clapping her hands and tapping her phantom feet.

Other times, it was a cart-load of cloth, block-printed and ready for dyeing. Then, the hut would fill up with the steam of Virginia's simmering pots as she coaxed the yellow out of acacia blossom, the green out of eucalyptus bark, a deep blue out of logwood chips, and crimson from the dried bodies of cochineal, plucked from the flesh of the prickly pear. I prepared the cloth, soaking it in a bath of metallic salts to encourage the dye, or brushing its detail with starch-paste to keep it in the clear. When it came to the dipping, we both hovered over the vat and watched as colour transmuted into mass; as the crude outline of the print took life. Violets bloomed against beds of black. A flock of miniature doves burst out of a washed blue sky. A windfall of bright apples surprised plain cloth. Winter never came.

So when Virginia told me she was still one hundred and four, that I'd been there with her 'no time at all, Anniewomun', I let myself believe. It was June 1719 when Anne walked down the beach away from me with her lantern swinging low in the twilight.

I settled on October. I could accept October. Four months at sea. (I said to Virginia, she'll weary of it soon.) I could not allow November or December. (She'd be twenty on the twenty-first.) I could not imagine the new year; not winter or spring on its way. I could not accept the distance of *five hundred days*. Cannot even now.

It's not as I remember it.

September 1720

That they, on the fifteenth day of September, in the year last mentioned, with force and arms upon the high sea, in a certain place about two leagues distant from Morant Bay, did piratically, feloniously, and in a hostile manner, attack, engage, and take seven certain fishing-boats; that they did make an assault upon certain fishermen, then being in corporeal fear of their lives; that they, there and then, did steal the fish and tackle, to the value of ten pounds.

Privately, it was agreed Mary Read was deceitful. Not to be trusted. Not much to look at. Bad luck. They'd had nothing but misfortune since she'd found her way into their crew. There was the squall; then the *guarda costa*; the days of fog; the wounding of the Captain; the loss of the slave cargo; humiliation at the hands of the Maroons; and now a miserable haul worth less than fifteen pounds.

George looked at Anne across the galley table. 'You're keeping quiet, Bonn. You knew about her all along.'

'I didn't, Fetherton.'

'Everyone knows you used to sniff round after her. You knew.'

'I knew as much as you did.'

'So it was Mark Read you were truly after? Is that what you're telling me?'

'I'm telling you to quit your lame-brain talk before you do yourself an injury.' She got up from the table.

'Just as I thought,' George said. 'He knew.'

'Aye,' agreed Patrick. 'Harbouring a woman. You can be keel-hauled for that.'

Anne found Mary alone in the darkness of the fo'c's'le, wide awake in her hammock. 'I thought you were on watch.'

'I thought so too, but John the Elder thought differently.'

'Where's Armand?'

'Bones has got him gutting fish on deck.'

Anne twisted the hammock's dangling rope. 'You love him.'

'Aye, improbable as we are.'

'Move over.' Anne eased herself into the hammock and rolled into the dip alongside her. 'So what will you do?'

'Go ashore at Kingston, I guess. Maybe make our way to Spanish Town.'

'We can't afford to lose you.'

'You can if I'm not allowed to take my turn at the watch or the windlass.'

'Give it time. They'll do as Jack tells them.'

'And what will he tell them? He has no use for me.'

'He *had* no use for you.'

She sighed. 'I'm the same person I was.'

'Aye, I know.'

'I must be.'

Quiet, as the hammock rocked to and fro, deep in the schooner's hull.

'You were right,' Mary said, speaking at last.

'About what?'

'What you said that day, after we made it past the *guarda costa*.' She spoke to the timbers. 'I did used to look at you.'

Anne felt a sudden pulse in one thumb and closed her fist over it.

'You were as wild as I was careful, as handsome as I was plain. I had to look. But, when I said I didn't know, it was true. I never thought.'

Anne measured her words. 'Yet I am the person I was.'

'Aye, and as you are, Mark would disappoint you. He's a coward to Fate, remember?'

Anne turned, rolling into Mary's warm side. Even so, her whisper was almost lost between them. 'Is he looking at me now?'

'He can't see you in this dark.'

Anne found Mary's hand and pressed it to her face. 'Here's my cheek. Here are my lips.'

Silence.

She had risked too much. She went rigid with shame, felt the sting of her own foolishness. But, out of the darkness, Mary's lips, tentative as a half-thought.

Anne's hand reached under her shirt. She felt a taut band of muscle give way under her palm. 'Kiss me,' she said.

Then, Mary's mouth, hard on her own. Teeth biting her lip. Fingers, light on her breast, and the press of thighs, warm even through the layers of rough cloth.

'Harbouring a woman,' Patrick said.

'Aye. Article Four,' said Noah, Chief Justice. He knotted the harness at her waist, then signalled to George, who heaved on the pulley.

She felt herself lifted up, high above deck. She waved to Jack who waved back with his lumpen arm. The crew gathered. She wished she had remembered to stitch up the hole in her crotch.

Then the plummet. The whining of the rope through the block. Jack still waving. Her mouth filling with water. Her body slamming into the ship's sharp keel. Her fingers clamouring for a grip on the crust of barnacles as they hauled her from bow to stern. She thought she'd be ripped in two.

'Anne!'

-son

'Anne!'
She opened her eyes. Could see nothing in the dark depths.
'We fell asleep.'

They climbed through the hatch into commotion. George was collapsed at the boom. John the Elder's hands were pressed to his ribs, trying to staunch the flow of blood while Bones ran for the medicine box. Armand, John said, had stabbed George with a gutting knife.

Mary found him bent double in the stern with the knife still in his hand.

'Armand. Qu'est-ce que tu as fait?'

He wouldn't look at her. 'Il disait que tu es l'amant d'Anson Bonn.'

'Et tu l'as cru?'

'Je ne sais pas.'

'Il y a un couteau dans ta main, et tu ne sais pas? Ils pourraient te fouetter quarante fois, et tu ne sais pas?'

'Alors, c'est pas vrai?'

'D'abord, dis-moi. Tu l'as cru?'

'Oui, je l'ai cru. J'ai eu peur. Je suis seulement le "net-boy".' He met her stare. 'Dis-moi que j'ai eu tort.'

'I don't want to lose you. Je ne veux pas te perdre.'

'Puis, dis-moi.'

Gently, she took the knife from his hand. Then she wrapped his fingers, still sticky with George's blood, in her own. 'Je ne peux pas dire plus que ça: je n'ai jamais aimé aucun homme que toi.'

John the Younger helped him out of his jacket and shirt. Tom and Richard tied him to the foremast. Noah took up the rope. Jack, reluctantly, gave the call. 'One.'

The rope hummed. Nine tarred tails striped his back.

'Two.' Noah aimed for the other shoulder. At the rail, Mary flinched as he found flesh.

'Say nothing,' said Anne.

'Three.'

Scored diamonds glistened across his back.

'They'll kill him.'

'Four.'

'No, Noah just wants to scare him.'

'He's scaring me.'

On the eighteenth strike, Mary saw his knees almost buckle. 'I lied to him. Partly.'

'I know.'

'How do you know?'

'He's still standing.'

The crew knew that it was losing strength. Their captain could no longer steer or fight. George Fetherton lay wounded below deck. Mark Read was an impostor. The French twins were curled up with rheumatism, and Armand's flayed back had refused to heal up under the repeated applications of lead paste. So when a single canoe bearing three men came into sight, just off shore of Poor Man's Corner, Noah decided they should seize the moment and give chase.

It was a mistake.

The three men in the pirogue had looked feasible enough to Noah from the other side of Jack's spyglass. The Negro at the back had a strong pair of arms and a good way with a paddle. The man at the front also seemed at ease on the water; he paddled in long, even strokes, even as the schooner gained on them. The third man, seated in the middle, pulled in his fishing-line somewhat inexpertly, but Noah put that down to haste. He tended to shovel the water rather than paddle it, but Noah concluded that *The Harbinger* was a schooner at any rate and in no need of paddling. Had he noticed the livid sunburn on the man's head and arms, or the large loyalist's ring on his finger, events might have taken a different turn at Poor Man's Corner that day, for here was no seaman or fisherman or pilot. Here was Godfrey Hill Esquire, regional deputy of that sprawling giant, the Board of Trade and Plantations, and, more important still, hopeful aspirant to the hand of Governor Nicholas Lawes' youngest daughter. Here was Master Godfrey Hill in his pleasure craft, ruminating on the best means to his success.

Unlike Hill himself, Sir Nicholas Lawes was not a man

susceptible to pleasure. A serious game of leap-frog in the Officers' Quarters was widely held to be his only diversion. The poet who penned the Pindaric ode, to celebrate the Governor's arrival two years before, had been happy enough to win His Excellency's reported 'forbearance'.

> Hark how the voice of joy breaks through the air.
> In pleasing strains that captivate the ear:
> Hark, 'tis the great Lawes they found!
> Echo bears the name around.
> And with great Lawes the vaulted hills rebound!

Godfrey Hill had committed it to heart lest it should ever prove opportune. He was all too aware, however, that strategy – and not poetry – would be his making.

So when he saw *The Harbinger* moving at speed towards his pirogue, and when his manservant assured him it could only be a pirate vessel, Godfrey Hill was at first loath to make for the shallows. His would-be father-in-law's most public concern was the plague of pirates that infected Jamaica's coastline; his more private fear, Godfrey knew, was that he was helpless to stop it. Hangings at Gallows Point had been less than frequent during his two years in office.

Not that Godfrey Hill entertained thoughts of sacrificing himself to the cause. He did, however, insist on exchanging paddle for spyglass as they made their getaway and, in so doing, managed to procure details of both ship and seamen aboard.

'Any closer, Noah,' warned John the Elder, 'and we'll run aground.'

'Damn him,' said Noah, visibly annoyed. 'If he's not going to paddle when we give chase, I'll not have him.'

Godfrey Hill was not meant for this story.

Noah should never have been at *The Harbinger*'s wheel to spy his canoe.

Jack should never have lost his hand and given up the wheel.

Mark Read should never have cut off that hand; it was a duel that shouldn't have happened.

And Anne should never have fallen in love with a man who wasn't meant to be.

Yet, by the time they made Port Royal, Lawes' man – a Captain Barnet – already lay in wait in a well-fitted sloop behind the Palisadoes. And Mary had promised Anne she wouldn't leave.

Chapter Thirty-Two

Thirty years before, Port Royal had been the Wickedest City in Christendom. It sat at the narrow tip of the Palisadoes Peninsula, a snaking spit of land that still shelters Kingston Harbour from the excesses of the Caribbean Sea. It was a city prone to excess. What started as a crude settlement around the base of Fort Charles grew into a city of thousands – some said six, some said eight – and people lived, all too literally, on top of one another. Buildings rose to three, five, six storeys, for the city could only grow up and not out. Rents soared accordingly, but money, it seems, was never a problem. Many a Port Royal man, it was claimed, made his home on a prostitute's belly.

For years it was a pirate haven. Spanish silver and gold was common currency. Merchants clamoured for space. Warehouses straddled the wharves, and nothing was in short supply: neither sugar nor drink nor tobacco nor meat nor fine quality cloth. Goldsmiths thrived. Strumpets wore London fashion and bought pews in the port's beleaguered churches. Taverns, rum shops and gaming houses spread like a rash – at last count, more than fifty across the city's half-mile spread – and men at sea dreamed of Port Royal.

So when the earth opened up on a clear June day in 1692 and swallowed two-thirds of the city, people started murmuring about retribution. When the sea rose up and engulfed the scene of destruction, people said it was the Lord's judgement come down on the Babylon of the West. More than two thousand died. Entire streets slipped into the sea. But survivors would claim it was the Royal Navy that spelled the end for that self-made city, for in the wake of disaster the Admiralty adopted Port Royal as its base in its war against piracy.

Under the banner of English colours, *The Harbinger* crept past the Navy dockyard. The wind was low. A sentry on each pier watched her slow progress towards Kingston Harbour. From sea, Port Royal looked quiet, almost still, as if it was a place not so much dead as fixed in a permanent attitude of surprise.

'Drop anchor,' ordered Jack. He was leaning on the rails, staring into the sea.

'What, here, sir?' From the wheel, Noah looked at the Captain like he'd lost more than a hand.

'Yes. Here. There's fresh water and food in Port Royal, the same as in Kingston, Noah. I've decided I don't want us loitering for longer than we need to.'

His crew exchanged glances.

'The last ship they're going to suspect', he explained, 'is the one that draws up under their nose. And it's not as if there's anything like a booty on board, now is there?'

'So what's our business then,' asked John the Elder, 'if anyone should enquire?'

'Sturdy gibbets, tell them. Good quality hemp rope. Suits of iron. Tell them what you like.'

There were rumblings – that he was drunk again, that they'd draw the attention of any incoming patrol ship, that it would be suicide for the lot of them. But, begrudgingly, they dropped the anchor and lowered the two boats.

'So who's going ashore?' he asked.

No one volunteered.

'Fine, I'll tell you who. Tom and Patrick, I'll see you on shore. Anson, you'll join me.'

Already he was climbing down the Jacob's ladder, with only the one hand to steady his descent and the old water-glass case clenched between his teeth.

'Right, Jack,' said Anne, paddling them away from the schooner's hull, 'so what are we doing out here?'

'Sssh,' he said. 'Listen.'

254

She lifted her paddle and strained to hear above the smack of waves on the side of their boat.

'What?'

'Can't you hear it?'

'Hear what?'

'Sssh.' A moment passed. 'There. The knell of Christ Church.'

'Don't go morbid on me, Jack.'

'Take us in closer,' he said.

'We should be following Tom and Patrick to the traders' wharves.'

'A little closer.'

She drew the boat in behind a disused Navy frigate.

'Can you hear it now? It's practically below us.'

And, for a moment, she thought she did hear the slow peal of a single church bell, pulled by the current.

'It's a graveyard down there,' murmured Jack, more to himself than to her.

Below her, she could make out the watery shapes of the sunken city: red-tiled roofs atop walls that stood, seemingly intact; a crooked church tower; a grounded sloop's twin masts; and what looked like a string of washing between the upper windows of two houses. She took up the paddle again and steered them in still closer to shore, pulling the boat into the shallows. In the distance, they could see the quarterdeck of Fort Charles. Ahead of them, a group of young sailors idled on a pier. She reached across and eased the water-glass out of Jack's hand. The leather case was warm from his grip.

'Let's have a look,' she said, 'since we're here.'

She got to her knees and peered over the boat's side. 'I can make out a sign,' she said. 'KICK-EM JENNY'S – a good name for a brothel if ever I heard one. And there's a belt buckle down there, and a spoon right below us. A ladies' hairbrush, just ahead, over that way – a snuff box too, I think. And a cutlass sticking out of that sand bar. Have a look for yourself. It's all just lying there.'

He shook his head.

'Go on, Jack. You wanted to see.'

'No. I didn't.'

'So what did you want then? A quiet word?'

He took up the paddle as if he'd row them away. 'Mary Read stays, I hear.'

'Aye. She can raise a sail as well as ever.'

'You ought to know, I suppose.'

Anne pressed the water-glass to her eye and searched for him in the blurred shape across from her. She could make out the black of his wig, and the tarred stump of his arm.

'I've told you, it doesn't work on the air.'

'No, it doesn't. So tell me. Why are we out here?'

'I want to give up the ship.'

'You don't want to captain her any more?'

'No, I want us – the two of us – to settle ashore. Kingston, or Spanish Town maybe. I want us to slip away. When we don't come back, they won't hang about, not here. They'll load the supplies and be safely gone. Noah will captain the ship.'

'No, Jack.'

'They won't wait. I've made sure of that by dropping anchor here.'

'What I mean is, no, I don't want to settle. I don't want to settle – with you, Jack.'

He looked away, changed the subject. 'Over there. In the surf.'

She turned and saw it too. A gold watch, bobbing in the tide. She dug the paddle into the sand below. Jack steadied it, and she climbed over the boat's side and into the waves.

He watched her wade into shore. When a wave rolled over her head, he stumbled to his feet, but she returned to the boat, up to her neck in water, and with watch in hand. 'It's only brass and it's stopped of course, but someone might be able to mend it.' She passed it to him and clambered back over the side.

He squinted for the date on its back: 1686. 'Six years before the city went under.' He turned it face up. 'Seventeen minutes to twelve.'

'Which is when everything stopped.'

'Everything. Yet, only the night before, somebody was winding this watch dutifully, some time between swilling out his mouth and kicking off his slippers.'

'So?'

'So, we're not going anywhere, Anne. Don't you see that?' He drew his arm far back and flung the watch back into the sea.

'What did you do that for?'

'Never mind.' He passed her the paddle. 'Tom and Patrick will be wondering where we got to.'

The Short Tale of Louis Galdey, or the Man Who Was Born Twice
By the time they pulled into dock, Tom and Patrick had already sold the stolen haul of fish.

'We got ten pounds for it, sir.'

Jack emptied his pockets. 'Take this then. It's the last dribble of our Spanish spoil. See what you can get with the lot of it, then load up the boats and get back to the ship.' He turned and started to go.

'And where are you going, Captain?' Anne asked.

'I'll make my own way back.'

'That's not what I asked, sir.'

'No. That's what I said, Anson.'

She followed him through the winding streets, a path which seemed comfortably familiar to him. Yet, as she passed fruit sellers and sailors, missionaries and slaves, she thought for the first time that Jack looked out of place; incongruous somehow in his feather-trimmed tricorn and his grand wig.

'Jack!'

He didn't turn around.

She followed him up a hill and into a tavern.

'Ah,' he said, seeing her at last. 'I thought you'd find me here.'

'You wanted me to follow you.'

'A gentleman never presumes.'

'It's not going to work, Jack. I've said they're not to go without us. I said, we're on our way.'

'And we are. I only wanted a last drink,' he said. 'I didn't expect our slim resources to stretch to barrels of ale.'

He took a seat on a corner bench, next to an old man who didn't so much as blink to acknowledge him.

'Anson Bonn, meet Louis Galdey. Louis has mostly lived on this bench since the Day of Judgement in 1692.'

'It must have been awful,' she offered.

He looked at her, stony-faced, then looked away again.

'Louis was walking along Lime Street at the time in a lazy rank of French refugees. They were heading for the fort, to do some re-pointing work on its west curtain wall, when Louis felt the need to relieve himself. So, as the group turned on to Cannon Street, he hung back for a moment – didn't you, Louis? – which is when the first shock came, and he found himself sliding deep into the earth along with the rest of Lime Street. He was buried alive. All over town, there was a terrible population of heads and straggling legs sticking out just above ground level, but Louis was swallowed whole.'

'Jack, he doesn't want to hear all this again.'

'His ears and throat were choked with earth. His nostrils were full of it too, and, as he struggled to hold the remaining air in his lungs, it occurred to him that he was suffocating, that this was to be the way he died. Not a bone in his body was broken. His head was not concussed. So he had a full minute or more to realize the weight of earth upon his chest – on his eyelids even – and to wait for the collapse of his lungs.

'It didn't happen. The second shock came within the minute, spewing him up out of the earth and casting him into the incoming wave. It was a moving wall of water. Had he been able to swim, it would have been useless. He went under, dragged down by an irresistible undertow, helpless as a piece of driftwood. The breath he'd regained in his flight from the earth was failing him. His mouth and nose filled with water. It was seeping into his lungs, yet he couldn't draw air to cough. He could feel such a pressure on his chest, he thought his ribcage was breaking, and once again he found himself waiting – thinking. More afraid of the dying than the death.

'But, like all waves, this one sank back, taking Louis out to sea. He landed unconscious on a sand bar, and was picked up by a passing fisherman from Hellshire Point and miraculously restored to life.'

'That was lucky,' said Anne, awkwardly. The old man still hadn't moved a muscle in his face.

'That's what everyone said. He was lucky. Blessed. Redeemed.

Chosen. Afterwards, he was famous in these parts. People were calling him the Man Who Was Born Twice.'

'Aye, I can see why.'

'Years ago now, he gave up telling them different.'

'Why would he? Why did you, Louis?'

'He always said they'd got it wrong. He'd not been born twice. The truth was, he'd died twice.'

'But he didn't die. That's just it. He's here, now.'

'Is he?' He looked at the old man. 'Well, are you, Louis? Louis? I'm asking you a question.'

'Leave him alone, Jack.'

'The pity of the human faculty, Anne, is this: knowing of one's own death – I mean, being able to ponder it, to sweat at the thought of it, to dream it – is death itself.'

She looked at the jar in his hand. He hadn't touched his drink. Ale spilled over the brim. His hand was shaking.

She steadied it with one of her own. 'Don't die, Jack,' she whispered. 'Don't die. Do you hear me?'

On the way back down to the waterfront, she took his hand and led him into a broken-down building that seemed once to have been a rum shop. A few bottles still sat on a shelf. Smashed glass covered the floor. A nest of wasps colonized a corner eave.

She took off his hat.

'Don't do this, Anne.'

She eased him out of his coat, pulling it gently away from his damaged arm. 'Don't do what?'

'Pity me.'

Her hands paused midway down the line of shirt buttons. 'It's only you pitying yourself. Where is the man who could charm the tiniest fern, the least of all living things?'

'He didn't charm you.'

'He didn't have to. It was never his charm I liked.'

'What did you like then?'

'That over-ripe tomato he first tempted me to bite a long time ago. That ludicrous love-apple.'

He pressed her to him.

*

259

Three smells mingled in the air as they walked back to the wharf. There was the tang of the saltwater breeze blowing in off the sea – she noticed it on shore in a way she never did at sea. There was the faint salt smell of semen still spilling down her thighs, clinging to her fingers. And, now and then, she caught a whiff of the salt marshes at Gallows Point, for the breeze was blowing out of the north, and the day was a hot one.

Chapter Thirty-Three

In the five hours it had taken for *The Harbinger*'s crew to drop anchor, load new provisions, and turn the schooner around again, no sentry had so much as hailed them. No patrol ship, coming or going, had demanded to know the nature of their business, or by what means they had purchased supplies. No harbour master had boarded the vessel to inspect the log book.

'It's odd,' said Jack, on deck once more, studying the dockyard through his spyglass.

'It's only as you said, Captain,' said John the Younger. 'Sitting here as we are, we seem to have nothing to hide. No one's interested.'

'Aye,' said Jack, still squinting, 'that must be it.'

Captain Jonathan Barnet had first come to the Governor's attention in the pages of a popular medical tract entitled, *Fortitude of Body, Fortitude of Soul: A Medical Enquiry into the Conditions of Life at Sea, with Particular Attention Paid to the Melodramatic Lives and Times of Hitherto Unknown Salty Seafarers of His Majesty's Fleet*. What had chiefly impressed Sir Nicholas was not the drama of Captain Barnet's life or the fortitude of his soul, but the unyielding brevity of his entry: 'a known and experienced stout, brisk man, of Jamaican waters'.

Anchored behind a crook of the Palisadoes Peninsula, Barnet's sloop did not fly the Navy's colours, nor did his thirty men wear the requisite uniform. To all eyes, HMS *Sea Hound* looked like any one of a number of small merchant ships that regularly made its way in and out of Kingston Harbour. Yet Captain Barnet himself was unlike most captains – naval or merchant – of his day. While publicly he knew his duty, privately he regretted his commission. Increasingly, it seemed to him, the shape of the world was changing. No longer were the continents of the earth surrounded by the vastness of water, but rather the seas of the globe were ever more circumscribed by land. Seamen – admirals and pirates alike – were now subject to planters' interests.

Nevertheless, when Barnet spied *The Harbinger*'s sails gliding out of the Admiralty anchorage and moving towards Fort Clarence, he did not hesitate.

The Harbinger pushed south-west, past Wreck Point and Old Harbour Bay, hugging the coastline in search of possible recruits.

'Where are we going, Jack?' Anne found him at the prow, watching each new wave spill from the figurehead's empty mouth.

'Ask me how far we'll get today, by sunset,' he said. 'I can answer that one.'

She didn't tell him that in the galley there was talk; that some of his crew were murmuring that he was unfit; that they wanted a vote. She only said, 'When we find more men, everything will be all right. We'll be able to plan again.'

'Maybe so.'

'We're all tired. The crew's had too much time on their hands.'

'Aye, it's true.'

That they, in the seventh year of the reign of our said Lord the King, did feloniously and wickedly consult and agree together to take all such persons, namely, subjects living in peace and amity with His said Majesty, which they should meet with on land or high sea; and in execution of their evil designs, afterwards (to wit) on the third day of October, in the year last mentioned, did, in a hostile manner, mount an assault upon two cattle-herds on the shore of Rocky Point, who having escaped into the encroaching woodland, did suffer two of their stock to be stolen and slaughtered, and their livelihood to be thereby diminished.

As the evening of the third drew in and the anchor was dropped for the night, Jack lit up the poop deck with half a dozen lanterns and summoned his crew from the galley. 'I want everyone up here, Bones too.'

His men gathered, as instructed, on deck. Tom and Patrick stood sulkily with arms folded. George, who had recovered sufficiently to be carried up to deck, muttered something to one of the French fishermen, who looked suspiciously at Jack. Armand, still bare-backed with the pain of his wounds, shivered in the open air.

'Right,' he said. 'We're all restless. I know that and you know that. It does little good us sitting in the galley bemoaning our plight over noggins of small beer. So, I am proposing, at the risk of being hissed off my own ship, an interlude. An entertainment.'

'Such as?' demanded Patrick.

'Such as a good yarn,' he ventured. 'Or some dramatic farce.'

'Like a mock-trial, you mean,' added George pointedly.

'Aye, like a mock-trial, in the style of the Admiralty Court, let's say. Why not? Noah, I give you the Judge's wig – my own linen handkerchief. Please remember, if ever our paths should cross again, that it was me who dressed your bald patch when it was without. And for the Judge's robes, what?'

'That piece of sailcloth will suit me fine,' Noah offered.

'A circumspect choice. Now, the Bailiff. Is there a bailiff among us? Come on. Inside every pirate is a law-abiding citizen waiting to get out. Who will be the Bailiff?'

Jack waited. 'Patrick?' Patrick shook his head.

'Does he get a stave?' asked John the Younger. 'I'm not doing it without a prop.'

Jack passed him a handspike. 'Next, a speaking role. Attorney-General of the Court. Thank you, Anson. And to play opposite, Counsel for the Defence, naturally a non-speaking role. Armand, it was made for you. Now, that much sought-after role, the hangman. Yes, I knew I could count on you, George. Here's the rope. I'll trust you to make your own noose. Finally, we need three criminals. I accuse Bones.'

'What is the charge, sirrah?' Noah enquired.

'The murder, your Lordship, of those steaks we ate tonight.'

'There is a case,' admitted the Judge. 'Who else stands at the bar?'

'Mary Read,' suggested John the Elder.

'On what grounds?' asked Noah.

'I thought that was obvious. Fraud.'

Mary looked uneasily to Anne, who winked at her.

'There is a case,' Noah judged, and he hit the rail with a rope mallet. 'And the final defendant?'

'Captain Jack Rackham.' George's words hung on the air like a dare.

'What is the charge?' asked Noah.

'There is no need to try me, sir,' said Jack, interrupting, 'for I confess to the wearing of calico underwear.'

'What is the charge?' Noah repeated.

George faced Noah. 'The charge, your Lordship, that the Captain is not in charge.'

For a moment, the crew shuffled awkwardly on deck. Even Noah seemed lost for words. Then Jack offered his wrists to be tied – difficult, given he was missing one hand – and smiled. 'You heard the man, Your Lordship. I stand accused.'

Act One

[Prisoners led out, unfettered, but sensitive to the point of Bailiff's stave/handspike. Bones the Cook trembles with credibility; Mary Read seems to shift balls in her breeches; and Captain Jack Rackham appears with head hanging low. Bailiff boots Bones in the backside, landing him first up at the rail/bar.]

ATTORNEY-GENERAL: An't please your Lordship, and you gentlemen of the jury, here is a fellow before you that is a sad dog, a sad, sad dog, and one that should be put out of his misery forthwith. He has committed piracy on the high seas, and we shall prove, an't please m'lud, that this fellow has escaped a thousand storms, nay, has even escaped the over-reaching grasp of the Don; yet, not having the fear of hanging before his eyes, went on robbing and ravishing man, woman, child, and it must be said, two cows, as well as plundering ships' cargoes fore and aft, burning and sinking ship, bark and boat, as if the Devil was in him. But this is not all, m'lud. He has committed worse villainies than all these, for we shall prove that he has been guilty of murdering healthy sides of beef, and your Lordship knows, that never was there a greasy Cook who was not slippery.

[Prisoner shakes his head, panic-stricken.]

JUDGE: Does his Counsel have aught to say in his defence?

COUNSEL: *Qu'est-ce qui se passe?* I do not understand.

ATTORNEY-GENERAL: Nor does anyone, m'lud. This man's wickedness defies all rational understanding.

JUDGE: Heark'ee me, sirrah, you lousy, pitiful, ill-looked dog. What have you to say why you should not be strung up immediately and set a sun-drying like a scarecrow?

PRISONER: Noah, let me go.

JUDGE: Hear me, sirrah, hear me. You must suffer for three reasons: first, because it is not fit I should sit here as Judge, and nobody be hanged. Secondly, you must be hanged because you have a damned hanging look. And thirdly, you must be hanged because I have laid a wager that you will be hanged, and no one would wish to see an honest man out of pocket.

[Hangman lassoes Prisoner.]

Act Two

[Bailiff offers Mary Read his arm, escorting her to the rail/bar all the while making vulgar gestures with stave/handspike. As they near the bar/rail, Attorney-General sticks out foot and trips Prisoner.]

ATTORNEY-GENERAL: An't please m'lud, here before you is a woman who is sorely fallen, a degenerate abuser of the virtue of Womanhood and a fraudulent impersonator of Adam, God's chosen child. Here stands – lies – she who could not accept the single rib which was her due. Here is a spinster with the audacity of two square shoulders! A damsel with the hubris of a flat chest! A vixen with an unnatural knack for tying a reef-knot! And here, m'lud, I must give pause to warn the gentlemen of the Jury that the exhibit to which I now direct their gaze is indeed the height of feminine transgression. (Attorney-General reaches into Prisoner's breeches and withdraws male organ/sawn-off stag horn. Gasps from the Jury.) Aye, gentlemen: a boastful six inches and perpetually . . . at the ready; reason enough for this Court to urge Your Lordship to decorate the said female with a necklace of hemp!

JUDGE (blinking): Counsel?

COUNSEL (to Prisoner): *Qu'est ce qu'ils m'attendent à dire?*

JUDGE: Silence! This court will not tolerate conspiracy between Counsel and Criminal. Heark'ee, wench, for maid though thou wast made to be, maid thou art no longer, having shared not only the same hammock, but the same pair of breeches with a man these several months past. Can you deny it?

PRISONER: I can, Your Lordship, but I do not.

ATTORNEY-GENERAL: Brazen, m'lud! I say, brazen!

JUDGE: Sustained. Mary Read, I convict you, not only on the aforesaid charge of fraudulence, but also for the more serious offence of daring to speak the truth!

ATTORNEY-GENERAL: She will hang then, m'lud?

JUDGE: Nay, you chuckle-headed pup! She will be detained at His Majesty's pleasure to bugger me later in my chambers.

Act Three

JUDGE: Enter the Prisoner.

[Captain Jack Rackham whispers something in Bailiff's ear.]

BAILIFF: The Prisoner has asked me to report, m'lud, that he wishes to enter but may not.

ATTORNEY-GENERAL: A ruse, m'lud! A ruse!

JUDGE: Will the Bailiff tell the Court why he may not enter?

BAILIFF: The Captain informs me, Your Lordship, that he is a man at sea, and therefore unavailable for trial.

JUDGE: You will inform the Prisoner that it is for this Court to decide whether he is or is not at sea, and that, accordingly, it is none of his concern. He will therefore enter as instructed.

[Bailiff shrugs his shoulder in the way of apology to Prisoner.]

ATTORNEY-GENERAL: An't please Your Lordship, here is a wretched case, a sorry example to sea-dogs everywhere.

[Bailiff barks.]

JUDGE: Overruled.

ATTORNEY-GENERAL: M'lud, cast your eye upon this wastrel of the lowest order. Here is a Captain who cannot command the natural elements – a man who gets wet in the rain, who is blind in the fog, a man whose vessel moves to the wind, and not the other way round. Here is a captain who cannot divine the evil workings of the Don, who cannot predict the furtive movements of the *guarda costa*! Here is a captain so undone in mind and spirit that he would sooner press a man into service alive than force him to work with a musket hole in his chest!

HANGMAN: Ballocks! Here is a man, more like, who almost drives his ship on to a reef to ground her in a storm! Who 'retires' below deck when his crew are to be shot to Kingdom Come. Who would sell slaves to Negroes. Who would slurp the dregs of a rum barrel to get a drink. Who's one hand short of a grip on the here and now. Here's a man who's lost his nerve!

Noah removed the handkerchief from his head and dropped the sailcloth from his shoulders. 'Perhaps, Captain, it would be for the best if we let a vote settle it.'

Jack nodded. 'I'll be in the galley.'

They voted him out, with a majority of five. Anson Bonn, John the Elder, John the Younger, the ever quiet Richard Corner and even Mary Read (who was permitted a vote) said 'Aye' to keeping him. George Fetherton, Tom Earl, Patrick Carty, the six Frenchmen (including Armand) and, surprisingly, Bones voted 'Nay'. Noah abstained.

It was agreed he would be permitted to remain a member of the crew. It was agreed that, if ever another ship was taken, he would be allowed to take it and any crew wishing to serve under him. There was some disagreement over whether he was owed any recompense from future revenues for the loss of his hand, as was Council policy. In the end, it was decided not.

Anne went below to tell him.

'I know,' he said, as she entered the galley. 'It's all right.'

There were no further dramas that month, on board or off – only a stealthy ten days spent careening the ship's keel in a nameless cove, and a chance encounter with a single woman they surprised in a canoe, just off coast of Great Padre Bluff.

Noah gave the wheel to Anne and shouted down to her. 'It's a bit rough just here for a pirogue, Madam. Shall we tow you back into the bay?'

'No,' she said. 'I thank you but it will not be necessary.

Indeed, it would be regrettable. I am collecting marine specimens, you see.' She gestured to a mess of barnacles and seashrimp in the bottom of her canoe. 'I am searching the bluff for that phylum of aquatic life which is dearest to my heart.'

'Why is that, madam?' queried Noah in a neighbourly way.

'The pursuit of knowledge, I suppose. The quest for revelation in the whorl of a sea-snail's shell. You may not know this, sir, but the common mollusc is an inspiring example of those seemingly unmarriable qualities, sensibility and survival.'

'I'll be,' said Noah. 'Barnacles too?'

She nodded solemnly. 'Barnacles too.'

Anne passed the wheel to John the Younger and drew up behind Noah. The new Captain continued to make small talk with the woman in the canoe, but Anne had already ceased to hear anything either was saying. She heard only the familiar seriousness of the voice. She registered only the woman's approximate age. She recognized only the accent – Irish, south coast, she was sure – and the slight but irrefutable wobbling of the woman's double chin.

Thomasina Manley. Her father's true daughter. Her half-sister. She was sure.

She had seen her for the first time on her seventh birthday, in the Great Hall, on the day she was breeched; on that nightmare day when she discovered she wasn't real.

'We must stop her, Captain,' she said, as if in a dream.

Noah turned to her, bewildered.

'She'll guess,' she heard herself saying. 'She's dangerous.'

'Keep your voice down, Anson,' said Noah, angrily.

'What's the matter?' demanded the woman below them. 'Who are you?'

'Do something, Noah.'

'I said, who are you?'

'Noah!'

'Quiet, lad! That's an order.'

'She'll tell, she'll tell someone.'

Again, the woman's voice from below. 'Tell what?' A long moment. 'I said, tell what?' Then she turned in her canoe and grabbed the paddle.

'Noah, for God's sake, she's getting away. She's going to report us!'

'Aye, Anson,' shouted Noah, 'you've bloody well seen to that!'

Below them, the woman was trying to make a desperate escape. Her strokes were awkward. In her hurry, she kept hitting the side of the canoe. A net of dripping barnacles, balanced across the canoe's rim, slid overboard.

Anne reached for the pistol at her hip. It wasn't there. 'Fire, Noah! You must fire.'

The woman looked over her shoulder, her eyes huge, then drove her paddle into a wave.

Noah seized Anne by the arm, so hard she felt it wrench in its socket. 'I'll not do anything of the kind, lad. Do you hear me? I'll not do anything of the kind.'

They watched her go, following her progress until she finally turned the wide corner of Great Padre Bluff.

Only once did she turn round to stare, she would later explain – at the sight of the terrifying young pirate who had spoken with the familiar lilt of her own West County Cork.

Chapter Thirty-Four

Captain Barnet's *Sea Hound* shadowed *The Harbinger* from less than a league behind, dropping anchor when the schooner dropped anchor; lying in wait in a neighbouring cove when her crew careened her keel. A month had passed, and still he had espied no suggestion of pirate activity aboard the vessel, and little that was otherwise worthy of note in his ship's log – only the headless skeleton of a cow rolling in the current near Rocky Point, and a lone woman in a pirogue, paddling with a vengeance for Great Padre Bay. When his look-out had hailed her, startling the quiet of the coast, she had turned round once, only to push on, faster still.

In the sparse comfort of his cabin, sipping stewed coffee and chewing on sticky handfuls of damp dried figs, Captain Barnet decided *The Harbinger* was no more a pirate craft than his own. Its crew was not big enough and its direction was unlikely; there were few trading vessels to be had on this bit of coast, apart from the logwood boats coming out of Black River, and already two such boats had sailed past the schooner, untouched. Winding his watch before sleep, Jonathan Barnet concluded that the case against *The Harbinger*'s crew was nothing more than Godfrey Hill's hopeful invention. He'd give it another day, then make for port.

That they, in the aforesaid pirate schooner, on the fourth day of November, in the year last mentioned, with force and arms upon the high sea, in a certain place about half a league distant of Bluefields Bay, and within the jurisdiction of this Court, did set upon, board, and enter a certain trading sloop whereof Thomas Dillon was Master; and then and there, did storm its hold and assail its crew in the peace of God and of our said now Lord the King, then being in corporeal fear of their lives.

The Unhappy Tale of Thomas Dillon

Thomas Dillon had never been a lucky man. As a young flax-spinner, he had left his native England to work as an indentured servant on a Jamaican cotton plantation, only to discover after his requisite five years of work that his papers were lost and his master was senile. Five years of labour stretched to six, and still his master ranted that he'd set the authorities on him if he tried to 'escape' the bond that was his due.

Being a young man, he made an escape and, being a young man, he was apprehended shortly thereafter. He would have been sentenced to hang had his old master not intervened, testifying he would set the lad to purposeful work on his plantation once more, and so Thomas Dillon went from indentured servitude to out-and-out slavery.

After three more years, however, he had an idea; he smuggled himself out, substituting the length of his body for the wooden bolt in a ream of unbleached cotton, and suddenly the future, once more, seemed a prospect. He was transported by donkey cart to the coast. He was loaded into a ship's hold. He was discovered as a stowaway, pressed into service aboard, and found to be quite a natural at sea.

When the crew was arrested for piracy, he would have been sentenced yet again to hang had his late master's son, seeing the banns for the trial, not remembered the name of Thomas Dillon, and decided the former hand could yet be of use to his estate. He pleaded Dillon's case with 'Christian compassion' (according to a local postmaster), moving Governor Lawes to pardon the 'miscreant'. For a time, the master's family had been suffering inordinate losses to the middlemen of the sea, ships' masters who charged insupportable sums for the transport of fabrics to Kingston Harbour and Montego Bay. Once more, Thomas Dillon was pressed into service, outfitted this time with a run-down sloop and a meagre crew, and reminded of the sentence on his head should he stray from the designated trade routes.

When his crew mutinied and forced him to steer the ship into hiding along the peaceable south-west coast, he was not altogether displeased. When they were set upon by the first band of pirates, who carried away the entire cargo and most of the provisions, he tried to comfort himself with his sudden freedom from cotton: from calico and huckaback; from the bleached and the unbleached; from the glazed and the stiffened. But when his crew fell prey to the second band of pirates, he sat down on his binnacle box and buried his head in his hands.

'The hold's empty, sir!' shouted Patrick Carty from down below.

'And the galley too, Noah!' called John the Younger. 'There's a few barrels of punch and some salt pork, but little else.'

'Just tell me what I need to know,' said Noah, 'and we'll leave you be. Where's your cargo, sir?'

Already three of Dillon's six men had up and joined the pirate crew. He shook his head. 'I have no cargo.'

'A cargo ship without a cargo is an unusual thing,' said Noah, patiently. 'Have you offloaded it on shore perhaps? I'm told your hold is taking on water.'

'It is,' he said, morosely. 'Worm-rot.'

'Well, take heart,' coaxed Noah, 'we're not interested in the vessel. She's not worth the towing. However, the cargo and, I might add, the barrels of punch would not go amiss.'

'Lost,' he said.

'Lost where?'

'To pirates.' He looked up. 'Not three days ago.'

'The devils.' Noah kicked the binnacle box.

As promised though, he summoned his crew and left the man in peace.

So when Thomas Dillon's despondent sloop drifted out to sea on the prevailing winds, it was with Jonathan Barnet's vessel that it nearly collided. Later, over stewed coffee and sticky figs, Captain Barnet would hear everything: how *The Harbinger*'s pirate crew hadn't actually injured ship or body; how they hadn't forced three men into their service; how the Captain had threatened nobody; and how they had made away with nothing but three barrels of cheap rum punch.

Barnet struggled with a bit of fig in a back tooth. The punch would have to serve.

*

At *The Harbinger*'s wheel, Anne was badgering Noah. 'We've got three new men. That's crew enough to see us back to New Providence.'

'See sense, lad. A crew will not be pardoned twice.'

'Cuba then.'

'It's no less Spanish now, Anson, than when we left.'

'Hispaniola.'

'To what end?'

'She's reported us, Noah. I know she has.'

'I expect you're right, but I would also expect that her message has only just reached Port Royal; that it is, perhaps, a little thin on nautical detail, though she may have got you right enough; and that some commander somewhere is likely wondering whether we are worth the effort. He'll know that we're at least a coastline – and several schooners – away.'

'But—'

'We'll see who else we can find in the way of crew, and then think again. In the future, though, I'll ask you to bear in mind that there are better ways of impressing women. If it happens again, lad, I'll quickly decide you're a risk not worth taking. Do you take my point?'

'Aye.'

'Then we'll say no more about it.'

There was plenty that Anne didn't say. She didn't tell Noah how the sight of her half-sister had turned her bowels to water, or how a childish fear possessed her still, clouding her mind. She couldn't say that, for a moment that morning, she had mistaken the sudden outcrop of Negril Point for the Old Head of Kinsale, seeing its stony Day-of-Judgement face there under the Jamaican sky; or how she had, the night before, crept half-asleep into Mary Read's hammock and laid her head on the dream of my shoulder.

It was later that morning though, at the ship's prow, that she heard a call so faint, so distant, she almost lost it to the roll of the surf. *Disembark . . . Daughter . . . shall then . . . retrieve you.* She found herself lifting one foot to a gunport; then the other. She got hold of the gunwale with both hands and leaned into the wind. She felt for the shape of the locket under her shirt, flat

273

against her breastbone. The muscles in her calves were taut. She was poised on the tips of her boots, unable to move, when the canoe came into view.

Ten men paddling at speed. All the crew they needed.

Her shout cleared her head. 'Fine on the larboard bow!'

But it came too late. By the time her call was relayed down the decks and Noah had yelled for more sail, the canoe was already landed. The ten men stood on the beach, studying the schooner from a safe distance.

'Too late,' said Noah. Jack had joined him at the wheel. 'They were too fast.'

'And too wary,' said Jack, eyeing them up through the spyglass. 'Draw in as close as you dare, Captain.'

'If they were interested in joining us, Jack,' said Noah, frustrated, 'they'd not have fled for shore. There's no hope of pressing them into work. They nearly outnumber us.'

'They're young and able-bodied,' he said, still behind the spyglass. 'Draw in a little closer, Noah. What harm can it do?'

Noah nodded to John the Elder. 'We'll tack towards shore.'

The beach was luminous in the midday sun. The ten, most of them bare-footed, shifted uncomfortably on the sand's white heat.

Jack yelled from *The Harbinger*'s prow. 'We're English!'

No one yelled back.

'Turtlers, are you?'

Still no reply.

He noticed the beached canoe. 'A good-sized canoe you've got there! Pretty sea-worthy too, from the look of it.'

A few turned to go, heading up the beach.

'Did one of you carve it?'

A man with a head of ginger hair and a pair of powerful shoulders turned round begrudgingly. 'I did.' He looked at his mates. 'As you're so interested though, we'll trade you it for the schooner.' He nudged his friend in the ribs.

'It's silk-cotton wood, am I right?'

'So?'

'The Devil's tree, some say. Natives in these parts never built vessels with it. Said the devil-wood canoe would always come to a bad end.'

'What are you getting at?'

'Only this: I'm offering each of you a place with this vessel's crew and a chance to make your way on the high sea.'

'Bloody pirates. We thought as much.'

'That's right. Bloody pirates. And if you'd rather be governed by laws that rich men have made for their own profit, that's up to you.'

There was some discussion on the beach.

'Everyone knows the Navy's cracking down on pirates,' said the ginger-haired man.

'And what do you think that really means?'

He looked blank.

Jack leaned on the rails, teasing out the moment. 'It means they're desperate. It means they can't find pirates to hang. We dropped anchor in the Admiralty's own waters, and no one was any the wiser.'

'All the same—'

'Join us on board over a bowl of punch, at least. We're getting tired of our own company.'

They hesitated.

'We've three barrels of the stuff and all day to drink it.'

'And how do we know it isn't a trap?'

Jack smiled broadly. 'You don't.'

There was more muttering on the beach, then the ten carried the canoe back down to the water's edge and launched it.

Noah gave the order to haul in the sails. He watched as the length of the anchor's cable slipped free of the windlass. He heaved with the others to ensure the hook was grounded and reminded them to take up the slack. He tied the ship's wheel. He checked the sail pins. He released the watch from duty, just for the day. Finally, he called for a barrel, and not a bowl, to be heaved on to deck, and he nodded to John the Younger, who tossed the Jacob's ladder over the side. The ginger-haired man moored the canoe to the schooner, and the ten climbed up to deck, cutlasses swinging at their sides.

Noah wasn't pleased. 'You'll have no need for weapons. One of my men will store them below deck for you.'

'We'll disarm when your crew does,' insisted a boy with an angry birthmark across his cheek.

Jack spoke before Noah could. 'Personally, I can't manage a cutlass and a mug of punch at the same time.' He displayed his stump and grinned. 'But when forced to choose, I know where my loyalties lie.' He withdrew his cutlass and threw it on to deck.

A smile got the better of Noah. He dropped his sword, then his pistol. The others followed suit. Tom and one of the new men from Dillon's ship, Jim Dobbins, carried the load below deck.

By the time they reached the bottom of the first barrel of punch, Jack was convinced that he and the ginger-haired man, both originally of Massachusetts, were distantly related on his mother's side, and was weeping. Across the deck, Noah – his bald head blushing with the effect of drink – was teaching three of the younger men to dance the quadrille, having amiably agreed to dance the woman's steps himself. Mary was happy with her stag's horn, pissing over the ship's side with a few of the new men. John the Younger had passed out. Bones had ventured out of the galley. But Anne was still not herself, and the punch had only worsened her mood. She climbed into one of the ship's boats and disappeared under sailcloth.

By the time they reached the dregs of the second barrel, several of both crews had fallen asleep on deck in the late afternoon sunshine. Others who could swim were jumping naked from the stern into the shock of cool water. Back at the bow, Bones had tried twice that afternoon to drown himself in the punch barrel. Mary and Armand had disappeared below deck. Noah was confessing to Jack that he'd never wanted to be anything more than an ordinary seaman, and Jack confessed to Noah that he was in love.

As the third barrel was heaved up through the main hatch, Jack stumbled off in search of Anne. Noah fell asleep against the ship's wheel. Two of the canoe's determined crew prised the new barrel open. George Fetherton was arguing with one of them, and somebody else was yelling, even louder, from the stern where the men had been jumping overboard; the skinny fellow who was called Tim hadn't come up again.

Three or four who were still on their feet gathered, drunk and frightened, at the poop rail, searching the limpid water below.

The one with the birthmarked face had raised the alarm. 'He's gone under the hull. He must be under the hull.'

'He could be anywhere,' said Tom. 'How long since he went under?'

'Three, four minutes, I don't know.'

His brother was crying. 'We jumped on the count of three. I thought he'd made it back first.'

Jack had joined them at the rail. 'Christ.' But he wasn't looking with dread at the water below; he was staring out to sea. A white flash of sail had appeared off Negril Point.

'Weigh anchor!' he yelled at their stunned faces. 'Now!' He turned and ran, stumbling up the deck, kicking men awake. 'Damn it, get up and set those sails!' Then he fell against the boards and vomited over the deck.

Noah was coming to. 'What in God's name . . .'

'Don't even think about it!' Jack shouted, oblivious to Noah's confusion. A few of the turtlers were gathered by the ladder, about to clamber down. He straightened, steered himself their way, hauled up the ladder, and untied the rope that moored their canoe. 'Now set those fucking sails.'

One of them started to scramble over the rails.

Jack got him by the neck and pulled him backwards; he crashed on to the planking. 'Take orders, the lot of you!'

'Jack!' Noah tried, his gaze now fixed on the approaching sloop. 'We don't know it's Navy.'

'Will we wait to find out, Captain?'

Noah untied the wheel and took up Jack's call. 'Spread canvas! Fore and aft!'

Bodies came haltingly to life. Blood pumped with fear. Oaths were flying. Hands and feet slipped in the rigging, and somewhere the brother of the drowned man was moaning for him.

Anne awoke in the ship's boat, dazed by the noise, and crawled out into mayhem. Before she could so much as take in the scene, she was rolling. Under the press of so much sail, the schooner's lee rails had dipped under the surf. Her head hit the boards as a wave crashed over the deck.

Struggling to her feet, she hauled herself windward and saw Barnet's sloop for the first time, giving chase and gaining on them. Sea-foam leaped from its bowsprit, a host of carronades lined its decks, and its sails blazed white under the twilight sky.

Anne's first thought was not of doom or of panic; it was a flicker of memory. Of something small. Of a sugar galleon with a flutter of sails and a rank of carronades, each no bigger than her thumb. Of three white masts lost in the tilting vastness of the Great Hall that day. For the first time in her twenty years, she felt resigned.

She would have slipped quietly below deck to wait – for the crack of the first strike or the jangle of grappling irons – had she not glimpsed Mary in the rigging overhead, her face as pale as the underside of a leaf in a storm.

She let the hatch door fall shut.

When *The Sea Hound* came within hailing distance, Captain Barnet shouted from her bow. 'What ship are you and what's your business?'

Everyone looked to Noah at the wheel. 'Go down below,' he told them, 'and collect your weapons. I want all the powder and shot you can muster.' As his men stumbled through the main hatch, still groggy with punch, he refused to answer the call. Instead, his lips started moving to the memory of sea ports. One-time destinations. Thriving communities that had disappeared at sea in the ravelled skein of coastline. They came slowly at first. *Bristol. Boscastle. Vigo. Lisbon.*

Barnet shouted again.

Trepassey, Long Island, Charleston, Cape Fear, Nassau, Cumana, Porto Bello . . . Cities, settlements – some only guessed at in a harbour's fog – gathered into a furious prayer in his mouth as he watched the sloop's bowsprit slide past his stern; as *The Harbinger*'s hull shuddered on contact with *The Sea Hound*'s gunwales.

A cutlass and pistol landed at his feet. He bent down wearily to collect them. All around him, boots were drumming the planking and, already, men were spilling over his rails. Bile, sour with rum, rose to his mouth. A few feet away, somebody was sliding through a tide of punch. He couldn't see who. He couldn't focus, not in this light. Something was rolling like thunder towards him. He squinted. The third rum barrel. He would have hidden inside if its girth could have taken him. In a moment – confused and breathless – he would stop his blade just short of John the Younger's back.

In the bow, Jack couldn't grab the pistol at his hip for fear of dropping his cutlass, but already his arm was trembling, unused to the weight of iron in his left hand. His opponent saw it too, and Jack's awkward manoeuvres gave way to frenzy. He slashed the air between them, hopeful only of keeping his enemy at bay. When he felt the tip of a blade skim his cheek, he thrust his boot up and unbalanced the man. Then he kicked – ribs, back, groin, head – like he was kicking Death itself, until the body under his boot jerked to a stillness, and he ran.

At starboard, Mary was yelling at Armand from across the deck, pleading with him to go below, when she felt the cold bore of a pistol press against the nape of her neck. 'Drop your weapon.'

She did as she was told.

He was reaching for the pistol at her hip when the sudden force of his weight sent her crashing to deck. For a moment, she struggled for life under him until, quietly, unaccountably, he rolled off her and on to his back – his spine skewed on the shaft of Anne's dirk.

The two of them held that end of deck, back against back, armed with swords, pistols and whatever else they, or Armand, could lay their hands on: handspikes, boarding axes, rope mallets, deadeyes. It wasn't until the lanterns were lit on the enemy sloop that they saw.

Most of their own had fled.

Anne darted to the nearest hatchway, nearly tripping over the body of the ginger-haired turtler. When she threw the door back, all was quiet below. 'For Christ's sake, we're under attack up here! Jack?' she peered into the darkness. 'Noah? George?' A nervous hush. She jumped through the hatch, and saw them, scattered through the fo'c's'le and galley, too ashamed to speak. Tom Earl was bleeding over the galley table. John the Elder was being sick in a corner. Jack was crouching at the bottom of the ladder. She stared at him.

'I can't – hold – a ruddy sword.' His chest was heaving. 'I can't even load a god-damned pistol.'

Overhead, Mary was yelling for her.

'We need you up there, Jack. I need you, now.'

'Stay here,' he said, reaching for her. 'Stay with me.'

She turned on the ladder and scrambled back up to deck, pausing only to shout a final time. 'Is anyone coming?'

Silence.

She fired her pistol into the darkness, then let the door crash shut.

Later that evening, Jonathan Barnet would note in his log that the action had been brief, the end having come within forty minutes of *The Sea Hound* clapping on; that seven good men had been lost and four of the alleged pirate crew; that mortalities had been mercifully few because surrender had come early, with the crew's unexpected retreat; that few of *The Harbinger*'s number had persisted with any notable show of force. (He turned a page and entered two names with care. His fingers, he fretted, were growing stiff these days.) There had been a minor incident as the prisoners were transferred to *The Sea Hound*, but the details were not pertinent to the record.

The water was as black as the sky by the time *The Harbinger*'s crew had been coralled in her stern. Over the murmur of panic on deck and the slapping of waves below, still a voice in the vortex of Anne's ear.

Daughter, we cannot see you for the night . . .

She felt for the locket between her breasts.

Somebody with a watch in his hand was demanding her name.

'Sorry?'

'Your name.'

It was on the tip of her tongue. When she jumped, hurdling

the rail, her only thought was of escape – of the flight through air, of the weightlessness of her body in water.

When her jacket grew heavier than lead, she panicked. When the struggle of her limbs failed to keep her afloat, her shout filled with water. Between waves, she glimpsed Mary's eyes in the lantern light above, searching for her without seeing her, and she knew she was drowning, after all.

She stopped struggling, finally. Old words lulled her in the dark.

> *Dada is riding,*
> *Mama is biding,*
> *Baby is hiding*
> *at the bottom*
> *of the*
> *wishing well.*

Jack's arm came like a choker round her neck. He pulled her, gasping, out of the black, hauling her into the night air with a violence that threatened to crush her windpipe, even as he yelled at her to breathe. Her lungs heaved. She retched salt water. A wave went over their heads and she twisted in his grasp, climbing up his arms, his shoulders, his head, greedy for air.

He dragged her, finally, on to his chest. He held her in the crook of his handless arm as he back-paddled them to the side of the schooner. He got her feet on to the ladder. He wrapped her fingers around the ropes. He made her climb, one rung at a time, supporting her trembling legs with his own.

Concluding his entry, Jonathan Barnet noted the pertinent discovery of one derelict punch barrel on the fugitive vessel's upper deck, with markings matching those described by the aforementioned ('See 4 November') Thomas Dillon, Master.

Chapter Thirty-Five

Virginia Lazarus said to me, 'When yu go?'

'Tomorrow.' I was standing in her doorway, watching the bats in the angel-trumpet tree.

'Wit de calico-man.'

'Aye. He goes back by way of the shore.'

'She not dere.'

'She might be.'

'Doin what? Yu tell me dat.'

I folded my arms across my chest.

'Yu hopin she wit she nogoodman in she nogoodleanto agin?'

'No.'

'Yu hopin she mek de acquaintance o de hangin Gov'nor agin?'

'No.'

'Den may be yu hopin dat Jack be Gov'nor o Providence by now and yu girl, Firs' Fancywoman. May be yu tink yu bump inta dem one day on a Sabbit-day saunter. Is dat it, Anniewomun?'

I held my tongue.

'Fine, yu go, yu go wit de calico-man, an when yu cum back an find me dead in me bamboo chair, yu mus pardon me when I don get up. A womun's only got so much miracle inside her.'

She gave me her hand, and I took it.

On shore, nothing was familiar. The beach had disappeared under a waterfront's rank of wharves. Merchantmen crowded the harbour. The luggers and the coasters, the cutters and the tubs, the skiffs and the smacks were gone. I stumbled into a hubbub of trade, past a garrison patrol, and searched for landmarks I couldn't find.

The Brunty brothers' hammocks were gone, palm trees and all; a warehouse had swallowed their former site. I found the Admiral's flag-pole – a code of military colours now flew stridently from its summit – but not the Admiral. There was no sign of Salt Beef Peg's washing line, or of Peg, or of her several offspring. Nor had I any hope of finding Unconscionable Nan; preachers on the wharves were damning the few strumpets who still dared solicit in the great outdoors.

In the distance, on the hilltop, the Hermit Governor's ramshackle fort had been transformed into a provincial stronghold, while the old population of outcasts and renegades had been purged to make way for the new citizens of the island's capital. Nassau, as locals now knew the town, was a place I'd never been.

At the far end of the shore, a fallen-down shingled wall marked the spot where I guessed our lean-to had been. I hauled it into the shade and sat down, feeling my age.

Half a sea away, outside the town Court House, the Crier of St Jago de la Vega was ringing his bell.

He had a touch of catarrh that day: blocked ears, a phlegmy throat, rheum in the nasal passages. 'All manner of persons that can inform this honourable Court, now sitting, of any piracies, felonies or robberies, committed in or upon the sea, or in any haven, creek or place—' He reached for the tiny pouch of ginger in his pocket and inhaled, deep into his sinuses '—or elsewhere in the West Indies by those—' A profound sneeze '—by those whose names shall follow, let them come forth, and they shall be heard. Hear now the names of those who stand accused. Believed to be lately of Providence: Noah Harwood, John Davies, John Howell, Patrick Carty, John Rackham, Anson Bonn, George Fetherton, Mark Read, William Boniface. Lately of Hispaniola: Pierre Cornelian, Jean Cornelian, Gilbert Robicheaud, Simon Timard, and Armand Leblanc, mulatto. Lately of Jamaica: James Dobbins, Thomas Bourn, alias Brown, and John Fenwick, alias Fenis.'

Hucksters shut down their stalls on the square. An entire punch house emptied. Women passed their baskets to children and sat them down to wait on the steps of St James'. A stream of people poured through the Court House doors and spilled into the gallery at the back.

His Excellency Sir Nicholas Lawes, President of the Court, entered, took his solemn oath and assumed the bench.

The Bailiff led the prisoners into Court and set them before the bar.

The twelve Commissioners took their seats.

The Registrar then addressed the Court. 'Articles exhibited at a Court of Admiralty, held at the town of St Jago de la Vega on the island of Jamaica, the sixteenth day of November, in the seventh year of the reign of our Sovereign Lord George, for the trying, hearing, determining, and adjudging of piracies, felonies and robberies upon the high sea.' He looked up from his document and stared at *The Harbinger*'s accused. Powder from his wig made a gentle snowfall on his shoulders. 'Let it be known that as Registrar of this Court, I am duly appointed and sworn against one Noah Harwood, late of the town of Philadelphia in the province of Pennsylvania, Mariner and late Master or Commander of a certain pirate schooner, *The Harbinger*; also against one George Fetherton, one John Davies, one John Rackham, one Patrick Carty—'

'Your Excellency, a word, please.' Jack had raised his tarred arm.

Sir Nicholas looked up, surprised. 'Sirrah, this Court cannot indulge interruption in its procedure. You will be asked to enter your plea in due course.'

'There is an error in your records, sir.'

'I must clarify for the Court,' Lawes intoned, 'that the information before us has been faithfully gathered by one Captain Jonathan Barnet on behalf of His Majesty's Admiralty.'

'Noah Harwood is cited as ship's Master, sir.'

The crew raised their heads.

'Indeed. The testimonies of Captain Barnet, one Thomas Dillon and of some eight turtlers – who are, I note here, to be separately tried – identify Harwood as master. Please explain, for the benefit of this Court, sir, this apparently universal confusion.'

'Noah was not master, Your Excellency. He was helmsman. After my injury, I was unable to take the wheel.'

'You are suggesting, sir, that you were captain?'

'I am informing the Court that I was.'

'I see, and do any of your crew remember otherwise? Speak now, prisoners at the bar, if any one of you was given to believe, understand, or generally entertain the notion that Noah Harwood was, latterly, your captain.'

Jack eyed Noah. Noah looked at the floor.

Nobody spoke.

'Fine. The Court will understand that Jack Rackham, late of the province of . . .' He consulted his notes '. . . of Massachusetts, was commander of the said pirate schooner.'

'Your Excellency?'

'Rackham, you are forestalling the business of this Court.'

'I hope to spare you needless effort, sir.'

'Save your confession. The law states that you and your crew have the right to a trial.'

'There are individuals at the bar, sir, who have no place in these proceedings. The men of Hispaniola, for example, were pressed into service aboard our vessel; Armand Leblanc has the whip marks on his back to prove it. They hardly speak a dozen words of English between them. And William Boniface, sir, was only the ship's cook. He scarcely showed his face on deck.'

Nicholas Lawes sat back on the bench. 'Are you quite finished?'

'No, sir. It is, I believe, in the interests of this Court to know that two other prisoners at the bar have been mistaken for crew.'

'Jack, no!' Anne felt the blood drain from her cheeks.

Lawes stared at her. 'Any further outbursts from any prisoner, and the said man shall be removed from the Court and convicted without a trial.'

In the gallery, the crowd pressed in closer. Somewhere, a baby was crying.

'Now, Captain Rackham, finish your wild claim and let us be

done with it. Which members of your crew here assembled are so suddenly not members of your crew?'

Titters from the crowd.

'Mark Read and—' He turned to Anne. She stared at him, her arms clenched behind her. 'And Anson Bonn.'

'Please explain to the Court, Rackham, precisely how these two men came to be with your crew and yet not with your crew.'

Confusion was spreading down the line of men at the bar.

'You will answer my question, Rackham. Why do you now assert that these two men are not crew?'

'Because, Your Excellency . . .' Jack saw the anticipation on the faces in the gallery. He saw Anne, head bowed, body braced. 'Because, sir, they are both women.'

Clamour in the gallery and confusion at the bench brought the Court to an unscheduled recess.

Neither the substance of Jack's claim nor the avowal of each woman could be admitted, in the end, by the Court's Registrar. There could, he explained to Sir Nicholas, be motives at play, dissembling strategies that aimed to undo the business at hand. Certainly, the more he studied the shapes of these two individuals who now stood before them in the presidential chamber, the more equivocal the situation seemed to become. Sir Nicholas was inclined to agree.

In the end, the Governor's own physician was summoned to bear witness. The two senior officials judiciously removed themselves from the chambers to await professional opinion, while the Bailiff was asked to avert his eyes.

In the gallery, people were laying bets.

At the trial's resumption, Dr Simmons would, under oath, testify to 'the fact of breasts, which were very white, in the case of each of the persons in question'. Over the crowd's ballyhoo, the Governor would order a separate trial for 'one Anne Bonny, alias Anson Bonn, and one Mary Read, alias Mark Read'. And later, in the darkness of the lock-up, Anne would lay her head on Mary's lap and cry.

*

The Harbinger's crew were, that same day, convicted on three charges of piracy and sentenced to hang.

In his closing speech, Sir Nicholas acknowledged the aforesaid acts of piracy might be alleged to be petty by some – 'to wit, the theft of fishing tackle and catch, of two cows, of three barrels of punch' – but it had been clearly established that this crew's piratical activity would not have stopped there. Indeed, recent additions to their seafaring number would have, most certainly, augmented the evil of their designs. Furthermore, it had been established that several among them had already been pardoned by virtue of His Majesty's grace on the island of Providence, little more than two years ago. If a man would return to his wrongdoing 'like a dog to its vomit', what hope could he have of mercy? Finally, Lawes concluded, there was no such thing as 'petty piracy'. 'It is', he insisted, 'a flagrant contradiction in terms.' He paused to work a cramp out of his leg. 'However . . .'

The prisoners at the bar looked up.

'However, as a compassionate gesture to the perhaps undeserving, this Court has agreed to release the following men: Pierre and Jean Cornelian, Simon Timard, Gilbert Robicheaud, Armand Leblanc, and William Boniface. There is a condition, that is to say that the Frenchmen must return forthwith to Hispaniola, and the ship's cook to New Providence. That understood, you are free to go in the peace of God and our said Lord, the King.'

Bones held fast to the bar, unable to move.

A few more words were spoken. Then the Bailiff nodded, and the crew filed wordlessly past. Jack, the last to fall into line, replaced his tricorn, with care, before crossing the floor.

The Bailiff – who had not averted his eyes – was partial to Anne, which was fortunate. As the sole occupants of the women's cell, she and Mary found they were not mistreated. He was generous with the rations, supplementing their bread, mash and small beer with titbits of his wife's own cooking. He was persuaded to lend them a lantern (what hazard could it pose to a building made of stone?) and to keep them in wicks and fish oil. And when townspeople appeared wanting a glimpse of the pair of 'sea amazons' – 'One breast or two, Bailiff?' – he turned them away.

Two. White and sweet of shape, with nipples like sunbursts.

When Anne asked for ten minutes alone with Jack Rackham, the convicted Captain, the Bailiff hesitated. It was not within his power to say yes, but he could not bring himself to say no.

He led her, after dark, to the men's lock-up and shut her in a cell that stank of urine.

'What's this about?' she asked. 'I thought—'

'Ssssh.' He looked over his shoulder, then pointed to an iron grating in the corner; it allowed air to pass between that cell and the neighbouring one. 'Ten minutes,' he said.

She got down on the earthen floor, and whispered through the grating. 'Jack? Jack, it's me.' She slid her wrist through two bent bars and grasped at the dark. 'Are you in there?'

'Aye.' Fingers closed round hers. 'Where else?'

'The Bailiff let me in. Do you have company in there?'

'No. The Navy recognizes rank, you see.' His voice was leaden.

'I don't know what to say, Jack.'

'Now that I'm about to hang, you mean.'

'Now that we're both about to hang.'

He pressed his face to the grating. 'Lawes ordered a separate trial. You two will get off with a prison sentence.'

'Why should we? The charges will be the same. My friend the Bailiff has said as much. The witnesses will be the same. The sentences will have to be the same. The Governor only feared that the sensation of Mary and me might hamper the business of your convictions.'

'Tell them I forced you aboard at New Providence.'

'They know I can handle a sword and pistol, Jack. Barnet's entire crew have made that much clear. I killed one of their men and wounded at least four others. There's not a lot I can say.'

'God, Anne, I wish you were still with that skulking, son-of-a-bitch husband of yours. I wish you'd never laid eyes on me.'

'You don't, Jack. Forget the speeches. There isn't the time.'

He squeezed her hand, lowered his cheek to her palm. 'Tom and Richard are better off already dead.'

'No, Jack, we're still alive. We're alive *now*.'

His voice dropped to a whisper. 'I'm scared, Anne, and I'm scared of being scared. At the hanging.'

'You'll bluff with the best of them.'

'Not this time. I've not had a lot of call for gallows humour in my time. I know the one about the pirate and the priest.' His voice turned falsely merry. 'What did the pirate confess to the gallows priest?'

'Stop it, Jack.'

'"Forgive me, Father, for I was caught." What did the pirate say to the Devil? "Sorry I'm late. I came at breakneck speed."'

'I said stop it.'

'You take my point.'

'We have minutes, Jack. Minutes.'

'Do you remember that day in Port Royal? The two of us.'

'Of course I do,' she said impatiently.

'I wanted us to quit the ship and settle down somewhere.'

'I know you did.'

He was playing a silent game of 'One Little Piggy' on her fingers. 'It wouldn't have worked, us under some palm tree together, would it?'

'No.' Her eyes were stinging. 'You knew as much before you asked that day.'

'And you knew you couldn't swim before you jumped that night. I wonder which one of us took the greater risk.'

She curled her hand into a small fist in his palm. 'I love you, Jack. I do.'

He pretended not to hear. 'You didn't drown. I'm glad – thankful – for that.'

'It was down to you.'

'But . . .'

'But what?'

'Say it, Anne. For me, say it.'

'Say what? Say what, for God's sake?'

'Say that if I hadn't cowered below deck, we might not be here now.'

'It's not true, and I won't waste time talking about it.'

'Say it. I don't want it going round in my head when the hood drops over my eyes.'

Her free hand started sweeping a mound of loose earth back

and forth beside her knee. 'The crew shouldn't have voted you out, you know. It wasn't fair.'

'Say, "If you'd fought like a man, Jack, you wouldn't be hanging like a dog."'

'You did right by Noah in Court though, even if they're going to hang him anyway.' Her face was wet. 'You did right by him, Jack.'

'Please, Anne.'

She wiped her sleeve across her nose. She pushed the hair out of her face. 'If you'd fought like a man . . .'

'If I'd fought like a man, what?'

'If you'd fought like a man . . .' She clenched his fingers in hers '. . . you wouldn't be hanging like a dog.'

They sat until the silence was broken by the over-earnest jangling of keys.

Chapter Thirty-Six

Less than a week later, the Bailiff opened the door of the women's cell to find Mary vomiting in the corner.

'She's not well,' said Anne.

'I can see that.' He hovered awkwardly at the entrance. 'It's not surprising, mind you.'

Monday, November the 28th, 1720
Court met according to Adjournment
Court called, by making Proclamation Three Several Times
His Excellency, Sir Nicholas Lawes, Knight, Presiding

The gallery was full. The Court House steps were full. Crowds jostled at the windows while the more able-bodied had climbed scaffolding that had been left in place for roof repairs. In the square, someone was selling 'genuine pieces of the sea-maids' apparel': tarred trous, cow-horn cod-pieces, pearly-buttoned fear-nought jackets.

Inside, all went quiet as the Registrar rose from his seat. 'Enter the prisoners, Anne Bonny, alias Anson Bonn, and Mary Read, alias Mark Read, late of the Island of Providence, spinsters.' The two women followed the Bailiff across the Court to the bar, their heads lowered. Each wore an ill-fitting skirt and bodice. The lapel of Mary's jacket was stained with vomit.

'Articles exhibited at a High Court of Admiralty, held at the town of St Jago de la Vega, the twenty-eighth day of November, in the seventh year of the reign of our Sovereign Lord George for the trying, hearing, determining and adjudging of piracies, felonies and robberies committed within the jurisdiction of His Majesty's Admiralty. Hearken now, Anne Bonny and Mary Read, to the articles that are laid against you.'

They did not need to listen. The twelve Commissioners did not need to listen. The crowd in the gallery did not need to listen. The substance of those articles was already well known in St Jago and beyond.

Seven fishermen's tackle and a netful of flying fish.

Two beef cows.

Three barrels of cheap rum punch.

'Anne Bonny and Mary Read, what have you to say?'

Anne looked at Mary, pleadingly. Mary shook her head.

The Registrar was impatient. 'If you have anything to say, you must say it now.'

Neither spoke.

Governor Lawes tried. 'You would be wise to bear in mind the Court's view of your particular cases. We are specifically concerned by the charge levied against you, and all it entails. We are, however, more generally troubled by the apparent duplicitousness of your daily conduct. Will you explain?'

Sir Nicholas waited. The twelve Commissioners waited. The people of St Jago waited.

'Anne Bonny?'

'I'm a married woman,' Anne tried.

'Not a spinster then?'

'No. I've a husband in New Providence.'

'And why are you not with this husband now?'

'I had to leave.' She looked to the Commissioners. 'He wouldn't do a day's work.'

Guffaws from the crowd.

Sir Nicholas leaned forward. 'If every wife with a lazy husband were to leave that man, and every man with a nagging wife were to leave that woman, where would that leave us?'

'I don't know, sir,' said Anne, despondent.

'My point exactly, Mrs Bonny. It would leave us *confused*. Mary Read, please tell the Court, are you similarly confused?'

'I am not married, your Excellency, if that's what you mean.'

A much-quoted reply with the crowd. Even a Commissioner suppressed a smile.

'Would it be fair to say that you know your own mind?'

'It would be.'

'Please tell the Court then, do you recognize this as a Court of law?'

'I remain hopeful, sir.'

'But doubtful.'

She said nothing.

'You think we are rigid, inflexible perhaps.'

'I will suspend judgement, sir.'

'This "judge" thanks you, Miss Read, and he will endeavour to prove his pliancy. What if I were to say to you, for example, that the choice of justice is yours? What if I were to offer you a sentence based on the time-honoured tenets of English law – or the fate that lies, let us say, in a riddle's answer? What would you say?'

The Registrar sat up. 'Your Excellency—'

'I would say, what is your riddle, sir?'

'You choose a riddle, then, over the law?'

'I choose to hear it. I might not choose to answer it.'

Sir Nicholas smiled. 'Or find yourself able to do so. The riddle is this: "I am a room within a room within a room. What am I?"'

The gallery went quiet. Mary looked to Anne, then back to the Governor. She met his eye. 'I don't like your riddle much, sir.'

'No?'

'I don't like what it hides.'

'It is ironic, Miss Read, that you should object to concealment, as you and your friend seem to be so very good at it. Your deceptions, I understand, came as a surprise even to your own crew.'

'I would argue, sir, that concealment is not the same as deception.'

'And I will tell you, Miss Read, that the two are one and the same. Distinctions, unfortunately, do not come easily to you.'

'Distinctions, sir?'

'Yes, distinctions: between truth and untruth, between the natural and the unnatural, between man and woman.'

The Registrar reasserted himself. 'The plea, Sir Nicholas. We must have the plea.'

'Then get it, man.'

The Registrar turned to the accused. 'You have heard the charge laid against you. Are you guilty, or not guilty, as charged?'

First Anne, then Mary. 'Not guilty.'

Chatter broke out between a large family at the gallery rails, but the Registrar wasn't finished. 'Your Excellency, I now call four witnesses to give evidence.'

Sir Nicholas nodded.

'I call Jean and Pierre Cornelian to be duly sworn in and examined by you, the President of this Court.'

The two men appeared at the Bailiff's door and sheepishly crossed the Court. An interpreter followed, who translated the oath, before taking it himself.

'Mr and Mr Cornelian,' began Sir Nicholas, 'you are recently freed men and, as such, you understand the urgent role of the Court in establishing the facts of any given case. We have before us two women who stand accused of piracy and all that it implies: robbery, assault, lawlessness. It is, perhaps, difficult for many of us to see the pirates for the women. Tell us, if you will, what you remember of *Mark Read* and *Anson Bonn* on board the pirate schooner.'

The interpreter listened patiently, then turned to Sir Nicholas. 'We remember them well. We were not so many, you see, and it was these two, among others, that forced us aboard their ship off Hispaniola.'

'Did they seem to you to be detained by force?'

The two men gesticulated as they spoke, glancing once at the two accused. 'No, they seemed to be there of their own free will. They seemed content.'

'Did you actually observe them engaged in piratical activity?'

'Yes, a few times, though there were failed attempts. Most recently, they boarded a small trading sloop—'

'For the record,' interrupted the Registrar, 'they refer to the sloop of the aforementioned Thomas Dillon.'

'Yes, they threatened its crew with swords and pistols.'

'Did it ever occur to you that they might, in fact, be women?'

'Never,' said John Cornelian.

'Not once,' replied his brother.

Sir Nicholas motioned to them to step down, then nodded to the Registrar. 'Call in your next witness.'

'Your Excellency, I call Thomas Dillon, Master.'

'Please describe, for the benefit of this Court, Captain Dillon, the events of November the fourth, as you remember them.'

Never in his twenty-eight years had Thomas Dillon imagined that he would be lucky enough to be on this side of the bar. He spoke, almost, with force. 'My sloop was, on that day, lying at anchor, sir, in Bluefields Bay. It was still early morning when two of my men spotted a strange schooner coming into the bay, sir. They thought little of it until, without warning, she fired in the direction of our vessel. The rest of my crew and I immediately climbed to deck. There was a hearty exchange of gunfire, sir, and we held our own, it must be said. But they were drawing ever closer, and something had to be done. When distance permitted, I boldly hailed them, sir, suspecting the worst. One of them, by the name of Harwood, yelled to me what I had feared all along: they were English pirates, he said. He also said, not very persuasively, sir, as you can imagine, that we need not be afraid; they were interested only in new recruits and the ship's cargo. My men and I defended the sloop like any crew would, but they boarded at last.'

'And when they did?'

'It was all pirates' talk, sir, but three of my men fell for it, I regret to say, and now are to die for it.'

'And the cargo?'

'Well, there wasn't any to speak of, was there?'

'For the record,' interrupted the Registrar, 'Captain Dillon's cargo was carried away by another group of pirates only three days before.'

The crowd enjoyed this aside.

Sir Nicholas ignored the disruption. 'Captain Dillon, do you recall the individuals who stand accused at the bar?'

'I do, sir.'

'Despite the petticoats.'

'Despite the petticoats, your Excellency.'

'Continue.'

'They both boarded my sloop with maybe six men, and they were very profligate indeed, sir, if I dare say so, cursing and swearing with the best of them, and very willing and ready to do anything at hand. One of them – the one called Anne – had a pistol in her hand, and I had no doubt but that she knew how to use it, though it would be true to say, sir, that I had no inkling that she was a she all the while.'

'Thank you, Captain Dillon. You may depart the Court, but please remain outside. Registrar, you will call your fourth and final witness.'

'Your Excellency, I call . . .' He checked his record. 'I call Miss Thomas.'

A side door opened and the woman from the pirogue appeared, crossing the Court in measured steps. Anne saw her nod politely to the Commissioners as she passed their bench. She saw her smooth her woollen skirt as she approached the Governor's bench. She saw the earnestness in her face as she repeated the oath, and she heard again the soft Irish lilt in her voice. It was only when the name was repeated, in full, that Anne's legs went weak.

'Miss Dorothy Thomas, you understand the nature of these proceedings?'

Anne felt for the chair behind her.

'I do, sir.'

It was not Thomasina Manley. It had never been Thomasina Manley.

'Anne Bonny, you will remain standing as instructed.' Sir Nicholas returned to the woman from the pirogue. 'Miss Thomas, your accusation, as you have been informed, does not constitute a specific article of this trial. However, I understand you offer your testimony to corroborate the evidence supporting the charge of piracy.'

'I do, sir.'

'Then describe to the Court your encounter with the said pirate schooner on the day of October the twenty-third.'

She turned to the Commissioners. 'I was in my pirogue, gentlemen, alone as is my habit, just off coast of Great Padre

Bluff. I am a devotee of the natural sciences, you see, and was, on this day, scavenging for molluscs – barnacles, sea-snails, shrimp, *et cetera* – creatures which I have studied avidly for some months now. All was quiet that afternoon until the said schooner came into view, and a mariner hailed me from the stern. He enquired, with seeming solicitude, whether my pirogue was sufficiently sea-worthy and whether I was perhaps in need of a tow. I thanked him, but declined, explaining the nature of my pursuit. He appeared interested and I elaborated, as best I could, for I am still a novice myself, it must be said. It was then that the young man joined him at the rails—'

'Can you identify that young man in this Court, Miss Thomas?'

'I can. He – she – stands at the bar now, with the dark hair.'

'Please continue.'

'The young man joined him at the rails and seemed, un-accountably, to take against the very sight of me.'

'Was there a dispute between the two men?'

'Indeed there was.'

'And was it intelligible to you?'

'Intelligible, yes. Comprehensible, no. I was, according to the young man, to be stopped, for what reason I could not fathom. I tried to right the confusion, and then it emerged: he wanted "to stop me" to prevent me coming against them afterwards. It was then, sir, that I realized I was in the company of pirates.'

'What did you understand by the young man's desire "to stop you"?'

'At first, I hardly knew myself. I knew only that I had to get away as quickly as my paddling would permit. I had only just cleared the stern, however, when I heard the young man yell at the other man to draw his pistol.'

'Did this man draw?'

'No, I believe he refused to fire, as I was a woman.'

'Yet the young man had no such qualms. Did you speculate as to why?'

'I did more than speculate, your Excellency, if you will pardon the strength of my feeling. I went over that quarter of an hour again and again, and finally I remembered a single detail.

Something that would, in most circumstances, be entirely inconsequential. Yet not so here.' She stared at Anne so fixedly that Anne had to turn her face. 'When the young man first appeared, he leaned for a moment on the rail. He seemed to be listening to what I was saying without actually hearing it, if that makes sense. It was no more than a fraction of a moment, but the particular memory resurfaced later, upon recollection.'

The Governor, the Registrar, the Commissioners and the crowd waited on her words.

'He had breasts. The day was very close, even there on the water, and his jacket – which was of a very stiff cloth – and his shirt were both open at the neck, about three buttons down, I'd say. Leaning on the rail, on his arms, as he was, there was a sudden and fleeting elevation of the breasts – which I was particularly well situated to observe – and a subsequent hint of a bosom; to wit, a glimpse of cleavage where the shirt and jacket were open.'

'Thank you, Miss Thomas, for your frank deposition. Do either of the two accused wish to question this witness, or to recall either of the three previous witnesses?'

Anne's voice was almost inaudible. 'No, sir.'

'Do you have any witnesses of your own whom you wish to call?'

'No, sir.'

'You will then depart this Court, under the surveillance of the Bailiff, to await the Commissioners' verdict. The public will please clear the gallery until Court is resumed.'

The crowd held its ground. Mary gave Anne her arm. 'They're waiting for us.'

Anne started across the Court, still dazed. 'I thought she was my father's daughter. I was sure . . .'

Mary prodded her, trying to ease the moment. 'And there was me thinking you were your father's daughter.'

Anne looked up. 'What's "a room within a room within a room"?'

'It doesn't matter now.'

'Tell me.'

She pulled Anne close. 'A woman – in a box – in a grave. Keep walking.'

The eyes seemed to multiply as they passed the gallery. 'I'm going to tell them. When we come back in, I'm going to tell them.'

'The answer to the riddle, you mean.'

'You *know* what I mean.'

'So we'll draw an even bigger crowd when we're hung? No, Anne.'

The doors were open again in less than twenty minutes.

The decision, Sir Nicholas informed the Court, had been both difficult, given the unusual circumstances, and straightforward, given the established evidence. 'Our verdict was, in the end, unanimously agreed.' He did not look at Mary and Anne, but to the Bailiff, who stood just to their right. 'You Anne Bonny, alias Anson Bonn, and Mary Read, alias Mark Read, have been found guilty as charged. You are to go from hence to the place from whence you came, and from thence to the place of execution, where you shall be severally hanged by the neck, till you are severally dead. And God in His infinite Mercy be merciful to both of your souls.'

A hush – only the sound of a child playing marbles in a back corner.

'Where some would plead sympathy, we felt it our duty to remain true to the civic and the moral law of this land, for does it not say in the Holy Book, "The woman shall not wear that which pertaineth unto a man and neither shall a man put on a woman's garment; for all that do so are abomination unto the Lord thy God"?'

Some of the Commissioners were nodding.

'I must now ask if either you, Anne Bonny, or you, Mary Read, have any reason why the sentence of death should not pass upon you?'

A formality. Already, the onlookers had started to chatter softly between themselves.

'I ask you again, can you offer anything material which might mitigate the punishment you have brought upon yourselves? Mary Read.'

Her voice revealed nothing. 'No, sir.'

'Anne Bonny.'

She hesitated.

'I repeat, Anne Bonny, do you have anything material to offer?'

She raised her face slowly. 'Only our bellies, sir. We plead our bellies.'

Sir Nicholas stared, blinking, at his two accused. He turned angrily to the Registrar, and back again. He shouted at the crowd for silence and climbed down from the bench. Then he crossed the Court and stood face to face with Anne. 'You will make yourself perfectly clear, Anne Bonny.'

She spoke again, louder this time. 'We are, both of us, with child, sir.'

Chapter Thirty-Seven

The Governor's physician was summoned to Court a second time. But Dr Simmons, the Court was informed, was visiting the Navy base that afternoon, a distance of fourteen miles over land to Kingston, and three further miles by water to Port Royal. He was rumoured to be advising a local Commander on remedies for motion-sickness.

A messenger was sent. Anne and Mary were detained at the bar. Sir Nicholas withdrew angrily to his chamber. The twelve Commissioners informed the Registrar that they would be conferring at a local drinking establishment. The general public held their places.

The Court's messenger – the Registrar's own clerk – did not meet the Doctor on the road to Kingston. Nor was there any word of him at the town piers when he arrived, late in the day. Two fishermen in a skiff offered to ferry him across to Port Royal for an audacious sum. When the lad flatly refused, they told him to climb in; they'd take him over anyway.

They rowed more painstakingly than one would have thought physically possible, extracting from him, by slow degree, the unabridged account of the events that had precipitated his journey. Under duress, the lad described, in full, the Governor, the Court House, the two women pirates, the lady witness, the size of the crowd and the weather in St Jago when he'd left. Drawing up at last to the Admiralty wharf, they enquired, quite cheerfully, whether he wanted them to wait.

Arriving at the said Commander's home, the messenger was, not surprisingly, told he was too late: the Doctor had left about a quarter of an hour ago. He might catch him at the wharf.

He made it back to the waterfront just in time to see the Navy boat, with the Doctor in it, moving out of shouting distance. Meanwhile, the two fishermen still sat in the shallows, whistling with feigned nonchalance. The Registrar's clerk emptied his pockets and climbed aboard.

The skiff caught up with the Navy boat just off shore of Gallows Point, at which time the Registrar's lad bid good riddance to the two fishermen.

'A message, sir, from Governor Lawes,' he announced breathlessly.

'Just a minute.' The Doctor was staring at the scene on the Point.

'An ugly sight,' said one of the oarsmen.

Three bodies dangled in the distance.

'The one in the middle's the Captain,' said the other.

They lifted the oars out of the water, and allowed the boat to drift in towards shore.

Noah and John the Elder still hung from the gallows, swaying slightly in the stiff sea breeze. Jack's body had been stuffed into a suit of iron and was gibbeted on high.

Looking on, in the last of the afternoon's light, the four passers-by would silently observe the Captain's bare legs – the boots and stockings, the Doctor guessed, must have been stolen from the man's body. They'd notice also the dark stump of an arm squeezed against the iron brace; the gold lace cravat under the slumped chin; the fine quality of the coat; the bare, wigless head.

Doctor Simmons, however, was more interested in the small group of women who stood at the feet of the hanged men, with their little ones in their arms. He had heard tell of such practice: common women bringing their babies to gallow sites and pressing the infant foreheads to cold legs and limp hands. He looked about. There was no boat waiting to return them to Kingston; they could only have walked the seventeen-mile length of the Palisadoes, bearing their children on their backs. And why?

New life, old wives claimed, was strengthened by the touch of those stiff in the noose.

As a medical man, he disapproved. As a moral man, he was unsettled. As a frustrated anthropologist, he was compelled.

'Did you want the Governor's message yet, Doctor Simmons?'

On shore, one of the babies had started to wail. 'No, but you may give it to me anyway.'

It was the messenger's moment. 'He's sentenced the two women pirates to hang, sir.'

'He can do that without me, lad.'

'He needs to know if they're 'indisposed', sir.'

'Indisposed how?'

'Indisposed *with child*, sir.'

On shore, a woman who stood at the feet of Jack Rackham's corpse suddenly noticed the Doctor observing her from the Navy boat. She faced him and stared angrily back.

'Carry on,' he instructed, coolly.

His cheeks were burning. He felt like a thief in a church.

As the boat turned in the water, nosing itself towards Kingston, the Court's messenger saw the Doctor steal a last furtive glimpse. The woman's back was turned to them. Her arms were bare and straining under the weight of the child in her hands. High above her head, her little one was fingering the soles of Jack Rackham's feet.

The Court was adjourned until the following day. Anne and Mary were escorted back to the lock-up. They refused their plate of mash and crawled under a thin blanket.

'You shouldn't have told them.'

'We had nothing to lose, Mary.'

'And nothing to gain. Lawes will simply use your revelation to give himself extra moral leverage when he confirms our sentence tomorrow: Anne Bonny, adulterous wife; Mary Read, sinful spinster.'

'You don't know that.'

'If we were nine months pregnant and ready to drop, I'd say he might be squeamish, but, even then, we'd get a stay of execution at best. He'd have the nooses round our necks before we could so much as give suck. Nothing's changed. It's best that we realize that now.'

Anne sat up. 'You mean, it's best that I realize that now.'

'All right. It's best that you realize that now.'

'Because then I can lie down and die, like you.'

'For Christ's sake, Anne, you don't even know for sure that you're pregnant.'

'I know you are, and funnily enough your life seemed to me more important than our dignity.'

'You know that's not what I'm saying.'

'I don't know what you're saying any more.'

'I'm saying, we're going to die, Anne. *Pirates die. Freebooters get caught. Sea-thieves get strung up.* It's not news to us, is it? And it's better, in the long run, that we accept it now rather than go on pretending we can outwit the inevitable. If they didn't see fit to lighten the sentence because we're women, they're not about to lighten it because we've got ourselves pregnant.'

'You're one to talk about pretending.'

'And what does that mean?'

'It means that you're trying to pretend your fear is really foresight. You're trying to persuade me that the sentence is justice or Fate or Providence, or whatever you want to call it, but that's only because it's less terrifying to believe *that* than to hope against hope that something might change.'

'You're making our circumstances into more than they are. You've got this kind of . . . of dramatic righteousness, Anne, and it's . . .' She hesitated.

'It's what?'

'Sad. It's sad. Our situation's more ordinary than you'll ever admit. We're a nuisance to the Governor; we are not the knife-edge of some moral predicament for him. Or for the Commissioners. Or for the crowd. It'll not tax anyone's conscience if we go to the gallows pregnant. There'll even be those who'll say it's for the best that our "bad blood" goes no further.'

'What's truly sad, Mary, is that you *want* to die.'

'What are you talking about?'

'You want to die because you're afraid of that baby growing inside you. You're afraid of what Queen Nanny said.'

'I don't even remember what she said.'

'Don't you? "Three babies on your back: one long dead, one new dead, one maybe yet to die. The first is the second is the third." Whatever that means. Remember?'

Mary's voice shrank to a whisper. 'Aye. "You must teach that child to walk or it'll get so heavy, it'll kill you."'

Anne pulled the slipping blanket back over Mary's shoulder and wrapped an arm around her. 'It won't kill you, Mary. Those were just words.'

'It might.'

'No. It'll be a helpless babe all new in your arms, and all your ghosts will disappear with it.'

Speech was an effort for her. 'I sent Armand away.'

'When?'

'Last night. He came here, last night, in the middle of the night.'

'What about Lawes' ruling?'

'He didn't go back with the others. He's been lying low, with some French family near here.' She spoke to the dirt floor. 'He wanted to see me.'

'And what did he say when you told him?'

'Told him what?'

'I might as well be talking to that wall, Mary. What did he say when you told him you were pregnant, and that maybe you wouldn't hang?'

'Why would I tell him that?'

'Well, the Court's adjourned now, isn't it?'

She sighed, frustrated. 'They're just waiting for the physician to return, Anne. That's all.'

'All right, but what did he say?'

'I didn't tell him.'

'Jesus, and I thought I was stubborn. What *did* you tell him then?'

'That the Court would sentence us to hang; that I didn't want him to wait any longer in case he was caught; and that I didn't want to see him at the gallows.'

'You sent him all the way back to Hispaniola? You didn't ask him to wait even a day?'

Mary didn't answer.

'Well, did you or didn't you?'

'There was no point in him waiting.'

The following morning, the two women were conducted into the presidential chamber and examined by Dr Simmons. It was an awkward affair, on the hardwood floor behind the Governor's mahogany desk, under a portrait of his third wife. The Bailiff waited outside the door.

'Well?' said Anne, as Simmons scrubbed his hands in Sir Nicholas' wash basin.

'I'm afraid I am not at liberty to say. A full report will be made to Governor Lawes.'

The Bailiff escorted them back to the lock-up.

Mary was sick on the way, under a bloodwood tree.

At three o'clock that afternoon, the twelve Commissioners were summoned to the Court House for a private meeting with Sir Nicholas. At half-past, the Crier was again ringing his bell, proclaiming the resumption of the 'infamous case' and the impending announcement.

Stalls shut down, the punch-house emptied and children were again deposited on the steps of St James'. A crowd swelled in the Square.

When the Bailiff unlocked their cell door, Mary was standing, ashen-faced, ready to go. Anne was still sitting in the far corner, sparking a piece of flint off the stone wall.

'Come on, Anne,' he said gently, 'it's time.'

'We don't need to be there. They'll get on just fine without us.'

Mary turned to her, looking through her. 'Get up. You know the Bailiff has no say in the matter.'

'I don't want to force you, Anne. Not in your condition,' he added, supportively.

'But you'll watch them hang me, in my condition, won't you?'

'I hope not. You know I hope not.'

'Anne, get up. I want this over and done with.'

'I know you do, that's half our problem.' A spark seemed to

306

leap from her fingers. 'Maybe I'll tell them who my father is. He'll have trade connections in these parts, you know.'

'Who your father was,' corrected Mary.

'I don't know that he was killed in the war.'

'What war?' said the Bailiff, confused.

'The Indian War in Carolina, five years ago. Get up, Anne. You're the one who wanted all this. You're the one who's hopeful, remember?'

The air in the Court House that afternoon was close, and Dr Simmons' report was thankfully brief. It was addressed to Sir Nicholas, the Commissioners and the people of St Jago.

Sir Nicholas read for the benefit of the Court. '"As per my examination of Mary Read, alias Mark Read, spinster, I am able to confirm that she is quick with child. It is my professional opinion that she is in her third or fourth month and that she demonstrates the attendant signs: that is to say, cessation of the menses; a slight swelling of the abdomen which cannot be attributed to bloating; nausea; and an increased production of the facial and scalp oils. I also note here that the results of an internal examination have proved concordant with my general findings."'

Sir Nicholas paused to look at Mary, who stared at the floor. He considered, fleetingly, her poor posture; the pronounced curl of the shoulders, surprising in a woman still relatively young. Then he addressed his attention once more to the report in hand. '"As for my examination of Anne Bonny, Mrs, alias Anson Bonn, I have not found that she is with child."'

Anne wavered on her feet. Mary grabbed her hand.

Sir Nicholas huffed on his reading glass and wiped it. '"Nor have I found that she is *not* with child. It is possible that it is too early to say. My statement is, therefore, necessarily qualified. From my interview with the said woman, there would appear to have been "relations" as recently as two months ago. There are also one or two nascent physical signs which are indeed telling, if the woman is to be believed. I can only assure the Court that time will reveal all, if time she has. On this note, I conclude. Yours faithfully, Dr Northrop Simmons of St Jago de la Vega."'

307

The Governor folded the Doctor's testimonial, returned it to its envelope and leaned back on the bench. 'The people of St Jago, and indeed of Jamaica itself, will appreciate that our tradition of English law is our sacred legacy. They will also understand that it is, given our mortal predisposition towards sin, a legacy which is all too easily eroded. I would be doing every man in this land a disservice if I were to acknowledge anything less at this particular juncture.

'Mary Read and Anne Bonny have both been found guilty of piracy. As citizens of His Majesty's Kingdom, they have transgressed. As women, they have transgressed. They stand before us now, pleading this Court's mercy for the unborn lives they carry or, in the case of Anne Bonny, which they claim to carry. It is, without doubt, a sorry situation, and one which this Court must resolve as best it may.' He smoothed out some papers on his desk.

'I met latterly with the Court's twelve Commissioners, and these were the issues addressed. Firstly, if hanging is the requisite punishment which we believe it to be, would not the gift of life, in these instances, be an irrefutable reward for wickedness?'

Anne could feel Mary's hand cold in her own.

'Secondly, the death of the unborn child would be, without doubt, a tragedy. Should we not, however, similarly consider the quality of the lives that would be? What sort of lives would await the children of women convicted for piracy? Thirdly, should this Court, as an organ of the greater social good, accept ultimate responsibility for the pitiable circumstances which have arisen, or must that responsibility be laid squarely at the feet of the mothers-to-be, if only for the instruction of others?'

His rhetoric had persuaded the crowd. They were eager for judgement.

'Our decisions were thus.'

The Bailiff's knuckles were white on his stave.

'One: that the award of life in prison for Anne Bonny and Mary Read would, in this instance, be a miscarriage of justice. Two: that an unborn child cannot be sentenced for its mother's evil. Three: that the aforesaid death sentence must yet be upheld.'

Anne dropped Mary's hand, winded.

'However, in the interests of the two lives now growing helplessly within, it has been decided that a stay of execution shall apply until each woman is either delivered of child or proven to be fraudulent in her claim.' Sir Nicholas stood up. 'This Court is adjourned.'

Both women remained silent as Sir Nicholas and the twelve Commissioners filed out of the Court. Then Anne turned to Mary. 'It's happened, Mary. We've got time. Months. Anything could happen.'

Mary turned to the Bailiff. A clammy sweat clung to her forehead. 'I'm ready to go back now.'

The Court's leniency surprised everyone. In time, talk would spread, however, from the Commissioners to their wives, from their wives to their intimates, from their intimates to the public at large.

Governor Lawes, it transpired, had argued at length for a stay of execution 'for the sake of the illegitimate babes'. His own Commissioners had been taken aback by the force of his opinion and were moved by his compassion.

In later days, his wife would drop an incautious word.

Sir Nicholas, it seemed, was born the son of a staunch loyalist landholder – and a girl who'd worked in the laundry. At the age of fourteen, he'd been taken aside and discreetly informed that his mother had been good with starch.

Chapter Thirty-Eight

('Mary? Mary?')

Seventeen-twenty-one was to be a good year for Robert Baldwin, St Jago's only printer. The continued spread of local plantations had guaranteed him a cheap supply of pulp. The Governor's official support of 'the dissemination of public knowledge' was more than he'd hoped for three years ago when Lawes had arrived on the scene. And Lawes' pledge to 'rescue the illiterate from the abyss of ignorance' could only be a good thing. People were stopping in the streets of St Jago to read his banns and notices.

Court News, January 1721

Let it be known that, on the ninth of January, one Zachary Heptonstall, indentured servant, was found guilty of the theft of his master's gold-headed cane. Mr Heptonstall pleaded a lesser charge, informing the Court he'd only been after the whiskey which was secreted within the aforesaid cane and not the cane proper, but the Court was not convinced. It sentenced Mr Heptonstall to eighteen months in the lock-up, to be served after the completion of his bond.

Let it also be known that, on the eighteenth of January, eight turtlers, lately of Negril Point and not known to this parish, were sentenced to hang for aiding, abetting and generally consorting with the former crew of the notorious pirate schooner, The Harbinger.

The hearing of Hannah, domestic slave to Samuel Young of this parish, continues. The woman stands by her confession; to wit, that she is a 'ligarou', or a witch, and that she flies at night to get blood. Sir Nicholas Lawes, President of the Court, has found that she is not a 'ligarou' and that she must return forthwith to her duties. The woman contests the findings.

('Mary!')

Of Public Interest, March 1721

The *Jamaica & Madeira Coffee House* will, as of the first of April, be
the new meeting-place for the local chapter of the Colonial Anthropologi-
cal Society, est. 1719, Doctor Northrop Simmons, founder.

Planning is currently underway for the annual First of May Fair.
Activities will include horse-racing, cudgelling, bull-baiting, wrestling
for belts, leap-frogging, and troll-madam. Any good citizen who is
prepared to assist in one or more of the aforementioned events, should give
his name to Mr Jonah Dean.

Escaped slaves: Tom, a young cotton-picker of William Fink's
plantation; Bolo, a general labourer of Tory Randall's plantation; Cob,
a sturdy cane-picker of Thurston Pringle's plantation. The public are
asked to be vigilant.

Births, Deaths & Forthcoming Marriages, April 1721

Governor Nicholas Lawes is happy to announce the betrothal and
forthcoming marriage of his youngest daughter, Caroline, to Godfrey
Hill, Esquire, Local Deputy of the Board of Trade and Plantations.
The marriage will take place in December of this year in the Cathedral
of St James.

A kindly neighbour of one Thomas Dillon, only recently of this
parish, regrets to announce Master Dillon's untimely death in unfortunate circumstances. Doctor Northrop Simmons has confirmed.

Court News, April 1721

Let it be known that, on the fourth of May, John Sadler, Commissioner
Charged with the Accounts of Court (to wit, bail sums and punitive
payments), resigned over 'alleged discrepancies in the ledgers of Court'.
Governor Lawes will elect a new Commissioner to Court forthwith.

Let it also be known that the prisoner Mary Read, found guilty of
piracy on the high sea, sentenced to death in November last, and granted
a compassionate stay of execution, was prematurely delivered, on the
twenty-fourth of April, of a stillborn child. The said prisoner sub-
sequently fell ill with puerperal fever and was discovered dead by the
Bailiff the following day.

('No, Mary. Please, no.')

Of Public Interest, May 1721

The public are advised that travel to Kingston is hazardous at present.
Torrential rains have flooded the principal road. All secondary paths are
believed to be deluged.

Governor Lawes has recently announced the forthcoming visit of the President of the Board of Trade and Plantations. Sir Nicholas and Lady Lawes will be hosting His Lordship, the Earl of Westmorland. Master Godfrey Hill, Deputy to the Board, and his betrothed, Miss Caroline Lawes, will be in attendance throughout this much anticipated visit.

Of Urgent Public Concern, May 1721

The Bailiff of the Court is appealing to any member of the public who might have witnessed the disappearance of the prisoner, Anne Bonny, convicted pirate, from the town lock-up on the eighth of May. She is wearing garments of grey serge and is heavy with child. It is expected that she will try to make her way to the Kingston waterfront as soon as the floods abate. The public are urged to exercise vigilance and to declare any sightings of the said felon.

No moonlight. The sky was thick with rolling cloud. She was mud-soaked and lost, wading through a marsh that had swelled into a flat sea.

When the doctor had passed her the lifeless body of Mary's child, it had seemed unreal in her hands, slippery and wrinkled as the pit of a peach. She had pushed her finger into the mouth and felt the warm pink of a tongue. She'd pulled an eyelid back with the tip of her thumb and seen a dead blue eye. She'd watched his skin grow purple and mottled as she'd held him in her arms, and she'd felt her own babe turn in its sleep, quickening in her womb.

Months ago, in the middle of the night, someone had whispered hoarsely into the darkness of their lock-up. ('Two womin wit child mus not sleep side by side, no no. De strong baby will draw de life of de weak an dat child will be born still as de wind at sundown.') Mary hadn't stirred, and in the morning Anne had said nothing; she would not allow them to be separated.

Now she was wet and numb with cold, and the weight at her middle seemed too great to carry. The rain had started again. She was sinking with every step, fighting against the pull of sleep – against the flickering dream of slipping out of her own skin.

Chapter Thirty-Nine

I gutted fish. I stripped conch from the shell. I wove palm leaves into roof thatch and stitched canvas into sailcloth. I lived under a tent of my own making at the far end of shore, and combed the Nassau waterfront for word of her.

I heard that she was pregnant; that a Mark Read was the father of her child; that the child had been born blind; that Jim Bonny had turned up looking for her. Someone said she'd joined the Maroons in the John Crow Mountains. A Jamaican deckhand said she'd vanished; that the Bailiff had given her his wife's second-best set of clothes, and looked the other way. No, said a turtler at the docks, her father in Virginia had used his planter connections to get her the Governor's pardon.

When I heard from a trader that her body was dangling at Gallows Point – that his own brother-in-law in St Jago had seen her hanging, slack-necked as a newborn, at the entrance to Kingston Harbour – I sank to my knees in the mud below the pier.

I did not move as the afternoon slipped away. The tide eddied at my waist. My eyes turned to sea.

I don't know who carried me back up the shore. I weighed nothing, my bones as light as hoar-frost.

In the night,
  'Is it Mrs Fulworth?'
  Mr Manley, is that you?
  'Mrs Fulworth?'
  Aye. Oh, Mr Manley, you've come.
  'Someone will know her.'
  I don't know anyone in this place.

'She's dreaming.'
For the love of Jesus, it's me, Mr Manley.
'Aye, let her sleep.'

My days narrowed to the width of a tent.

I stopped going to the waterfront. I stopped altogether. Mornings were white tent-light searing my sleep. I'd wake with sand in my mouth and blink at the strangeness of canvas.

By day, I drank the rainwater that collected in the dip of my roof. I ate the smashed fruit that children with dogs dropped outside my tent. (I liked their shadows on my walls; I liked their noise.) When they scratched at my tent flaps with long-fingered branches, sometimes I'd scratch back.

I told myself things in the quiet of the night. A piece of bread between the lips saves tears when you're cutting onion. A slice of raw potato will draw the pollution from a sore. A pig has a good head for soup. A rub of sweet herbs keeps a good table. Rue for her who rues love in the night. Hail holy Queen, mother of mercy, to you we cry, poor banished childen of Eve, to you we send our sighs, mourning and weeping in this our valley of tears, turn your eyes towards us, and after this our exile, show unto us the blessed fruit of your womb, Jesus. For soda bread: a pound of wheat flour, two fistfuls of oats, the cream off a cup of milk that has soured on the sill, a good sprinkling of soda, sea salt, a pat of butter, milk mixed with water to make a soft dough, and a Cross-of-Jesus on the top of each loaf.

Tap, tap, tap.

Three taps on the window for a death in the family. *(Not her. Not her.)*

Tap, tap, tap.

I sat up and pulled the flap back to the suddenness of morning. There was the smell of rain, and my heart in my mouth, and a small black girl sitting outside my door. I eyed her and she eyed me.

'Shoo,' I said. 'On your way.'

She didn't move. Her hands were wrapped around a wooden mug.

'And just what do you have there?'

She licked her lips. 'Molasses,' she whispered and showed me her mug.

There was nothing in it.

'I see.'

She looked at me in a new way. 'Yu see molasses?'

I hesitated. 'I said I did, didn't I?'

'Me too.'

'Are you wanting some bread with this molasses then?'

She nodded.

I shaped a loaf of bread out of wet sand, and cut its Cross with a broken stick. 'There now. Eat up.'

She scooped a wet hunk into her mug and pretended to eat, staring at me all the while. 'How old are yu?' she asked.

'Old,' I said. 'As old as winter.'

She didn't know about winter. 'Once, de mun who is steamy for me Aunt Seraphine show me a womun so old, she already die once. Yu know her?'

I was scratching at the mould on my skirt. 'I don't know anyone in Nassau.'

'Yu know me Aunt Seraphine maybe?' A fisherman walked past, staring.

I was short with her. 'Does she know me?'

'No.'

'Well then.' I wanted her to go. I wanted to crawl back into my tent.

She got to her feet, shrugged her narrow shoulders and started to walk away. I could see a smear of wet sand on the back of her calico skirt – red apples on white cotton. I knew those apples.

I got to my feet and called after her. 'This old woman . . .'

She turned.

'She had no legs?'

'No, she got legs. Two,' she added with hindsight.

'Ah.' I sat down again.

She hovered for a moment, stirring the sand in her cup with the end of her finger. 'Leastways, I see legs jes fine till Hosea shout at me an say, girl don yu know it not manners ta clap yu eyes on de afflicted. Den I blink and lo, dey were gone. Hosea

always tek a big mountain o clot ta her on de back o he donkey
cart, an a li'l while ago wen me Aunt Seraphine was in she bed,
sick wit love (dat's wat Hosea say), he lemme ride wit him inta
de wood. Yu know Hosea may be? He has a fuzzy beard.'

'Aye.' I was nodding. 'I do.' We'd hardly spoken during all
his to-ing and fro-ing, but I knew Hosea. Virginia Lazarus'
calico-man.

It felt like grace.

She was sitting in her bamboo chair under the angel-trumpet
tree, throwing seed to her hens. The sun was dropping out of
sight. 'Well, Anniewomun, yu bin gone so long I turn a
hundredanfive.'

'I didn't find her.'

'I know. I know.'

Hosea unloaded the cart. I sat down by her phantom-feet and
laid my head in her lap as the hens scattered. 'They hanged her,
Virginia. They put a noose round her neck and hanged her.'

'An dat Jack too, I spose.'

'Aye.'

She sighed.

'I thought she'd come back, she said she'd come back. I should
have got on the first boat to Jamaica.'

'An how yu ta know, eh? Yu tell me dat?' She stroked my
hair. 'Ssssh . . . Yu got no more tears ta cry.'

'When she was born, I didn't want her.'

'So? I 'spect she di'nt wan yu neither, but dat's not here or
dere.'

'She frightened me.'

Hosea disappeared through the door of the mud-and-grass
hut, laden with cloth. In a moment, he was out again, almost
buried under a snowfall of bleached calico.

'Tank-yu, Hosea,' she shouted, 'I see yu wen I see yu.'

He loaded the cart, kicked the donkey and trundled away.

'I'd swaddled five children,' I murmured, 'but I couldn't
swaddle her.'

'Sssh now.'

'Some stranger will have wound her body in a sheet . . .'

'Let us go inside, Anniewomun.'

'I used to think she'd never be at peace.'

'Come now, de night air is getting under me skin.'

I got to my feet and wheeled her chair over the rough patch of ground. 'She was always restless, even in her sleep.'

'Well, not now.'

'You don't know that, Virginia.' I pulled back the muslin curtain and pushed her chair into the hut. 'Even at one hundred and five, you don't know that.'

'Oh, but I do, Anniewomun. I do.' She lit a rush taper. 'Jes look.'

On a mat in front of a burned-out fire, under a sheet of white calico, was Anne, fast asleep.

'She bin sleeping two days now. She asleep on she feet wen she cum troo dat door.'

'You didn't say a word.' I couldn't take my eyes off her.

'When yu climb off Hosea's cart, yu sick wit grief. Who am I ta say, never mind dat, an by de way?'

'Her face is thin.'

'And she belly is great. Not yet ready ta drop but not so long ta wait neither.'

'Did she ask for me?'

'No, she only ask if I 'member her an when I say yes I do, she ask me if she can sleep on me floor for a bit. Den she pull off her wet tings, climb under de sheet, an dat's de last I hear.'

I took a seat. Virginia folded her hands in her lap, and we waited.

'She said she'd come back,' I reminded Virginia.

'Yea, she did.'

I crossed my legs, then uncrossed them.

Anne turned in her sleep.

'Do you think she's feverish?' I was halfway out of my chair.

'No.'

'Cold?'

'No.'

'Oh.' I sat down again.

'Yu jumpy.'

'No.'

'No?'

'Maybe.'

'An may be yu tink I don know a lie wen I hear one.'

I looked at the shape of her, curled on her side, her knees tucked up to the round of her belly. 'She's a stranger again.'

She sighed, I sighed, and slowly the night drew in.

When I awoke, Virginia's hens were roosting between my feet. I looked up. They had settled in her lap, on the tabletop and in the fire grate.

She opened one eye. 'I like de company dese days.'

I looked to the mat by the hearth, then stumbled to my feet. 'Where is she?'

'Stay, Anniewomun, she only washing she self in de waterhole.'

I took my seat. I smoothed my skirt. I stared at the liver spots on my hands. I watched the curtain that swayed in the doorway. I tapped my foot. A plump fowl started pecking at my toes, and I swatted it with the back of my hand.

There was a fury of feathers.

'Oh go den, for de peace o me and me hens. Tek her dat piece o huckaback for she ta dry she self, an don cum back till yu settled. Jes a few eggs dis day would be a fine ting indeed.'

I walked out of the hut, over the rough patch of ground, and past the angel-trumpet tree. I could feel my heart, fluttering like a bird in my chest. I smelled water. I heard splashing. I almost tripped on a root. Then I saw her, swilling her armpits in the middle of the waterhole, naked as the day she was born.

'Annie.' She stopped in mid-motion, her breasts too large, her belly an impossible outcrop.

'You didn't wake me.' Already, I could feel tears welling behind my words. 'Why didn't you wake me?'

She straightened slowly. 'I thought I'd leave you to sleep.'

'*You died.*'

'Oh, Annie.' She waded to the muddy edge, awkwardly.

'*They hanged you.*'

'I'm sorry . . .'

I stared at a blank patch of sky. 'When you were born, the cord was tangled around your neck.'

'I came back, Annie.'

'You were so blue, I couldn't think fast enough.'

She climbed out of the water and sat next to me, streaming. Her legs were bruised and cut.

'When I heard they put a noose around your neck—'

'They didn't.'

'I was so angry . . .'

'I'm here.'

'Now you're here like some miracle sitting next to me, and I'm afraid.' I turned to her. 'I'm afraid of you.'

'Don't say that.'

I gave her the piece of huckaback and got to my feet. 'I'm going inside now.'

'Wait for me.'

'Virginia will be wondering where I got to.'

'Annie, it's me.'

'And who are you?' I shook her hand from my leg. '*What* are you?'

She almost slid in the mud, but she managed to catch me by the arm and pull me around. Her breath was hot on my cheek. 'Unnatural,' she spat. 'Say it.'

She had cravings. She longed for calaloo, snapped fresh from the stalk.

'No, no,' clacked Virginia, 'it tasty in soup, but eat it raw, girl, an it gnaw at yu innards like a hundred tooth. Yu know dat.'

'Cassava juice,' she said. 'I'm so thirsty.'

'Uh-uh,' said Virginia. 'Sprinkle it on clot, an it turn ta starch. Drink it, an yu stiff long before yu die.'

'An apple from the manchineel tree,' said Anne. 'Just one.'

'What yu tinking of? It soften ta worms deep in yu belly. Tink of yu child.'

Virginia said a fortnight. I said a month. Anne said, 'I don't want it.'

'Of course you do,' I told her. 'It's a part of you.'

'I will drown it like a kitten in the waterhole.'

We waited. A fortnight passed. Then a month. Her breasts were heavy and tender. Her nipples dribbled milk.

At the table one day, over a silent meal, she suddenly spoke. 'You never asked me how I got away, how I got to the harbour.'

I looked up from my bowl of mash, surprised. Her face was unreadable.

'I prayed to my mother.'

I put down my spoon. I looked at Virginia, then back to Anne. 'And she led you to safety?'

'She left me for dead. An oyster-picker found me face down in a salt bog.'

Another month passed. Her back ached with the weight. Her feet and legs were badly swollen.

'Something's wrong,' I said to Virginia.

'Yea, dat baby wants out.'

'It's long overdue.'

'Sometimes wit de first, tings tek a little longer . . .'

'Something's wrong, Virginia.'

She made an infusion from Anne's hair and a handful of palma-christi seeds. 'Drink dis,' she ordered. 'Go on.'

Anne did as she was told.

'It strong, but good.'

In the night, she was rocked by spasms in her stomach, but the baby held fast.

'I want it out, Annie. I want to be rid of it.'

'In its own time,' I said.

'It jes shy,' tried Virginia. 'It afraid ta put its head round de door.'

'What if it goes on growing?' she said.

'It won't,' I said, convincingly.

'Talk ta it,' said Virginia. 'Speak gentle. Maybe den it hear yu an grow bold.'

'Say what?' she fretted.

'Dada is riding . . .' I began.

She answered, slowly. 'Mamma is biding.'

'Aye.'

'Baby is hiding . . . at the bottom of the wishing-well.'

I lay next to her that night. We stared into the dark, listening to Virginia's hens clucking in their sleep. 'Soon,' I whispered.

Anne's Bringing Forth

At first light, her place was cold.

'Virginia, wake up, where's Anne?'

'For pity's sek, I don know.'

'She's not in the hut.'

'Den I reckon she outside de hut.'

I pulled back the curtain and shouted for her. 'Anne!' I listened. 'She doesn't answer.'

'I got ears, don I. Go find her.'

'Where would she go? It's not even light.'

'Sometime, wen a womun or an animal know her time to deliver is cum, she go off on her own.'

'Not Anne.'

'Go see.'

I walked over the rough patch of ground, past the angel-trumpet tree and into the wood. I pushed past sprawling ferns, prickly pears and oozing aloe leaves. 'Anne?'

A mockingbird rattled at me from a nearby branch.

I threaded my way through climbing-moss and needled boughs. 'Anne!' Lizards rustled under dry leaves. A bird screamed overhead.

I turned back.

It was the boot behind the angel-trumpet tree that brought me up short. 'Anne?'

Silence.

A stone's throw away, one of her stockings. Grey worsted with a hole in the toe.

'Anne!'

Its mate, ten feet overhead, hanging from a fir bough.

'I've had enough, Anne!'

Thrown over a bush, her shift. And under the same bush, her other boot.

At the waterhole, no one. I walked a little closer, cupping my hands to my mouth. 'Anne, please . . .'

In the distance, I could hear Virginia calling. I sat down at the edge and rubbed the sleep from my eyes. Already, the air was still with the day's heat. I yawned. I watched a stray cloud's progress in the water's mirror. Then, bubbles.

I stood up, squinting. There were bubbles trembling on the water's surface.

I pulled off my boots and stockings and started to wade in. There was no shock of cold or of wet. More bubbles. I moved slowly, wary of ripples, of unsettling that reflected world in which I stood.

I was hauling up my skirts, worrying about the mud on the hem, when the force of her head shattered the surface like a fist.

I reeled. 'Sweet Jesus Christ!'

Her face was smeared with hair. She was sucking the air, trying to draw breath.

'What in God's name are you doing?'

Her face was white and strange, hovering over the water's surface like some terrible bloom.

'I've got your things over there. Come on now.'

She pushed a mat of wet hair out of her eyes. 'Go away, Annie.'

'Didn't you hear me calling?'

She stared at me.

'What did you think you were hiding from?'

'Go back to the hut.'

'Not until you come with me.'

'No.'

'No?' I looked at her, stunned. 'But the baby—'

Her eyes were steely.

Suddenly, I could hardly breathe. 'Jesus, Mary and Joseph . . .' I plunged deep into the water.

'No, Annie, no!'

I got hold of her arm and dragged her, fought her, to the edge. Up to my ankles in water, I stood blinking.

The round of her belly was gone. I could see the rise and fall of her ribs.

'Where is the baby?' I demanded.

She hugged her own body with shame. 'I don't know.'

I hit her so hard, her knees buckled. 'What have you done with it, Anne?'

'No, Annie, I promise—'

'Where is the baby?'

I struck her again.

'I don't know!' she screamed.

Soda bread: a pound of flour, two fistfuls of oats, cream from a cup of soured milk, soda, sea salt, enough milk and water to make a soft dough, and a Cross-of-Jesus on top. Virginia took the warm loaf from me and wrapped it in white calico.

'It isn't possible.' The same words kept surfacing on my lips.

'Who are we ta say?'

'There was a woman once in my village – she had this way of walking that made people take against her. When she lost her baby, everyone said she'd gone to see Mother Midnight in the dark. But she died swearing she'd conceived the child in a dream and that, when she came to her senses months later, her belly had just subsided like a wave.'

'De body is more dan blood an bone, dat much I know.' She turned to Anne and offered her the warm bundle. 'Sometime, when a slave womun's babe was tekkin from her, de other womin go an steal her a loaf o round bread from de pantry an wrap it in clot.'

Anne looked past her.

'Jes press it ta yu for a bit, girl. It will ease yu pain.'

'I don't need to hold a loaf of bread, Virginia.'

'Yu create dis child wit de seed of yu want. Tek it.'

'There is no child, Virginia,' she snapped.

'There is no baby wrigglin in yu arms, it's true. But dere is a child an only yu know its shape.'

She turned to the wall, her back resolute.

'A phantom baby in de womb is de same as de phantom in de house. It want layin ta rest.'

'Silence.

'Why dis baby haunt yu?'

323

'I don't know.'

'Yu do know. Is it sad?'

'Maybe.'

'Why it sad?'

'I don't know.'

'Tell me.'

'Maybe it's . . .'

'Maybe it's what?'

Anne's voice was bitter. 'The copy of its mother.'

Virginia laid the loaf on the table and sighed. 'I leave yu two now.' She turned her chair round and pushed it towards the door. 'I'll jes be outside, stretchin me legs, if yu wan me.'

Anne turned round at last. 'I didn't kill it, Annie.'

'I know.'

'What's wrong with me?'

'There's nothing wrong with you.' I toed the earthen floor.

'I used to feel it move.'

'I know, ssssh now.'

'I didn't want it, Annie.'

I searched her eyes. 'And you did.'

She hesitated. 'And you didn't want me.'

'And I did.'

She looked away. 'It doesn't matter now anyway.'

'It does matter.'

'I feel old, Annie.'

'You don't know what old means.'

'I'm so tired.'

I crossed the room. Stood beside her. 'Anne—'

'Is that my name?'

'Of course it is. Your mother's choice.' (Old words, strange and familiar . . .)

'I had no mother.'

'Don't talk so foolishly. Do you think you gave birth to yourself?'

She took a lungful of air. '*Aye.*'